SPRING MISCHIEF

SPRING MISCHIEF

...a tale of stargazing,
skulduggery and stagestruck
saddlebacks

Caroline Kington

WINDSOR
PARAGON

First published 2010
by Bed & Bolster
This Large Print edition published 2011
by AudioGO Ltd
by arrangement with
the Author

Hardcover ISBN: 978 1 445 85918 7
Softcover   ISBN: 978 1 445 85919 4

British Library Cataloguing in Publication Data available

Printed and bound in Great Britain by
MPG Books Group Limited

For my beloved Miles

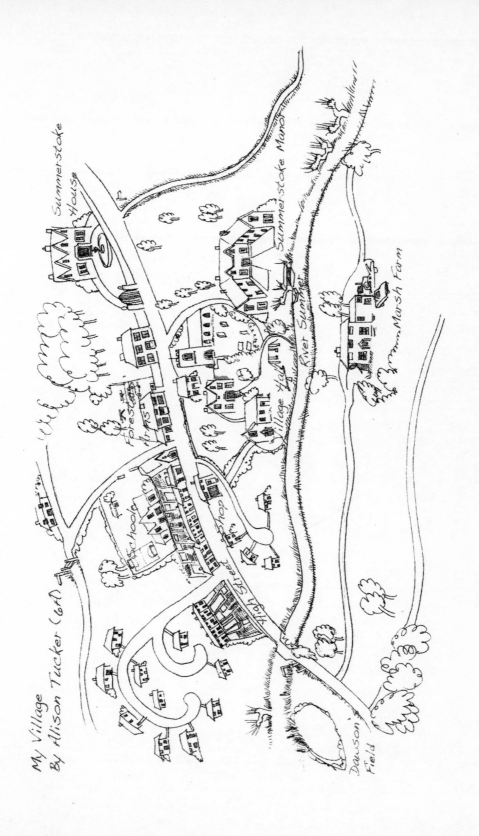

My Village
By Alison Tucker (6A)

Summerstoke House

Summerstoke Manor

Brooms Marsh Farm

River Summer

Village Hall

Forester's Arms

School

High Street

Shop

Dawson's Field

1

'I'll tell you what I think, George, since you ask. I think you should stop moonin' about and find yourself a wife. A farmer needs a wife—never a truer word was spoke, in my opinion. You've been a widower far too long. Little Richie needs a Mum, Emily needs to stop worryin' about keepin' house and holdin' down that teachin' job of hers, and young Will needs to have a bit of fun; not be shoulderin' half the burden of runnin' the farm. You owe it to them, George—find yourself a wife.'

Jilly's voice quivered and broke off; for a few seconds the only sound in the room was the sharp pinging of a radiator.

Then someone sniggered, somebody else laughed outright, others joined in, and the applause was enthusiastic with relief, the script being far better than experience had taught them to expect.

'Great. Thanks a lot. Thanks.' Marcus Steel loved this moment: the start of a new production, when his actors were virgin territory, their individual foibles not yet headaches, his crew were still willing and grateful for their jobs, he and the director (Emma Knight, in this case) hadn't yet fallen out in any major way (she would see he was right about the casting), his budget was not yet overspent, and the commissioners were still enthusiastic . . .

Sitting at the head of a long table in the bland, institutionalised comfort of a hotel conference room somewhere in the centre of London, he

1

surveyed the assembled mix of performers and crew and congratulated himself. With this cast it was going to be a strong production and the director of photography, Colin James, could make the inside of a pig's ear look attractive.

'We'll decamp next door for some wine and nibbles in a minute, but before we do, questions anyone?'

Jilly Westcott raised her hand.

Marcus respected Jilly. She was plump and cheerful, with a crown of white curly hair and shrewd blue eyes behind her specs. She had a great sense of fun and an infectious laugh, but he knew she was seriously committed to her work, no matter how small or trivial her role.

'Will we get to see the other episodes before we go on location, Marcus?'

'We've got the next two episodes to give you when you leave this evening, plus the outlines of the remaining three, so read them in your own time. Obviously Graham and his team will get the scripts to us as quickly as possible and we've built time into your schedules to have a read-through, at least, before shooting.'

Half way down the table, Ben Dacres, a handsome man in his mid-fifties, leaned forward.

'In the opening sequence I'm described as herding cows down the High Street. I don't mean to be difficult, but cows and I . . .'

He ran his fingers through his shock of greying hair and displayed the rueful smile, which during a long and successful career on television had made him irresistible to countless female viewers.

His presence in this comedy would do a lot to promote its success. He knew that, Marcus knew

2

that; but Marcus also knew Ben was a vain, rather silly man and that other directors had found him a pain to work with.

'How will Emma deal with him?' he reflected. She'd not met Ben before the castings and Marcus had watched with detached amusement as Ben had trowelled on the Dacres charm.

He nodded at his director. 'Over to you, Emma.'

Emma responded. 'Right, thanks for that Ben. This is a question that will come up time and again, I'm sure. After all, it's a drama set on a farm and there are farm animals involved . . .'

Deftly dealing with Ben's concern, she moved on to take other questions, allowing Marcus to sit back and appreciate the dextrous way in which she moved the meeting on whilst allowing some of the bigger egos to have their say. The likes of Ben Dacres would present her with few problems.

She was younger than him—about thirty-five or so. She was not pretty, exactly—her nose was too long and bony, and she was thin and wiry. Her dark brown hair was scooped up in a sort of coloured bandana around her head, and her features and her hands often looked cold and pink. But she had large, expressive eyes and when she was roused, was so animated it was hard not to be drawn along with her enthusiasm.

He'd not worked with her before, but she'd been identified as someone who produced classy, interesting work, and he'd been pleasantly surprised when she'd agreed to take on his rural comedy.

A series of six one-hour programmes, it was loosely based on the activities of the Tucker family he had met some while ago. Scenting a possible successor to *The Darling Buds of May,* he had sent

3

a writer, Graham Lawrence, to stay with them. The result, *Silage and Strawberries*, he'd successfully pitched as an updated, grittier version of the HE Bates books about the Larkin family.

Ben Dacres was to play the widowed farmer, George; Jilly, his mother; the lovely Juliet Peters, his daughter, Emily; Jason Hart, his older son, Will; and Harry Hobbs, the ten-year-old Richard.

Marcus hadn't been keen on having a juvenile in the cast—he saw them as troublesome—but he'd accepted Graham's arguments for including a child in what was designed to be a family show.

'Think of the pathos, Marcus—a kid growing up amongst animals that have to be slaughtered. "Why does Buttercup have to go to market, Daddy? Can't we keep her for ever and ever, like Grandma?" We'll have the country weeping buckets, Marcus. Think of it . . .'

So Marcus had cast Harry Hobbs as the youngest son of the farmer. He was a small fifteen-year-old with a freckled face, skin as smooth as a baby and huge troubled eyes that could fill with tears at the drop of a hat.

'So what's this place we're going to?' The enquiry came from Jason Hart, and his tone was prickly with suspicion.

*   *   *

'Jason Hart—why on earth choose Jason Hart?' Emma had stared at Marcus with disbelief. The casting, up to that point, had been pretty harmonious. The casting director had done her stuff and the quality of the performers they'd had to choose from had been good. Then Emma noticed they'd auditioned nobody to play the pivotally important role of Will.

So Marcus came clean. Following his instructions, the casting director had gone headhunting in a different direction.

Emma was appalled.

'He's a stand-up, Marcus! He's had no acting experience, let alone any training. You know how tight our turnaround is. What are you up to? Just because he's big on the comedy circuit doesn't mean he can act. We can't afford any lame ducks, let alone one in such an important part. Are you mad?'

She was not mollified by his explanation.

She had a point, he accepted that—as director she would expect to have the casting vote over who played what, but at the end of the day, she was an employee like anyone else, and what he said, went.

The media had a love affair with comedians—they could do anything, and they could do no wrong—so casting Jason Hart, tipped as one of the most promising young comics of the day, in a central role, had sealed the deal with the programme commissioners.

The casting agent had suggested him because not only was he a favourite on the university circuit, but he had no discernible physical defects. Yes, he was unremarkable in appearance almost to the point of being quite plain, but he was not spotty, or too hairy, or chubby, or scrawny; he was not a beanpole, nor a shorty; his nose was not too big, his hair was thick, cropped and spiky; his chin didn't disappear under his bottom lip; his ears didn't stick out; and he didn't have a broad North Country accent but spoke with a definite estuary twang,

5

which the casting director insisted could pass for West Country.

Emma had fumed, but was helpless to do anything about it; Jason had been selected.

*   *   *

He might look unremarkable, reflected Marcus, but seldom had he come across someone with so large an ego and Marcus harboured some sympathy for Emma, not that he'd ever admit it.

During the reading, Jason had slumped back in his chair, doodling on his script and yawning at regular intervals. His posture hadn't changed when he had to read and his reading was flat and uninterested.

Not a good beginning.

'The address of the location is on your schedule, Jason.' Emma replied calmly. 'Marsh Farm; near the village of Summerstoke. It's about twenty miles from Bath, ten from Summerbridge.'

'Never heard of it.'

'No, well it is quite small . . .'

'And you want us to stay there for twelve weeks? Three whole months? In the middle of nowhere? Did you tell my agent?'

'It's clearly spelt out in your contract, Jason,' Marcus cut in smoothly, disguising his impatience. 'Of course you won't be needed all the time, but the central characters should be resident there for the duration of the shoot.'

Jason snorted and muttered under his breath.

Emma turned to Juliet Peters. 'I've only been to Summerstoke once and it seems really pretty. Juliet, you live there, don't you? Perhaps you could fill us in?'

Juliet dimpled and shrugged her shoulders, 'When I came back from Hollywood, I thought it was heaven on earth. Yes, it's small and pretty and nothing much appears to happen there.'

Like Ben, Juliet was a well-known television face thanks to a soap, and one of those ads that run and run. Marcus, who knew her socially, having once gone out with her husband's twin sister, knew she'd had Hollywood ambitions. These had gone nowhere and this job, for her, was a consolation prize, he knew. But he didn't mind; she was very lovely and although she was thirty-three playing twenty-three, he was glad to have snapped her up.

Her dimples deepened as she looked round the gathering.

'But Summerstoke is a typical English village and if you need a brief on village life, you should watch *Midsomer Murders*, or read Agatha Christie.'

She was sitting next to Nicola Scudamore, a pretty girl in her mid-twenties, who had a small part as the love interest in the first episode of the drama. Judging from the shrieks when they met, the two had worked together before.

Marcus laughed. 'Thanks for the warning, Juliet. Any problems from now on, folks, Ross Manvers, here, is the second AD and he's your man. He's got your schedules, which should contain all the information you need. Now, I think it's time we had a drink, don't you?'

2

The logs crackled in the large open fireplace; the dancing flames flickered gold over her supine, naked body and stabbed at the shadows in the darkened room; her large blue eyes held him, locked.

'Charlie' she whispered. 'Charlie, I want you so much.'

He bent over her. She stretched out an arm and languorously undid the buttons of his shirt. He stroked her fine blond hair then his hand, descending slowly, caressed her cheek, her throat, her breast . . .

The van lunged, hitting a particularly deep pothole, but Charlie Tucker didn't notice, so completely absorbed was he in one of his favourite daydreams.

Isabelle's marriage had disintegrated some four months ago, so their relationship, though passionate, had not yet stood the test of time. Therein lay his problem . . .

'I need to know it's not just a knee-jerk reaction,' she'd told him, 'and not just for my sake, and yours, but for the children . . .'

So Charlie, never the most patient of people, was trying to be just that.

And he was finding it difficult. The desire to sweep Isabelle up in his arms and make mad passionate love whenever they met was confined out of the sight of the children, to snatched hugs and intense, burning kisses. 'Oh' he groaned aloud, 'Oh Isabelle . . .'

Naked, he lay down beside her, his hand gently playing with her soft bush. Her hand, cool and gentle, reached out and firmly encircled his throbbing erection . . .

The squawk of his mobile rudely interrupted.

'Charlie. Just a quickie to check we're fine for Monday.' Marcus Steel was brisk. 'I understand everything is on course but I just wanted to make sure that Marsh Farm is ready for this invasion.'

Charlie had been enlisted by Marcus Steel not only to prepare Marsh Farm and its buildings for occupation by Marcus's outfit, but to help Clive, the location manager, enlist local support for all sorts of services, including accommodation, taxis on demand, fresh food, and the names of those prepared to be extras.

'No probs, Marcus. The only thing I'm concerned about is the weather. It's been bucketing down the last few days. I just hope the field we're using for your base won't become a quagmire.'

'Ross has been warned; they'll bring all that's necessary. By the way, I understand your support has been sterling, Charlie, so thanks a billion for making this happen.'

'No worries, mate, I've enjoyed it. The only headache was trying to accommodate you lot. I never realised just how many you have in tow.' Charlie grinned, 'I've had to do an awful lot of sweet-talking. I reckon there's not a spare bed left in the village.'

'How are the village taking it?'

Summerstoke, where Isabelle lived with her two little girls, nestled on the other side of the river from Marsh Farm. It had one main street, a church, a shop and a school, and not much happened

9

outside the usual rituals of village life, the greatest excitement and gossip being provided by the behaviour of the villagers themselves.

And now a film crew was going to descend on them for three whole months . . . It was hardly surprising there was talk of little else.

'As you might imagine,' Charlie shrugged, 'a fair bit of grumbling from the moaning minnies who can't see beyond the ends of their nimby noses, but you've got the shop and the pub all in favour, of course, and with these B&B deals raking in the cash, the antis are well in the minority.'

'That's good. Makes life a lot easier. How are your plans for the farm launch coming along?'

'We're gonna discuss it all tonight; we aim to open over Easter weekend.'

'And we've scheduled in a filming break that weekend, so we'll be out of your hair.'

'That'll be sweet music to Steve.'

'He okay?'

'You know what Stephen's like, Marcus. He's all for a quiet life and until this rare breeds centre is up and running, he'll grumble at his shadow. I've told Clive any problems, any requests—deal with me. Okay?'

'That's fine by me. I'll make sure Ross and Matt know; Ross's in charge of logistics, he's staying in one of your cottages on the farm, and Matt, who's lodging with Isabelle, controls the shooting schedule. I'll introduce them to you on Monday.'

'Great, is that when you're coming down?'

'I'm moving into my cottage on Saturday.'

'Fancy joining us for a pint on Saturday night?'

'Sure. I'll give you a call. Cheers, Charlie.'

'Cheers, mate.'

Lurching in and out of the next pothole, Charlie turned his attention to the family meeting.

The rare breeds had been Stephen's idea, a measure to redress the faltering fortunes of their dairy farm. It was a risk, they all knew it was, but Charlie was confident if they pulled together, they could make it work.

He acknowledged having the film crew descending on them at this time meant a hell of a lot of work, but he didn't think they would get in each other's way and it was worth it for the money they'd earn.

Charlie gave a little whoop of delight. He hadn't yet told the family how much they'd been offered; he was saving that for this evening. 'Even Stephen,' he chuckled, 'will have to admit it was a good business move.'

Then he sighed, a slight frown marring his habitual cheerful countenance. If only it was left to him, life would be a lot simpler. But Stephen was so very cautious, and objected, moaned, and complained at the slightest thing.

'I think he's become worse since he became engaged,' he muttered. 'I'm sure he never used to be such a stick in the mud. If that's what marriage does to you, I'm glad I'm not headed that way . . . yet.'

He'd nothing against Stephen's fiancée, Angela—he barely thought about her—but he did find it infuriating the way she always backed Stephen, no matter how unreasonable Stevie was being.

Look at the fight over the pigs.

'We have to have pigs,' he'd argued. 'They're a real draw, particularly when they've got piglets.'

But Stephen didn't like pigs, had never liked pigs; said they'd ruin the meadows; said as all their foodstuff would have to be bought in, they'd not be cost-effective and he didn't want anything to do with them. He only backed down when Jeff Babington, his mum's boyfriend and the best vet for miles around, took them to visit Northwood Farm, a rare breeds farm near Bath, and there Angela had fallen in love with a family of noisy, squealing piglets.

So Charlie had acquired two sows, one a saddleback, the other a middle-white, called Clementine and Rebecca, after Isabelle's two little girls, and they were due to farrow about two weeks before the Easter opening.

The van bounced into the yard and shuddered to a halt. He glanced at his watch: just time to check on his pregnant porkers before supper.

It was a shame Isabelle wasn't with him, but they'd spent the better half of the afternoon decorating the bedrooms she was renting to the film crew, so she'd opted for a quiet evening getting on with her own painting.

He sat in the dark of the van, listening to the engine cooling noisily.

The immediate future was choc-a-bloc, what with his work for the television company and the launch of both the farm and the holiday cottages. He'd invested all his time and money in these projects. But what did he really want? What did he, Charlie Tucker, want for himself? He knew his brother wanted to marry and eventually run the farm without him or their gran, a major shareholder, breathing down his neck. Was he going to stand back, take his money and do something else? And if not, where did he fit in . . . where did his future lie?

With Isabelle? Oh yes, yes! But here, in Summerstoke? Her prospects as an artist were looking good; her first exhibition for ten years was taking place in just over a week. Once she had found herself, would she really want to throw in her lot with a yokel, a free-wheeler, like him?

3

'You're kidding me, Ange? She ain't serious?'

Angela giggled at the note of horror in Stephen's voice and cuddled up as close to him as the broken upholstery of the ancient Land Rover would allow. She'd been working late in the library at Summerbridge, a town some eight miles from Summerstoke, so Stephen had collected her and now they were trundling back along narrow country roads, the wipers flipping back and forwards, smearing the drizzle into a fine grease on the windscreen, barely dislodging the caked grime that was a permanent feature of all their farm vehicles.

'She is, Stephen, she is. And she wants you to ask Mrs Merfield if we can perform in the grounds of Summerstoke Manor.'

'Why me?'

'Because Mrs Pagett knows you get on with the ladies at the Manor and you're more likely to get them to say yes than she would.'

Stephen groaned. 'That's as maybe, but we've got one helluva summer laid out for us already, Ange. What with opening, and the film crew here for three bloomin' months . . .'

13

'And our wedding!'

'Specially that, Ange. Do we want to be botherin' with The Merlin Players this summer? Specially with somethin' like this? We'd have our work really cut out.'

Angela looked thoughtful. 'I suppose it's because it's the Merlin Players' twentieth anniversary that I think we should make an effort, Stephen.'

'But Shakespeare? At the Manor? Supposin' it rains? What would we do then, eh?'

'Other companies do it. I think it'd be lovely—*A Midsummer Night's Dream* at Summerstoke Manor, in July. Just think—it'd be so romantic, Stephen. And because it's outdoors, there wouldn't be much of a set, or lights. It would be quite simple. She'll hire all the costumes.'

And Stephen realised that the formidable June Pagett, founder member and sole producer of the Merlin Players—an aspiring and not very successful amateur company that he and Angela had stage-managed for the last ten years—had won his love around.

'We'll see how the meeting goes. I'm not promising anything, Ange. The most important thing is to get this farm on its feet and I'm not gonna take any chances by not being here when I'm needed because I'm gallivantin' after the amateur dramatics, as Gran would say.'

'Is she going to be there tonight?' Angela knew better than to push Stephen any further for the moment.

'Of course. I know Gran has promised us her share of the farm when we marry, but she hasn't given it yet and she's still got her hands firmly on the reins, tho' she might pretend she ain't.'

14

Angela looked across at him, anxiously. 'Do you mind that?'

'I wouldn't mind being my own boss, one day,' he replied lightly. 'Just you and me—the farmer and his wife.'

Angela blushed happily. 'You and me and the children, Stephen.'

'Yes, of course, and the children,' he agreed, less happily.

His future was so clearly mapped out—he was going to take over the farm; get married; have children. He couldn't ask for anything more, but he was worried . . . supposing he couldn't have children? Supposing, horror of horrors, he was impotent? Sex was a subject he and Angela hadn't really discussed, although it was something that exercised them both. Although Angela was twenty-eight and Stephen thirty, they were virgins and Stephen (unlike Angela, who assumed that when they were tucked up in their honeymoon suite, all would be wonderful) fretted about it whenever he was alone.

In every other respect he thought himself the luckiest man on earth, and marvelled that it had taken him the better part of ten years to realise that Ange, his friend and steadfast companion, not only loved him but that he loved her and wanted to spend the rest of his life with her.

'But maybe that's the trouble,' he would argue to himself. 'Maybe it's because we've been friends for so long, making the leap and becoming lovers, lovers more than just kissing and cuddling that is, seems somehow, well, not right. And supposin' we did, well, try it, and I couldn't . . . well supposin' it didn't work out? Ange might call the wedding off.'

15

And at that, Stephen would break into a cold sweat.

4

It was no good, Alison Tucker could not concentrate on her maths; theories, theorems and equations danced before her and scattered, like balls of mercury.

She glanced at her mobile. It was six-thirty.

'Oh bollocks!' she grumbled, 'Where is he? He should be here by now!'

For the umpteenth time that evening, she left her desk and went to inspect her face in the mirror of the heavy old-fashioned mahogany dressing table her gran had given her.

'No, no spots—and no bags . . .' A miracle considering how little sleep she'd had the night before.

She'd already changed her mind twice since she'd abandoned a plain, long-sleeved, dark blue T-shirt which, she felt, made her look less babyish than most of her stuff (comprised principally of cast-offs from her best friend, Hannah; Hannah's taste in clothes was a lot more frivolous than her own), but which she'd discarded, thinking maybe it was just too ordinary.

Her reflection glared back at her, the green eyes narrowing as she surveyed her appearance.

Yep, she'd been right in the first place—the blue would be better; the white blouse was too frilly and with her hair loose over her shoulders . . . she looked as if she was headed for a party rather than an evening round the kitchen table with her family and her boyfriend.

Struggling out of the blouse, she tingled at the thought of Al, of his lean body, his stern, intensity when they made love, and his dark eyes that burnt the back of her skull whenever he looked at her.

A calendar, stuck to the mirror on her dressing table, was marked with a big cross on the date they'd finally made love; he'd been smashed up in a bike accident shortly after they'd met and so sex had had to wait. But when they did, oh—Alison's eyes went dreamy at the memory—wicked wasn't in it!

But Al was at Durham Uni, and they'd only managed to see each other twice since Christmas. Now, at last, with his arrival so imminent her whole body quivered with a hungry fire.

A bed had been made up for Al in the sitting room, but with her mother's bedroom and an impossibly creaky staircase between them, quite how they were going to manage to get it together tonight, she didn't know.

But Alison was determined and resourceful. She'd find a way.

It was a pity, she reflected, that Angela was staying the night. When she did, she slept in Gran's old room in the attic, while Stephen remained in his bedroom on the floor below.

'Does Stephen ever sneak up to Ange's room at night?' she wondered. Somehow she didn't think so. 'Have they ever done it?' Negative again. They were planning to get married in three months—how would they manage then?

'Maybe they've left it too late to take the plunge?' Alison shuddered. Before she met Al, she

17

thought she'd left it late enough.

Her thoughts were distracted by her inability to find the blue T shirt. Suddenly no other garment would do.

'Oh sod it—where the buggery are you?' she fumed, frantically tossing aside the discarded clothes before finding the T-shirt in a crumpled heap under her bed.

The trouble with Stephen was his shyness and his total inexperience with women. Maybe Charlie should take him on one side. Wasn't that what brothers were for? Charlie had never had any trouble on that score. Perhaps she should suggest it. She giggled at the thought of Charlie's reaction.

She smoothed the T shirt over her slim body and peered anxiously back in the mirror. It wasn't too creased? Perhaps she should tie her hair back—Al liked it loose, but it was getting a bit too long . . .

Her mobile rang and she snatched it up.

'Hi, Ali,' It was Hannah. 'Lover boy with you, yet?'

'No, not yet. He's due any minute.'

'You finished your maths yet?'

'As if! I can't concentrate.'

'Tell me about it.' Hannah chuckled. 'I haven't made a start yet, but if I stay up in my room, Mum thinks I'm hard at it. I've told her I've earned a night off, so me and Nick are going to the movies. Do you fancy coming along with Al?'

'Sorry, Hannah, no can do. We've got a farm meeting tonight and I've got to be here.'

'What about tomorrow, then? How long's Al staying with you?'

'Just the two nights. He's off to his aunt's the day after. He's got piles of work to catch up on because of his accident, and I've got my course work to finish, so we're gonna meet up as and when. But I'll ask him about the cinema.'

'You're such a keener, Ali.' Hannah sounded slightly censorious, causing Alison to respond defensively, 'How do you make that out?'

'You don't see your man all term and you still put schoolwork first. Where's your priorities? Won't Al think you're lukewarm? If I said to Nick, "Sorry darling, but shagging will have to wait, I've got an essay to write", I know what his response would be.'

Fortunately for them both, Alison heard the far-off sound she'd been waiting the last long hour for.

'Hannah, I've got to go. It's Al. I can hear his bike.'

5

'I'm gonna wash that man right outta my hair, I'm gonna wash that man right outta my hair, an' send him on his way-ay . . .'

In the kitchen of Marsh Farm, Jenny Tucker sang lustily, if not tunefully, as she stood at the sink, peeling potatoes. Twelve mouths to feed for tonight's supper, plus Isabelle's little girls—though they ate so little, they hardly counted—but the boys and Jeff had hearty appetites so it was an enormous pile to be prepared. It was not often, she thought with pleasure, that they were all together, boy and girlfriends as well as family, including Jeff her own, her own . . .

19

Even after seven or so months Jenny hesitated to call him her boyfriend. He was, but for goodness sake, she was in her early fifties—far too old to have a boyfriend—that was for teenagers and she felt silly calling Jeff that.

Her partner?

That sounded odd, and anyway, they didn't live together, so how could she call him that?

Her lover?

He certainly was that and she blushed happily at the thought, but to introduce him as that?

If only . . . if only he'd propose there'd be no problem, but he'd not mentioned it for months and she daren't for fear of discovering he'd gone off the idea.

'I'm gonna wash . . .' She loved old musicals and although she couldn't always remember all the lyrics, that didn't deter her, when she was alone, from belting out the words she could remember.

The door to the yard banged opened and caught her mid-warble.

'Hello, love,' Jenny smiled at her eldest son. He smiled back and whistled to the two dogs, who'd been alerted by the sound of the van and had sat up, their ears pricked, their eyes fixed on the door.

'Isabelle not with you?'

Charlie shook his head. 'No, she didn't want to muscle in on our pow-wow and she said you had enough mouths to feed as it is.'

Jenny tutted. 'She and her kiddies eat like birds. They wouldn't have made no difference. It would've been nice to have her here with the whole family.'

'Yeah, that's what I said. But she'd made up her mind.' He looked round, puzzled, 'I thought Angela was going to give you a hand, tonight?'

'She was, but the poor thing had to work late at the library. Someone's gone off sick. She was ever so apologetic, but she can't get here till seven. Stephen's gone to pick her up.'

Charlie frowned. 'Then can't Alison give you a hand?'

'She's trying to finish an essay before Al gets here. It's an important one; it goes towards her grade, she said, so I don't want to bother her.'

Charlie snorted. 'It'll be a good thing when she finishes these bloomin' As. They always seem to get in the way when there's work to be done.'

Pushing a loose strand of hair off her sticky face, Jenny was defensive, 'Now, Charlie, that's not fair. She's working really hard at the minute . . .'

He shrugged. 'If you say so. I'll just go and check on the porkers then you can set me to work. Come on then, Gip, Duchess . . .' And so saying, he left the kitchen, the two dogs dancing at his heels.

Jenny smiled fondly at his departing back and turned her attention back to the potatoes.

The hall door suddenly crashed open, and Alison, her green eyes sparkling with excitement, swept through the kitchen to the back door. Here she paused in her flight to bestow a rare smile on her mother. 'I think Al's arrived, Mum. I heard the bike coming down the track.'

Jenny smiled back. 'My word, you could hear a bat whisper, Ali. I haven't heard a thing.'

But then the roar of a motorbike entering the yard announced Al's arrival and before the splutter of the engine had died away, Alison had whirled out of the door.

A small pucker appeared on Jenny's brow. Alison's relationship with Al made her feel uneasy.

21

His family also farmed land in the village, but they couldn't be more different than the Tuckers: they were rich, and successful, and unscrupulous, and she knew they despised her family. No matter how much Alison might declare that Al was not like them, no way, and that he wanted nothing to do with them, she was not reassured.

'It ain't natural,' she thought. 'He's only twenty. She's his mother; he can't do that to her . . . I'd die if Charlie or Stephen said they was never going to see me again.'

She couldn't bear it if her baby, her bright, sparky, difficult daughter, got hurt.

She sighed as she filled a large pot with the peeled vegetables, covered them with water and slid them onto the hot plate of an old and rather encrusted Rayburn. Pulling the lid off a heavy casserole, she stirred the simmering goo with a large wooden spoon.

'Oh bugger me,' she declared, crossly. 'Why does it always do this?'

A vigorous scraping revealed a thick burnt coating of meat and gravy on the bottom of the pan.

The kitchen door opened again.

'Something burning, Jenny?' asked Elsie, her mother-in-law, entering, followed by Ron, her second husband. He beamed at her as if to sweeten the sourness of Elsie's greeting.

Jenny cursed inwardly. Elsie might be eighty, but nothing escaped her notice, least of all any mistake Jenny might make.

Elsie's bright eyes peered over Jenny's elbow. 'Well,' she commented, 'you have made a mess of that, I must say. I thought Angela was going to cook this evening . . .'

22

'She was, but . . .'

Not interested in Jenny's explanation, her exasperating mother-in law had turned away and was unpacking bottles from the basket Ron had placed on the table. 'I've brought up some of my blackberry wine, at least that will be palatable . . .'

'Now, now, Elsie, love,' Ron interjected good humouredly, 'I'm sure it will taste very nice. It's a lot of people poor Jenny has to cook for, single-handed, tonight.'

Elsie snorted, but her expression softened as she looked at him. 'That's as maybe. If Jenny had been a farmer's wife in the old days, she'd have had to cook not only for the family but all the farmhands as well. She's lucky she's only got her family to poison.'

Jenny stared, flushing miserably, into the pot. 'Why do I allow Elsie to get to me?' she brooded. 'After thirty-two years, you would think I would be able to stand up to her, fight back—just a little?'

True, the old bag had become easier since she'd married Ron, and they'd moved out of the farmhouse, but they ate their evening meals with the family and Elsie continued to goad Jenny at every opportunity.

'So where's Alison? Why's she not helping you? Ron, my dear, sort out the cutlery, will you, otherwise we won't be eating till midnight. You're too soft with that girl, Jenny. Exams or no exams, she should pull her weight.'

'She was coming to help, but she heard Al arrive, I'm surprised you didn't pass them in the yard. She'll be here in a minute.'

'We saw his bike. I used to ride one of them.' Ron chuckled. 'You never lose the passion for 'em.

23

Fancy getting up in leathers, Elsie, love, be my pillion passenger?'

'I wouldn't put it past her,' reflected Jenny. There was nothing frail about Elsie's tiny frame and although she had more wrinkles than a raisin, she had an energy and a zest for life that Jenny could only marvel at.

Elsie chuckled back. 'If you can get astride one of them things, Ron dear, then you'll find me on the back, right enough. Now Jenny, how many's we laying for?'

'Isabelle's not coming; Stephen's gone to pick up Angela, and Jeff will be here shortly. His surgery finishes at six-thirty, so he won't be late.'

'He popped the question yet?'

Jenny so wanted to say 'mind your own business'. Both Alison and Charlie got impatient with her for not standing up to Elsie. They certainly did and the sparks flew, but all she could do was blush and shake her head and murmur, 'It's early days, yet, Elsie . . .'

'Early days, my foot. Before you know where you are, Stephen will have married Angela and what's going to happen then, eh? You can't have two women running the farm kitchen. I knew when to retire—I handed the reins over to you as soon as my Thomas died.'

'But Angela wouldn't expect . . . there's Charlie to think of, and Alison . . . this is their home, I'm their mother . . . this is my house . . .'

'This is the farmhouse, Jenny; it goes with the job.'

Jenny was saved from making any further reply by the more or less simultaneous arrival of the rest of her family.

24

Angela, bobbing at Stephen's elbow and looking for all the world like a little dormouse in huge specs, rushed immediately to Jenny's side.

'I'm so sorry I'm late, Mum. I couldn't help it. And you've had to do it all. What can I do? Oh . . .' She caught sight of the burnt pan.

'If you can rescue a burnt stew,' commented Elsie, 'then you can perform miracles.'

'Oh, it's not that bad,' said Angela. 'Here, let me . . .'

Relieved, Jenny stood back. There was no doubt about it: her son's little fiancée might live a humble existence as a librarian, but when it when it came to cooking, she was in her element and she needed no encouragement to cook for the Tuckers, for which Jenny was grateful.

But if Jenny's role in the kitchen was to be handed over to Angela, Elsie was right, what was she to do? Housework? She was never very enthusiastic about that, either. Gardening? It didn't come naturally, and as for small livestock, she'd got rid of the hens and ducks years ago . . .

'Penny for them, Mum.' Stephen squeezed her shoulders and she smiled up at him. Not quite as tall, or as good-looking as lean, dark-eyed Charlie, Stephen was her secret favourite. He was plump, with big red hands, rosy cheeks, worried hazel eyes and short brown hair; he was shy, like her, and gentle. For many years she had fretted he would never find anyone to love him as he deserved, but he had, and now here he was: engaged to be married. Her eyes misted with happiness.

'Don't worry about supper, Mum,' he said softly. 'Ange'll sort it out. You sit down and take the weight off your feet, you look worn out.'

25

'So Isabelle's not coming, that's a shame.' Isabelle was a particular favourite of Elsie's.

'I think it was the thought of all us Tuckers frightened her off, Gran,' laughed Charlie, crossing the kitchen, dog bowls in hand, to a large sack of biscuits leaning against the dresser.

'Perfectly understandable,' agreed Jeff Babington, who'd followed Charlie indoors. 'You're a frightening lot! Hello, love.' He bent down and kissed Jenny on the top of her head. 'You look hot.'

Immediately Jenny became self-conscious about her sticky red face, her hair falling out of its comb and the spattered apron she'd vowed to remove as soon as he appeared.

'It's not surprising,' observed Charlie, 'it's like a furnace in here with those pots, bubbling and hissing on the stove. It reminds me of that Mickey Mouse cartoon we used to watch as kids, you know—*The Sorcerer's Apprentice.*'

'The potatoes,' Jenny leapt to her feet. 'They need to be turned down, Angela . . .'

'I've done it, Mum. Don't worry,' Angela soothed her. 'It's all in hand, I just need to know what vegetables to put on . . . Only I can't see any ready . . .'

'Oh, right, sorry, Angela. I've got a cabbage and some carrots in the larder. They'll just need a scrape . . .'

'What did I say?' said Elsie triumphantly. 'It'll be midnight before we eat.'

'Anyone for a beer?' Charlie returned from rummaging in the larder with vegetables under one arm and a six-pack under the other. 'Jeff? Stevie? Al?'

At the mention of Al, Jenny turned in time to see

26

him enter with Alison.

Al, normally so pale and fierce, looked flushed and happy; and Alison, her fair hair tousled, her green eyes sparkling and her cheeks red, was so animated the whole company was affected by their mood, and without further ado the table was laid, the carrots scraped, beer, cider, blackberry wine and water distributed, chairs found sufficient for the assembled company, and the noise of good humoured chit-chat filled the kitchen.

6

'I thought you hated Summerstoke, Juliet?' Nicola sipped her wine and looked at Juliet with curiosity. 'You used to go on about your husband's ghastly family—the freaks who lived in the manor house . . . Or are they all dead now and you're the lady of the manor?'

Juliet laughed. 'No, thank goodness! With Oliver's parents still hale and hearty, that frightful prospect is a long way off. The old ladies are still there, very much alive and kicking hard. We've a sort of armed truce now, mainly because of Jamie, my son. He's at the sixth form college in Summerbridge; they keep an eye on him when Ollie and I aren't about.'

'So you've moved into the village?'

'No, not exactly. We're buying a flat in Notting Hill, but Oliver has to have somewhere to live in his constituency—you know he's become an MP? So we're renting a place in Summerstoke. I'm there at the moment because the flat is being done up.'

'You've certainly fallen on your feet with this filming, then, Juliet. Plum part and right on your doorstep. I'm staying at the Stowford Country Club.'

'Very nice, darling. You'll be in good company.' Juliet cast a meaningful glance at the rest of the assembly.

Nicola followed her gaze. 'It's certainly a bit of a mixed bag, isn't it? Ben Dacres is very charming, but hard work. And what on earth is Jason Hart doing here? His reading was so flat! He was meant to be making love to me and it felt as if we were licking envelopes.'

Juliet pealed with laughter, attracting the attention of the subject under discussion who turned and stared at them.

Conscious of his stare, Juliet dropped her voice. 'Maybe he's got hidden depths, Nicola—saving it for the camera?'

Looking dubious, Nicola shook her head, 'I don't know. And he's very . . . well, nondescript to look at. Not at all sexy, unlike our Marcus. Have you ever been directed by Emma before?'

'No, have you?'

'No, but I hear she's good—a bit fearsome, though.'

'I met her once, at a first night; she was living with a guy called Jonathan Black. He's an archaeologist, who does stuff on radio and TV and writes a lot. Not that I've never read anything by him, but Ollie has; he says he's good.'

'Never heard of him, but then archaeology is not exactly my bag.' Nicola giggled at the idea and turned her attention back to the gathering. 'I'm glad Ross Manvers is our second AD; I've worked

28

with him before, he's a sweetie—nothing's too much for him.'

Juliet looked across at Ross as he moved about the room, re-filling glasses, chatting and joking with the other actors.

Although she'd not worked with him she knew of him as a long-time survivor in a business littered with casualties. As the second assistant director, he had one of the toughest jobs on a shoot, but as far as the actors were concerned the best ADs were those who made them, each and every one, believe their feelings and comfort were all that mattered, and Ross Manvers did just that.

Jason Hart, still with his eye on the two women, had grabbed hold of Ross's arm and was whispering in his ear. Ross turned, smiled across at them, then glided over, brandishing a bottle of wine in each hand, Jason Hart following close behind.

'May I top you up, my lovelies? Ms Peters, I'm so excited to be working with you. I'm a great fan of yours. And Nicola, it's my lucky day. How are you, sweetheart?' Without waiting for a reply, he continued, 'Jason, here, has demanded an introduction, although I wouldn't have thought he needed one. Anyway, chums, I'll leave you to get better acquainted.'

As he turned away, he winked at Juliet. 'I think we're going to have some fun and games on this shoot, don't you?'

And Juliet, who had started the day by throwing up with an unaccustomed attack of nerves, found herself laughing at Ross and realising it might just be possible she'd enjoy the next few months.

*   *   *

Jason Hart's gloom at his prospective exile on some stinking farm, in a remote corner of England, stuck with a bunch of luvvies, had also lifted a fraction.

So far the rest of the company had reinforced his prejudices: they spoke with overloud voices and called everyone darling; they kissed each other a lot, and were larded with makeup and perfume, and, the most galling thing of all, they didn't seem in the slightest bit impressed by his presence.

His star was rising and he'd joined that exclusive coterie of celebrities who never had to explain who they were, or what they did to earn a crust, or pay for a round, or fumble for ID when going into a club. So he didn't expect this bunch of nobodies to look down their snouts at him and make him feel like an intruder.

He'd just decided to go and buzz his agent and tell him to stick it—there was no way he would allow himself to be buried alive with this fossilised lot—when Ross Manvers had arrived at his elbow, re-filled his glass and told him how much he admired him and how delighted he was that they were going to work together, and that anything he could do to make the ride easier for him, all Jason had to do was ask, when this laughter trilled across the room. He had turned to see this red-headed popsy in conversation with the pretty dark-haired bird he'd read a scene with earlier.

He hadn't noticed her before (not so surprising: once he'd established from the cast list there was nobody he'd heard of, he'd lost interest in getting to know any of them). Jason had a long-term girlfriend, but that didn't stop him from hunting down anyone he fancied. The more difficult they

30

were to pull, the more he enjoyed himself. This particular skirt looked very delectable.

'Who's that?' he'd whispered to Ross, nodding in the redhead's direction.

'Juliet Peters. She's en route to Hollywood, dear boy; we're lucky she was available to do this; she's married to Oliver Merfield, a rising star of the Conservative Party.'

'Never heard of him, or her, come to that. Time to make amends. Introduce us, Horatio.'

She was even lovelier close to. Large, intense blue eyes looked up at him, dimples quivered in the corners of a perfectly shaped mouth; she had a small straight nose, her skin was creamy, and her hair was not red but a sort of red gold, tumbling in curls over her shoulders. Oh yes, she was definitely trophy material. And the wife of an MP: that was no deterrent, far from it—he'd never scored with one of those before!

*　　*　　*

'Pleased to meet you, Jason.' Juliet dimpled, a little disconcerted by the way he stood, without the glimmer of a smile, looking down at her. 'You know Nicola, of course.'

His gaze barely flicked across to Nicola. 'No. I don't know anybody here.'

'Yes, well, my mistake—reading through a love scene with someone doesn't necessarily mean you know them, in the real sense of "to know".'

He shrugged his shoulders, uninterested. 'So which part are you playing?'

Both Nicola and Juliet goggled.

'It's not much of a compliment if you have to ask

31

me that, Jason. Was my reading so unmemorable?'

He pulled a face. 'I wasn't really listening. It was so boring, I couldn't tell you who was reading what.'

This statement was met by a flabbergasted silence and both women stared at him.

Undeterred, he carried on, 'I'm new to this lark and I can't say I'm impressed so far. It's all so bloody slow, and up its own backside. I'm used to facing large and noisy audiences, dancing on the edge, bending 'em to my will, making 'em listen, making 'em laugh.'

'Then why are you taking on this?' asked Nicola, puzzled.

'It's part of the plan to shift me from late-night TV into the mainstream. With this under my belt, the next step will be to get my own show.'

'So three months with us in Summerstoke is the price you're having to pay?' Juliet said this lightly, but inwardly she seethed; what an obnoxious, self-satisfied jerk!

'Oh, it'll go quickly enough. With you guys around we can cut away from the luvvies and make our own fun, eh? Jools, you can introduce us to the high spots of—where is it, Summerstoke? There must be some.'

And he grinned.

His cold, rather sullen appearance was transformed. His eyes twinkled and crinkled, white even teeth flashed, his face warmed, the dull visage vanished and he became almost good-looking. It was the rare use of this grin that had won over the hearts and minds of his audiences. Half cheeky little boy, it had the girls swooning; half wolf, it had the blokes cheering him on as one of them.

Nicola melted.

Juliet, who regularly showed her dimples, or flashed her eyes and tossed her golden curls whenever she wanted something, was less impressed. Fun and games, Ross had said. It was certainly going to be that and cartloads more.

She glanced across at Marcus. 'What was he thinking of,' she mused, 'when he cast this antidote to charm, this nasty little jam-jar of worms?'

She knew he must have his reasons.

Marcus was intelligence personified—striking to look at, tall, with a closely shaven head and piercing blue eyes; a man who took no prisoners and was single-minded about his work. Which made it all the more puzzling, she reflected, that he should have allowed someone like Jason Hart under the velvet rope.

*   *   *

Marcus and Emma moved around the room, chatting with actors and crew alike. Both would have preferred to have spent the time comparing notes on the reading, but, as Marcus murmured to Emma when they exchanged the conference room for an identical space, described by the hotel as 'the reception room', there would be time for that when the party was over. As with the actors, some of the crew knew each other, others knew nobody, and so—with Ross's help—both producer and director concentrated on making everyone feel comfortable and to generate excitement about the series.

And also to reassure, as Marcus, surrounded by a deputation of the older actors, discovered.

'I say, Marcus, old chap,' Ben Dacres was wearing his rueful, between-you-and-me look. 'I hesitate to teach me Gran to suck eggs, but,' he dropped his voice to a conspiratorial whisper, 'are you sure about him?' He nodded in the direction of Jason Hart.

Jilly Westcott put her hand on his arm. 'We're not questioning your judgement, Marcus, of course not, darling. It's only that we're a bit concerned that he seems so . . . so . . .'

'Untalented, uninterested, and completely contemptuous, not only of us, but of the whole process, Marcus, darling,' chipped in another actor.

'Is he going to play ball when the time comes, Marcus?' Ben frowned. 'Will he pull out the stops?'

'Or is he going to be a permanent pain in the butt, to coin yet another cliché?' Jilly chuckled, but Marcus knew better than to underestimate the genuine concern behind their questions.

He was taking a risk, he knew it. But that was why, at the age of forty, people who mattered, i.e. the television commissioners, rated him. He took risks and, by and large, they paid off.

He'd joined the production company, Laughing Jackass, with a brief to develop light entertainment ideas and already he had a number of programmes to his credit. But he badly wanted a comedy drama series, and one that would capture the viewing public's imagination and run and run, not vanish without trace after a pilot.

He could see that *Silage and Strawberries* might do just that. He was well aware that with Jason Hart he'd introduced an uncertain player, an unpredictable element, a wild card, but equally he knew without him there might have been no commission. His casting had to work, but it wouldn't, he knew, unless he had the whole-hearted

34

support of the rest of the company.

'Don't worry,' he smiled at them with the assurance born of an unshakeable conviction in himself. 'It's going to be fine. He's inexperienced, but he's an entertainer, like the rest of us. He'll be fine. Just give him as much support as you can; it'll pay dividends, I promise.'

7

Sipping from his can of beer, Anthony Lester—Al to his friends—sat in the kitchen at Marsh Farm, watching the bustle, his fatigue ebbing.

This family, the way they were, the way they lived, couldn't be more different from his. In his mother's kitchen everything shone: the dishwasher, the fridge, the Aga, the tiled floor, even the fruit in the fruit bowl—no smudges, no grease, no cobwebs. Every pot and pan had its place; after meals everything would be tidied away, the work surfaces cleared of all evidence of food and the long scrubbed oak table left empty. It was not a friendly kitchen, not a place to linger and chat, or simply to sit and be comfortable.

Not like the kitchen of Marsh Farm.

Al had goggled when he first visited the Tuckers' farmhouse: he'd never seen anywhere like it. The kitchen was a long, low room, quite dim, as the only source of natural light came from a grimy sash window over the sink or, at night, from a central light bulb encased in a paper globe yellowed with age, hanging over the kitchen table.

The room itself had to be some future

35

archaeologist's dream, so full was it of domestic jumble, ancient and modern. Layers of out-of-date calendars and faded children's drawings plastered the walls; the shelves of a large old dresser were crammed so full of general rubbish, not an inch of space was visible and yet, at the shout of 'clear the table, someone', magazines, catalogues, newspapers, knitting patterns, gloves and a host of other bits and pieces were somehow crammed onto the shelves.

Not that the table ever looked any clearer. It was the repository for stacks of jam jars, balls of wool, cans of dog meat, bags of sprouting potatoes, packets of seeds, dried flowers, baking tins and withered fruit, all of which seemed to be in permanent occupation. Yet amongst all this the Tuckers found room for their plates of food as, perched on assorted wobbly chairs and stools, they jostled for elbow-room.

Alison had confided in him that things would change when Angela married Stephen and took over the kitchen. Much as he liked Angela, Al fervently hoped she wouldn't change too much. He thought of his parents sitting at this table and grinned.

'What are you smiling at?' whispered Alison, sliding into a seat next to him. 'Here, take this. I hope there's enough.'

His eyes widened: the plate was piled with a velvety dark brown stew, golden mashed potatoes, and a pile of carrots and vivid green cabbage glistening with butter.

'This is as much as I've had to eat all term. Are you trying to fatten me up?'

'Mum thinks you look a bit thin and pale . . .'

He snorted with derision but tackled the food with the single-minded drive of the half-starved.

The meal was a jolly affair but not lingered over. In no time at all every scrap of food was eaten, and Gip and Duchess, who had been closely following every movement of food to mouth, sighed heavily and slumped back in their baskets. Jenny sprang up and put a huge old kettle on the stove; Alison stashed the dishes in the sink and set to washing them; Stephen and Angela wielded tea towels, and Charlie, with constant reference to his mother because he never seemed to know where anything went, put things away.

It was only then, when the whole exercise was complete, did the farm meeting begin. Elsie presided from the wooden carver at the head of the table.

Stephen launched off with his report on the farm's last quarter with the projections for the next, and the progress being made on preparations for the Easter weekend opening.

Charlie reported on the conversion and usage of the buildings, and on the filming as far as it would affect the farm, since the unit would be with them for the duration of the next quarter.

When he'd finished, Elsie turned to the rest. 'Now I'm sure you've got lots to ask both Charlie and Stephen and that's the purpose of this meeting. We don't want to be here all night, so don't waste time with tomfoolery questions. I'm going to begin by asking Charlie, because as I'm sure you noticed, he neglected to tell us how much the film company are paying to use Marsh Farm. Charlie?'

This was the moment Charlie had been waiting for. The last few years of farming had seen their debt to the bank grow and grow, and although their fortunes had improved recently, the debt had not gone and the threat of bankruptcy still lurked.

With a solemn air he looked at their expectant faces. 'It's called a facility fee. Marcus has offered us a lump sum buy out for everything he wants. I said I'd run it past you, but I'm sure there'll be no objections.' He paused and grinned.

'You rat, Charlie, how much?' Alison shrieked.

'Seventy K,' was the nonchalant reply.

Their reaction was deeply gratifying.

The stunned silence that greeted his announcement gave way to a great shout. Stephen, red in the face and with a hint of tears in his eyes, thumped Charlie on the back, then hugged Angela; Alison threw her arms round him and gave him a smacking kiss on the cheek, something she hadn't done since she was about ten; Jenny sat, her eyes as round as saucers, shaking her head, murmuring, 'Seventy thousand pounds, seventy thousand pounds. How can they possibly afford to give us seventy thousand pounds?'

Jeff laughed and patted her hand. 'That's the film industry for you, love, more money than sense.'

Even Gran, Charlie noticed with satisfaction, looked impressed.

'It does seem a lot,' he said when they had quietened sufficiently for him to continue, 'but I did check it out and it would seem, if they paid on a daily basis, we'd get anything between five hundred quid to a thousand, tops, so actually, I think it's a good deal all round. It means, as if I have to tell you, we can clear the bank loan.'

'Yep,' said Stephen beaming, holding Angela tightly, 'and have some left over to put towards a new milking parlour.'

Charlie looked at him, a slight frown creasing his brows.

'Maybe, but let's see how the launch goes before we spend every last little bit. We might decide it would be better to invest in a kiddies' play area, something we've put on hold because of health and safety regs . . .'

'But when all's said and done, this is a working farm, Charlie, and we need to update our milking parlour, you know that . . .'

To Charlie's relief, they were diverted by a question from Al.

'What sort of animals are you going to stock, Steve? Ali's shown me the pigs—they're wicked—and I saw the Highlands on my way in.'

Talking about the stock brought a glow of excitement to Stephen's face. 'I'll show you around tomorrow, if you like, Al. We've got in a couple of Jerseys, which we're gonna milk with the main herd, as well as four dairy Shorthorns—they look nice and they're good-tempered beasts . . .'

'We were thinking of getting some Belted Galloways, weren't we, Stephen,' Angela chipped in. 'They look so unusual, but Uncle Jeff said they'd be a handful to manage, so we've got some Longhorns instead.'

'They're arriving next week, so Lenny is double-fencing all the paddocks,' Stephen continued. 'Not just the ones the Highlands are using.'

'Oh, you've decided to do the lot, then, Steve?' enquired Jeff.

Stephen nodded.

'It's a good idea.' Jeff explained to Al. 'Health

and safety. They'd prefer all horned creatures behind double fencing. And the important thing is to keep the animals moving around—stops the ground from developing high levels of parasites and the animals from picking up pathogens; this the sort of thing they teach you on your zoology course?'

'Yeah.'

'Well you could be very useful to us,' Jeff smiled, 'Particularly with some of our more unusual acquisitions, eh, Stephen?'

Stephen nodded with pride. 'Ange has set her heart on getting some ostriches, but they'd be purely for show. We might get some llamas or alpacas as well, but for the moment we're concentrating on good old farm stock. We've got some English goats and a couple of Golden Guernseys and a few sheep—some Wiltshires and some Cotswolds and a beautiful Portland ram. Then of course there's the chickens and ducks . . .'

'When Thomas and I farmed, we had chickens and ducks in the yard,' said Elsie. 'They were part of everyday farm life, not just show animals. They were the responsibility of the farmer's wife.'

She looked pointedly at Jenny.

'I'd love to have some to look after,' piped up Angela. 'Perhaps you could teach me how to go about it, Gran?'

'We're all going to have to muck in to make this venture work,' Elsie nodded her approval. 'It's our last chance to put the farm back on its feet.'

'We're all behind you there, Gran. I think we've more or less got everything covered.' Charlie smiled at his mother. 'Mum is going to be in charge of refreshments and the sale of produce, although, of course, that's going to be a bit slow to begin with.'

Jenny beamed. 'Jeff has taken me round to other farm shops so we've got some idea of the sort of thing that goes down well. We'll send the goats' milk out to begin with, but when we've got the small barn converted, we can invest in a little electric machine and make our own yoghurt. Ange is going to help me.'

'We'll need a commercial fridge, of course,' continued Charlie, 'and then we'll be able to sell our own pork and then perhaps our own milk, butter and ice cream, and maybe your cordials, Gran.'

'And my chutney and cakes,' added Jenny.

Elsie snorted. 'And then we'll have the environmental health office closing us down for poisoning the neighbourhood.'

'Gran,' protested Alison. 'Don't be so negative.' She turned to her mother. 'If you want my opinion, Mum, the one thing Ange and Gran can't do, which you can, is knit. You should concentrate on knitting things for people to buy. Look how well your little strawberry hats are selling in the village shop, and think how much those designer sweaters you knit for Mrs Whatsername go for—you could do really well. You could even knit farm animals for the kids.'

'That's a brilliant idea, Ali!' Charlie jumped in, enthused. Isabelle had drawn his attention to the fact that Jenny was in danger of being sidelined, however unintentionally, by her prospective daughter-in-law and he'd been racking his brains to find a way to divert his mother from her resolution to stock the farm shop with the results of her cooking.

'So that's the farm more or less dealt with,' Elsie

41

consulted her list. 'Except for the actual day of opening. We said Easter. Which particular day?'

'Good Friday.'

'Easter Monday.'

Charlie and Stephen spoke simultaneously.

'Steve,' Charlie was exasperated. 'It's gotta be the Friday. What's the point in opening on the Monday?'

Stephen looked stubborn. 'I don't see why its gotta be Friday. No-one goes anywhere on Good Friday except to the shops. Easter Monday is the real holiday and it gives us more time to get ready. Christ knows, Charlie, I've got my work cut out as it is. I'm gonna need all the extra time I can get . . .'

'It's no different for me. I don't see what difference three days is gonna make. If the crowds aren't huge on Friday, all to the good. It'll give us time to adjust things . . . learn from our mistakes . . . sort things out before we hit the big time. We don't want to waste three days' revenue while you pussyfoot around getting ready.'

'There are arguments to be made on both sides.' Elsie said sharply as her grandsons glared across the table at each other. 'From a business point of view, Stephen, I would come down on the Friday opening, unless, of course, we come into conflict with the film crew. Charlie?'

'No, Gran. According to their schedule, the whole of Easter weekend is a break for them.'

'Good. Then unless anyone has further objections, I think we should consider that matter settled.'

Stephen sat back in his chair, discontented.

Elsie, casting a quick look in his direction, consulted her notes and continued, 'Charlie,

42

the holiday cottages and the studio—what's the situation with them?'

'The studio is being taken over by the TV people. Marcus is setting up his production office in a trailer that's gonna be sited in the yard near the house, and the four cottages are ready, apart from finishing off the furnishings. I've got a pile of Ikea furniture waiting to be constructed and Mum's giving me a hand with curtains and stuff, so they should be finished by the time the film crew move in. That means they're fully booked until the end of June, and then, who knows . . .'

'What are you doing about the summer lets?

Charlie was tempted to say 'give us a break' to his gran, but he knew better than that. He sighed. 'I've got to sort out how best to advertise them, Gran, but in the first instance, I'm going to let the tourist centre in Summerbridge have our details.'

'What about your website?'

They all looked at Al with surprise.

Al's presence at this meeting was tolerated because he was Alison's boyfriend, but some of the family were uneasy. He didn't speak the same language; he'd gone to a public school and was at university. None of the Tuckers had ever done either, and found it difficult to believe he had really completely broken with his family. At heart he was a Lester and the Lesters had made no secret of the fact they wanted the Tuckers out of Marsh Farm. For him to be present this evening was an expression of trust on their part, but he was not expected to be asking questions.

'Website?' Charlie replied cautiously.

'Yeah. You're not going into this business without a website, are you? How will you expect

43

people to find out about you, or know what your USP is?'

'USP?' Stephen stared at him suspiciously.

'Unique selling point. You've got to have one, otherwise why should anyone visit this farm over all the others in the marketplace. And if you haven't got a website, how will people know you're here, let alone when your opening day is?'

'We're going to put brochures in the library, in the tourist information offices and in all the hotels around here, and we're going to let the local press know,' Angela replied, somewhat defensively. 'I'm working on the brochure, right now.'

Alison shook her head. 'Al's right. Brochures have their place, Angela, don't get me wrong, but we live in the 21st century and the first place anyone would go to find out what we have to offer is our website.'

'What would a website do that a brochure can't?' enquired Elsie.

'One, it's instant access, Gran. "What shall we do today? How about a farm visit?" Not "let's go down to the information centre and pick up some brochures", but "let's tap into Google and see what comes up". Two, we have nice little pics of the animals—click and watch the little piglets playing with their tails; click—see little Johnny having a pony ride on Bumble; click—watch Stephen milk the Jerseys. And three, we can update it whenever we want so whenever we've got anything special, like a new litter of piglets or chicks, or we're opening the farm walk, we can post it up.'

Elsie shook her head. 'Sounds extraordinary.'

'It is, Gran, but that's the way to sell businesses these days. We can't afford not to if we're to be

44

successful.'

Elsie turned to Al. 'So what do you see as our, what d'ye call it, our USP, young man? What will make Marsh Farm different from all the others?'

Al hesitated, but before he could say anything more, Charlie sat up, his eyes glinting with excitement. 'I know, it's obvious isn't it? What have we got that none of the other farms have?'

Stephen shrugged, nonplussed, and the others looked equally blank.

'The filming!' Charlie proclaimed. 'We're working so hard to make sure the filming doesn't interfere with our plans, we're forgetting it's there and we could make a feature out of it.'

'You're right, Charlie,' said Alison, excited. 'Click, see the filming in action; click on a pic of Jason Hart, see him walking across the yard . . .'

'Who's Jason Hart?' asked Jenny.

'He's an absolutely brill stand-up, Mum. Marcus told me he's going to be in it.'

'I thought Charlie said they're not gonna be filming the weekend we open?' protested Stephen.

'They're not, but I reckon we could do a deal with Marcus. We could organise a tour of the set. That's our USP! Al, how quickly can you and Ali get this website installed?'

Alison and Al looked at each other aghast.

'Charlie,' Alison finally spoke for them both. 'It's not that simple, and I really don't have the time, nor does Al . . .'

'We're all doing our bit, Alison,' said Stephen sternly. 'We know you've got these exams, but none of us really use computers like you . . .'

'Yes, but Stephen, designing a website that will look any good is a specialised skill. I can keep it running and feed stuff into it once we've got it, but I really couldn't set it up.'

Al nodded. 'She's right. You'll have to pay someone to design it.'

Stephen frowned. 'How much would that cost?'

'To do all the things you talked about, a good fifteen hundred.'

Stephen snorted. 'You're jokin'. I think we'll stick with our brochures, thank you very much.'

'That's so short-sighted, Stephen!' Alison spoke crossly. 'It would be money well spent, for God's sake. Do you think a few piddling little brochures are going to put the farm on the map—and how often would you be able to update them?'

'We could have a weekly newsletter,' said Angela brightly.

'And who's going to write it and distribute it? Let alone read it? You could put all that on a website.'

'It's a lot of money, Ali,' Charlie said slowly.

'Yes, it is, but think of all the money you've spent so far, think of all the money you're going to make from the film unit . . . Isn't a website as much of an investment as a pregnant Middle White?'

8

In the plush golden and cream richness of the master bedroom of Summerstoke House, Veronica Lester peered into the oval glass of her elegant Sheraton dressing table and removed the last vestiges of her makeup. She picked up a small, heavy pot, the label of which described the contents as extra-firming neck cream, and scooped out a liberal amount of the expensive unguent.

She had noticed a tell-tale puckering of the skin on her throat, an inevitable consequence of the onset of her forty-ninth year, but Veronica didn't 'do' age, and was determined to go to any lengths, short of plastic surgery, to banish all signs of the decaying process. On the whole she was making a good job of it.

Her figure, with the help of constant rounds of tennis and the daily exercising of a highly bred stallion, was trim; her hair, with the regular assistance of her hairdresser, was thick and blonde; and her skin, with the aid of the subtlest of makeup, presented to the world clear and wrinkle free.

While she was slapping the offending dewlap with the back of her hands, her husband, Hugh, emerged from the shower, rubbing vigorously at the silvery drops of water still clinging to his hairy torso. He was a short, fit, well-built man in his early fifties, his classic good looks permanently marred by a scowl or a sneer, dependent on his mood.

Tonight it was a scowl. He hated holding drinks parties, which he viewed as occasions when too much good booze was chucked down the throats of people who respected neither him nor his liquor.

Veronica eyed him in her mirror. 'Marion said something interesting to me this evening.'

'Makes a change.' Hugh was not interested in anything his wife's friend had to say.

Veronica ignored his tone and continued, keeping her voice light and unemotional. 'She said how nice it must be for us to have Anthony back home.'

Hugh stopped rubbing his hair and stared at his wife's reflection. 'What did the fuck she mean by

47

that?'

Veronica selected a pot marked "extra nutrient-rich night cream" and dipping the tips of her fingers into the jar, smoothed the cream onto her face, watching her husband all the while.

'She thought, Hugh, darling, that Anthony had come home. It would appear that when they were waiting at the traffic lights on the Summerbridge Road, he drew up alongside her on his ghastly bike. She'd just registered it was him when the lights changed and he shot off in the direction of Summerstoke.'

'She must have been mistaken. One motorcyclist looks just like another in all that clobber.'

'One would think so, but she was convinced it was him and she said Gavin agreed with her. He recognised the bike.'

She saw Hugh go very still as he digested this piece of news, an ugly frown replacing the scowl.

'Why the hell should Anthony come to Summerstoke? There's nothing for him here. Have you been in touch with him?'

'No, I haven't. Hugh, I agree with you—his behaviour was abominable and until he apologises . . .'

'Apologises!' Hugh snorted. 'He's got to do more than that, he's got to crawl!'

'Well I can't see him doing that,' observed Veronica. 'He's far too much like you. The question is what is he doing in Summerstoke? He's no friends here that I know of, except Cordelia, of course. Maybe she can shed some light on this.'

'You haven't asked her?'

'When have I had the chance? Anyway, Cordelia's not here, she's staying the night with

48

that friend of hers, Tamara whatsit. I'll ask her tomorrow when I pick her up.'

Hugh made no further comment and leaving his towel in a damp heap on the floor, climbed into bed, still frowning.

Veronica sighed at her reflection. Much as she would like to have gone straight to sleep, unless she did something to tease him out of this mood, it would overshadow the whole weekend.

She got up from her dressing table and without comment, picked up the towel and took it back to the bathroom, sprayed herself with a light scent kept there for occasions like these, and returned to the bedroom.

Sitting on the edge of the bed, she leant forward and kissed him full on the mouth, letting her breast, in its silky negligée, press against his naked chest. She could feel him relax, soften and yield as she kissed him. She trailed her fingers down the length of his body to his groin. He groaned.

A cold draught, playing across her back, distracted her and shivering in her negligée, she slid off the bed to shut the offending window. Drawing back the thick silk curtains, she paused for a moment and looked out over the darkened houses of the village. A trail of silver raindrops hit the windowpane.

She shivered.

'I wonder where he's staying tonight,' she said half-aloud.

'He'd better not be skulking anywhere on my property,' came the harsh reply. 'Now are you going to carry on faffing about, or are you going to take that silk thing off and come to bed?'

49

9

Emma Knight lay, in semi-darkness, on a battered sofa in the small sitting room of her flat in Notting Hill, listening to the comforting sound waves of Kathryn Tickell and Andy Sheppard and brooding over the first read-through. One hand was folded round the stem of a large glass of shiraz balanced on her stomach and the other dipped into a dish of salted almonds; one of the best ways to unwind, in her opinion, and didn't she need to do just that!

Could she have been firmer with Marcus when he first told her about Jason Hart? He might not have taken any notice of her, but she would have made her position crystal clear. It was too late to back out now—besides, she wanted the series. She'd done single dramas before and she knew she'd established a good reputation—that's why Marcus Steel had approached her. She was ready for something more light-hearted, but with longevity and with the added bonus of being shot entirely on location.

Three months away from London, the flat, and everything that reminded her of Jonathan. The bastard!

She took a mouthful of wine and swilled it around her mouth, relishing its tart richness and the way it made the inside of her mouth pucker. She'd have to make sure she put a case of the wine in the car; Summerstoke didn't sound like the sort of place she'd be able to buy a good shiraz.

She hadn't had time to go and check out her lodgings, but that wasn't unusual and Marcus had

50

mentioned the landlady was an artist, so it sounded as if it would be a pretty relaxed sort of set-up; just what she craved.

But what she didn't need was this prick, Jason Hart, to be foisted on her. Emma prided herself on being able to coax a performance out of the most unpromising material, but from today's read-through it was clear to her that Jason had neither aptitude, nor interest: a deadly combination.

It was all very well Marcus saying the project was sold on the back of having Jason Hart on board. If he remained on board, he would scupper the ship and she was not going to allow that.

A glint came to her eye.

She'd never worked with Marcus before, but she knew of him. He'd been variously described to her as determined, intelligent and ruthless, and 'a bit of a dish'. Which he was, in a way, but not her type, not at all, she reflected vehemently—well-built, but with not an ounce of fat—she bet he worked out in the gym every day, or ran, or played tennis; his sort did. His eyes were the brightest and shrewdest she'd ever encountered. She thought he was probably older than her—late thirties, forty even, but it was hard to tell. A force to be reckoned with; but then, she thought, with a challenging tilt to her chin, so was she.

She finished her wine, got to her feet, switched on a light and reached for her laptop.

Marcus Steel had made it clear he was not going to change his mind about Jason Hart, but she was equally determined that he would . . .

*   *   *

Yawning, Marcus poured himself a generous glass of Laphroaig, splashed in a smidgen of water, went over to his desk and opened his Mac. Included in the emails awaiting his attention was an invitation from his brother, Milo:

Hi littlel bro know your busy but i thought i'd drop a reminder about the jack vestric and isabelle langtons opeining at polly merfield's gallery see info attached bring your medai pals see youo milo.

Milo, Marcus's half-brother, had seized on the convenience of emails as the perfect excuse for never writing a letter again, but as he never bothered to correct anything he wrote there was often a fair amount of deciphering to be done.

Marcus clicked the attachment, looked at the invitation, thought about it for a moment, then printed it off. He had no great fondness for the stuff that Jack Vestric churned out, but Isabelle, Charlie's girlfriend, had worked for Milo, who was not the easiest person in the world, and the few times he'd bumped into her he'd liked her.

He continued scrolling then double-clicked on an email sent that evening.

Hi Marcus, just to say how much I enjoyed the read through today. I think the show is going to be a great hit and thanks so much for giving me the part of Josie. I love her.

See you on location,
Best wishes,
Nicola.

A faint smile flickered across Marcus's face. The part of Josie, the girlfriend who dumps Jason Hart's character in the first episode, was so small and limited Nicola Scudamore's gratitude could be seen as a little excessive. But he was well aware that while the last three episodes remained in a fluid state, Nicola, and the millions of other struggling actors like her, would dance on scorpions if it improved their chances of being written back in.

She was pretty, true. Petite, with dark glossy curls and bright blue eyes and a merry expression—it was why he'd cast her. And she could act—they all could, all the bright, pretty, young and not so young things, who went up for audition after audition, all desperate to be given the chance to demonstrate that they, too, had star quality.

The whole profession was a lottery even for those, like Juliet Peters, who were relatively successful. As a consequence it was rare to meet a performer who was not jittery and insecure, and almost without exception, demanded reassurance and love from the people they worked with as well as from the world at large.

Marcus pitied them but, by and large, did not seek out their company or make friends with them.

Nicola was still relatively young and came across as confident and flirtatious. Marcus was aware that, as a free agent, he would be considered fair game. Location filming was an intense, exclusive, other-world experience, with its own rules and codes of behaviour. Actresses like Nicola Scudamore had to be treated with caution.

'What will Charlie Tucker and his family make of these butterflies?' he wondered, and grinned at the thought.

He and Charlie Tucker had liked each other from the moment they'd first met. Charlie was no country bumpkin—he was, like Marcus himself, a bit of a maverick, but one who happened to be born into a way of life that would claim him, chain him, and drag him down unless he could find a way of fighting free.

When Marcus first met him he was thrashing around, thinking of taking his Gran's bequest and setting off into the unknown world of greener grass. But pragmatism had prevailed and then Marcus had snapped him up to act as an aide de camp to the location manager.

He'd done a bloody good job and Marcus wondered idly whether he could employ Charlie in the future; but there was no room for sentiment in the film business and when Marcus moved on, he doubted they would want to journey together.

The cursor hovered over an email from Emma Knight marked ominously, 'Jason'. With an exasperated grunt, Marcus opened it.

Hi, Marcus, sorry to bang on but I'm seriously worried about JH. I could see nothing in him to think that he will be other than a time waster. Can we/you afford this? Our time is tight enough as it is. It can't be too late to reconsider.

Otherwise, the rest of the cast and crew are great and I think we've got a good series here—but not with Mr Hart!

Emma

Marcus frowned, muttering 'How many times are we going to have this conversation?'

She had a point: Jason's woodenness and lack of enthusiasm had been painful, but he thought he'd made it clear to Emma he was integral to Marcus's agenda.

He was confident once Emma realised he was not going to change his mind, she'd get on with it; she was, in all likelihood, miffed he'd cast the guy without consulting her.

He sighed, impatient. He'd have to have a word with Jason, and, if necessary, with his agent, who was determined to see his client on mainstream telly. It was just unfortunate the guy was such an arrogant shit—and Marcus suspected that nursing him through the next three months might become a major preoccupation.

'Maybe,' he thought, stretching and yawning, 'maybe he'll take a shine to Nicola and that'll solve two problems at a stroke. I'll get Ross to make sure they have adjacent trailers.'

10

The booing and catcalls were good-natured and matched by whistles, shouts, cheers and table thumping. The room was crowded, illuminated only by dim wall lights with curling orange shades and the spillage of light from a minuscule stage, where a shaven-headed youth thanked his audience with a flurry of V signs.

Jason, with Daisy May, his current girlfriend, an aspiring singer, had arrived half-way through the night's line up, but he'd made his debut in this club and his subsequent success ensured that no matter how busy it was, whenever he patronised it a table was instantly forthcoming.

His ego had taken a battering at the script read-through and the party afterwards had not lifted his spirits. He'd got onto his agent when he'd got home, but was told, in terms that still rankled, that his contract was watertight and he would incur real financial damage if he ducked out now. The only way out was for the project to fold, or for him to be fired by the TV company and he didn't want that to happen, did he? Because that would put paid to a telly career once and for all.

When Daisy May had arrived back from a gig, she found Jason half way through a bottle of whisky, feeling very sorry for himself, so she'd dragged him out. For Jason, this club was home. True, it was no longer fugged up with fag smoke and he missed that, but the rowdiness and the bonhomie, the mix of adrenalin with the claustrophobic smell of too many bodies, the sour sweet smell of spilt beer mingling with a faint whiff of marijuana and lavatories, all that served to settle and comfort him.

'Hi Jayce, Daisy May,' Ted, the club's owner, stopped at their table and nodded. 'How're yer doin? Okay for drinks?'

'Thanks, mate, wouldn't say no to a refill. Pint of Stella would go down nicely.'

'And I'm drinking vodka and coke, Ted,' chipped in Daisy May. 'That last lad was a bit of all right, wasn't he? He been on here before?'

'Third showing. He's in training for Edinburgh . . . got a good slot in The Pleasance; should do well. Following in your footsteps, eh Jayce?'

Jason gave a non-committal grunt, causing Daisy May to interject hastily, 'But he ain't as good as Jayce was when he began. He had them eating out of his hands when he was still wet behind the ears.'

'Yeah, you're right, I did,' Jason slurped back the last of his beer and slapped the empty glass meaningfully on the table.

'Maybe you'd do a bit for us tonight?' The owner enquired, more in hope than expectation and picking up the empty glass, signalled to a member of his bar staff.

Jason shrugged.

'None of the kids we've had on tonight come near you, Jayce. You know that. They're good, but you'd knock the spots off them.'

'Yeah, I would, but this is a night off, Ted.'

'Anyway Ted, he couldn't do it just like that, his manager would have a fit.'

Daisy May's mention of his manager was an immediate irritant and Jason scowled. 'I'm fucking tired of being told what I may and may not do, so shut it, Daisy May. If I choose to do five minutes in my old club, what's he gonna do? Fire the goose that lays the golden whatsit? Not bloomin' likely.'

In a matter of seconds, word got back to the evening's compere that not only was Jason Hart in the house, but that he was up to doing a routine. The cheers that greeted this announcement brought Jason to his feet and he made his way somewhat unsteadily, clutching his fresh pint, to the stage.

For a moment he stood there, staring at his audience and when the applause showed no signs of decreasing, he held up his hand for silence and when that didn't have the desired effect, he bawled 'Shuttit!'

The noise subsided and he surveyed the expectant faces with a grim satisfaction.

'Prats!'

Then he grinned and the audience collapsed with grateful laughter.

'I'm very grateful for your applause—specially as I've done nothin', absolutely sod all, for it. You clapped me 'cos you know who I am. I know who I am—at least, I think I do. Who was the guy who said "I think therefore I am"? What a prat he was. Hadn't he met the dickheads what don't think?

There's billions of 'em, farting around, running governments, making countries bankrupt, screwing up wars; and then there's the celebs, earning billions doing nothin' but showin' their faces and makin' asses of themselves, or so called soccer stars, prancing about on the pitch, missing free kicks—that lot, they're full of "I-am", they fuckin' ooze "I-am", but they've very little brain, and I'm not talkin' about fuckin' bears.'

He paused, cocked his head and continued thoughtfully, ' "Pooh Bear"—that fellah ought to've been knighted for services to piss-taking for thinking that one up. I was sitting on the bus going to the airport, minding my own business, when this family clambered on board. It was the three bears—Daddy Bear was carrying the big, big suitcases, poor sod; Mummy Bear was carrying the travel bags, and Baby Bear had one of those ickle dinky back packs with Tractor Ted stuck on its pocket. They squeezed into their seats and Baby Bear wails, "Where's my Pooh, I want my Pooh". My jaw dropped onto my chest, I can tell you. Was this anal retention carried to an extreme—did this kid go travelling with his big jobs wrapped up in his travel blanket? And what would happen when they went through the X-ray machine at the airport—would it classify as combustible material?

'"What's this madam?"—"It's my son's pooh."—"You can't take that on board, it's an offensive weapon".'

He grinned. 'You can see it happening can't you? "Take me to the pilot or I'll rub this in your face . . . " In fact you wouldn't even have to take it in your hand luggage—just hold tight then when you're on board, hey presto—nip to the lav and

58

catch your jobbies in a napkin. I bet air security haven't thought of that, have they?'

His audience thumped their tables and screamed with unqualified laughter.

'But to return to my central thesis—self-centred, self-satisfied cocky fuckers with no brain, who'd come on this stage and lap up your applause, because, like me, you know 'em . . . But I digress and before I go any further I have a question. Any act-ors in the audience tonight?'

A couple of voices shouted 'yes'.

'Well you can fuck off out of here, for a start!'

The audience roared.

'I've just spent the last half day of my life with a bunch of act-ors and I tell you, my eyes have been opened.

'To be more specific, it wasn't theatre act-ors I was with. That sort graft like the rest of us and I take my hat off to 'em, learning all that Shakespeare and stuff. Anyway, my gripe is I've gotta spend the next three months of my fuckin' life with a bunch of telly luvvies and believe me, they are unreal, I mean, unreal!'

He minced around the stage blowing air kisses. 'Mwah, mwah, dahling you look divine, dahling, you read that beaut-i-fully, dahling, no–one would guess you're over the hill, dahling—how's dear Peter? Darling Judi? Dear Anthony?'

'They call each other darling because they can't remember anyone's name; they can't remember anything—even their lines are fed to them in tiny doses, just before each camera take—"lights, camera, action . . . " "Oh sorry, darling, what's my line?" '

In the face of this harangue the audience

59

continued to titter, but with less enthusiasm and as if sensing he was in danger of pushing his audience away, Jason switched tack and returned to more familiar territory, but not before promising them, on his return from three months' exile, a remorseless exposé on life with the luvvies on a farm in a rural backwater, run by straw-sucking country bumpkins.

In the dark recesses of the club, Ross Manvers sipped his beer and looked thoughtful. He was, in every respect, a very conscientious second assistant director. Not knowing the world of stand-up comedy and sensing that Jason was going to be a difficult customer, he'd decided a little research might come in handy and a couple of mates had suggested this club.

He hadn't known it was the venue that had given birth to Jason, or that it was a frequent haunt of his, so his appearance on stage took Ross completely by surprise, as did the content of his diatribe.

Whilst Ross didn't like a lot of the actors for whom he was responsible, he took pride in knowing all their foibles and vulnerabilities. For the duration of the project they belonged to him; they were his charges; their fragile egos were in his hands. He stood between them and the prying, prurient world, and they trusted him. If Jason Hart were serious and his charges were exposed and ridiculed . . . not only would individual reputations be destroyed, but the series would be jeopardised; his own competence questioned.

He frowned. Quite how he could stop him he wasn't sure, but he would. There was no way this nasty little cuckoo was going to be allowed to upset Ross's cosy nest.

11

'Mum, Mum, come and look!'

Staring out of his bedroom window, six-year-old Ryan Spinks, the eldest child of Lenny Spinks, Marsh Farm's only hired hand, bellowed with excitement. 'Mum, come up 'ere; come and see!'

His mother, Paula, responding to the urgency in his voice, left her three younger children tucking into sugary-coated nuggets of something purporting to be corn, and clopped up the stairs in her fluffy mules, grumbling gently.

'What is it, Ryan? You're gonna be late for school again if you're not careful. What is it, what are you lookin' at?' She followed his gaze out of the window and gasped. 'Oh my word . . .'

Like a travelling circus, the film unit's base camp had materialised overnight in a field across the river from the Spinks's cottage; an impressive encampment of trailers, caravans and lorries, with a double-decker bus at its heart.

'Your Dad said they was expected, but it rained so hard last night, he doubted they'd come on account of all the mud. It's huge, ain't it? Fancy them bringin' in all those vehicles, and I never heard a thing.'

'Can we go and have a look, Mum? Go on, let us go. Dad said they's on the telly.'

'Not now Ryan, you're late enough as it is. It'll have to wait till after school.'

But as soon as Paula had deposited her two eldest in the school playground, she wheeled the pushchair, containing her two youngest, straight for the field in the company of a small contingent of other young mums, all equally curious.

For as long as anyone could remember the village had used the field as if it belonged to them. It was where the kids played; where blackberries were picked; Guy Fawkes celebrated; the Mere skated on when the temperatures dropped low enough to turn the muddy water to ice, and where dogs were exercised all year round.

Now a sturdy barbed wire fence restricted public use to a narrow footpath running along the edge of the river; and as if to reinforce the changed status of their playground, a large security guard stood by the gate.

Paula and her mates arrived in time to hear this mighty mortal being harangued by a middle-aged lady inside a purple mohair sweater and tracksuit trousers. A muddy, overweight, chocolate Labrador sat wheezing at her side.

Paula greeted her cheerily, 'Mornin' Mrs Godwin. We've come to have a dekko at the camp. Seen anyone famous, yet? Oh my word, you do look muddy.'

'I am,' snapped Rita Godwin. 'I was explaining to this gentleman here that if we can't use the field, the footpath, which is muddy enough already, will turn into a quagmire.'

'I'm sorry, madam,' interjected the security man politely, 'but you must understand, in the interests of security . . .'

'So you keep on saying, but this field is used by the village; we should have been consulted. I'm going to have to bring this up at the Parish Council. It really is too bad!' And so saying, she marched off, dragging the weary Labrador behind her.

The guard watched her go with a shake of his head then turned, a wary expression on his face, to confront the assembled young women with pushchairs.

'Well, ladies, what can I do for you?'

By common consent, Paula, on account of her 'doing' for Juliet Peters and because her Lenny worked at Marsh Farm, was their spokesperson.

She spoke up boldly. 'We live in the village and we was wondering if you could show us around. Most of us are gonna be extras, see . . .'

The 'extras' recruitment had not yet taken place and, in reality, most of the young mums shrank at the idea. But not Paula; she had idolised the film star, Joan Collins, for most of her life and she dreamed that one day the cloud of drudgery would lift. One day she would be spotted and launched on the dizzying stairway to the stars. One day she would join her idol and have it all—fame, glamour, bubble baths, chocolates and champagne.

The TV crew coming to Summerstoke, as she saw it, was her first big break.

The security man smiled at her.

'I'm sure my boss would be happy to sort summat out. Not today, mind. It being the first day, we're pretty busy . . .'

Paula peered past him into the camp. It looked deserted.

'Don't look that busy to I. Where is everybody? Where are all the actors to?'

The man shrugged. 'If they're working today, they'll be on the set, not here. That's where all the action is, if you can call it action. If you're gonna be an extra, you'll find out soon enough that's the last thing it is. To be honest it's a lot of hanging about with not much happening. I did it once—never again. My job guarding the base camp's much more interestin'. I gets to meet them all and they all know me by name.'

'So when are they goin' to come back here, then? The actors, I mean?'

'Not till lunchtime, I should think.'

There was not much more to be said and disappointed there'd be no sight of anyone famous that morning, the young women wandered off.

12

'Oh, bollocks!' Al, exasperated, pushed his chair back from Alison's computer with an irritated sigh.

Looking over his shoulder, Alison chewed her lip, disappointed. 'It's not registering.'

'No, and I can't see why fuckin' not. I've done everything they said. I just don't see where it's going wrong.'

'Er . . . shall I have a go?' ventured Angela.

It was her day off and she had arranged to meet Alison and Al, first thing, to help set up the farm's website. She'd not spent much time in Al's company before and his truculent attitude disconcerted her. Stephen never swore, at least not in her presence, and she winced every time Al did.

Unsmiling, he looked at her. 'Be my guest, but I think you're wasting your time.'

'It may just be that I'll pick up on something you've missed,' Angela said in a small voice. 'That often happens at the library—trying to source something, it's so easy to overlook a link and then . . .'

With an impatient snort Al got up and stalked over to the bedroom window.

'Go on, Ange, see what you can do,' Alison encouraged her. 'It will be so frustrating to have got this far and then not to be able to open the website.'

'It's what I said,' remarked Al. 'It's all very well loading the information, but you need a proper designer for something as complex as this should be, and if we can't even put up the opening page . . .'

'Let Ange try,' Alison went across to him and perched on the sill, looking up at him. 'Don't look so cross,' she coaxed, adding softly, 'If we don't succeed, it'll reinforce what we said to Stephen and Charlie: we need to invest a decent sum of money to get it set up.'

Al glanced over at Angela, hunched and preoccupied over the keyboard, then leant forward and pushed his tongue into Alison's mouth. Her body sizzled and stifling a groan, she returned his kiss, keeping one cautious eye on Angela.

His hand moved under her jumper, slipped inside her bra and caressed her breast; before she could stop him, he had undone the fastening and was fondling her nipples.

Still watching Angela, she undid his belt and had just released the top button of his jeans, when Angela shouted, 'Don't do that!'

Alison flushed and hastily pulled her jumper down.

'Oh no! It's gone, don't do that, you silly machine!'

With an impish smile at Al, Alison went back to

Angela's side. 'No luck?'

'No.' Angela shook her head and turned round. 'I couldn't get anywhere with it. Oh dear.' She looked as if she was going to burst into tears. 'I so hoped we could do it ourselves. It seems an awful waste of money if we have to pay someone else. And it's money that could better be spent elsewhere—that's Stephen's point.'

'Yes, but see it as an investment, Angela,' said Al, his belt and trousers now intact. 'You can't afford not to get someone else involved.' He gave her a fleeting smile. 'I think you'd be better off getting together as much material as you think we might need. The copy you've provided is great, but we need pictures, digital ones. Have you got a digital camera, either of you?'

Angela shook her head.

'No, not really—but my mobile takes pictures,' said Alison.

'No, no—the resolution wouldn't be nearly good enough.' Al frowned. 'What about your friend, Hannah? Or Nick? Ask around; see if you can borrow one, and I will, too. Between us we should come up with something'

'Angela! Angela!' Jenny called from the bottom of the stairs.

Angela jumped up. 'I've got to go. I promised Mum I'd go and look round the camp with her this morning. I would've liked to able to help you more, but if there's any additional writing you want done, just let me know.'

She opened the bedroom door and shouted, 'Coming, Mum,' then turned back to them. 'I'll catch up with you later. I'm really sorry to have to leave you to it. See what you can do.'

66

Seconds later they could hear her footsteps running down the stairs.

With a wicked smile, Al turned to Alison, 'I think we should obey her instructions, and see what we can do, don't you?'

And slowly, deliberately, with his eyes fixed on her face and a teasing half-smile playing over his features, he unzipped his jeans.

13

A breeze had picked up. The uniform grey of the sky was dispersed and replaced by rolling whorls of pearly cloud, patches of pale blue and occasional shafts of weak sunshine. Glistening gold celandine danced in the wind and the snowy-white blossom of the blackthorn, growing alongside the river, fluttered into the air and settled lightly on the black surface of the water. But in the field occupied by the film unit there was little other activity in evidence until halfway through the morning when Jenny Tucker, accompanied by Angela, arrived at the gate.

Jenny's hair was pinned back and she'd applied lipstick; the habitual pinafore had been discarded and over an unremarkable skirt she wore a beautiful, multi-coloured sweater—a reject from the designer for whom she knitted.

Excitement and the exercise of walking up the long track from the farm had brought a becoming flush to her face, and the security guard, who was well into his fifties, gave a soft wolf-whistle. (He had been warned that wolf-whistling was not 'appropriate behaviour' and could lead to him getting a reprimand, if not the sack; but it was an instinct born of his generation and he couldn't see why he shouldn't give what he saw as a compliment to a pretty woman.)

Jenny, who'd attracted plenty of wolf-whistles before she married and very few subsequently, smiled, assuming it was directed at Angela who bobbed along at her elbow, plain as plain, eyes wide behind her enormous glasses.

'What can I do for you, ladies?'

'Marcus Steel said we was to ask for a Mr Ross Manvers. He's goin' to show us around the camp,' Jenny replied.

'Right-ho, love—and who shall I say is callin'?'

'I'm Jenny Tucker, and this is my son's fiancée, Angela Upton. We farm this land, see.'

The guard spoke into a small walkie-talkie, which spluttered and spat in reply, then whistled across to a man leaning against a car, reading the paper. He looked up.

'Hey, Joe, would you be so kind as to take these two lovely ladies to our leader.'

Ross met them at the door of his trailer and smiled a greeting, talking simultaneously into his mobile.

'Fine, will do, no probs, Matt. Be with you in just a tick, ladies.' And he punched in another number and instructed whoever it was who answered that their presence on the set was required immediately. Finally, he turned his attention to Jenny and Angela, with a cheerful smile. 'Marcus says I'm to give you the gold-star tour. I'm not sure what he means by that, but I can show you round and then we can end up here in time for coffee or tea and

68

bacon butties, which are due in about ten minutes. How does that sound?'

'That's really kind of you, Mr Manvers. Are you sure you've got the time?' For Ross's mobile had gone off again. Apologising, he dealt swiftly with the call before replying, 'Of course, so long as you'll excuse my enslavement to this thing—if it rings, I have to answer. And please, call me Ross.'

Jenny instantly liked Ross. He was, at a guess, in his early forties. Not tall, he was clean-shaven, with short brown hair peppered with grey, lean and wiry, with a sharp nose, an oval shaped face and bright eyes, and the sort of smile that seemed personal and warm. Normally Jenny was quite shy, but to her—and Angela's—amazement, she became almost chatty as he showed them around.

'We call this area of the camp Beverley Hills,' he waved at a line of trailers, most of which had nameplates stuck on the door although all appeared unoccupied.

'Why? What are they used for?' Jenny asked.

'They're for the actors; they're the dressing rooms. The costumes are laid out ready for them first thing, so they'll change here and wait till they're wanted. The actors who are in for the whole run will have a trailer for their sole use.'

He stopped outside one. 'This is Ben Dacres's. He's gonna spend a lot of time in here. In fact he's about this morning.'

Jenny went quite pink with excitement. 'Is he in there now?'

Ross grinned. 'I hope not—he should be on set. They're filming the opening scene.'

'May we look inside?' asked Angela.

'Not in his, obviously, but I can show you one

69

that's not being used. We have quite a lot of actors who come down for the odd day's filming, so the name on some of the vans is constantly changing. Here, have a peek inside this one while I take this call.'

Angela and Jenny clambered up the steps and looked inside. Each trailer was divided into two dressing rooms just large enough to contain a compact divan tucked under a window, a small dressing table and mirror, a narrow wardrobe and a minuscule bathroom with a shower.

They joined Ross outside.

'They're very small, aren't they?' observed Angela. 'And not very . . . very, well, luxurious.'

'Not what you'd expect someone like Ben Dacres or Juliet Peters to have. I thought they'd be full of velvet curtains, flowers and champagne,' murmured Jenny.

Ross laughed. 'Can you imagine the amount of space we'd need if we had luxury caravans for everyone who thought they deserved one? They're only for daytime use, so they're adequate.'

'Do the actors have somewhere else to go, like a Green Room?' asked Angela, determined to demonstrate that if not knowledgeable in the ways of television, she was in the practices of the theatre.

'No. They can go to the dining bus for meal breaks or to collect drinks, but we like them to stay in their trailers when they're not on set. I'm afraid it boils down to the old cliché: time is money. If we can't find them when they're called for filming because they're not in their trailer, we waste time looking for them, we fall behind schedule, and I get a terrible bollocking, if you'll excuse my French. Now, here we have our makeup department.'

Ross led the way in and out of the vans and, in between calls, introduced them to the makeup staff, showed them where the costumes were hung, where the props were stored, and trailers full of electrical equipment and other gear.

He introduced them to the cook and his assistants; to the drivers who ferried anyone from the base to the location, and to others described variously as runners, chippies, standby props and standby riggers, all of whom seemed to have such different, incomprehensible jobs, Jenny's head span.

'Here we are, the dining room and just in time for bacon butties.'

Ross led the way onto the double-decker bus, the inside of which was transformed by rows of tables and chairs. There was a serving hatch at one end where one of the kitchen assistants was dispensing rolls, tea and coffee to members of the crew.

'Grab a seat, ladies; Chris, here, will get you want you want, I'm needed in my office. Chris, will you bring the ladies back to my van when they've finished? Ta.'

Chris, a youth in his late teens, with a pale, acne–pocked face, light brown Rastafarian locks and over-sized droopy trousers, obligingly fetched Jenny and Angela bacon butties and steaming mugs of tea.

'So you're from the farm then?' asked one of the crew.

'Yes.' The question had been directed at Jenny, but her mouth was too full of bun and bacon to do more than nod.

Angela, who always nibbled at her food, answered with pride. 'My fiancée is the farmer—

we're going to get married in the summer.'

'Oh, so that would be Charlie,' said another.

Angela reddened with annoyance. 'No, Charlie's Stephen's brother, he works on the farm.'

'Oh, sorry, Marcus said he was the farmer.'

She bridled and retorted, 'Well he's not; when we get married, Stephen will be the major shareholder and he looks after all the animals. Charlie just does the crops and looks after the buildings and stuff.'

At this, Jenny felt a twinge of concern. While she adored Stephen, she didn't want Charlie to be undervalued. 'Charlie's my eldest son,' she explained. 'The boys are partners. Charlie's developing the business side, looking at all the other ways the farm can make money.'

'Sounds a bit like our script,' commented another. 'Have you read it?'

'No,' confessed Jenny, 'I haven't. Marcus said it was a comedy. I can't wait to see it. It'll be so funny seeing our farm on the television, and oh, I just can't get over the fact that the likes of Ben Dacres is here, on our farm . . .'

'But we ought to read the script, Mum,' Angela frowned. 'Has anyone in the family seen it?'

Before Jenny could reply, she was distracted by the arrival of a distinguished man, in his early fifties. He looked familiar, or rather he looked like a rather washed-out image of someone she knew very well; it was his voice that more immediately identified him.

'I hope you ravenous hordes haven't eaten the last of the bacon butties, I'm starving! Plenty left, oh good, be a sweetie would you and bring a couple to my trailer.'

Jenny squeaked with excitement and clutched

Angela's arm. 'It's him, Ange. Oh my Lord, it's him!'

Fans were almost as indispensable to Ben Dacres as fresh air, and he had a highly developed internal radar for sensing potential admirers. At the first squeak he'd swung round and homed in on the excited, glowing face of Jenny.

He turned back to the serving hatch. 'On second thoughts, darling boy, I'll eat them here.' Taking the proffered plate, he moved across to Jenny and Angela and twinkled at them both. 'I don't think we've met, have we? May I join you?'

Jenny could feel her insides dissolve, perspiration break out all over her body, her mouth go dry and her face go scarlet. She tried to speak, but no words came. Fortunately Angela, who didn't have a television in her bedsit and so was not so familiar with Ben Dacres's winning personality, was less overcome.

'Feel free,' she said, and when he was seated, asked, in all innocence, 'Are you one of the actors, then?'

The twinkle left Ben's face. 'You could say that. And you are?'

'Oh, we're from the farm. Stephen, the farmer, is my fiancée . . .' But she got no further.

'How nice for you.' He cut her off, the dead tone of his response making it clear he was not interested in her forthcoming nuptials. Ignoring her unhappy blush, he turned to Jenny and tried his twinkle again. 'And you are?'

It worked. Jenny beamed, her green eyes shone, and she was finally able to ask, in her soft, sweet West Country voice, 'Is it really you? I'm not dreamin' am I?'

The various members of the crew, assembled for their elevenses, had taken to Jenny, so the general laughter that greeted her remark was sympathetic rather than derisory.

'Oh it's him alright, Jenny . . .'

'Better watch yer step . . .'

'Every woman's heart-throb . . .'

'Dreamy Dacres . . .'

'Beddable Ben.'

'It's him, alright.'

Ben laughed, flashing perfect white teeth. 'Okay, fellers, okay.' He turned back to Jenny, grinning. 'Impudent groundlings—trouble is, they know me too well. I've worked with a lot of these chaps before. Yes, Ben Dacres at your service. And whom have I the honour of addressing?'

Jenny, ignoring the catcalls and laughter, thought she hadn't met a more pleasant, courteous, and, yes, handsome man in her life.

She blushed and dimpled. 'I'm Jenny Tucker. My two sons run Marsh Farm, where you're filming.'

'And Mr Tucker, your husband—has he retired?'

'Oh no. He's dead. I'm a widow; have been these last ten years.'

'I'm sorry to hear that.' His voice softened so sympathetically that Jenny, who hadn't wept for her Jim for some considerable time, felt tears spring to her eyes.

'I lost my first wife some years ago. It's something you never get over, is it? So sudden— she was killed in a car crash. Tragic.' He shook his head sorrowfully. 'And your Jim? He must have been quite young?'

'He weren't that old. He was making silage when he suddenly keeled over with a massive heart

74

attack.'

'Silage?' Ben Dacres choked.

'Yes. He was standing on top of the clamp. It was horrible. Poor Jim. But your wife—a car crash, you said? That's really sad. Where you there? Oh please . . .' she put out a hand and timidly touched his arm, distressed to see his eyes fill with tears.

'How stupid of me. I didn't mean to upset you.'

With a manful effort, Ben controlled his emotions. 'Not stupid at all, you know how it is—even after all this time, a sympathetic enquiry can bring it all back.' He gave her a brave smile and patted her hand.

Jenny felt her heartbeat change gear.

'Do you believe in astrology?'

'Astrology?' Jenny whispered, finding the volume switch on her vocal chords unaccountably turned almost to zero.

'Yes,' he replied, dropping his voice nearly as low as hers so that she had to lean forward to hear what he was saying, effectively excluding Angela, and the rest of the crew who watched on, amused. 'The stars.'

'Oh, well, er . . .' Jenny always read her horoscope, but she didn't know whether she believed in it and she didn't know whether it was something she could admit to without appearing stupid.

He settled that for her. 'I do. And I think you do to. What star sign are you, Jenny?'

It was the way he said "Jenny". Her heart flipped again. 'Cancer,' she croaked.

His hand squeezed hers. 'A water sign, that's beautiful—like Princess Diana. I knew as soon as I saw you that you are kind and compassionate—a nurturer—and that we'd get along, that we'd be compatible. I'm a Leo.'

'Oh.' She really couldn't think of anything else to say; her brain appeared to have seized up, along with everything else.

'So when is your birthday?'

'Uh . . . it's on the 23rd of June.'

'That's wonderful. I think we'll just be finishing filming then so we'll be able to celebrate with you.'

Jenny was so overcome she gave up the struggle to say something sensible and simply beamed.

'Ah, there you are, Ben.' Ross swung himself onto the bus. 'I thought you were going straight to your trailer. They need you back on set; slight change of plan. Joe . . .' Ross turned to one of the drivers. 'When you've dropped off Mr Dacres, would you go the Country Club and pick up Mr Hart.'

'But I've wiped off my makeup, Ross. I thought they'd finished with me this morning. It's a bit early in the day to start changing the schedules, isn't it?' Ben looked displeased.

'Marianne is on set. She'll fix you up there. Sorry Ben, but we don't want this scene to run on into the afternoon.'

With that he was gone.

Ben shrugged and turned to Jenny and Angela. 'Alas, dear ladies, duty calls, but I do so hope we meet again . . .'

'Oh, I do hope so, too, Mr Dacres,' replied Jenny with fervour. 'Will you be at the party, on Friday, you know, at the Foresters' Arms?'

'Ben, you must call me Ben,' he said. 'Truth to tell, I'd forgotten about Marcus's party, but now . . . Yes, we shall dance till dawn!' He tilted her chin

76

and looked in her eyes. 'What lovely colour eyes you have, Jenny. Adios.'

And with a half-gesture of farewell to the rest of his audience, he left.

It was as well Jenny was still seated as her head was spinning. 'Well I never; who'd have thought it; well, well, well . . .' was all she could say.

Angela, looking at her watch, brought her to earth. 'I think we should go, Mum. It's getting a bit close to lunch and I haven't cooked the potatoes for the shepherd's pie yet.'

Ross was on the phone when they got back to his trailer and he waved at them to take a seat while he finished his call.

His trailer had been converted into a fully equipped office, complete with landlines, a computer, printer and photocopier. Displayed on the walls were a number of photographic portraits, each labelled with an actor's name and identifying their role in the TV series. Jenny identified Ben Dacres's picture and then looked to see how many other faces she could recognise.

'It's a nice one of Juliet Peters,' she whispered to Angela, 'she's a lovely girl. And look, Jilly Westcott—I haven't seen her for ages . . .'

Angela joined her, not much interested.

'Sorry to keep you, ladies.' Ross came off the phone. 'I've asked Joe to give you a lift back to the farm; he should be waiting for you by the gate.'

'There's no need for a lift. We can walk back, can't we Angela?'

Angela's reply came in the form of a strangled squeak. She was staring at one of the photographs.

'It's not . . . she's not . . . she can't be . . .'

Puzzled, Jenny scrutinised the photo that

appeared to upset Angela. A pretty girl smiled back. She looked vaguely familiar, as did the name. She shook her head. 'What's wrong, Angela, do you know her?'

Ross looked over Angela's shoulder. 'Nicola Scudamore. She's playing the part of Will's girlfriend in the first episode. Pretty little thing, isn't she? Do you know her?'

Angela bit her lip and said curtly, 'Yes, yes, I do know her. She was in our theatre company, The Merlin Players . . .'

She gave a poor imitation of a light laugh, which caused Ross to stare at her curiously. 'Fancy her turning up like this. I'll have to tell Stephen . . .'

In the car taking them back to the farm, Angela lapsed into an uncharacteristic, broody silence and Jenny's attempts to get her to agree that Ben Dacres was one of the 'dishiest men to walk the earth' was met with a snapped, 'Well if you think that, Mum, where does poor Jeff fit into it all . . .'

Which left Jenny thinking about Jeff and about Ben Dacres, and then about Jeff again. But her thoughts kept returning to Ben's last words to her, 'What lovely colour eyes you have, Jenny . . .' Jeff had never said anything like that to her.

Never.

14

'There you go, girls—eat yer fill.' Charlie slit the twine holding the bale and tipped it into the feeder, deftly avoiding a pair of sharp horns as he did so. He stood back, for a moment, watching the shaggy, russet beasts toss the hay with their massive heads. 'They are beauts,' he remarked to Lenny as he clambered back into the tractor.

'Yeah,' agreed Lenny, changing gear and heading back towards the farm track, 'but I wouldn't like to cop one of those horns. Could do some damage.'

'You're right—we need to get those signs up, asap. I'll give the shop a bell and collect them tomorrow, when I'm back from London.'

'When are you off, then?'

'I'm picking Isabelle up at three. We're going to stay the night with Polly and she has booked us into some fancy restaurant after the bash.'

'Well, Boss, who's the lucky bugger—you've got it made! She's a lovely girl'

Charlie grinned happily at the prospect. ' 'Bout time, Lenny, 'bout time.'

'So who's lookin' after the kiddies, then? Isabelle ain't said nothin' to Paula—you know they could've stayed at ours?'

'I know, Lenny; you and Paula are fantastic the way you help her out, but with school the next day, she thought they should stay put. Alison's going to spend the night at theirs. She's great with them and,' Charlie grinned, 'if I'm not much mistaken, she'll have that boyfriend over to keep the bedbugs at bay.'

As they reached the gate, a car bumped passed them going down the track to the farm and one of the occupants waved vigorously.

Charlie waved back. 'It's Mum,' he explained to Lenny. 'She and Angela were booked in for a tour of the camp. You should have seen her over breakfast this morning. She was so excited she used animal bran to make the porridge.'

'Did it taste any better?'

'I can't say—I never eat it, anyway, but Steve was fair pissed off.' Charlie chuckled at the thought.

'Seems to 'ave become a habit with him these days, Charlie. Like a bear wiv a sore 'ead, he is. What gives?'

The laughter faded from Charlie's face. 'I dunno, Lenny. You'd have thought he'd be delighted to have paid off the mega portion of our debt to the bank, but I've never known him to moan so much. Anything to do with the filming is a cause for complaint and they've only just started. And as for the rare breeds—he's gone into a terminal sulk because Gran sided with me over the opening date, and I can't talk to him about the publicity.'

'Perhaps,' said Lenny thoughtfully, pulling the tractor up at the entrance to the next field, 'he's frightened.'

Charlie jumped down and opened the gate, distributed the hay to an enthusiastic group of Longhorns and climbed back in the cab.

'You might be right, Lenny. But what's frightening him the most? The filming—hardly; the rare breeds—it's a gamble, I grant you, but we're all in it together; so that leaves . . .'

'Wedded bliss.'

'Angela . . .'

They bumped along the track towards the farmyard.

'I've nothing against her, Lenny. She's very nice. She's a brilliant cook and she dotes on old Stevie.'

'Maybe that's the problem, boss.'

'How do you work that one out, my old potato? You dote on Paula, she dotes on you. It's a

80

marriage made in heaven and the pizza parlour—
you've told me that, often enough.'

'Yeah, but . . .' Lenny sucked the air through the
gap where his front teeth once were and steered
the tractor into the yard. 'Paula and me—like, we
know each other—she don't expect me to do things
I don't want ter do, and the same goes for me wiv
'er—and our sex life is bloody fantastic. Whereas
Stevie and Angela . . .'

Charlie sighed. 'I take your point. Poor sod.
Frightened—he's probably terrified!'

'Charlie!' Stephen's voice bellowed across the
yard.

Lenny grinned, 'He don't sound so terrified to
me, boss. He sounds bloody mad.'

Charlie groaned and climbed down from the
cab. As he did so, an irate sound-recordist emerged
from the large barn where most of the interior
sequences were being shot.

'Do you mind?' he said, fizzing with indignation.
'We're filming, for Chrissake. Keep the bloody
noise down—didn't you hear Dave, there, asking
for quiet? Then we get the noise of the bloody
tractor and someone bellowing. Dave, if you can't
keep control here, better get someone up from base
to help you.' He turned on his heel and strode back
into the barn, muttering, with Charlie and Stephen
staring after him, abashed.

'Sorry, guys.' Dave, the runner, approached them
apologetically. 'I should have seen you coming. My
fault. We're about to do another take. Is the tractor
going to start up again?'

'We can wait,' replied Charlie. 'Sorry about that,
Dave. Tell us when there's a break—we need to
pick up some more bales and then we'll get out of

earshot.'

'Charlie,' hissed Stephen. 'I need to talk to you—now!'

'What is it?' Charlie whispered angrily back. 'What the fuck are you making all this noise about?'

'Is it true you've promised them my cows?'

'What?'

'My cows,' whispered Stephen, almost beside himself. 'You said they could film my cows!'

Charlie stared at him. 'So?' he whispered back. 'What's the problem? We've cows—they want to film cows; why can't they film ours?'

'Why can't they film their own?'

'Oh, Stephen!' Charlie groaned through gritted teeth.

'Guys!' came the warning whisper from Dave, hovering anxiously nearby.

'We can't discuss this here,' Charlie whispered, 'I'll give Lenny an early lunch break and meet you in the kitchen.'

It wasn't just Stephen who greeted his arrival in the kitchen with a challenging look, for Stephen had evidently shared the cause of his grievance with Angela. She stood defensively by her fiancé's side and glared at Charlie, while Jenny, hovering unhappily in the background, ostensibly busied herself laying the table for lunch.

'Now what's all this about?' Charlie tried to keep his tone light, but Stephen was squaring himself up for a slugging match,

'You've no right to tell them they can use my cows, Charlie, that's what it's about. My cows are working animals, in case you've forgotten. They produce the milk that keeps this farm going and I'm not going to have their routine upset by any bloody

82

stupid camera crew.'

'Ross, the second AD, told Mum and me that when animals are used in filming, they bring in their own, with their handlers,' chipped in Angela.

'So what's different in this case? Why did you agree and why did you not consult me?'

Charlie felt his temper rising. 'Because Stephen, if I consulted you on every little thing, nothing would ever get done. Yes, they asked me about the cows, and yes, I agreed—there's no big deal. They want shots of cows in the fields—it's impractical for them to bring a strange herd in. Be realistic, for Christ's sake.'

'It's not just in the field—they want to film the cows walking through Summerstoke.'

'So?'

'I'm not going to waste my day taking the girls through the village when they're not out in the fields yet. It's out of the question.'

'Then I'll do it; I'll use the heifers and the dry cows—they won't know the difference between them and milkers. And anyway, Stephen, it's all very well you getting your knickers in a twist, but you're forgetting when we accepted their fee we agreed to put the farm at their disposal as far as we reasonably could. I think this is a reasonable request.'

'Well, I don't!' Stephen had gone puce and thumped the table with his fist.

Attracted by the shouting, Alison entered the kitchen.

'What's going on? Why all the shouting?'

Ignoring her, Stephen continued, 'I knew it—I knew it. Now you've taken their money, you're in their pocket . . .'

Both Jenny and Alison gasped. Alison attempted a protest, 'Stephen, that's bloody unfair, you know . . .'

But he ignored her and drove on. 'Well? I might remind you that this is my farm and these are my animals you're playing fast and loose with. If you want to use any of them, you've to consult with me first . . .'

Charlie boiled over. 'I've taken their money? *I've* taken their money? That's rich, Stephen, that really is. I might remind you that the film fee has paid off the *farm's* debt to the bank, not mine; that I have put all the money Gran gave me back into the farm on the understanding that we're equal partners; and that, so far, *you've* done nothing but whinge, or jump up and down about your cows, which are not, I might point out, producing a profit, and if you had any sense, you'd sell the herd and invest in something else. But you're just too stupid to see beyond the end of your nose. Now, if you'll excuse me, I've got work to do. If you've anything further to say to me, it'll have to wait till I get back from London, tomorrow.'

And trembling with rage, he slammed out of the kitchen, sending a cork board, hanging on the back of the door and full of invoices, receipts and other vital information, crashing to the floor in a puff of dust.

An uncomfortable silence followed his departure.

Stephen sat, staring, red-faced, into his hands. Jenny, sighing heavily, crossed to the door, picked up the board and retrieved the bills that had scattered over the floor. Angela turned to the potatoes sitting on the stove and started to pound them with a masher.

Alison, staring at her brother with shocked amazement, finally broke the silence. 'Well, aren't you going after him?'

Stephen did not look up. 'Why should I?'

'To apologise? To say you didn't mean all those stupid things?'

At that he did look at her, 'Oh, so you think I'm stupid, too, do you? I might have known you'd side with him.'

'I'm not siding with anybody, but to suggest Charlie hasn't got the farm's best interests at heart is stupid.'

'And I haven't? I work all hours of the day on this farm so I think I have some claim to know what's best, and I don't think you're in any position to interfere.'

'I'm not interfering. I just can't bear to see you and Charlie fall out. It's stupid. We're meant to be pulling together . . .'

'Oh, so how are you helping? Encouraging Charlie to spend money that should go into the milking parlour on some stupid computer program when Ange has done all the work already?'

Alison was growing increasingly exasperated. 'We agreed it would be the best way to promote the farm—you know we did. And Ange is helping me get all the material together, so nothing she's done has been wasted.'

At that, Stephen's face went pale. He turned to Angela who, having reduced to the potatoes to the consistency of whipped cream, still continued to pound them.

'You didn't tell me you were doing that, Ange. I thought you agreed with me?'

Looking a little like a trapped mouse, Angela turned. 'I thought . . . since the decision had been made to go ahead, it would be stupid not to . . . it does make sense, Stephen . . .'

Stephen slowly rose, feeling betrayed and utterly desolate. 'I see, so you think I'm stupid, too . . . So that's what you all think of me!'

'Stephen . . .' Angela wailed, dropping the saucepan onto the floor where the potatoes, now looking more like semolina, flopped out to form a large creamy puddle.

Indifferent to the fate of the mash, she stretched out trembling arms towards her fiancé, but he pushed passed her, skidding on the potato as he went.

'Stephen!' Jenny, too, was close to tears, 'what about your lunch?'

'I'm not hungry, Mum. I'll see you later.'

And he slammed his way out of the kitchen, leaving slimy, white footprints in his wake.

15

Angela stood at the entrance of the track to Marsh Farm, waiting for the bus that would take her to Summerbridge. It had started to rain—a cold, pitiless, April rain that made a mockery of Spring. Her hair rapidly turned to rats' tails, water dripped down the back of her neck, and her brand new raincoat was no defence against the unremitting wet.

She'd no idea how long she'd have to wait; she'd never had to catch the bus before, Stephen usually gave her a lift. But when it became apparent that her swain was not going to return for his lunch, or for a reconciliation with his loved one, she had cobbled together an excuse and left, despite Jenny's entreaty that she should stay and wait for Stephen's return.

This, her first quarrel with her beloved, had devastated Angela. Mild-mannered and timid she might be, but she had a strong sense of fair play and she felt Stephen had been wrong in the accusations he'd hurled so liberally around the kitchen that morning. That, and the fact that he'd included her in his condemnations, really hurt.

Tears started to her eyes and once she started to cry, she couldn't stop. Her glasses misted up, tears dripped down her cheeks and her nose ran. The only tissue she could find was crumpled and damp, and she was trying ineffectually to blow into it when a voice caused her to look up.

'Erm, can I help you?' The enquiry was devoid of any enthusiasm.

She hadn't heard the approach of the car. It was a Volvo estate of uncertain years, as was its owner who regarded her with the look of someone already regretting the impulse of humanity that had caused her to stop in the first place.

'No, it's alright,' gulped Angela. 'I'm just waiting for the bus to Summerbridge.'

But for all her brave intentions, her voice ended in a helpless wail, the flimsy tissue gave out and as she groped in her coat for something to replace it, the tears flowed freely.

The woman sighed, irritated. 'The bus has just gone. The next one is not for two hours.' She paused and then added, with obvious reluctance,

'I'm going into Summerbridge myself, if you'd like a lift?'

'Oh thank you, thank you so much!' Angela's relief and gratitude was so heartfelt and so profuse that when she had settled in the car, the woman unbent enough to pass her a box of tissues.

'Thank you,' said Angela for the umpteenth time. 'You're very kind.'

The woman, who hadn't been feeling very kind at all, sniffed, casting her passenger a sideways glance. 'You looked so upset . . .'

'Yes, I . . . er . . . yes.' Angela was not ready to share her first argument with Stephen with anybody and her voice trailed away.

Unfortunately for Angela, her rescuer was one of those women who thrive on other people's business; worse, a gossip and a bit of a bully. The solitary woman standing, weeping in the rain, at the entrance to Marsh Farm, had fired her curiosity and it was this that caused her, against her better judgement, to stop. Now she had Angela in her car for the next twenty minutes; Angela would have needed to be made of sterner stuff not to tell her more than was good for her.

'You're cold,' she said sweetly, and turned up the heater. 'My name's Sally Green, by the way. I live in Summerstoke. I don't think we've met, have we?'

By the time Sally Green dropped Angela in the middle of Summerbridge, Angela had told her about her prospective marriage, about the plans for the Rare Breeds centre and how they were relying on its success to pull the farm out of the doldrums, described how the advent of the television crew had reversed their fortunes but caused terrible tension between her beloved and his elder brother; and how she was terrified, just when everything on the horizon was looking so rosy, the animosity between the two brothers would get worse and would, indeed, threaten everything she and Stephen had set their hearts on.

'Seems to me,' said Sally Green, pulling up outside Summerbridge library, 'and do forgive me if you think I'm interfering, but I think you and your fiancé should run the farm yourselves. Too many cooks and all that. You need to find a way to buy that brother out.'

'Yes,' said Angela, shaking her head sadly. 'But how? How on earth could we raise that sort of money? We don't want to get into debt again.' She looked humbly at Sally Green. 'Thank you so much for listening, Mrs Green, you've been very kind.'

Sally Green gave her a condescending smile. 'Not at all. I know how much it helps to get things off your chest. I'll pop into the library when I'm next in Summerbridge, Angela, and see how you are.'

16

'You finished then, Jeff?' Roger Jones, Jeff Babington's partner, looked up from the cage where he had just placed an unconscious cat, and observed his colleague winding a vivid, multi-coloured woollen scarf around his neck. 'If you want to hang on for five minutes, we could have a pint. Sarah's gone to her book group tonight so I'm in no hurry to get home.'

'Sorry to disappoint you, Rodge, but I'm going

89

over to Jenny's.'

'You virtually live there these days, old man. No longer the life of a gay bachelor, eh?' Roger, a short man in his early fifties, with fair hair verging on ginger, a plump rosy face and thick glasses, beamed cheerfully at Jeff.

'I don't think I was ever that. A comfortable bachelor, maybe.' Jeff grinned as he shrugged on a battered old Barbour. 'But I like things the way they are. Jenny suits me and I've always felt part of the Tucker clan. I can dip in and out of family life as I like. Can't be bad.'

Roger cocked his head on one side and gave him a shrewd look. 'You not got any plans to marry Jenny, then, Jeff? Not that it's any of my business,' he added hastily. 'But we've known you for a long time and Sarah was asking me, just the other day, if you were going to get hitched.'

Jeff shrugged. 'Jenny's got her family to think about. I don't think now is the right time to take her away, even if that's what I wanted to happen.'

Driving over to Marsh Farm, he mulled over his conversation with Roger. He wasn't given to much self-analysis and generally took life pretty much as it came. It was true: he did like things the way they were. Jenny and he had a lot of fun together and the very thought of their sex life made him tingle. But would he want her to move into his house? He didn't mind that she was a chaotic housekeeper and couldn't cook. It was just that he was now in his fifties and his wife had died so long ago, he was used to living by himself; did he really want to move over to make room for somebody else? 'Yes', he answered himself, 'yes, one day. And it would be Jenny. But not yet, not yet.'

He had a standing invitation to join the family for supper whenever he wanted and self-interest determined his visits generally coincided with the nights Angela was cooking, and Angela, Jenny had told him yesterday, had volunteered to cook for the family tonight as it was her day off.

When he walked into the kitchen, it was immediately apparent that all was not well. For one thing only half the family appeared to be present: no Alison, no Charlie, and more significantly, no Angela. Stephen sat at the table, working his way through a large plate of bread and jam, looking as miserable as Jeff had ever seen him; Ron attempted a smile, but he looked pale and to Jeff's eye, rather sickly; Elsie, in the process of pouring water into a teapot, nodded at him, a grim expression on her face, and Jenny, flushed and flustered, was standing by the stove, struggling to open a pack of bacon.

She attempted a smile when she saw Jeff. 'Sorry love, supper's going to be a bit delayed this evening.'

'A bit!' snorted Elsie, 'You've only just started. And eggs and bacon. Really—I could do those at home.'

'It was a bit of a mix up . . . I thought Angela was going to cook this evening and when I realised,' Jenny stuttered with a glance in Stephen's direction, 'that she hadn't . . . that she wasn't . . . that I should . . . and poor Stephen missed his lunch and he's starving, so I thought I'd do something quick and easy. How many rashers would you like, Ron?'

'Not for me, dear. I'm not very hungry this evening. A boiled egg is about all I could eat.'

Elsie gave him a keen look. 'Me, too. I

can't understand why you use all that oil to fry bacon, Jenny. It makes everything so greasy and indigestible. Drink up your tea, Ron love. We'll go back to the cottage and I'll boil you a nice fresh egg. The smell of fried food in a dirty kitchen is enough to put anyone off their food.'

Jeff hated to see Jenny wilt under Elsie's barbs. He put his arm around her shoulders. 'Make poor old Stephen his supper, love. Then you and I'll go out for a Chinese.'

Half an hour later, a considerably more cheerful Jenny climbed into Jeff's car.

'So what was all that about?' Jeff asked. 'I've never known there to be such an atmosphere. Where's Charlie? Where's young Alison?'

'Charlie has taken Isabelle to London for her art show and Alison is over at Isabelle's looking after the two girls. Perhaps we should drop in there and see how she's doing?'

'On the way back, maybe, love. I'm starving. So tell me, why was Stephen looking so miserable? Have he and Ange had some sort of argument?'

'Not just him and Ange. Oh Jeff, it was dreadful!' And Jenny described the fight between Charlie and Stephen and Angela's subsequent flight.

'Stephen was wrong, Jeff, and he's got to apologise. But supposing he doesn't? He can be so stubborn. I couldn't bear it if they don't make up. Stephen's been so happy since he and Ange decided to marry.

'I wouldn't worry too much, love. One or two little spats won't do them any harm. It's all part and parcel of learning to live with someone else, isn't it?'

Maybe, thought Jenny, that's the problem with

us. We haven't had any spats at all. Maybe we're just too comfortable and Jeff doesn't want to change that.

'Yes,' she said aloud, 'I suppose so, but . . . And what do I do about Charlie? He was so angry. The boys have squabbled before, but usually it's Charlie who pushes Stephen too far. I've never known Stephen to be so unreasonable.'

'If they're going to make this rare breed venture a success, they're going to have to pull together.' Jeff sighed. 'Stephen knows I rate his abilities. Would you like me to try and talk to him?'

'Oh Jeff, I'd be so grateful. He always listens to you.'

Jeff squeezed her hand. 'And you, my love, what are we going to do about you?'

Jenny's heart gave a massive flip, her stomach turned a triple somersault, and her breathing stopped. Had the moment finally arrived? Was he about to propose?

'Me?' she croaked.

'Yes. When are you going to start to stand up to Elsie? Tell her she can't carry on treating you the way she does? She's not like that with anyone else.'

Jenny's disappointment was so intense, for a moment she had to struggle with tears.

Jeff glanced across at her and concerned, reached for her hand. 'I hate to see you reduced to tears by her. You've been so good to the old battleaxe all these years. She doesn't deserve you.'

'That's what she'd say,' replied Jenny bitterly. '"What have I done to deserve a daughter-in-law like you? You can't cook, you can't keep house . . ." She can't wait till Angela is in charge of the farm kitchen and I'm,' she gulped, 'and I'm out of

93

the picture.'

'Out of the picture? Why should you be that?' He patted her hand. 'Cheer up love, I'm sure things aren't nearly as bad as they seem. You and little Angela are friends, aren't you? Life will be a lot easier for you when you can share the workload.'

*　　*　　*

But that's not what I want, she thought. Not what I want at all. Now, now is the time to ask him about us. Go on, Jenny, ask him what his intentions are!

But before she could summon up the courage, Jeff pulled the car over and turned off the engine. 'Here we are—the Beijing Palace,' he said and so cheerfully, Jenny wanted to hit him.

17

Alison gazed up at the cool Italian tiles, the great gilt-edged mirror, and the thick, fluffy, coffee-coloured towels hanging from a heated rail, and thought of the bathroom back at Marsh Farm.

There bathing was an experience to be endured rather than savoured: the bathroom was cold and damp, heated by a small single bar fire; the bath was an old cast iron affair with a surface rough from having been re-painted a number of times, and the taps, green and gummed up with scale, reluctantly spat out limited amounts of hot water and fountains of freezing cold. The linoleum on the floor was always icy and the thin bath mat permanently damp. The deep windowsill, now a repository for soaps, oils, talc and shampoos, had been used by her brothers in their teens to store bottles of fermenting ginger beer which they sold to supplement their meagre pocket money, a practice banned when she was five years old.

She'd just had a bath, she remembered, when suddenly there was a loud explosion, followed by another and another. Hearing Alison screeching fit to burst and the sound of what she thought were gunshots, her mother had rushed in to find every bottle had burst its cork and her daughter drenched in ginger beer.

Far from being sorry for her, her brothers had roared with laughter. In those days, she reflected sadly, they were as thick as thieves.

A chink of glass brought her out of her reverie.

'For someone who is about to have mad, passionate love made to her, you look pretty down in the dumps,' commented Al, looking down at her, a bottle in one hand and two glasses in the other. 'Or maybe it's that prospect that fills you with gloom?'

She smiled up at him. 'Idiot. I was just thinking about Stephen and Charlie.' She made a face. 'Stephen was always the kind, soft one. I didn't like what I saw in him today.'

'Possessions are poison.' Al pulled a wry face.

'Do you think that's it? Do you think by promising him her share, Gran's driven them apart?'

Al shrugged. 'It's possible. But it's possible Stephen is just plain envious.'

'Of Charlie?'

'Yeah—good-looking bloke, nice guy, nice bird, and he doesn't have to milk the cows twice a day.'

Alison gave a slight laugh. 'True, but he does work bloody hard and Stephen can't manage without him.'

'And that must make Stephen feel sour, too.' Al pulled off his T-shirt. 'But they've got to sort it out for themselves, there's nothing much you can do.'

'There is one thing.' Alison was thoughtful. 'I still have my share of the farm, don't forget. Gran's been encouraging me to give it to Stephen as a wedding present; she'd reimburse me and I must say the cash would be much more use to me than owning one sixth of a farm. But maybe I won't; maybe I'll just hang onto it, or maybe I'll sell it to Charlie, instead.'

'Whatever.' Al unzipped his trousers. 'But enough of farmyard machinations,' he leant forward and kissed the tip of her nose. 'You look really fit, like something out of one of those old movies; I do hope you're not wearing a cozzie under all those suds?'

'Come in and find out for yourself,' Alison flicked a soap bubble in his direction.

'I will. But first . . .' He picked up the bottle, popped the cork and poured the sparkling wine into two glasses. 'Only cheap Cava, I'm afraid, but we can dream on.'

'Hmm, this is pretty dreamy, anyway.' Alison reached out an arm and took a glass. 'I wondered what you were up to. I was afraid one of the girls had woken.'

'They certainly took their time getting to sleep. All the way through that last story, I was mentally undressing you, very slowly, till you were completely naked. I was on fire!'

'And how are you now?' she laughed.

'Hot,' he said, discarding the last of his clothes and stepping into the bath, 'red hot.'

18

'Bugger!' Veronica Lester, deep in thought, almost overshot the entrance to the Stowford Country Club. She stabbed on the brakes and swerved into the drive, causing the driver behind to hoot angrily.

'Shouldn't be so close,' she muttered, dismissive.

The club was approached by a long drive that wound through glades of rhododendron and gnarled old oaks, their branches clad in a skin of lichen, glistening a fluorescent green in the spring sunshine; pale primroses glowed in the dappled undergrowth and sunny yellow daffodils poked through the dead bracken.

But Veronica was not in the mood to appreciate these manifestations of spring. All she could think about was her son, Anthony, whom she'd caught sight of as she was driving down the hill through the village. He had pulled out of a gateway on his bike and roared off down the road. It was, unmistakably, him.

For one mad moment she'd toyed with the idea of putting her foot down and speeding after him—the Porsche was certainly capable of catching the bike up—but what held her back was the thought of being seen; there were those in the village who would gleefully make hay with the news that her car had been spotted in a high speed chase with her son's bike.

And anyway, if she'd caught up with him, what

would she have said?

So with a mixture of emotions, she had watched him accelerate out of sight. What was he doing in Summerstoke? Was he planning to come and see her? Did she want to see him? And what was he doing coming out of the driveway of the Old Vicarage?

The Old Vicarage—why the Old Vicarage?

Not long ago it had been the home of her erstwhile friend and confidant, Richard Garnett, but some five months had passed since he'd left the village, his wife and his children. She'd never been a particular friend of Isabelle's and the two women had not spoken since. So what was Anthony doing coming out of Isabelle's house at nine o'clock in the morning? Was that where he'd been heading the time Marion said she saw him—when was it—two weeks ago?

But what would Anthony be doing with Isabelle Garnett? An affair? Ridiculous—Isabelle was twelve years older than Anthony. But what was he doing coming away from her house? To be leaving at that time in the morning would strongly suggest he'd stayed the night.

She'd heard that Isabelle was taking in lodgers to make ends meet, but she'd been told they were television people. And anyway, having vowed never to return or see either of his parents again, it did seem a bit unlikely for Anthony to have taken up residence in the village and run the risk of bumping into them.

Veronica didn't like mysteries. She had to find out, but how? How? Who would know—and would tell her?

Veronica was not on good terms with the village

network. She was contemptuous of gossip and tittle-tattle unless it suited her purposes, and she had offended one too many people in the past to have access to ready information. She'd already asked Cordelia if she knew why her brother had come back to Summerstoke and had met with a blank response; as far as Cordelia was concerned, if Anthony wasn't in Durham, he was staying with his aunt, in Bath.

Veronica pulled a sour face at the thought. She and her younger sister, Anthony's godmother, had been estranged for years; it was so typical of Anthony that he should find refuge with her.

'It's no good, I'll have to enlist Sally Green's help,' she concluded, pulling into the only vacant space in the crowded parking area outside the club. It was marked 'disabled' but Veronica never bothered with niceties.

Sally Green was on the village shop committee, the epicentre, in Veronica's opinion, of nosiness and gossip. 'I'll invite her and her dreary husband to our next drinks party and she'll be so grateful, she'll do anything I ask.'

Veronica and Hugh had a large circle of acquaintances, privately classified by Veronica as A, B or C.

An A classification was conferred on friends, regular dinner guests who might be invited to ride one of the Lesters' cherished horses; B acquaintances would be invited to parties and occasionally to dinner; if, however, they were C, the best they could expect was the occasional invite to a drinks party when Veronica was more interested in quantity than quality.

Richard Garnett had been a category A and the

only other inhabitants of the village who might also have been As were Oliver and Juliet Merfield, but there existed such a degree of dislike between the two families, they seldom met socially.

Sally Green barely made the C grade and was so delighted on the rare occasions she and her husband were asked, she would deluge Veronica with reciprocal invites, all of which Veronica, with regard to Hugh's disinclination to dine with any but the most influential and wealthy, had to find some reason to decline.

'Morning, Ms Lester.' The unctuous day-manager handed her a locker key with a smile. 'Hope you don't mind, but we've a special request to make of you . . .'

'Oh?' She replied with all the discouragement she could muster, suspecting what was to come. Acknowledged as one of the best players in the club, the hotel would sometimes approach her to give guests a game. This morning she was not inclined to be obliging.

Undeterred, the manager pressed on. 'Yes. As you know, at the moment we are privileged to have resident here some of more illustrious members of the acting profession who find themselves quartered in Summerstoke for the duration of their filming . . .'

'I know. The club, along with every spare bedroom in Summerstoke, has been taken over by this band of light fantasticals.'

'It so happens one of our guests,' his voice dropped almost to a whisper, 'is Ben Dacres—you may have heard of him, he's dominated the small screen for some twenty years, I believe . . .'

Veronica stared at him, impatiently. 'I really

100

don't watch much television, Robert.'

'No? Well, take it from me, Ben Dacres is very popular. The thing is, Mrs Lester, he's asked me to arrange a game for him this morning and as both our professionals are booked through till lunch, I wondered whether you might consider . . . ?'

Veronica sighed heavily and looked at her watch. 'I'm due to meet Gavin Croucher at ten-thirty, and I planned to have a session in the gym first . . .'

Her impatient and disagreeable tone gave no hint of the satisfaction his request gave her. The club had a reputation for tennis and for a guest of this importance she knew the pros would have been consulted.

She looked coolly at the day manager. 'If he's available within the next half hour—you know what these actors are like, he's probably still in bed.'

'Well actually, Mrs Lester, he's in the gym right now. I'll introduce you.'

In a very short while, her troublesome son forgotten, Veronica found herself on the number one court, serving to one of the most handsome and agreeable men she'd met for a very long time.

19

'I'm really sorry, Ross. I've done my best. What d'ye expect me to do? Go up and drag him out of his bed?'

In the hotel's reception, Joe, the unit driver, was on his mobile, exasperated at being caught between the devil and the deep blue sea, which was how he described his predicament to the sympathetic girl

101

behind the desk.

'Boss, I've dialled his mobile but he's not picking up; reception has rung his room but he's not answering; someone has gone and banged on his door and all he said was he'll be down when he's ready . . . Right, Ross, yes, I know, you're the boss, but I can't see as . . . no, I've got that. I'll do me best. I'll ring you back.'

With a heavy sigh he pushed the phone back in his pocket.

'I've had me orders,' he said. 'I know it's against your house rules or whatever, but I've got to go and bang up Mr Hart meself. Where's his room?'

'I'll get the manager for you. I'm really sorry, but I can't let you do that without permission. It's more than my job's worth.'

'And it's more than my job's worth if I don't get him back to the unit in the next few minutes. I've been here half an hour already. It was meant to be a quick pick-up.' He consulted his watch. 'Oh my gawd, there's going to be tears before bedtime.'

*   *   *

'Game, set, and match. Well done. You're a fine player. I'm only sorry I didn't put up more of an opposition.'

For a man who had just been trounced, thought Veronica, Ben Dacres was incredibly gracious. She glanced at her watch. She just had time to cancel Gavin before he left for the club.

'I had to work jolly hard for those last points. I think you were just getting into your stride,' she spoke encouragingly. 'Have you got time for another set? Or are you needed on set?' She simpered at her joke and Ben chuckled.

'Not until this afternoon. That's very sweet of you. But have you got the time? I understand you're very much in demand on the courts.'

He couldn't have said anything to please her more.

'I just need to make a quick call and then I'm all yours,' she said archly.

'It's my lucky day,' he twinkled back.

Gavin Croucher was not at all pleased to be cancelled just as he was about to leave and he made it quite clear he was not impressed by Veronica's excuse that she'd somehow double booked, but Veronica cut him off in mid-grumble and turned to Ben with a smile. 'No problem. Ready? And we could go up to the club for a drink afterwards, if it's not too early for you?'

'That would be delightful. Then you can tell me all about yourself. Playing tennis is not conducive to much conversation beyond "in", "out", "net" and "your serve", is it?'

Veronica was right—Ben started to play with more strength and conviction and she had to work harder to keep her lead. Then, in the middle of a really exciting volley, he became distracted by something off the court and her ball slammed home inside the line. 'Forty—thirty' she called out, cheerfully. 'That was good, carry on like that and I'm dreadfully afraid you might win.'

But he made no attempt to answer her, or to retrieve the ball, but walked off the court towards a man standing on the other side of the fencing, waving at him.

Veronica was just close enough to hear their conversation.

'Hi, Joe. Is it me you're after? You know I'm not scheduled on set till this afternoon?'

'Yes, Mr Dacres. I'm really sorry about this, but Ross wants you right away.'

'What, you're kidding?'

Veronica could tell from Ben's change of manner that he was not pleased at all. Disappointed and annoyed that her plans for the morning had gone awry, she derived some pleasure from seeing that he, too, was put out. And he was gratifyingly apologetic when he returned to her side, took her hand and kissed it, saying with a melancholy sigh, 'This is unforgivable; I've got to leave, just when, as you said, I was getting into my stride. But duty calls and I am to be whisked away. My dear Veronica, I am so sorry . . .'

'Please, my friends call me Vee . . .' she began, but he brushed that aside with a shake of his head.

'No, no. Ver-ron-nica, it's such a beautiful name.' He looked deep into her eyes. 'My dear, you suit it. You are Veronica, the Queen of the tennis courts.'

Veronica's insides appeared to disintegrate and the cool, calculating, clever, conniving Mrs Lester succumbed, for the first time in her life, to feelings quite outside her control; an emotional state, if she had been thirty-five years younger, which she might have recognised as a crush.

She blushed; she perspired; she could hear a squeak in her voice that defied control. 'We could make another date . . . to play . . . you're going to be here for some time, I understand . . .'

'I'd love that.'

'I'll leave my card with reception. You can phone me any time. And you must come and have dinner with us . . . I live in Summerstoke. It would be lovely. And do you ride? We could provide you with a mount any time you wanted . . .'

He laughed, holding up his hands. 'That sounds all too wonderful. Thank you. I must go. I look forward to our next encounter.' And with a slight bow, which Veronica found utterly charming, he was gone.

Dazed, she stood alone on the tennis court, watching his retreating back until he was completely out of sight. She had the whole of the rest of the morning in front of her and no partner now to play with but she didn't mind and wandered back to the clubhouse, reliving the whole encounter with Ben Dacres and planning how soon she could feasibly see him again.

By chance the only other occupant of the changing rooms was Sally Green. Veronica was surprised to see her there. Sally's husband was a solicitor in the nearby town of Summerbridge and although she supposed they had enough to live on, she didn't think his salary would run to meeting the very high cost of a club membership.

She frowned. There was something she was going to ask Sally, but, for the moment, she'd forgotten what it was.

'Vee!' Sally got in first. 'I wondered if I might see you here. Aren't these facilities amazing? Philip bought me a day pass as a birthday present—to see if I liked it. I thought I'd go to the gym first. Are you going there—oh, but you're dressed for tennis. Have you finished your game? The tennis courts are fabulous, aren't they? I wish I played better than I do, I used to be quite good when I was at school . . .'

Sally Green was a heavy, plain woman, with

small, light brown eyes and hair a little too blonde. She was slightly younger than Veronica, in her mid-forties, but, in Veronica's opinion, she looked older. She worked part-time in her husband's office, but Veronica had no idea what she did there and no interest in finding out. Sally Green was, in her opinion, a dull, dull person whose conversation revolved around the particular achievements of her dull children, her dull husband, and the comings and goings in the dull village in which both their families lived.

Oh yes, she suddenly remembered, that was why she wanted Sally Green: to find out who was lodging with Isabelle Garnett and why Anthony should have paid at least two visits there.

First, the carrot . . .

'Sally,' she drawled,' I'm thinking of having a drinks party—to welcome some of the actors on this TV thingy to the village. Would you and Philip like to come?'

Sally Green's piggy eyes gleamed with excitement. 'Vee, we'd adore to. What a lovely thought . . . Oh, I say, talking of the television people, I had the funniest encounter, yesterday . . .'

Vee sighed impatiently. Sally gave every sign of being about to embark on some long and, no doubt, utterly tedious tale of how she'd met one or other of the actors. But what Sally Green had to tell her was interesting, very interesting indeed . . .

Never before had Sally Green found Veronica so attentive a listener and encouraged, she left nothing out.

'And so,' she concluded, 'I advised her to think of buying him out. Too many cooks, I said. Though, if you ask me, Vee, I think they've bitten off more than they can chew—what with this rare breeds and the television. They're bound to come a cropper.'

'Yes,' said Veronica thoughtfully. 'Yes, you're probably right.'

20

Instead of heading straight to makeup, Ben made for Ross's trailer, where he found him on the phone.

Maintaining the flow of conversation, Ross beamed at Ben, but the actor was not to be wooed. He stood there, arms folded, oozing annoyance until Ross finished his call.

Ross barely had time to greet Ben before he was cut off with an icy, 'What's going on, Ross? I am not scheduled to be here till this afternoon. This is the second time in less than a week I've been fucked about. What's the point in issuing a schedule if it means sweet FA?'

Helplessly, Ross shrugged his shoulders. 'You've every right to be annoyed, Ben. I'm sorry, I really am. Word came through from Matt there's to be a change in the shooting order and they want to do your scene this morning.'

'Why? What's Matt up to . . . or doesn't Emma know her arse from her elbow? Does Marcus know what's going on? Is he about?'

'Marcus is in London today.'

'Well unless I get a decent explanation for this farting about, I'm going to have a word with him. I'm sorry, Ross, I know you're just obeying orders, but I am well pissed off.'

And he turned on his heels and stomped out of

107

the trailer.

Ross stared after him and pulled a face. Ben Dacres in a mood was not a pretty sight, but at least Ross could rely on him to do everything that was expected of him and to be on set when required. Not like Jason Hart. What a pain in the backside he was and although Ross would do his level best to prevent dissent between the actors, he knew full well it was only a matter of time before Ben discovered just why his schedule had been changed that morning.

And not only Ben; Ross'd had to stand down Nicola Scudamore till the afternoon, so she was hanging round, twiddling her thumbs, and he'd had to pull in Jilly Westcott—not that she'd complained, she was a sweetheart—but the danger was they might confer and the last thing he wanted was a gang of disaffected actors. Disaffected actors behaved badly; meat and drink for Jason Hart's savage ridicule.

Ross thought for a moment, then opened his laptop and typed:

Hi, Marcus. Sorry to bother you, but a little problem has arisen that might get out of hand unless there's a timely nip and I think you're the one to give it . . .

''Lo, Ross,' a voice interrupted him. It was the youngster, Harry Hobbs, standing, unsmiling, in the doorway. 'Frank came to collect me. Is that right? Only I'm not meant to be on till this afternoon and Mrs Jones is right pissed off.'

'Yes, sorry, Harry. Change of plan. Mrs Jones is your tutor, isn't she? I'm really sorry to have mucked her about. Tell her I'll try to make sure it doesn't happen again.'

Harry shrugged. 'It's fine by me; she's a hag. An'

she's so boring, she does my head in.'

'Oh,' Ross stared at the boy, sighing inwardly. Child actors and their associated needs he regarded as a pain in the backside and he hadn't warmed to this particular specimen. 'Sorry to hear that.' He attempted a smile. 'I guess I found all teachers boring when I was your age. It's just something you have to put up with.'

'Is it? I don't see why I should put up with being pushed around without anybody ever asking what I want.' And with that, Harry Hobbs turned and stalked out of the trailer.

Ross frowned. It was bad enough having a bunch of adult temperaments on his hands, but if the juvenile starting playing up as well . . .

He turned back to his email.

21

'A few more days, my lovelies, then you can go out into the fields. The weather's set fair and the grass is looking good.' Stephen spoke softly to the four Jerseys.

Devoted to his herd of Holstein Friesians, in the short time the Jerseys had become resident at the farm, Stephen had fallen in love with their gentle looks, their general good manners, and the rich creaminess of their milk. Already he was dreaming of building up the herd and of the day when they could sell Marsh Farm Jersey milk and, with Angela's help, Marsh Farm Jersey ice cream.

Thinking of Angela, the heavy lump of misery that had descended on Stephen since yesterday's fight with Charlie reasserted itself. When hunger had driven him back to the kitchen, he discovered that Angela had left and taken the bus back to Summerbridge; Alison pointedly refused to speak to him; there was no sign of Charlie, and even his mother, who usually championed him against the rest of the world, looked at him reproachfully and said she thought he'd been a little unfair and that he should apologise both to Charlie and to Angela.

With a heavy sigh, he turned and walked away from the cow palace. He would finish up in the dairy, then go and check the fencing Lenny had been working on. Not that he didn't trust Lenny, but some of the new arrivals were pretty feisty and better to be safe . . .

Angela was back at work today and this evening they were due to attend a meeting of the Merlin Players to discuss the summer production. Stephen groaned at the thought of it. He had enough on his plate at the moment and the idea of doing an outdoor production of Shakespeare made his heart sink. Angela had showed him a copy of the play and explained it was a romantic comedy. He couldn't see that; it was all gobbledegook to him. His job would be so much harder: if he couldn't understand what they were saying, how could he be expected to get his lighting and sound cues in the right place?

He knew, too, Mrs Pagett would give him a hard time because he hadn't asked Mrs Merfield if they could use Summerstoke Manor. He and Angela had planned to go and see them yesterday afternoon, but as Angela had gone off in a huff . . . And what about the party on Friday? They so rarely got invitations, let alone one like that . . . Marcus said it was for them to meet the actors and the film unit.

Ange had been so looking forward to it.

Should he swallow his pride and say sorry? Shouldn't she apologise to him? After all, she'd gone behind his back, helping Ali with this stupid computer thing. It was so unfair—they were all on Charlie's side and there was no way he was going to apologise to Charlie; he'd meant what he said. Charlie was bending over backwards for this bloody film crew and making his job a lot harder, but what thanks did he get?

No, he didn't see why he should apologise and he wasn't going to.

But he didn't feel any better for having reached this decision and, shoulders hunched, crossed the yard towards the dairy.

'Stephen?'

At the sound of the sweet voice, he froze then turned.

'Nicola,' he croaked.

Wrapped in a dark Puffa jacket, she was sitting in the sun, on a flatbed cart, swinging her legs and smiling at him.

He walked slowly over to her.

'Hi, Stephen; surprised to see me?'

For ten years, until he'd finally recognised the true value of the steadfast Angela, Stephen had a crush on Nicola. She had been the star of the Merlin Players when he'd first joined and he'd been smitten from the beginning.

The path to enlightenment had been painful; she'd never taken him seriously and flirted with him for her own amusement. Unable, in the past, to talk to her without blushing, Stephen could now look down at her pretty face, her dark curls and

111

sparkling blue eyes and reply, without colouring or stammering.

'I didn't realise you were in this thing, Nicola. I don't remember Marcus mentioning your name . . .'

'Oh.' Nicola pouted. 'I play Jason Hart's girlfriend.'

'Who's he?'

'Stephen,' Nicola protested. 'You haven't heard of Jason Hart?'

'No,' replied Stephen, without interest.

'He's a really famous stand–up; he's playing Will, the farmer's son. I ditch him in the first episode.'

'I should think you'd do that really well.' His comment sounded more acerbic than he'd intended and Nicola cocked her head, looking at him with interest.

'I hear you've taken on the farm from your brother and that you're about to expand. Is that right?'

Encouraged to talk about his beloved farm, Stephen unbent a little. 'Yes. We . . . I . . . am opening a rare breeds centre. In three weeks, with any luck. Most of the animals are here already— we've got some lovely beasts.'

'How exciting. I saw the Highland cattle on my way in, this morning. The baby looks so sweet.'

'She is, but you can't go near her yet, her mum is very protective. There's lots of other things, too. Goats, sheep, hens, longhorn cattle, a couple of sows about to produce piglets . . .'

'Piglets! Oh how lovely. Will you show me them?'

Angela had fallen in love with piglets, Stephen remembered with a pang. He shrugged. 'They're about two weeks off, but we've got lambs and kids if you're interested.'

112

She smiled at him. 'Oh, yes please, I'd adore to see them. I've nothing to do till this afternoon.'

Stephen looked at her. She really was pretty, far prettier than Angela, but not worth one inch of her, he knew that. Angela didn't like Nicola; she would not be at all happy to learn not only that Nicola was on the farm, but that this conversation was taking place; and as for him showing Nicola around . . .

Stephen was not sure where the impulse came from, but instead of saying he was sorry, he was far too busy and he'd get someone else to show her the animals, he looked as his watch.

'Give me thirty minutes, I've got to finish off in the dairy.'

He looked at her footwear—dainty little feet dangled from the flatbed, clad in neat leather lace-up boots. 'You need to find some wellies, though. It's quite muddy across the yard.'

'I'll get some from wardrobe. They've brought enough to shoe an army.'

'Right. Good. I'll meet you back here then, in half an hour.' And feeling an odd mixture of guilt, confusion and elation, he walked off to the dairy.

*   *   *

Swinging his van round into the yard, Charlie saw a young woman leaning against a cart. She was small, slight, and very attractive.

'Hi,' he said, getting out of his van. 'You waiting for someone?'

'Yes,' she said in a sweet voice, her cupid's bow of a mouth curving into a smile. 'The farmer; he's going to show me some animals.'

'Stephen?' Charlie couldn't quite conceal his

113

surprise.

'Yes, isn't it kind of him. I've got time on my hands between takes—I'm here with the filming—and rather than go and sit in my trailer for hours, I thought I'd have a look around, so he's offered to take me.'

'Well, well,' thought Charlie. 'Our Stephen's full of little surprises.'

He smiled at the girl, 'That's a good idea, I should have thought of it . . . we'll arrange a tour of the farm for anyone in the company who's interested. I'll talk to Marcus about it. Make sure Stephen takes you to say hello to the Saddleback and the Middle White. They like visitors. They are going to farrow pretty soon and then we'll have lots of little piglets to show off to visitors.'

'Yes, I will. Do you work on the farm as well, then?'

'You could say that. I'm Stephen's brother, Charlie. He's the stockman; I'm what you might call the diversification and development man. I am, if you like, responsible for you lot being here.'

'Oh.'

Charlie could not know it, but Nicola, being in between boyfriends, had a weakness for attractive men and Charlie was attractive, there was no doubt about that. The difference between him and his brother was striking—he was tall, tanned and lean, with a thick mop of brown hair, laughing brown eyes and an energy about him that she found alluring. What a pity it was Stephen who was going to show her around and not this Charlie. But there was nothing she could do about it—she could see Stephen walking across to join them.

The coolness between the two brothers was

marked. They nodded at each other, barely speaking, and before Nicola could tell Charlie her name, or interest him in her further, he had turned on his heel and gone.

Stephen had not seen Charlie since their quarrel and he was not best pleased to come across him in conversation with Nicola. Irrational though it was, he felt, yet again, as if Charlie was muscling in on his scene, particularly when Nicola said brightly, 'If you're too busy to take me now, Stephen, I can wait. Charlie said he'll organise a trip round the farm for us all.'

'It's okay,' he said coldly, 'I've got time.'

The Stephen who showed Nicola around was rather different from the diffident, clumsy, country bumpkin she'd known in her Merlin Players days. After a little coolness on his part, he relaxed, and animated by his enthusiasm for the farm and its future, and boosted by the flirtatious manner of Nicola, who couldn't bear not to be admired, he found himself enjoying their excursion as much as she apparently did.

She asked him all sorts of questions about the farm, his family and his plans for marriage.

'And what about your brother?' she asked. 'Is he married?'

'Charlie? No. He's what my Gran calls a flibbertigibbet, can't settle down to anything for long. He's going out with a woman in the village at the moment; she's married with two kiddies, so I can't see it lasting. What about you?'

'Oh,' said Nicola lightly, 'I'm footloose and fancy free at the moment; I'm not ready to settle down, either.'

'Are you going to be around for the Players'

summer production?'

'I don't think so. My agent would throw a hissy fit if I left London for any length of time. What are you planning on doing?'

'June's got it into her head to do this Shakespeare outdoors . . . at Summerstoke Manor. Dream something.'

'*A Midsummer Night's Dream*?'

Stephen nodded his head. 'That's the one.'

'You're kidding, not really?' Nicola threw back her head and laughed.

Stephen looked at her anxiously. 'I think it's a daft idea. Do you?'

'I can't think of anything dafter. June Pagett's got delusions of grandeur. Oh Stephen, you really can't let them do it. No-one will ever take them seriously again. Have you all agreed? What does Angela think?'

'Angela is in favour, I don't really know why. We have a meeting to discuss it tonight. You're right, I'm glad you agree with me. I've got to stop 'em making fools of themselves.'

22

Alison's mobile sang out. Half asleep, she rolled over to retrieve it from the floor under her bed. It was Hannah. 'You sound really dozy, Ali.'

'That's 'cos you woke me up.'

'But it's half way through the afternoon!'

'So? I'm having a siesta.'

'Ooh, there's posh for you. Maybe you didn't get much sleep last night?'

'Maybe I didn't.'

Hannah giggled. 'Fantastic. Are you going to tell me all?'

'Certainly not! But,' Alison lay back on her pillow, her body tingling with the memory. 'It was fantastic. I told Isabelle if she ever wanted to have a night off again, I'd be more than willing to babysit. Al was terrific with the two girls and they were as good as anything.'

'Does your Mum know?'

'About Al staying? No way, and as Charlie didn't ask, I don't think he plans to say anything, thank God.'

'Cool. Hey, how about you, me, Al and Nick renting a caravan, somewhere for a weekend.'

'What, now?'

'No, idiot, once we've finished our exams. We could go down to Padstow.'

'Could be good, but I'm not sure about Al's movements. His term finishes so much earlier than ours and he's talking about staying up in Durham to get a job.'

'So what will you do? I'd die if Nick went a million miles away.'

'It's not a million miles, dopey. But it's a bit of a blow, I admit. Something will work out.'

'You're so calm about everything, Ali. When are you going to see him again?'

'This Friday, at the film unit party.'

There was a small pause at the other end of the phone and when Hannah spoke again she sounded awkward. 'Hey, Ali—this party . . . is there any chance you can wangle an invite for me and Nick? I know what you said about it being invite only, but I'd love to come. I've never met anyone on the TV

117

before and I'd die to meet Jason Hart. I've been looking at his website and he's really fit.'

Alison suppressed a sigh. Ever since it became news the TV crew were going to hold a party for the Tuckers and people in the village associated with the filming, she'd a number of calls from friends asking if she could get them in. She'd fobbed them off, knowing that Marcus didn't want it to become a free for all. But Hannah was different, Hannah was her best mate; Hannah had bent over backwards to include her in whatever she could, invited her to billions of parties and lent her clothes and makeup because her own wardrobe was so impoverished. She couldn't say no to Hannah.

'I'll ask Marcus, Hannah—see what he says.'

'Brill. Thanks Ali—ooh, that would be wicked! Have you seen Jason's website? It's something else. Have you met him yet?'

'No. The barn they're using for all the interior stuff is on the far side of the yard. I haven't met anyone much . . . just the two guys who stop you going up and down outside every time the camera is running, or something. They're pretty cool.'

'You never cease to amaze me, Alison Tucker. All those TV stars on your doorstep and you haven't been to have a look. Aren't you curious?'

Alison laughed. 'I don't watch as much television as you do. I will go and look, sometime, but they're pretty busy and I don't want to get in the way. The only one I've heard of, apart from Juliet Peters of course, is Jason Hart and I suppose I hope I'll bump into him in the yard, casual like, you know. Although I'm not even sure I'd recognise him. Seeing someone on late night TV is probably very different from meeting them in the flesh.'

118

'Then check out his website.'

'I will. I'll give you a ring back when I know about the party.'

'Cheers, Ali.'

Alison slid off her bed and opened her laptop. Jason Hart's website was clever, funny, and very intricate.

'He must have paid a fortune for a site like that. It's shit hot—if only we could have something like that for the farm.'

She glanced at her watch—nearly five; perhaps Marcus would be in his office, and then she'd take Bumble, her pony, out for some much-needed exercise.

'I wonder if Marcus knows anything about website design?' she thought, as she made her way across the farmyard to the trailer Marcus used as an office.

His voice answered briskly to her knock, 'Come in'.

As she peered round the door he looked up from his computer, looking so stern, she shivered. 'He's a formidable person,' she thought. 'I'd hate to diss him.'

But on seeing her he smiled. 'Alison, come in. This is a rare treat.'

'I hope I'm not disturbing you?'

'No. I've got five minutes before I'm due to see someone. Sit down. What can I do for you?'

Alison liked his direct manner. 'A couple of things, Marcus: I've got to set up this website for the farm, but it's really beyond me. Maybe our computer is just not up to the job and my IT skills aren't either. I just wondered if you had any ideas as to where I might find someone who could do it

119

for us, for not too much money. Your company's website is pretty swish . . .'

'And pretty expensive, too; I'll have a think. A number of the guys on the crew here have their own websites. They might have some ideas. I'll ask around. And the other thing?'

'It's the party on Friday.' Alison hesitated. 'Um, I know you said you didn't want a free for all, but I wondered if . . . The thing is, Hannah, my best friend, has always included me in everything she's done.' She frowned. 'I would feel very uncomfortable being there with Al and not her as well.'

She looked at him anxiously. If she couldn't get an invite for Hannah and Nick, then maybe she shouldn't go herself.

Marcus smiled. 'Is your friend going to sign up to be an extra?'

'Oh yes. Are you kidding? Nick, her boyfriend is, too. At fifty quid a day, I should think you'll find half the county queuing up to sign on.'

He laughed. 'A large number of them will be disappointed, but not so disappointed as those that are picked. Take a tip from me, if you are called upon, make sure you take a good fat book.'

There was a knock at the door.

The smile left Marcus's face. 'Ah, business calls. Give the names of your mates to my secretary, Rosie; she'll add them to the list.'

Alison rose. 'Thanks, Marcus.'

'And have you thought of going to the IT department in your college—they might have some ideas.'

'Yes, I will. But it's closed for Easter and the farm is due to open on Good Friday.'

120

'I see. I'll do my best.'

There was another bang on the door, more impatient this time.

Marcus rose and opened the door to let Alison out. A man in his late twenties stood scowling on the top step. 'I was about to bugger off,' he snarled at Marcus, completely ignoring the presence of Alison. 'I knocked twice—I thought you weren't here.'

'Please come in,' said Marcus smoothly. 'See you later, Alison.'

The visitor pushed past, nearly sending her flying.

'And that,' she thought as she walked across to Bumble's stable, 'is the fabulous Jason Hart. What a prick.'

23

Jason slammed his way out of Marcus's office, so furious he could hardly breathe. He stood at the bottom of the steps and stared around him. In the short space of time he'd been here, he'd grown to loathe this mucky yard, the big shabby farmhouse in front of him, the sheds, the machinery, the stink of alien beasts, breathing, stamping and defecating somewhere out of sight; but most of all he loathed the film crew—they were lurking everywhere, shepherding him and the rest of the useless bunch as if they'd got no minds of their own—'don't go here, wait there, be quiet, put this on, take this off, do that again, do it differently . . .'

There was, he felt, very little difference in the

way performers and farm animals were treated, except the animals didn't get ripped apart by some fucker if they decided to have a lie-in.

They'd all known he was for it, and not a smidgen of solidarity from any of them. He'd been treated like a piece of dead meat the cat had brought in when he'd turned up for the afternoon's shoot. Even his mate, Ross, had been a little cool.

His face burned, recalling Marcus's look of contempt when he'd tried to defend himself. Then Marcus had given him a warning.

'We're not so far into the shoot as to make you indispensable,' he'd said. 'I know you think we need you more than you need us, but when you act like this it means we start to lose money, real money, and I won't stand for it. There are plenty of actors who'd make a good job of your part, but we went out on a limb with you and you were prepared to play ball with us. But if you're going to fuck us around like some petulant rock star, then, Jason, I am not interested in playing ball with you. Get it?'

He got it all right.

Ignoring the car waiting for him he marched across the yard, through an open gate and along a small track that went slightly uphill away from the river, with fields on either side.

The track was flanked with thick hedges, black thorny shrubs, bare of leaves but smothered with a mass of white blossom. The grass verges were lush with bright green shoots, glistening celandines, wild daffodils and the early tight buds of bluebells. But Jason was so angry, his surroundings impinged on him not at all, except for when he tripped over the occasional stone, or splashed in a puddle, or skidded on a pile of fresh manure, all of which

122

exacerbated his sense of injury.

He was not going to take this humiliation lying down; some way he'd get his own back on the lot of them—the stinking countryside, the film crew, the actors—the whole lot of them. Somehow—somehow he'd screw them up, good and proper, the bastards!

*   *   *

'Hey—hey, you! Stop him! Stop him!'

Some half an hour later, having worked the edge off his fury, Jason was walking back down the track when he heard the girl's voice. He turned and saw a huge bundle of wool and a pair of fierce horns charging down the track towards him.

'Stop him!'

Far from stopping the beast, Jason's instinct was to run but as he did so he skidded on a malodorous pile and fell, by sheer coincidence, full length across the top of the woollen monster, who as shocked as much as Jason himself, was stunned into immediate submission.

Fortunately for them both the girl was upon them before either had a chance to recover.

'Fantastic, well done!' she shouted exuberantly. 'What a brilliant dive. I've got him by the horns. You can get off him, now.'

Jason fell off rather than got off, glancing up at the girl tugging at the gigantic horns of the beast. He recognised her as the girl he'd bumped into coming out of Marcus's trailer. Angry and frightened as he was, he could appreciate she was one scrumptious bird, and while her physique was slight, from the way she hung on to the animal, that frailty was clearly deceptive,

'Push him from behind, would you. He's escaped from the field back up the track. It's not far, but the stubborn bastard's too strong for me . . . What are you waiting for? Push!'

Never in his twenty-seven years had Jason Hart, the darling of the late night comedy circuit, experienced anything quite like this. He was trapped, with his shoulder wedged up against the backside of a recalcitrant ram, pushing for all he was worth. Helpless to do anything else but obey the girl's instructions—any relaxation and he'd be trampled—his fury and frustration bubbled up in equal measure and he cursed everybody and everything that had landed him in this situation.

Then, without warning, the beast shot forward and sent him sprawling backwards on the muddy track.

'There . . . that's him sorted, for the moment.' The girl slammed the gate shut with a triumphant clang and turned to him.

Completely filthy, shaken, and trembling with the sudden release from his Sisyphean ordeal, he was ready to hurl every foul expletive he could muster at this girl. But looking at her, for some reason not entirely obvious to himself, he held fire.

She was quite a bit younger than he was but looked at him with a cool self-possession that disconcerted him. His first impression had been accurate—she was poised, very pretty, with the most amazing green eyes.

Her composure further fuelled his anger—he felt and looked a mess. He'd been through hell and the need to make someone pay for it was overwhelming . . . to hell with reason or rationality;

he held her entirely responsible; she'd suffer; he'd crack that self-possession . . . Yes, she'd pay for his humiliation, and he'd have some fun making her pay . . . he bloody well would!

'Thank you so much,' she said. 'I'm really grateful. He only arrived this morning. He's one of our prize animals and it would have been terrible if he'd escaped.'

'No problem,' he shot her a cool look, 'I've a thing about rams' bottoms.'

She gave a faint smile. 'He's not just any ram—he's a Portland, he's classy.'

'Give us a hand up, will you,' he held out a hand and after a moment's hesitation, she took it and pulled him to his feet. Not letting go of her, he smiled the famous smile.

'I know you've some weird country customs and I've heard of gut-barging; but ram-barging is a new one on me, particularly as a "how-de do?" I'm more used to the eyes-meeting-across-a-crowded-room format.'

'Well, we like to do things differently around here.'

Her voice was sweet, with a hint of the soft West Country lilt. She dropped her eyes from his face to her hand, still held by his, and before he could tighten his grip, she stepped back, disengaging herself as she did so.

His dislike grew; that sort of move was his prerogative. If he wanted to hold someone's hand, then he would do so until he'd had enough.

She looked at him with sympathy. 'I'm afraid you're terribly muddy. I'm really sorry. My Gran's cottage is very near here, if you would like to use her shower?'

He shrugged. 'No matter. I'll get a lift back to the place I'm staying and get some clean clothes. My name is Jason Hart, by the way.'

To his further chagrin she did not look in the slightest bit impressed even though she replied, 'Yes, I know. I recognised you. You're in this TV sitcom, aren't you? I'm Alison Tucker. I live on this farm.'

'How come? I've not seen you around.'

'I live on this farm because my dad, before he died, was the farmer. I'm not around because I'm busy.'

The sudden harsh call of a crow caused her to glance up and he followed her gaze. The sun had gone, the colour had drained from the sky and a low dark cloud was rapidly obscuring the remaining light.

He shivered.

She looked at him, concerned. 'Look, the weather's changing and you're really damp as well as muddy. If you don't want to go to my Gran's, then I think we should get back before your mates go off duty and you lose your lift. If you start walking, I'll fetch Bumble and catch you up.'

She started off up the track without a glance back. He stared after her, puzzled and pleased. For whatever reason, she wasn't going to be an easy pushover. So much the better, it was more fun when his quarry had a bit of fight in them.

He called after her, 'Bumble, who's Bumble?'

'My pony; I was out for a ride when I spotted the ram. He won't have gone far.'

In the descending gloom she disappeared round a bend. He hesitated, inclined to wait for her return, but another shiver brought him to his senses and he started to hobble back down the track.

It wasn't long before he heard the gentle clip-clopping of a horse's hooves. He turned to see her astride the fattest pony he'd ever seen.

'Blimey,' he laughed derisively. 'That's some fat horse.'

'He's a pony, not a horse, and he's overweight because he's elderly and he doesn't get enough exercise.' She patted the animal's neck, 'I should take him out more, but it's hard to find the time at the moment.'

He limped alongside her. 'So what are you so busy doing? You don't do stuff on the farm, do you? You don't look like my idea of a farm girl.'

'With round rosy cheeks, big bosoms and straw in my hair? I am a farm girl, nevertheless, and I do my bit, but at the moment I'm studying for my As.'

'Oh, what?'

'Maths, biology, physics, and environmental science.'

'Blimey. A bit of a bright spark, eh?'

She shrugged but made no other reply.

After a moment's silence, which she clearly was not going to break, he began again, trying a friendlier, more engaging tone. 'So what's there to do around here? I take it you do go out to play sometimes?'

'Of course.'

He persisted, 'So where do you go, what do you do?'

She relented and opened up a little. 'It depends. I've friends in Summerbridge. We have parties, we go to the cinema, go to clubs in Bath if we can afford it, go to the pub, listen to music, go to the theatre, sometimes; there's a good one in

127

Summerbridge and they get a lot of stand-ups there. You might know some of them.'

'Not the sort who would bother to come all the way down here. They must be desperate.'

'On the contrary, we get some good ones—Al Murray was down last month—and they like coming 'cos they get good houses. You should check it out.'

'I will—if you'll come with me?'

She turned and stared down at him. 'Me? Why?'

'Because,' he put on his most appealing look, 'I find myself stranded in the middle of the country, working with a bunch of self-obsessed wrinklies whose idea of relaxation is spending every spare moment in the gym; or doing su-bloody-do-ku if they've given up bothering about their weight, then knocking back glasses of champers in the bar, playing the "dahling-I-know-more-famous-people-than-you-do" game with the volume switch full on. I tell you, I'm desperate for some normal company!'

'They can't all be like that? There are lots of people around who seem quite normal, particularly the crew.'

'They might be,' he said bitterly. 'But it's an unspoken rule: actors and crew don't mix.'

She shook her head in disbelief. 'Sounds a bit odd. But you're all going to Marcus's party on Friday night?'

'For that evening, we'll put on a show—all united and jolly, and when it's over, they retire to their side of the line and we to ours. It's a reinforcement of the bloody class system—above and below stairs. I've never been forced to stay above stairs before, and I don't much like it.'

And he pulled such a tragic face, Alison laughed.

'Well I really don't have much spare time, but if you're serious, I'll get hold of a programme and if there's anything you fancy, we'll get tickets.'

They had just reached the perimeter of the yard when they heard a faint shout. 'Jason!'

'Over here,' she shouted back.

Seconds later Joe, the driver, appeared and seeing them, muttered 'Thank Christ for that,' before turning away to speak into his mobile.

She looked at Jason with an enigmatic smile. 'Looks like there's been a search party out for the young master. I must get on; Mum'll be wondering where I am. I'll leave you to tell them about your adventure with the ram. Thanks a billion for coming to my rescue.' She patted the pony. 'On Bumble, giddy up, there's a good boy.'

'Will you be there on Friday?'

'Sure. My boyfriend's coming, too. It'll be fun. Cheers.'

'Yes,' he said to her vanishing form. 'Yes, it will be. Lots of fun.'

24

Stephen reached through the ivy and tugged at the bell pull. He could hear the bell resounding inside the old house and as if in response, his stomach gave an audible rumble.

He sighed.

The only way he could get to see the Merfield ladies before collecting Angela in time for the production meeting was to miss his dinner. It was some sacrifice—Stephen loved his food and didn't function well with an empty belly—but following his conversation with Nicola, he'd convinced himself the best thing he could do was to go and see the Merfields himself, without Angela. That way he could put the Merlin Players' request to them, but make it clear that he, Stephen, didn't think any good would come from granting it.

By nature Stephen was a shy man and he'd never paid a visit to the Manor alone before. He found the four old ladies who lived there quite formidable, but Mrs Merfield, the eldest, owned fields he farmed and he thought her a fair and benevolent landlord, and Angela had struck up a warm friendship with Nanny, who had lived with the Merfield family since time immemorial.

Nanny it was who usually answered the door to callers, but when, this evening, the great old oak door was pulled open, a tall, skeletal lady, dressed in red crimson wool, a red chiffon scarf swept round her neck and with a streak of red in her thin blond hair, stood there.

'Ah, Stephen Tucker,' she drawled, 'how unexpected.'

'Yes, sorry, Miss Charlotte. I should have rung to say I was popping by ...'

'Well do pop in quickly, for goodness sake. I'm freezing to death standing here!'

The door slammed behind him, the sound echoing round the great stone flagged hall, and Stephen, feeling very uncomfortable, wondered if it had been such a good idea after all. As if to affirm his doubts, his stomach gave another enormous rumble.

Charlotte appeared not to notice his discomfiture. 'My sisters are in the drawing room.

130

Nanny is at a village shop committee meeting if you were hoping to speak to her.'

'Er, it was Mrs Merfield I wanted to see, Miss Charlotte.'

'Then follow me.' She crossed the hall to a far door.

With trepidation, Stephen followed.

Nanny's absence was a blessing in a way. Although she was by far and away the most human of the four old ladies who occupied the Manor, it occurred to him that Ange might well have told her about the Merlin Players' plans and she would be surprised by any reservations he might express about the project.

The drawing room was at the back of the house, overlooking lawns that swept down to the river. This evening thick, dark green velvet curtains had been drawn shut against the chill air. A fire crackled in a wrought iron grate, setting the crystal inside a tall, glass-fronted cabinet alive with a thousand twinkling refracted sparks. In the centre of the room a polished oval table stood, laden with bottles and decanters, an ice bucket, and little dishes containing olives and slices of lemon.

Around the fire a selection of upholstered chairs had been set and on one of these sat the rigid, upright figure of Mrs Merfield. She was dressed entirely in black, the only colour on her person provided by the flash of a diamond brooch as it caught the firelight.

Her sister-in-law, the youngest Miss Merfield, was the antithesis of such sobriety. Attired in a swirl of apricot silk, her silver cropped hair was adorned with an apricot coloured feather and she wore the highest pair of heeled slippers Stephen had ever seen.

Not for the first time, Stephen wondered who these elderly ladies dressed for and why they bothered. He thought of his own grandmother, also in her eighties, also a force to be reckoned with, but dressed, in his opinion, entirely appropriately for her age—no fancy silk for her!

Charlotte drifted past him to the fire, murmuring, 'My dears, we have a visitor.'

His stomach grumbled again, as if to affirm his presence.

Mrs Merfield turned and fixed her gaze upon him as he stood, hesitating, at the open door.

'Ah, Mr Tucker. This is an unexpected pleasure. Do come in and please, shut that door. At this time of year we do feel the draughts, you know.'

'I'm just fixing Charlotte and myself a gin. Would you like something to drink, Stephen?' enquired the youngest.

'Er, no thanks, Miss Louisa. I've got to drive into Summerbridge after, so I'd better not.'

'How sensible,' murmured Charlotte, taking the glass handed to her by her sister. 'But do help yourself to one of these little cheese straws,' she pushed a small dish into his hand before sinking onto a chair close to the fire. 'Nanny makes them and they are simply delicious.'

Mrs Merfield raised a bejewelled claw.

'Please take a seat, Mr Tucker, and tells us what we can do for you. I take it this call is not entirely social?'

'Er no, no it's not.' Stephen sat down, clutching the bowl and eyeing the crisp, golden pastries. He ached to eat the whole lot, and wondered when he could politely put one in his mouth, but held off, remembering his mother's constant nag not to talk when his mouth was full.

'Then how can we help you?' prompted Mrs Merfield.

Taking a deep breath, Stephen launched into the purpose of his visit, describing the Merlin Players, his and Angela's relationship with them, and their ambition to use the Manor grounds to stage a production.

'I promised them,' he said, in conclusion, 'I'd ask you. So that's what I've done. I quite understand if you say no, but at least I've asked, and I hope you're not offended.'

Perspiring slightly, he breathed out and courage up, took a large bite of a cheese straw. It was delicious; his stomach expressed its appreciation.

The three ladies looked at each other; it was impossible to read their reactions.

'What is the play, Stephen?' Charlotte enquired. 'You haven't told us which play they wish to stage here?'

Stephen blushed, swallowing a mouthful of buttery cheese. 'I should've written it down; I can never remember the names of the plays we do unless it's something straightforward like *Grease*.'

'*Grease*?' Louisa gave a small giggle. 'Is there a play called *Grease*?'

'Yes—well, it's more of a musical, really. We did it a few years back. It was quite good. But this one, Dream something, by Shakespeare, is a different kettle of fish.'

'Do you mean *A Midsummer Night's Dream*?' asked Charlotte.

'Yes, that's the one.' Stephen helped himself to another straw and chewed it as quickly as he could before the next question.

'Hmm, Shakespeare,' said Mrs Merfield. 'Very respectable.'

'Unlike something called *Grease*,' tittered Louisa. 'What a lark.'

'It could work well in the rose garden,' commented Charlotte. 'But perhaps we should talk to Nanny about it before we come to any decision?'

'If little Angela is involved, I can't see Nanny saying no . . .' drawled Louisa.

His mouth full of another cheese straw, Stephen became alarmed. He hadn't expected them to accept the idea so readily. He had vaguely plotted to fan their objections and lead them to a refusal without making his position too blatant. Such subtlety was now quite beyond him . . .

'Er,' he said, blowing a fine dust of pastry crumbs over his knees. 'Um, thing is . . . it's not . . . I don't think . . . I don't want . . .' He could feel himself growing red in the face and as the three ladies looked at him, clearly surprised at his interjection, he grew even redder, a stentorian rumble from his stomach capping his embarrassment.

Charlotte was the first to speak. 'I don't think you've given us the entire picture, have you, Stephen? What is it you don't think and you don't want?'

For a moment, Stephen looked at them in utter misery, then his worry found voice.

'Thing is,' he said, 'to be honest with you, I'm bothered. I think it's too big—they're biting off more than they can chew, so to speak. They're going to be trampling all over your garden, making idiots of themselves, in my opinion that is. To be fair, Ange thinks they should do it, but Ange

134

always looks on the bright side and truth to tell, I feel awful, going behind her back like this . . . But I have to say they're really not doing themselves any favours. I've worked with the company for ten years, I know what I'm talking about—they're going to come a cropper if they go ahead, believe me.'

An astonished silence greeted his little speech. Miserably he picked up the last cheese straw in the dish and bit into it.

'So,' Mrs Merfield raised a hand to her brow; her eyes, dark in their sunken sockets, glinted. 'If I understand you correctly, you have come here to ask, on behalf of your theatre company, if they might use our garden for a performance of *A Midsummer's Night's Dream*, and you want us to refuse the request. Am I right?'

'Yes,' said Stephen unhappily, running his finger around the empty dish to catch up any residue of cheese dust. 'Yes, that's it, in a nutshell.'

25

Paula Spinks sat on the edge of the bed and leant forward to peer into the mirror of her dressing table. The cottage bedroom was too small to accommodate more than the double bed, a small cabinet and the dressing table, but she didn't mind. One day her and Lenny's fortunes would change and then she would have plenty of room for a stool. It would be covered in mink, she'd decided, and she would sit upon it, in a silk negligée, to do her makeup, adjust her hair, or fix her jewels.

She pouted her lips and applied a generous layer of a deep rose pink, then added a further layer of thick black mascara onto eyelashes already heavy with previous applications.

Sitting back on the bed the better to view the results, she smiled at her reflection, puffed up the glistening lacquered beehive balanced on the top of her head and looked at the photo of her icon kept in pride of place on her dressing table.

'Well Joan, that's as good as I get, I reckon. If they don't pick me, then they don't know what . . .'

'Paula? Paula? Where are you? Where's my tea?'

She scrambled off the bed. 'I'm up here, in the bedroom, Lenny, love. Just a sec.'

Pushing her feet into a pair of high-heeled, imitation crocodile skin winkle-pickers, she picked her way along the landing and down the narrow stairs, carefully stepping over the toys and other hazardous objects littering the way.

She found Lenny in the kitchen, his head in the fridge.

''Lo darlin',' she said seductively.

'What's to eat, I'm starvin'?' He withdrew his head and looked at her. His jaw dropped. 'Blimey!'

His look of admiration and the wolf whistle that followed was heartfelt. Pleased, she gave a little twirl.

'How do I look?' she demanded, smoothing down the short, very short, faux leopard skin skirt and fluffing up the imitation cheetah fur ruff around her neck.

'Fantastic—bloody fantastic! A dog's dinner. Come here!' And he grabbed her buttocks and pulled her to him so that her ample breast squashed against his chin and her fur tickled his forehead—in

136

her heels, she was nearly six inches taller than him.

She giggled and returned his embrace with equal enthusiasm.

'You're a right cracker,' he said finally, breaking off. 'I come home from work, sweatin' and starvin' and what do I find but a vision of loveliness. If it wasn't for the kiddies, I'd have you here, on the kitchen table.'

'If it wasn't for the kiddies,' replied Paula, 'I'd have a big fur rug ready and waiting on the sitting room floor.'

'We ain't got no fur rug.'

'No, and that kitchen table's so wobbly, it 'ud collapse the moment I lay on it.' She chuckled. 'Well I better get these clothes off and get you your tea. I'm sorry it's a bit late, I got carried away.'

'No worries, I'll crack a cider and 'ave some crisps to keep me going. Anyways, my little flower, what's it all in aid of, eh . . . this dressin' up?'

'It's for tomorrow.'

'What's happenin' tomorrow? The party's on Friday.'

'Tomorrow is the auditions; you know, Lenny, for the extras. They want everyone who's interested to be at the Village Hall at seven. Mum's coming and we're goin' to take the kiddies.'

'Why?'

'cos they said all ages. They might want kids in a crowd scene. And it's fifty quid a day, Lenny. That's not to be sniffed at.'

Lenny whistled. 'How many people do they want, then?'

'Dunno—but all the folks from the village is goin'. This is my chance, Lenny.' Her voice thrilled with excitement. 'I could be spotted!'

'They certainly couldn't overlook you, lookin' like that, love,' he replied, his voice full of admiration. 'You'll turn everybody's head.'

'Why don't you come too, Lenny? I bet you're the sort of person they'd want. They said they'd like people from the village an' you've lived here all your life.'

Lenny grinned. 'Give me half a chance, my lovely, and I would. Charlie's been a bear with a sore head since yesterday and Stephen's so grumpy, he's almost impossible to talk to.'

'What's wrong with Charlie?'

'I dunno—he had a bad hangover, that's for sure, but it was more than that. I asked him about London, but he didn't want to talk about it. And then I got it in the neck from Stephen for Baldy's escape.'

'Baldy?'

'Our Portland ram; he only arrived this morning; worth a fortune. The gate wasn't fastened properly and somehow he got through and was making off down the track when he met one of the actors. Luckily the guy grabbed hold of him and then Alison turned up to give him a hand to push him back into a field.'

'That was some luck—but why did you get the blame?'

''Cos I put him in the field in the first place—but since I took real care to shut the bloomin' gate, I don't see why I should carry the can.'

'And didn't Charlie stand up for you?'

'No, he buggers off when Stevie turns up.'

'Well, thank your lucky stars that actor was around.'

'Yeah, Quite a surprise, really. I thought he was

a bit of a berk. Joe, the driver, was bellyaching about what a pain he was, never on time and keeps him waitin' like some bleedin' servant, then he turns up, covered in mud and tells us about Baldy.'

'Blimey, he was brave. If I saw a ram running towards me, I'd be over the fence in no time.' She started out of the kitchen, 'I'm goin' to get changed.' Stopping at the bottom of the stairs, she cocked her head winsomely and said, with a note of appeal, 'Do come tomorrow night, Lenny. Just think, if you gets picked, it would be an extra fifty quid in the kitty.'

'But I'm working flat out at the moment, sweetheart.'

'Yeah, and little thanks you seem to be getting for it. You don't have to say nothing to the Tuckers. If you gets called, you could throw a sickie.'

26

Stephen stood in the porch of June Pagett's house, a large, thirties bungalow on the outskirts of Summerbridge, and pressed the bell. Having achieved the answer he wanted from the Merfields, it was a matter of some irony that he couldn't remember when he last felt so miserable.

He'd gone straight from Summerstoke Manor to pick Angela up from her bedsit, but she had not been there. 'She said to say she's gone on, if you called,' the landlady informed him and with his heart in his socks, he had driven on to the production meeting alone. It was the first time, ever, he'd not picked her up before going to the

Merlin Players.

The inner circle of the Players had been summoned to June Pagett's home and it was Mr Pagett who let him in. 'They're waiting for you, you're the last,' he said, showing him into an over-heated, crowded sitting room.

His eyes immediately sought out Angela. She was perched on the end of a sofa and when she saw him, she coloured and would have turned away but he sent her such a look of abject misery, she immediately relented and patted the sofa beside her.

There was no time for any other communication between them for as soon as Stephen was seated, Mrs Pagett called the meeting to order. Briefly she outlined her plans to celebrate twenty years of Merlin Players with a summer production no-one would forget.

'We are going to do *The Dream*,' she said melodramatically, her voice husky from too much nicotine. 'In the grounds of Summerstoke Manor.'

Gasps of amazement and paeans of praise for her courage and spirit of adventure followed, much to her evident gratification.

'That has always been The Merlin Players' way. Nothing is too difficult for The Players to take on. We did *The Merchant* for our tenth anniversary, and those of you who remember it will support me when I say that it was superb. *The Dream* will be even better, particularly in the garden of the Manor, which dates back to the Tudor period, I believe.'

Stephen wriggled unhappily in his seat.

'Have the owners agreed to let us use it?' someone finally asked.

'Stephen, here, is acquainted with Mrs Merfield,

140

the owner, and will ask her on our behalf. I hoped they could have confirmed everything this evening but Angela tells me they've not yet had the opportunity to pay the good lady a visit.'

She turned and looked sternly at Stephen. 'We really do need to know as soon as possible, Stephen. There's a great deal of work to be done, and the sooner we can get started . . .'

Stephen felt his colour rise. 'I went to see them,' he blurted, aware of an exclamation of surprise from Angela. 'Before I came here, I went to see them. I knew you'd want an answer this evening, so I missed my tea and went.'

'Oh Stephen,' whispered Angela, fully aware not only of the courage it must have taken Stephen to go without her, but of what missing a meal meant to him. 'Well done!'

'Good,' said June briskly. 'And?'

'No. They said no.'

He couldn't have put it more bluntly and for a moment June Pagett gaped at him, unable to believe that 'no' is what he'd said. A murmur of disappointment rippled round the room.

June found her voice. 'Well, I must say, that's very disappointing. Very disappointing indeed.' She was loud in her displeasure. 'I understood from Angela it was a strong possibility; you have a good relationship with them. Did they say why not? Is there room for manoeuvre? I think you should try again; see if you can persuade them to change their minds, Stephen.'

Angela squeezed his hand sympathetically and for the first time since that whole awful episode in the kitchen with Charlie, Stephen felt a small warm glow of happiness.

'Mrs Merfield said no,' he repeated firmly. 'She and her two sisters are elderly ladies, Mrs Pagett. They're concerned about their privacy.'

'I quite understand their concern and The Merlin Players would respect that. Perhaps they don't understand what would be involved; we could certainly set their minds at rest. All they need is reassurance; I think I should go and see Mrs Merfield, myself.'

Far from feeling alarm at this pronouncement, Stephen's instinct told him a visit from June Pagett, who was everything the Merfields were not—loud, bossy, nicotine-stained, thick-skinned and stout— would cause the old ladies to feel they'd had a lucky escape.

So he shrugged. 'If you think you can persuade them, then go. I don't really want to bother them anymore.'

'I think it was very good of you to ask, anyway, Stephen,' said Angela, loyally. 'Now that they've been introduced to the idea, Mrs Pagett might be able to persuade them to change their minds.'

At this Stephen felt another spurt of happiness and squeezed her hand in turn. It suddenly didn't matter who was right or wrong over the business of the website, he loved her and couldn't bear it when they weren't friends.

27

'Emma, darling, your glass is empty. We can't have that.' Ben Dacres sashayed across the room, brandishing a bottle, and refilled her glass. He looked round.

'Anyone else ready for a top-up yet? No?' Ben had decided to throw an impromptu party at the Country Club for a select few of his colleagues.

'It's been a helluva day,' he'd said emphatically to Juliet and Jilly Westcott as they finished work, 'and tomorrow looks like being even worse, so I think we deserve a little party.'

He'd invited Juliet and Jilly, Nicola, Emma, Ross, Matt, Colin and Marcus, although Marcus had not yet turned up, and he had pointedly issued those invitations when Jason was not about.

Harry Hobbs, the only one present not to be invited when the party was first discussed, went home in a sulk, even though, as Juliet had said, in an attempt to console him, a bunch of adults drinking could be of no possible interest to a fifteen-year-old.

Colin, the director of photography, had stayed for a fruit juice then made his excuses and left. Emma watched him go with a certain amount of envy. He was a nice guy, refreshingly untemperamental. He had a close relationship with his own team but did not mingle much with the rest of them.

'That way,' he'd confided to her one evening over supper at Isabelle's, where both he and Emma were billeted, 'I'm not drawn into any factions or unholy alliances.'

She sympathised. It was undoubtedly one of the hazards of a long shoot, and this was longer than any she'd been involved with before. But as the director, his sort of detachment was denied her: if she'd refused, or had one drink then gone, she knew it would be taken amiss by everybody. She would have been happier, however, if Jason, for all the problems he was causing, had not been so specifically excluded. As she saw it, just by being here she was party to that exclusion and that made her uneasy.

She sipped from her glass and shuddered. Ben's generosity in throwing this party did not extend to his choice of wine.

'Well, Emma,' Jilly Westcott stood over her, beaming, 'how do you think it's all going, so far? Apart from the troubles with our young friend, that is?'

'It's early days, yet,' replied Emma, cautiously, 'but it's looking good. And I'm sure once Jason feels his feet . . .'

'He's an arrogant little shit,' sniffed Ben. 'You're too soft with him, Emma. You need to tell him to stop wasting our time.'

'I agree,' growled Matt, pushing his wine glass away and looking across at the bottles on the table. 'Got any beer, Ben?'

'That's what Marcus is for,' said Emma firmly, frowning at Matt for his indiscretion. Her remark was picked up by Marcus as he walked into the room.

'What is Marcus for?' he asked, raising a quizzical eyebrow.

'For coming to our rescue, darling, when things

144

go a teensy bit ape-shit,' dimpled Juliet, 'and for rapping our knuckles when we deserve it.'

'I hope I do a bit more than that,' he smiled down at her and accepting a glass from Ben, sat between her and Emma.

He nodded at Matt. 'How're you getting on with your quiz team, Matt? I'm sorry I can't be in it, but you're probably better off without me.'

Matt, the first assistant, was a tall lean man in his mid-thirties, with endless amounts of restless energy. He was, as was already clear to everybody in the crew, highly competitive. He grinned at his boss. 'If you say so, Marcus . . . pity though, we'd have made an awesome partnership. Ross has also chickened out.'

'When would I have the time?' responded Ross, good-naturedly. 'I shouldn't really be here as it is. I've got my work cut out at the moment.'

'Not helped by that little prick giving us the run-around,' grumbled Ben, determined to air his grievance. 'Three changes to the schedules in as many days, and all because of him.'

'Oh don't worry about him,' Ross murmured, 'I've got his measure.'

'Changes happen for all sorts of reasons, Ben. You're a seasoned player—you know that.' Marcus was polite but brisk, and closing the subject of Jason, he turned back to Matt. 'So have you had the opportunity of checking out the opposition at the Bunch of Grapes yet, Matt?'

'Tomorrow night's quiz night; me and Colin plan to go on a recce. I can't imagine we'd have much to worry about. I've taken on some of the best in London. A little yokel affair—it should be a walk-over. Come and join us if you fancy a pint. It's

145

a nice looking pub, I'll give it that. Some good guest beers.'

Marcus shrugged. 'I'll see how things go, thanks.' He turned to Emma, 'I promise not to talk all shop, but as I've got you, Matt, and Ross here, is everything sorted for Friday?'

Ross answered for them, 'Sure, Marcus. Charlie has okayed the herd and the village is being prepared. We reckon on closing the High Street for no more than two hours.'

Ben shuddered. 'Can't say I'm looking forward to that little sequence. I do hope you're not expecting me to mingle intimately with the beasts, Emma?'

She smiled at him with sympathy. 'Charlie is taking your place for the wide shots, Ben. Please don't worry—they're only cows.'

'But cows can do very nasty things,' chipped in Nicola, who'd been chatting politely to Jilly while half-listening to the main conversation, waiting for the moment when she could join in. 'You occasionally hear of people being trampled to death by them.' She shuddered. 'I've lived in the country, but I always give them a wide berth if I can. They're so big!'

'My sentiments exactly.' Ben nodded, turning to this new ally. 'My darling, how neglectful of me, your glass is empty . . .'

'I have a friend who was attacked by cows,' said Juliet. 'She was crossing a field, on a public footpath, when they surrounded her, knocked her to the ground, and . . .'

'Oh my God,' Ben, about to pour Nicola a glass of wine, froze, then turned and went to sink into the sofa by Juliet's side, his face quite livid. 'What happened? How did she escape? Was she badly

146

hurt?'

Nicola stared at her empty glass, frustrated. Her attempt to move in centre stage had been thwarted; her role was to look on and listen. As indeed, did the four members of the crew, unable to intervene, as Juliet, her audience in horrified thrall, told her tale with great relish.

'She tried to get up, but every time she did, they knocked her down; two, three, four times . . . she was shrieking and crying, screaming for help. There was a bunch of people, picnicking in the corner of the field, but not one of them came to her rescue; they just stood there, watching, terrified. The cows had formed a circle around her; then, when she was on the ground, one of them rolled over her. Deliberately. They were determined to kill her . . .'

'They're huge—wasn't she squashed to death immediately?'

'And it wasn't an accident? It was deliberate? They were deliberately trying to kill her?'

'I read in the paper about a lady being trampled to death by a herd.'

'It's true, it really happens. And yet farmers put them in fields where there are public footpaths.'

'You won't get me going near a cow again.'

'What are you lot so excited about?' drawled a voice from the doorway. 'My, my, I seem to be missing a little party.'

There was a split second's silence as they registered Jason standing there. But just as Emma was about to leap up, Nicola got there first. Abandoning her empty glass and the unenviable position of being lodged between Jilly's bulk and the end of a sofa, she danced up to him.

'Hi Jason, we were wondering where you were.

147

Ben decided to throw a party after we finished, but you'd vanished.'

His eyes flickered over her, his expression quite cold; he didn't move.

Nothing daunted, she fluttered in front of him. 'We've been comparing notes, about cows of all things. Juliet's just telling us about a friend of hers, who nearly got trampled to death.'

'Come on in, pal,' Ross got to his feet and picking up a glass, held it out to him. 'Where've you been?'

Jason shrugged and with a second glance at Nicola, moved to take the glass. 'Not communing with cows, that's for sure. If you want to know, I've just had a close encounter with a ram. We had a wrestling match and I won.'

The effect was gratifying.

'What?'

'A ram?'

'You're kidding?'

'Oh come on, Jason, pull the other one.' This was from Ben who didn't want Jason to gatecrash his party and certainly did not want to be upstaged by him with some fabrication.

'No, it's true.' Jason made for the wine. 'There was I, taking a stroll, minding my own business, breathing in the country air, thinking "this is meant to be good for me, but, by God, does it stink", when down the track, hurtling towards me like some demonic escapee from the jaws of hell, comes this bloody great hairy beast, with massive horns and the most evil eyes you ever saw . . .'

He picked up the bottles, one by one, examining the labels as he talked.

'For a moment, I was stuck in a cliché, the whole

of my life—birth excepted, I couldn't remember that—flashed before my eyes; but I'll spare you the details, you can read those in my autobiography, *You've Gotta Laugh*, due out next month, only £15.99, available in any supermarket near you. So there I am, facing certain injury, if not death, and I knew I couldn't outrun him, and I couldn't leap over the hedge, it was too high; so I did the only thing I could do in the circumstances, I hurled myself at him and grabbed his horns before he got me.'

'Jason! My God! You could have been killed!' Nicola's shriek was a mix of horror and admiration; Jason glanced at her again and shrugged, nonchalantly. 'As I said, quite possibly—those horns looked pretty lethal. He wasn't expecting to be leapt on, that's for sure.'

'I don't believe a word of it,' snorted Ben.

'Trampled by cows, attacked by rams . . . I thought the countryside was meant to be a peaceful place,' exclaimed Jilly Westcott.

'You stopped him all by yourself?' Ross's voice was sharp. 'Wasn't there anybody else about?'

'Yeah. I'd just got him under control when this farm girl comes up and says he'd escaped. She fairly licked the mud off my boots, she was so grateful. Seems he was pretty valuable.'

'But you could have been badly hurt.' Emma shook her head. 'You shouldn't be exposed to risks like that.' She turned to Marcus.

He nodded. 'I agree. Not like the Tuckers to be so careless with their animals. I'll have a word with Charlie tomorrow.'

'Lucky you weren't hurt, Jason, then my schedules really would have gone to pot.' Matt grinned at him. 'A quiz question for you—was he a golden ram, by any chance, and what's that to do with you?'

Jason regarded him coldly. He didn't like Matt. 'Why?'

Emma laughed. 'Oh very clever, Matt—but a bit obvious, I think. Jason—he means your namesake: Jason, the ancient Greek hero and his band of merry men from Argos, the Argonauts, who went after a ram with a golden fleece.'

Jason's expression was sour. 'Did he? Bully for him. I'm afraid I didn't stop to inspect the beast's outfit.'

'And now that you've inspected all those bottles of wine, would you like a glass?' asked Ben, with exaggerated politeness.

Jason put down the bottle he was holding. 'No thanks, I've tasted this house wine and it's shite. I'm off to the bar for something decent.'

On his way out of the room, he paused in front of Nicola. 'Fancy coming with? I can't imagine this funeral party is your bag. The bar's gotta be a better laugh.'

28

A pale grey light filled the valley. Wisps of mist drifted across the ridge and rose slowly from trees where a froth of blossom and a hint of bright green smudged stark wintry silhouettes.

The dawn symphony was well underway, chirruping, whistling and warbling, a distant cockerel gustily contributing a strident solo. The sky was busy with winged traffic intent on breakfasting and re-establishing territorial boundaries.

The early morning air was sweet and soft, and Stephen lingered outside the barn housing his milking herd and breathed in deeply, appreciatively. Spring really had arrived.

Turning back to the milking parlour, he bumped into a young boy—at least, he looked like a young boy. He stared at the child, bemused. 'What on earth are you doing here?'

'I'm with the filming' the boy replied perkily. 'My name's Harry Hobbs. I expect you've heard of me?'

Stephen shook his head slowly, 'Nope, can't say as I have.'

'Never mind, you're probably too old. What are you doing here?'

Far from taking offence, Stephen quite liked his cheeky directness. 'I could ask the same question of you, I've been milking my herd, if you really want to know and now I'm about to go and clean the parlour. So I'll ask you again—what are you doing here?'

The boy pulled a face. 'We've been pulled in to film some scenes we missed yesterday.'

'But it's barely six-thirty!'

'Tell me about it! I had one piddling scene, which we've just finished, and then I've got to hang about, doing nothing, till this afternoon. They take me for granted, this lot. It's so bloody boring!'

'Haven't you got anything else to do?'

'Oh, like what?'

'Well, I don't know—shouldn't you be doing school work, or something?'

The boy sighed with disgust. 'Typical—you grown-ups are so unoriginal. Yeah, yeah, I've got

151

schoolwork, for what it's worth. But it does my head in and that cow who supervises me is the pits.'

Stephen looked at him curiously. 'How old are you?'

'Fifteen. And before you say anything else, I'm well hacked off with being told I look about six . . .'

'Well I wasn't going to say that, exactly . . .'

'Good, because it's the way I look that's putting the greenbacks in the bank; that, and my acting of course. I've been professionally employed since I was five, you know.'

'Blimey. Do you like doing it?'

The boy pulled a face. 'Not much. And I especially don't like this outfit. There's nobody of my age about, plus no shops, no movies, no bowling alley . . . Three months, stuck here in the dead end of nowhere—I'm going to die of boredom!'

Stephen could think of nothing to say to this beyond, 'Yes, well, we all have to do things we don't want to do. Like cleaning the milking parlour.' And then in a philanthropic rush of generosity towards this hothouse kid, who probably didn't know what physical graft was and might enjoy learning something about life in the raw, he added diffidently, 'If you've got nothing to do, you can come and give me a hand, if you like.'

The boy flashed him a look of complete contempt. 'Hell, no, I ain't that desperate.'

*   *   *

Inside the barn, converted into a studio for most of the interiors, real time was suspended, and night had descended on the kitchen set.

'Standby for rehearsal,' shouted Matt, and his

words could be heard echoing down the line until it reached the furthest reaches of the yard where the runners and general dogsbodies, Chris and Andy, stood, waiting to clamp down on the movement of animals and humans when the camera was actually running.

Colin leant across the camera operator and looked into the camera's eyepiece, then checked back on the small TV monitor by his side. At the same time, makeup, props, sound, continuity, and every other professional involved in how the scene looked, peered into the nearest monitor with the utmost concentration.

Emma, the only one concerned about the actual performance, was behind one of the flats, perched on a stool beside Matt, staring at her own screen, her lips pursed, her body tense.

Juliet sat at the kitchen table and breathed in deeply. If only she didn't feel so sick. She glanced up and caught sight of Jason leaning on the other side of the door through which he was due to make an entrance. He was yawning and looked pale, even with his makeup.

'Bastard!' she thought, savagely. 'He's the reason we've been called at this ridiculous hour.'

She'd never been very good at getting up at the crack of dawn, but she prided herself on being thoroughly professional—if it had to be done, so be it. But the fact that it was Jason who was the cause of this early start irritated her and her irritation was aggravated by her feelings of nausea.

Ben Dacres was poised, waiting for his cue on the other side of the set. She could tell from his fixed expression that he, too, was equally out of sorts. 'I never thought I'd find myself drinking with Ben

153

Dacres till the early hours of the morning, moaning about another member of the cast,' she marvelled. 'I deserve to feel as sick as a parrot. That's what sodding Jason Hart has done—removed all my common sense.'

Ben turned to see her looking at him and threw her an expressive, eyebrows raised, 'What-are-we-doing-here-it's-all-you-know-who's–fault' look. It was conveyed so exquisitely she wanted to giggle, an impulse she hastily concealed by burying her head in the schoolbooks her character was meant to be marking.

'And—action!'

'We can't carry on like this, Phoebe. If Will doesn't start pulling his weight, I'm going to have to re-think the farm's future.'

Ben paused, looked towards the door and caught sight of Jason mid-yawn. 'I am going to have to re-think the farm's future,' he repeated louder and with more emphasis.

Jason heard him the second time. 'Oh sorry,' he muttered and pushed the door open. He stood in the entrance, swaying, the drunken son returning home. 'A reception party, how nice. But you shouldn't have waited up for me.'

Juliet stood up, gathering her books, 'I'm going to bed.'

'What a good idea,' Jason looked at her and winked. 'Mind if I join you?'

Throughout the studio there was a frozen silence, then Emma, bristling with annoyance, came onto the set. 'Jason . . .'

'Sorry, sorry!' He held his hands up and smiled disarmingly at her. 'Just a little joke.'

His smile had no effect and she snapped, 'I'm

not laughing. And when we're working, I'm not interested in any jokes not in the script.'

'Oh, are there any?' he replied, a note of belligerence creeping in. 'I thought I was brought in to up the laughs, but I can't see, for the life of me, where the fun in this pile of shite is to be found.'

'Can we continue this conversation some other time, some other place, please.' Matt interjected with ill-concealed impatience. 'We need to get this scene wrapped as soon as poss, otherwise our schedule today, like yesterday, is going to be on the skids. Positions, please.'

Emma retreated from the set and Jason returned to stand behind the door. Catching Juliet looking at him, he winked again and grinned.

She turned back to her books, amused in part, but also annoyed, and the annoyance was tinged with fear. Although she'd set her sights on Hollywood, like everyone else involved with *Silage and Strawberries*, she wanted the series to be commissioned beyond the pilot, but if the destructive antics of Jason Hart continued unchecked . . . 'He really is outrageous,' she brooded. 'He just doesn't give a damn about anyone else. If he's not brought under control, he's going to sabotage this show, single-handed. Perhaps I should talk to Ross. He seems to be the only person Jason listens to.'

'Action.'

With a long-suffering sigh, Ben delivered his line. 'We can't carry on like this, Phoebe. If Will doesn't start pulling his weight I am going to have to re-think the farm's future.'

On cue Jason pushed the door open.

With a resounding crash it fell forward,

155

just missing Juliet and forcibly carrying Jason, still clutching the handle, along with it until, bent double, he let go and staggered forward, head-butting Ben in the stomach before Ben had a chance to get out of the way.

With an agonised 'oof', Ben crumpled to the floor.

Juliet was violently sick.

29

Veronica Lester, who normally exerted an iron grip over her emotions, had never felt so unsettled. Although she assured Hugh she had effectively banished Anthony from her thoughts, his absence periodically pricked her comfort zone and these tantalising sightings did not help. The news of trouble at Marsh Farm also served to unsettle her. The final rift with Anthony was the direct result of his parents' attempts to bankrupt the Tuckers, and now Sally Green's news intimated at a crack in their armour. But how she could use that to her advantage, or how she and Anthony could become reconciled, were conundrums with no immediate solution. So she put them to one side and succumbed, mind and body, to her most pressing preoccupation, Ben Dacres.

It was as if she'd fallen into a nettle patch; every inch of her body twitched and sang, and half tormented, half ecstatic, all her self-control appeared to have evaporated.

Fortunately, Hugh didn't seem to notice, except to comment that the melba toast for the foie gras they'd had for supper the previous night was a little on the charred side.

She'd thought about raising the idea of a drinks party for the film crew over supper, but knowing his dislike of most things that didn't involve horses or making money, and, in particular, his contempt for artists of any sort, she decided to bide her time and hope the opportunity to see Ben Dacres again would soon present itself.

It was just twenty-four hours since he'd kissed her hand, looked deep into her eyes and said 'Ver-ron-nica'.

Twenty-four hours!

Every minute of those twenty-four hours had weighed heavily on her and following an unmemorable ride on her horse the morning after her encounter with the most beautiful man in the world, she rushed back to the house to pick up the telephone message she was convinced would be waiting.

No messages.

Zero calls.

Nothing.

Paralysed by an overwhelming sense of disappointment, she stared at the unblinking machine, then looked towards the closed kitchen door from whence came the muted sounds of the radio.

'Carol,' she called, sharp and impatient. 'Carol.'

A pale freckled face with thin, pencilled eyebrows pulled together in a suspicious frown, peered round the kitchen door.

'Yes, Mrs Lester?'

'Has anyone called while I've been out?'

'No Mrs Lester, leastways, I don't think so. I

didn't hear no phone . . .'

Veronica curtly cut her off. 'I'm going to have a shower. Bring the coffee through to the sitting room in half an hour.'

She climbed the staircase to her room, scolding herself.

'It's no use behaving like this. You only met yesterday; he knows you're a married woman; why should you expect him to call you?'

The hot fizz of the water cleared her head.

Why should she wait for him to make the next move? When had passivity ever got her anywhere? Didn't she always get what she wanted by being pro-active? She knew what to do—a two-pronged attack: tennis and the party. She'd already done the groundwork; all she had to do was to phone and leave a message suggesting a game tomorrow to make up for their aborted match. If he couldn't make it, he'd be honour bound to suggest another date. And as for the party . . . she knew how to play Hugh, of course she did.

As if on cue she heard her husband enter the bedroom and shout through the bathroom door.

'Vee, are you in the shower? I'm going to grab some coffee then trawl through that paperwork Ranwell is bleating about.'

Concealing the soap behind a bottle of shampoo, she called languorously, 'Hugh, Hugh.'

He opened the bathroom door.

'Odd time of day for you to be taking a shower, Vee,' he commented.

'I know, darling, I was late back from my ride. Be a sweetheart and pass me the soap from the basin, will you. The stupid girl appears to have cleared it away.'

From that point it was but a short step to encourage him to remove his clothes and soap her body and then move onto other things.

Veronica did not encourage sex outside the bed, or outside what she called bedtime hours, so Hugh, delighted and completely taken aback by this unexpected seduction by his wife, was in an uncommonly high humour when, half an hour later, she joined him in the sitting room for coffee.

'Well,' he said, taking the cup she proffered him. 'You never cease to amaze me, Vee. How many years have we been married?'

'Twenty–three,' she replied with a smile.

'And you still turn me on. Amazing!'

'You're a handsome man, Hugh, and . . . well, it's good to do the unexpected every now and then. It stops us becoming middle-aged, predictable and boring.'

There was just enough edge to her voice to cause him to look up. 'And you think we're in danger of becoming that?'

'No, no darling—not us, not you . . . But a lot of our friends are.'

She laughed lightly and pressed on. 'I thought that at the last party we gave, you hinted that you felt much the same. True, we have to have people here for form's sake as well as for business, but the others . . .' She groaned dismissively, sipped her coffee and then resumed her offensive. 'The trouble is I do like giving parties . . . if only we could meet a different set of people.'

He shrugged. 'Short of moving somewhere else, I am not sure how we'd achieve that.'

She laughed lightly and, kitten-like, curled back in her chair, tucking her feet up. 'That would be a bit extreme, darling. I'm not suggesting that. But why don't we take advantage of the fact that Summerstoke has been invaded by a television crew . . .'

He shot her a sharp look. 'Juliet Peters and her gang? You're not serious?'

'I think we can safely say that Ms Peters wouldn't come, but that wouldn't stop the others. There are one or two really charming people billeted at the Country Club . . . some quite well-known, I understand . . . and they are stuck here, bored to tears. I'm not suggesting the groundlings, of course not, but we could invite the better-known actors, and the director and the producer; a sort of intimate, exclusive, welcome to Summerstoke affair.

Hugh pulled a face. 'Can't say the prospect excites me, Vee.'

Veronica sighed. 'I thought it wouldn't. Mind you, you could take advantage of the occasion. I'm sure you've one or two business cronies who might be impressed at the presence of a few TV celebs in our house. Sweet as he is, Gavin Croucher, the "ex-Olympic gold medallist", is wearing a little thin as our star attraction.'

And Hugh, because he was feeling very much in the mood to please his wife, gave a rare smile. 'You've got a point there.' After a moment's reflection, he put his cup down and got up. 'Let me know when you've fixed it and who these "star" players are. You're right, there are one or two I might like to invite.'

As he left the room, a triumphant smile spread across Veronica's face. 'Ye-es!' she hissed. 'Clever girl!'

160

30

As if to make up for the last disagreeable twenty-four hours, Angela pulled out all the stops cooking the family's supper.

'Wow,' said Stephen looking at her with adoration, 'Spaghetti bolognese and apple crumble. We don't deserve you, Ange.'

Angela beamed happily back at him as she stirred the sauce. 'I love cooking for you, Stephen. Now, if you like to lay the table, I'll just grate some cheese and it'll be ready.'

'I'll do that,' said Jenny holding her hand out for the grater.

'No, it's alright, Mum, I've already started.'

'Shall I'll make the custard, then?'

'No, no, Mum. It's all in hand. You just sit and relax.'

Feeling uncomfortably redundant, Jenny picked up her knitting and listened to the chatter of Alison and Hannah, who was going to the casting with them that evening, but since their conversation was all about music she'd never heard, films she'd never seen and people she didn't know, she couldn't join in.

'Those film people were in a right tizz this morning, Ange,' chuckled Stephen as he counted out the knives and forks. 'Bit of their set collapsed right in the middle of filming. They was running around making a hell of a din.'

'Was anyone hurt?'

'Not really. Seems Ben Dacres got butted in the stomach . . .'

'Oh no!' Jenny looked up, concerned. 'Is he all right?'

'Their medic said he was okay, just winded. Made a helluva fuss, though. And Juliet Peters was so frightened she threw up all over the set. These actor types—they're nervy creatures; far too pampered, if you ask me. Anyway, they got everything back up and running fairly quick, so there was no harm done.'

The door to the kitchen opened and Jenny looked up, hoping it would be Charlie, who seemed to have missed out on every family meal since the quarrel with Stephen, but it was Elsie and Ron.

'Ah,' said Elsie brightly. 'Glad to see you're in harness tonight, Angela, dear. Poor Ron is feeling a little poorly and we need to tempt his appetite back.'

Ron did indeed look pale, thought Jenny, but he smiled and nodded at her. 'You're looking very pretty tonight, my dear. Is Jeff taking you somewhere special?'

On cue the door opened to admit the vet. 'Hope I'm not too late for supper. My, that smells good, young Angela. What a lucky family this is.' He kissed Jenny on the top of her head. 'I haven't had time to pick up the cinema tickets, love, but I don't suppose we'll find it difficult to get in.'

She looked up at him, appalled. 'But Jeff, I'm not going out with you tonight? Have you forgotten? It's the extras auditions.'

He looked at her blankly. 'The what?'

'The extras . . . the film people are having a meeting, tonight, to sign people up.'

'Oh, sorry, I forgot. So no cinema, then?'

'No.' Jenny was concerned. The last thing she

wanted was to let Jeff down. 'I'm really sorry, Jeff, but . . .'

'No matter,' he said cheerfully. 'It wasn't a film I wanted to see much anyway. It'll give me a chance to do my VAT.'

'Yes, I suppose it will.' Jenny felt a bit empty. He was just a little too cheerful about doing his VAT instead of going out with her. 'You haven't forgotten about tomorrow night, have you?'

'Tomorrow night?'

'The TV people are throwing a party for us at the Foresters Arms? I can't remember when I last went to a party where there's going to be dancing and stuff. Marcus says they've taken over the function room at the back and there's going to be a proper DJ and lots of food. I was so looking forward to it; you haven't forgotten, Jeff, have you?'

'No, no, of course not. I'm on call, but it shouldn't be a problem . . .'

'Food's ready,' Angela called out. 'I'll dish it out over here if you'd like to bring your plates.'

'What about Charlie? Aren't we going to wait for Charlie?' asked Jenny, anxiously.

'I'll put some on one side for him—he can have it when he gets in,' replied Angela briskly. 'Now, Gran, how much would Ron like?'

*　　　*　　　*

Everything had been cleared away and washed up by the time Charlie arrived back. He wolfed down a half-congealed plate of food before giving Jenny and the girls a lift to the village hall, then wishing them luck, drove on to the Old Vicarage.

Becky, Isabelle's older daughter, met him in the

163

hall.

'Mummy's in the kitchen with Emma,' she told him, 'An' Clemmie 'n me are makin' our Easter cards. D'you want to help us?'

'Love to,' he grinned. 'I haven't made cards since I was at junior school . . . the same one you're at now, Becky.'

'Did you have my teacher?'

'Mrs Jones? No, I reckon she's a bit too young to have been around when I was there.'

Emma was sitting at the kitchen table, sawing off a large chunk of bread from a loaf and chatting to Clemmie, who was sitting at the other end of the table, surrounded by pots of poster paint, card, paper, glue and scissors. Isabelle, ladling out a bowl of soup at the Aga, turned and smiled at Charlie's arrival.

'Hi Emma,' he nodded, crossing to Isabelle to drop a kiss on the nape of her neck. 'Hi, sweetheart; hmm, that soup smells good. I suspect you're a better cook than you let on; Ange had better watch out.'

'If mixing an assortment of ready-made soups makes me a good cook, Charlie, then you're right,' Isabelle laughed. 'We're taking it in turns and Colin's chicken curry last night put me to shame. Would you like some soup, or have you eaten already?'

'I'd love some,' he said, the cold plate of spag bol an unappetising, unsatisfying memory. 'If you've enough that is; what about the other two?'

'Oh don't worry about them, they've eaten already,' said Emma. 'They've gone into Summerbridge, to the cinema. I was going to go, too, but Marcus is coming over.'

164

Charlie raised his eyebrows, 'So you lot aren't going to the extras meeting?'

'No. That casting is left to the third assistant director, Sarah Thornby. It's her little empire; we don't interfere.'

'I hope she gets a good turnout. People are funny about being on camera.'

'From the way Paula's been going on, I don't think you need have any worries,' said Isabelle, bringing two bowls of soup to the table. 'Here, sit down and cut yourself some bread. According to her, most of Summerstoke's going to be there tonight.'

'My friend Ryan's going. He's in my class an' I wanted to go too, but Mummy said I couldn't,' Becky pouted.

Emma smiled at her. 'You'd find it very dull, Becky. Most of the time it's standing round waiting for something to happen. I don't think we're likely to need any children, but if we do, I'll be sure to ask your mum.'

Clemmie looked up. 'Me too, Emma. Me too?'

'I wouldn't dream of leaving you out, Clemmie.'

Isabelle pulled a face but said nothing.

'How was the filming today, Emma?' Charlie enquired. 'I heard you had a bit of trouble.'

Emma frowned. 'Yes, I was telling Isabelle about it. That's why Marcus is coming over. Fortunately nobody was really hurt, but he'll want to go over it all in minute detail and, I have no doubt, apportion blame and rap knuckles.' She sighed. 'And the trouble is, because of it, yet again we fell badly behind schedule. He's not going to be at all pleased.'

Charlie looked at her with sympathy. 'But how

165

can he blame you, he's not unreasonable?'

She gave him a bleak smile. 'Isn't he?'

'There, I've finished,' announced Clemmie waving a card in the air. 'Look at my chicken, Charlie.'

Charlie got up and went and looked over the little girl's shoulder.

'Don't look much like a chicken to me,' commented Becky.

'Does, too! Doesn't it, Charlie?'

Charlie grinned. 'It's got four legs.'

'So?' Clemmie's bottom lip wobbled.

'Look at me, Clemmie,' Charlie tucked his hands into his armpits and with bent knees and bowed legs, started to cluck and weave around the kitchen. 'What am I?'

'A chicken,' yelled the two little girls and scrambling off their chairs, attempted to imitate his actions.

'Watch me . . .'

'Look at me, Charlie!'

'No, no, look at me!!' Emma shouted and leaping up from her chair, to the amazement of Isabelle who in the limited time she'd known her had found Emma quite reserved, folded her arms and bringing her knees right up to her chin, paraded around, cocking her head from side to side and clucking louder than the rest.

'Come on Mummy, you too,' yelled Clemmie, and Charlie pulled her to her feet.

Isabelle, almost doubled with laughter, pulled a large feather out of a vase, stuck it in her hair, and joined the parade.

They made so much noise, gobbling, clucking, crowing and shrieking with laughter, nobody

166

heard the doorbell ring and Marcus's arrival went unnoticed by all of them until Emma was brought up short by the sight of him, standing, quite amazed, at the kitchen door.

31

The village hall was filling up rapidly with people, many of whom Jenny didn't recognise. Only the front two rows were relatively empty, although right in the middle, at the very front, sat Paula, resplendent in her fake animal skins, with Lenny by her side, his blond ponytail looking unusually shiny and fluffy. Paula's mum, in her best coat with a big furry collar, sat on her other side, trying to control the four little Spinks, almost unrecognisable with their faces washed, hair combed, and eyes bright with excitement.

Jenny slid into the seat her friend, Rita Godwin, was keeping for her. 'Rob not coming?' she asked, peering round.

Rita gave a short laugh. 'You must be joking, Jenny Tucker. He thinks this whole TV thing spells trouble. Suits me though. If I get picked, he can mind the shop, bad back or no bad back.'

Jenny looked at her friend curiously. 'I thought you were in two minds about having the television crew in the village? You've moaned enough about the way they've take over Dawson's field.'

Rita pursed her lips. 'I am in two minds—I think they may spell trouble with a capital T. But I tell you, Jenny, it's early days but they use my shop a lot more than the village does; my takings have really picked up this week and that man that does their catering, he's putting some really good orders my way. So if they're going to pay me fifty quid to hang around in my own village, I'd be daft not to take it off them.'

It appeared a fair number of villagers shared Rita's point of view, including Lavender Grey, the vicar's wife, and Sally Green, the solicitor's wife.

Just when the hall had become so full it seemed impossible to cram anybody else in, a thin, dark-haired woman in her late twenties, a clipboard in her hand, emerged from the back room. She was flanked on either side by two young men whom Jenny had seen working with the unit at the farm; one of them carried a Polaroid camera.

The woman held up her hand and the hall fell silent. 'Thanks for coming,' she said. 'I wasn't expecting such a big turn-out, I must admit, so this might take a little time. My name is Sarah Thornby; I'm one of the directors on *Silage and Strawberries* and I'm responsible for the crowd casting. I think you all know we are looking for a number of people who we can use to dress the location shots. A lot of the filming is self-contained as the story is set on the farm, but occasionally we see the characters in the village, in the pub, in the shop . . .'

Rita squeaked and whispered, 'That's rich, they haven't asked me . . .'

'They'll pay you, Rita,' Jenny whispered back. 'They're really generous.'

' . . . so obviously we need people in the background. This particular drama,' continued the woman who had, Jenny noticed, not smiled once, 'is unlikely to require many extras so I am afraid quite a number of you will be disappointed. We employ on a half-day basis. If you're needed, we'll contact you the day before, tell you what to wear and where you're to be. Hot drinks and snacks are provided, as well as lunch. I should warn you that, inevitably with filming, there's a lot of waiting around so if it's a cold day, you'll need something warm to wear on top of whatever it is you have in the way of costume. Andy here is going to hand out forms, so if you're interested, please fill them in, and before you go, Chris will take your photo and that'll be attached to your details.' She looked around the hall, her eyebrows raised. 'Any questions?'

After a moment's hesitation, one or two hands waved in the air.

'Don't you want to hear us read something?' asked one.

She sighed a little impatiently. 'No, we're looking for bodies, not voices; you won't be expected to say anything.'

'How often is this going to happen?'

'As I said, it's when there is an outdoor location which requires people, and so far there isn't a lot of that in the script.'

'If we get chosen, will you want us more than once?'

She shrugged. 'We might do. It's hard to say at the moment.'

'How many of us do you think you're going to use?'

'I'm not sure—twenty, thirty. No more than that, I should think.'

A rumble of disappointment went round the hall.

'How do you choose?'

'The first assistant director tells me when he needs people and the sort of impression the director wants to make. I look at the mug shots, make a selection, check availability, and we take it from there.'

'What about the kiddies?' This was from Paula.

The woman frowned. 'If we use children, and I'm not sure yet that we want to, we expect a responsible adult to accompany them and they must have written permission from school, if they should be in school that is.'

She glanced at her watch. 'It's going to take some time to get through the paperwork and take the photos, so I think we'd better press on.'

A number of people left without bothering to leave their details, but a large majority persevered and soon the queue for the camera snaked all round the hall. Progress was slow and the excited buzz present at the start of the evening was replaced by low grumbles of discontent and whispered comments and gossip.

'Why don't they have two cameras?'

'I thought they was going to have proper auditions, not just some boring meeting.'

'They should've provided tea and biscuits at the very least.'

'Or wine and cheese. This is cheapskate.'

'I'm starving—I missed my tea to get to this on time.'

'If that little Spinks boy barges through once more I'm going to clip his ear.'

'They're letting the kids run wild, somebody should say something.'

'Fancy Mrs Fairfax turning out . . . Are they going to pay extra for her Zimmer frame?'

'Why do they want to know my age; what business is it of theirs?'

'That Paula Spinks—who does she think she is?'

'Acting the film star already.'

'Mobile number? I don't have a mobile.'

'We're going to be all night at this rate.'

'They should take the kiddies home. She said they probably weren't going to use them, anyway.'

'Who's that pushing in? What a cheek.'

'She's took Paula and the kiddies to the head of the queue!'

'Very sensible.'

'That's not fair. I might have kiddies waiting for me at home for all she knows.'

'Trust Paula Spinks.'

'Is it worth it? I ask you, is it worth it?'

After nearly an hour of waiting in line, Alison was not alone in asking this question.

Hannah shrugged. 'Who knows, but you'll kick yourself if I get picked and you don't 'cos you couldn't be bothered to wait a little longer.'

Alison sighed. 'I s'pose you're right. I just have to keep thinking "fifty quid, fifty quid . . . " But you heard what she said—twenty to thirty people at the most.'

'But you could count the number of people our age on one hand. Unless they want it to look like a village of wrinklies, we're in with a good chance.'

*　　　*　　　*

'Don't be ridiculous, Emma,' Marcus's voice was cold. 'You're letting your dislike of the guy get the better of you; something I didn't expect from you.'

Emma glared. 'I am not being ridiculous. I've worked with people I don't like before and I've never allowed my personal feelings to cloud my professional judgement. It may be I'm wrong, but I don't think so. There was nothing wrong with the door until he went behind it after his little outburst.'

Marcus shook his head, impatiently. 'You want him out, so you're leaping to a conclusion . . .'

'Which is the right one. Marcus, believe me, he's not taking anything seriously and he saw it as another opportunity to have a little fun at our expense. The chippy found the door pin lying at the back of the set. Jason must have pulled it out just before he pushed the door . . .'

'You've absolutely no proof of that.' Marcus interrupted her, his tone icy and contemptuous. 'It sounds much more like the chippy's mistake. I'll have a word with him myself. We can't have pieces of the set collapsing when we're working. Health and safety will give us a bad time if they get wind of accidents like these.'

'Have a word with him, by all means,' Emma was furious, hating him and hating the fact that the colder Marcus became, the hotter she got. 'Don't you think that's the first thing I did? And Ross did, too. He's adamant he put the pin in and he was backed up by his number two.'

'It would be surprising if he wasn't. A mistake like this could cost him his job.'

'And doesn't he know it? He's as angry and upset as anybody. But I believe him, Marcus, I really do. The first time Jason opened the door, it held. If the pin wasn't in it, the door would have collapsed then and there.'

'And you're seriously suggesting that Jason went behind the door and because of some little spat with you, pulled the pin out, for a laugh?'

'Yes,' Emma hissed, thoroughly put out. 'Yes I am because he's made it clear he doesn't give a damn about the project. He's just having a good laugh at our expense.'

'Well, I'm sorry,' Marcus was positively glacial. 'I don't buy it.'

32

'Were you looking for something in particular, Jenny?' Behind the shop counter, Rita watched Jenny shuffle through the greeting cards on display.

'Hmm,' Jenny replied a little self-consciously. 'I was looking for a get well card. Have you got any, only I don't see . . .'

'With Easter coming up, we're a bit low on much else, but there should be a couple.' Rita lifted the lid of the counter and came round to join Jenny. 'Let's have a look . . . Ah, here's one.'

She produced a card showing the picture of a teddy bear, lying in bed, a thermometer stuck in its mouth.

Jenny shook her head. 'That's more of a kiddie's one.'

'Who's sick?' asked Rita, curious.

Jenny bent to pick out a card at the bottom of the rack, but not quickly enough to hide the sudden blush to her cheeks.

'Who is it, Jenny? Not Jeff?'

'Oh, no—one of the actors. He had a bit of an accident yesterday and I thought it would be nice to send him a card, you know.'

'What sort of accident? Who was it?' This was

exactly the sort of gossip Rita loved to peddle and her curiosity was thoroughly roused by Jenny's evident embarrassment.

Fortunately for Jenny, they were interrupted by the shop bell, announcing the Reverend Grey, vicar of St Stephen's, in pursuit of his *Telegraph* and daily allowance of pear drops.

A tall scholarly man, old before his time, he found conversation with most of his parishioners painful, but a sense of duty drove him to try when no escape routes were obvious.

'Ah, good morning Mrs er . . . er . . . I don't mean to interrupt . . . take your time, my dear Mrs Godwin, take your time . . . No hurry, no hurry at all . . .'

'That's alright, Vicar, Jenny's looking for a get-well card and I'm sure she don't mind if I serve you first.'

'A get-well card?' The possibility some sick parishioner might expect a visit clouded the Vicar's face with apprehension. 'Is somebody ill?'

'Jenny was just telling me. One of the actors, apparently, met with an accident yesterday.'

'An accident? Dear me, I hope he wasn't badly hurt.'

With the vicar's and Rita's eyes on her, Jenny was forced to elaborate. 'No, no, I think he was just badly winded. A bit of the set collapsed and sent him flying. He was lucky not to have been knocked out.'

The Vicar frowned. 'Extremely fortunate. I hope these film people know what they are doing. Lavender told me there was a very large turnout at the village hall last night . . . we don't want any accidents in the village . . . dear me, no.'

174

'That'll be one pound forty, please, Vicar. Thank you.'

'Thank you, Mrs Godwin. Good morning. And a good morning to you Mrs er . . . er . . .' And tipping an invisible hat, he made his escape.

'Found one?' Rita turned her attention back to her friend.

'Yes, there's this . . .' Jenny proffered a card decorated with a bunch of irises and embossed in gold letters with 'Get Well Soon'. 'It's not exactly right, but I think it'll do. What do you think?'

Rita opened the card and read the lines inside, aloud.

'So sorry to hear you've been laid low,
We miss your smiling face, you know.
So 'Get well soon' you hear us shout,
We want to see you up and out.'

She glanced at Jenny. 'That's nice, isn't it? Just the ticket.'

Jenny looked doubtful. 'I'm not sure it's quite right . . .'

'Well, that's all there is,' Rita was brisk, 'unless you get a blank card and write your own message.'

Jenny was horrified. 'No, that's no good; I wouldn't know what to say. I'll take this one.'

Rita took the card from her, looking at her closely. 'You haven't said which of the actors it is, Jenny?'

'Haven't I?'

'No?'

'Oh,' Jenny tried to shrug casually. 'It's Ben Dacres.'

'The one that tried to chat you up?'

'He didn't try to chat me up. He was just very nice to me.'

175

Rita stared thoughtfully at Jenny. 'You want to be careful of those actors, Jenny. You don't want to lose your head, now. He might flatter and flirt with you, but it's all a game with that lot and you're no spring chicken, don't forget that.'

'I'm hardly likely to with you and Elsie constantly reminding me,' snapped Jenny, snatching the card from Rita's hand. 'Two pounds ten, I think. And what do you know about actors, anyway? Ben Dacres was a perfect gentleman . . . he didn't have to be nice to me, did he? And I don't think sending him a card means I'm losing my head, so I'll thank you to mind your own business.'

And she marched out of the shop, leaving Rita looking after her with amazement mingled with concern. In the thirty years they'd been friends, never before had Jenny told her to mind her own business.

33

'Oh hi . . .' Veronica, in a haze of her most expensive perfume, her blonde tresses floating loose over her shoulders, her makeup immaculate, and her tennis clothes Persil-white (she'd decided in favour of this outfit since it showed off her tan to perfection as well as drawing attention to her long slim legs), stood at the reception desk of Stowford Country Club, trying to act normally.

Since her manner towards any underling was seldom other than arrogant, peremptory or dismissive, the smile that currently adorned her features completely disconcerted the receptionist.

'Good morning, Mrs Lester,' she replied, with caution. 'How may I help you?'

'I wonder if you mind giving Ben Dacres's room a buzz for me. He's been enquiring about a game of tennis and at last I've got an hour or so free . . .'

'I'm sorry, Mrs Lester, but we've had instructions that Mr Dacres is not to be disturbed this morning, on any account.'

Veronica's smile froze. 'I'm sure, in this instance, he wouldn't mind. He was very keen to play . . .'

'I'm sorry, Mrs Lester.'

If the girl, Veronica reflected sourly, was sorry, she didn't look it. The thought of Ben in his room, not knowing she was in the lobby, frustrated her; she was not good at dealing with frustration. But short of finding out his room number and going to knock him up, herself . . .

'What's his room number?'

'I'm sorry, Mrs Lester, we're not able to hand out that information. You must understand we need to protect our residents' right to privacy.'

'But . . .'

'I'm sorry.'

Veronica could have sworn the girl smirked as she said this. She turned away from reception and walked through to the club bar, simmering with annoyance.

'Coffee—black—and bring me some writing paper and an envelope,' she snapped at the waiter.

A note was despatched and Veronica, confident Ben would appear within minutes, settled down to wait.

And wait.

She was halfway through her second jug of coffee

when her mobile rang. She snatched it up, her heart palpitating with excitement and caffeine.

'Hello,' she said, as seductively as was possible feeling as breathless as she did, with a mouth so dry she could hardly speak.

'Is that you, Vee?' It was a woman's voice.

'Yes,' Vee replied curtly, so disappointed she very nearly cut the caller off.

'Sally, here, Vee . . .'

'Oh.' She couldn't imagine anyone whom she less wanted to talk to.

'Are you alright, Vee?'

'Yes, of course I am,' she snapped. 'What is it you want, Sally?'

'Only you sound a little . . .'

'I'm fine. What do you want?' Vee, her eyes fixed on the door to the hotel lobby, was barely polite.

'You wanted me to find out who's living at Isabelle Garnett's, or Langton, as she now calls herself. I think that's a shame, don't you, when the mother takes a different surname from her children. But still, it takes all sorts . . .'

'Sally, I am expecting an important call . . .'

'Oh, sorry. Anyway I asked her when I phoned to talk about the next village hall meeting. She's missed quite a few and I . . .'

'Sally!'

'It wasn't that easy, Vee.' Sally sounded hurt and rather sulky. 'You can't just ask someone outright who's staying with them. It would be so odd.'

Vee sighed, her impatience bubbling over. 'I'm sure you were the soul of discretion, Sally, but really, I can't . . .'

'Well, yes, I managed it pretty well. I said a friend of mine, not mentioning your name, was convinced an old school friend was part of the film crew. That's right, isn't it? Anyway, I jotted the names down later. Here they are—Emma Knight, Colin James and Matt Morgan. Recognise any of them?'

'No, no, I don't know any of them . . .' And at that very moment, she spotted him.

Framed in the doorway of the lounge, with a pale blue cashmere sweater draped over his shoulders, a white linen shirt with sleeves casually rolled up and dark blue chinos, he could have stepped straight from a feature in Vogue. He was leaning against the door-jamb, one hand pressed to his brow, a picture of elegant, restrained suffering, and it seemed from the way he cast his eyes around the room that he was looking for someone.

Her? It had to be. In her note, she'd said she'd be in the lounge. Veronica's heart leapt into her mouth and she started up, cutting off Sally Green in mid-flow.

'Darling!' he beamed, and held out his arms. 'There you are.'

Veronica squeaked and half–fainting, stepped towards him. He swept past her and she turned in time to see him embrace an unexceptional, plump woman, older than himself, her hair quite white, wearing a thick cotton smock, trousers and a pair of spectacles dangling from a chain around her neck.

'You heard what happened to me, Jilly, darling?'

For a second, Veronica froze, stunned and humiliated. She glanced at her nearest neighbours—had they noticed he'd cut her dead? But along with the rest of the room, they were listening to the conversation between Ben Dacres and his companion.

'He head-butted me.' His melodious voice reached every corner of the room and he made no attempt to lower it. 'I didn't have a chance to get out of the way. It was simply excruciating . . .'

Veronica didn't hear the reply. Her mind was racing, sorting out her next move. He hadn't recognised her . . . or hadn't seen her. It didn't matter, she was not one to fall at the first hurdle, never had been.

'I'm feeling a lot better now, darling, thank you. But it was a shock. A real shock, you know. And why did it happen? Why?'

Veronica moved in. 'Ben. How nice to see you again. Did you get my note? I want to finish off our tennis game—it was getting exciting.'

On hearing his name, Ben had looked up and regarded her blankly, but at the mention of tennis, a glimmer of recognition flickered across his face.

He got to his feet, adopting a rueful smile. 'Forgive me, my dear . . . I've had so much on since our game; I've quite forgotten your name.'

It was a blow, but Veronica forgave him, he looked so handsome, so penitent. 'Veronica, Veronica Lester. But my friends call me Vee.'

'Ah yes, of course, Veronica. Meet my friend and fellow thesp, Jilly Westcott.'

Veronica nodded at the older lady: she might be an actress, but she looked positively ordinary . . . clearly no rival for Ben Dacres's affections, but a friend of Ben's could not be ignored.

'Pleased to meet you,' she purred. 'Ben and I met on the tennis court the other day. He was within an inch of thrashing me when he got called away.'

Ben smiled modestly, 'Oh I wouldn't say that. You were putting up a pretty good defence.'

Ordinarily Veronica would have bridled at this total misrepresentation of her prowess but for once her pride was swallowed without effort. 'We must finish the game, Ben.'

'We must.' He smiled at her and her insides seemed to dissolve once again. 'But not today, alas. I had a bit of an accident on the set, yesterday, and my abdomen is still very sore. Next week, perhaps.'

'Whenever you're ready.' Veronica feigned a warm, relaxed smile. 'I was rather hoping to tempt you all over to Summerstoke House next week, for a little drinks party. A "welcome to Summerstoke"?'

She turned to the woman he called Jilly. 'You will come, won't you? It must be so boring for you stuck out here in the country, with so little to do.'

'Not really,' the woman replied. 'We're working, after all. We're very good at making our own entertainment.'

'But a party is a jolly nice idea,' Ben interjected. 'It's very sweet of you. What day, what time, and are you issuing us with an open invitation, or do you want a select few?'

Veronica shrugged, trying to look as casual as she could.

'Whatever you think best; I suppose all of you would be rather a lot, wouldn't it? Perhaps I could ask you to put together a list for me, Ben. Unless that's too much of an imposition? And let us say next Thursday evening at eight? For wine and nibbles?'

'Lovely. Jilly and I will put our heads together and come up with the crème. You won't want "Uncle Tom Cobley and All", believe me.'

'Are you coming to our party, tonight, Veronica?' Jilly enquired politely. 'It's for the cast

181

and crew down here, and for anyone involved with us in Summerstoke. It's being held in the pub, in the village. I don't remember its name.'

'The Foresters Arms. No,' replied Veronica, rather stiffly. 'I . . . er . . . I didn't know about it.'

'Then you must come,' said Ben, grandly. 'You shall be my guest.' He patted Jilly's hand. 'Be my aide memoire, darling, and make sure I put this dear lady's name on the guest list.' He turned, took Veronica's hand and kissed her fingers with a flourish. 'You shall go to the ball! And we will dance the night away; I'm sure you'll be as light on your feet on the dance floor as you are on the tennis court.'

Veronica, overcome with an excess of emotion and too much coffee, collapsed in the nearest armchair, quite incapable, for once, of a suitably sophisticated riposte.

'Coffee, Veronica?' Jilly Westcott waved the coffee pot in her direction and although her body screamed at the thought of any more caffeine, all Veronica could think was that by accepting the offer of coffee she could legitimately stay in Ben's company a bit longer. 'Thank you, that would be lovely,' she croaked. 'Just a little one.'

Jilly turned to Ben. 'Are you going to be up for this afternoon, darling?'

For a moment Ben looked haggard. 'I had toyed with the idea of asking Emma if I could postpone it till next week; the prospect of any more battering is beyond me. But she's assured me I shall be perfectly safe; they won't allow the beasts near me and you know, darling, we're behind enough already after that little shit's antics. It's up to me, to us, to show him how a true professional operates.'

'Spoken like a real trouper,' Jilly chuckled and patted his hand. 'I'm sure you'll have nothing to worry about.'

'What are you doing this afternoon?' asked Veronica, curious.

'I've got to escort a herd of cows,' Ben's face darkened. ' I'm apparently driving them to pasture through the centre of the village.'

34

'Yeah, that's great. Maybe I'll see yer there, Trace, bye.' Paula Spinks finished the call and stared at her mobile phone.

No, there were no messages, definitely.

The Merfields had made it plain they didn't approve of mobile phones, but she'd put it on silent while she cleaned, and tucked in the pocket of her mini skirt, she'd have felt the vibrations. That call, from her mate, Tracy, was the first of the morning. Tracy had rung in great excitement as the crowd casting person had phoned to book her for action that afternoon.

Paula was pleased for her, but . . .

She pulled a face, turned up the collar of her PVC mac against the drizzle, and tottered down the drive of the Manor, her stilettos sinking with every step into the soft gravel surface.

'It ain't twelve o'clock, yet,' she chided herself, 'there's plenty of time for a call, so you better get yourself home and ready. If you're to go filming this afternoon, you want to look your best, Paula, girl.'

*   *   *

'Some enchanted evening, you may see a stranger
. . .' Jenny sang, indulging in the most wonderful
daydream. Only instead of Jeff, it was Ben Dacres's
handsome features that admired her from across
a crowded room. They drifted together—he, tall,
distinguished, in evening dress; she, twenty years
younger, twenty pounds lighter, in a diaphanous
gown of pale blue silk . . .

There was a tap on the door.

'Come in, door's open,' she called putting down
the rather blunt knife with which she'd been trying
to dismember an elderly cauliflower.

It was Isabelle, carrying a bulging bag, her
battered duffel coat glistening with damp. 'I hope
I'm not disturbing you . . .'

Jenny smiled to see her. 'Come in Isabelle. What
a nice surprise. You don't pop in often enough.
Would you like a cup of tea?'

'Only if you're having one,' Isabelle smiled back.
'I'm just returning the shirt and trousers Charlie
wore in London. He might want them for this
evening. I've ironed them for him.'

'That was nice of you, dear, just leave them on
the table. Take off that coat and hang it by the
Rayburn. I didn't realise it was raining. It was so
bright earlier. Real April weather, isn't it? The
kettle's hot so it won't take long to make a cuppa.'
She bustled with mugs, milk, tea bags and sugar,
and found a packet of custard creams.

'I haven't heard much about your do in London;
I've scarcely seen Charlie to ask him. Did it go
well?'

'I think so,' said Isabelle with diffidence. 'I found

184

it all a bit overwhelming, to tell you the truth . . . so many people. But I sold two paintings, and I've got a commission. I'm really excited about that!'

'That's very nice for you, dear. You deserve some nice things to happen to you.' Jenny beamed at her, and Isabelle lost some of her reserve.

'Thanks, Jenny, I'm just keeping my fingers crossed that it's going to last. You know . . . that my work is not some sort of fad: all the rage one moment and forgotten the next.'

Jenny had the haziest idea of the sort of pictures that Isabelle painted. Rita Godwin (who always knew exactly was going on in the village) told her Isabelle had painted on a freshly decorated wall at the Old Vicarage. Rita described it as a 'mad, messy explosion', but Polly Merfield, who ran an art gallery in London, had been impressed and had encouraged her.

Abstract art was something Jenny did not understand, so she had never gone to see the mural just in case she was obliged to give an opinion and would be found wanting.

She picked up her knitting.

'Are you looking forward to the party, tonight?'

Isabelle, sipping her tea, reflected, 'I suppose I am. I'm not a great party person, actually. But I'm looking forward to meeting the actors and the rest of the crew. The ones I've got staying with me are very pleasant and it'll be interesting to put faces to names. Charlie said you'd met Ben Dacres?'

Jenny felt herself blushing. 'Yes, on Tuesday. Me and Angela were being shown round their camp and he turned up. He was ever so nice . . . not at all stuck up.'

'No reason why he should be.'

185

'No, but with him being so famous you might think . . . but he wasn't, he was really friendly.'

Isabelle smiled. 'Perhaps he'll ask you for a dance tonight—that would put Jeff on his toes!'

'If he's there—he's on call, Isabelle. I ask you, the first proper party we've been invited to and it's quite likely he won't be there.' Jenny sighed heavily. 'I'd like to dance with Ben Dacres though . . . that'd be . . . oh . . . s o wonderful. But I don't suppose he'll ask me.'

'Why not?'

'Because,' Jenny looked miserably down at her knitting; it was an insurmountable problem that had completely clouded all pleasurable anticipation of the party, 'and don't laugh at me, Isabelle, because I feel silly saying it at my age, but I haven't got anything to wear.'

She had tried confiding in Angela, but Angela had looked amazed and said she couldn't see what the problem was and why it should matter what other people thought she looked like, and that she should put on what Jeff liked her in best.

The trouble was Jeff rarely made any comment about anything she wore. She'd not been able to afford new clothes since Jim's funeral ten years ago and she'd put on a fair bit of weight since then. And she wanted, if not to attract attention at this party, at least to maintain the impression she had created when she'd met Ben Dacres; she'd not been impervious to the look of admiration in his eyes.

'You looked lovely in the jumper you were wearing last night, Jenny.'

'Yes, that's my reject sweater. It is lovely. But I can't wear it to a party, Isabelle. It would be too hot; I'd sit there sweltering, and if I danced, I'd melt.'

Isabelle glanced at her watch. 'I've got a few minutes; why don't you show me what you've got? I might be able to help out.'

Jenny looked across at her son's slender girlfriend. Wearing a paint-spattered long blue shirt pulled into shape by a wide leather belt, faded jeans tucked into black leather boots, a long multi-coloured striped scarf wound round her neck and loops of intertwined coloured metal dangling from her ears, framing her delicately boned face, there was nothing expensive about anything she wore, but she had style and she had a figure.

Jenny felt wistful. She'd once been slender and pretty; now she was middle-aged, plump, and yes, dowdy, and whatever Isabelle might come up with, she was stuck with her basic shape and there could be no disguising it.

'No, it's all right. That's kind of you, but I expect I'll find something; as Angela said, it's silly of me to worry about what I look like.'

Isabelle leant forward and squeezed her hand. 'It's not silly. It's important to feel good when you go out. If you start out feeling drab, it'll make it much harder to relax and have fun. I've found myself in that situation so many times in the past. I won't, if you really don't want me to, but let me have a look and maybe I'll come up with something.'

So Jenny led the way to her bedroom and shyly revealed the paucity of her wardrobe to Isabelle. Dressing up, swapping clothes . . . all that was something she hadn't done since she was eighteen and lived at home with her sister and certainly not something she'd expect to do with Charlie's girlfriend, of whom she had always been a little shy.

But pulling out the clothes and discussing the merits of each item as if they were model gowns, all awkwardness between them evaporated.

'Here, put this on, it's a lovely colour.' Isabelle held up the plain dark blue dress Jenny had bought for Jim's funeral.

'I don't know as it'd fit me,' confessed Jenny sadly, taking it and wondering if Isabelle would think it daft if she went to change in the bathroom.

'Try it anyway. I'll wait outside; give me a shout when you're ready.'

She just managed to do it up and her heart in her mouth, she looked at herself in the mirror. She groaned out loud. It was no good; true she could get into it . . . but only just; the material stretched across her bust, and, unforgiving, followed every contour of her midriff, exaggerating the roundness of her belly and bottom.

Isabelle put her head round the door, 'Did you call?' She entered the room and thoughtfully considered Jenny.

Jenny hung her head, feeling tearful. 'It's no good. It's too tight.'

'That only really shows around the middle,' said Isabelle carefully. 'The colour really suits you and the skirt is lovely. Would you mind if I lent you something for the top part . . . if you feel comfortable enough wearing the dress, that is?'

Jenny looked doubtful. 'Do you have something that would fit me, then?'

'Yes, I have. I've a lovely multi-coloured kaftan top. You know the sort of thing—one size fits all— it's a sort of drape, and it's made from chiffon, so it's light and floaty. It would work really well with

188

the material and colour of your dress, if you'd like to try it.'

'Oh, Isabelle,' Jenny could feel the tears in her eyes. 'I don't know how to thank you.'

'I shall need a pair of your shoes.'

'My shoes?' Jenny looked at her blankly. 'My shoes, why?'

Isabelle laughed. 'I want to paint them. It's no good going to the ball if you haven't got the right slippers, is it?'

35

'Right,' Emma, tension sharpening her voice, addressed her crew. 'We don't have the luxury of endless takes on this one so we've got to get it right first time. The camera's on a long shot looking down the High Street with everyone going about their daily business. Okay, Sarah?'

Sarah Thornby nodded, 'Woman with pushchair, Jilly Westcott with shopping basket, chatting outside the shop and when cued, Jilly waves to Ben; man getting into car, and a couple of gossips.'

'Fine. Cows appear over the brow of the bridge, camera tracks in to fill the screen with herd, Ben visible, driving them in the background. Okay Colin?'

He nodded and Emma continued, 'We cut and set up the reverse shot; long track, following them up the High Street, Ben's shoulder framing edge of shot. Are we going to get away with Charlie doing this, Matt?'

'Ross says he's in make-up with Ben now.

They've padded out an identical jacket to make him broader in the shoulder and Fleur is working on his hair in case his head gets in shot. Ross says she's pretty confident, but I should warn you, he says Ben is in bit of a funk.' Matt's lip curled. 'Too many cow horror stories if you ask me.'

Emma snorted with impatience. 'We're doing our best to accommodate him. Is the animal trainer ready with the dog?'

'Yep, standing by.' Matt glanced at his watch. 'It's now one o'clock. I suggest we take half an hour for lunch, then the crew can finish off setting up and be ready to go at two. Okay Colin?'

'Should be. Shame it's so overcast. I've got Sparks pumping some floodlight on the houses to try and make the stone look less dingy. He's nearly there. How many cows, by the way?

'Thirty, Charlie says.'

'Sounds a lot; I assume they'll stop before they reach me and trample my camera?'

It was an innocuous enough question but Emma and Colin immediately picked up on the slight hesitation before Matt's impatient reply. 'I'll double check with Charlie on how he plans to control them. For Christ's sake don't you go soft on me, Colin! They're only cows . . .'

*   *   *

'You're joking?' Charlie stared at Matt. 'Ross asked me for a herd of cows to walk down the High Street. Something they are well used to doing, so I agreed. They are not used to being told to stop half way, turn round and go back to the beginning. They're only cows, Matt, and their main interest is to get to

190

that nice juicy grass waiting for them at the other end of the village.'

'You mean to say once they start walking, we're not going to be able to stop them?' For once, Matt looked flustered.

'You could try, but they'd get very confused and that wouldn't be such a good idea in the middle of the village.'

'Oh God! Look Charlie, this is not good news. We're set up to do two main shots—one of them walking down the street towards the camera, and the other following them, so we need to be able to change the camera position and have the cows walk twice.'

'Why can't you use two cameras and do it once?'

'Because they would be in each other's shots.'

Charlie pulled a face and considered the problem. 'There is a way we could do it,' he said slowly, 'but I'd have to ask for Stephen's help and I can't say I'm too thrilled at having to do that.'

'Charlie, mate, please help me out on this one . . .'

*   *   *

'You're joking?' Stephen's reaction was as unhelpful Charlie had anticipated. 'You know what I feel about them using my cows. Why should I help you? I've got a busy afternoon.'

'Suit yourself,' Charlie shrugged, feigning indifference. 'But as you constantly point out, they're your little darlings and I thought you'd rather take them down to Summer Meadow than let Lenny do it.'

It was a calculated shot. Lenny was a brilliant

mechanic who kept all their collapsing farm vehicles going, but he had no time or sympathy for the stock.

'Lenny? Why should Lenny take them? You can't let him do that.'

'I don't see as I have any alternative if you won't help. The obvious solution to their problem is to divide the herd in two . . . one cow looks much like another to that lot. As the first herd goes on through, they switch camera positions and I'm standing by to take the second lot through.'

'Why can't you take the first lot through then come back for the second?'

'It would take too long and they want to use my back view; they think they can make me look enough like Ben Dacres to get away with it. That's why,' Charlie pulled off his cap, 'they've curled my hair.'

Startled, Stephen stared at his brother. Charlie's hair, normally dead straight and floppy was now anything but; furthermore, Fleur had sprayed his sideburns grey. Framing Charlie's youthful, tanned face, the effect was very odd indeed.

Stephen snorted. 'What a prat you look.'

'Thanks, Stephen. Well, I'd better be off and brief Lenny, I'm running out of time.'

For one, indecisive second Stephen watched his older brother walk away across the yard, then panicking, he shouted after him, 'Okay, you win, Charlie. I'll help you, but just this once, mind.'

*   *   *

In the end, over an hour elapsed before everyone was ready to commence the afternoon's shoot.

Following Charlie's advice, the tracks had been abandoned and a flatbed truck found to accommodate Colin's camera, thus rendering it less vulnerable to any unwelcome attention from the cows; meanwhile Charlie and Stephen divided the herd in two.

The half-hour delay neither helped Ben Dacres's nerves, nor the tempers of the extras who'd been summoned an hour earlier and were fed up with hanging around in the sullen east wind that blew straight down the High Street.

'Right,' said an exasperated Emma, for the umpteenth time, 'Are we ready to go, Matt?'

'Ready?' Matt muttered into his talkback and instantly the High Street was bathed in warm light.

'Ready?' Emma looked at Ben, who replied merely with a tense nod.

'Ready?' asked Charlie of Stephen who was waiting behind the camera truck.

'Come on, let's get on with it,' came the morose reply.

'Turn over.'

'Turning.'

'Mark it.'

'Action.'

The cows ambled out of their pen assisted by the encouraging cries of Charlie in the rear and Gip, the farm's dog, running to one side. As they gained the brow of the bridge leading down into Summerstoke High Street, Ben took Charlie's place and the animal trainer released the dog (the farm dog in the series), to replace Gip who was called back by Charlie.

At the sight of the strange dog one of the cows stopped and turned to confront it and others, following her, did likewise. The dog froze and dropped on its haunches, growling nervously. Running into a bunch of immobile cows, seemingly intent on terrorising the dog, Ben squeaked with terror and flung up his arms for help.

Jilly, thinking this was the cue, waved vigorously back, causing one of the lead cows to jump backwards into another. For a moment, chaos threatened.

Fortunately for the crew, Stephen intervened: seeing the lead cow distracted by the disarray in her ranks, he sang out to her. She turned towards him, hesitated, then surged forward, bellowing to her troops to follow. Thus called to order the cows moved on, throwing an occasional curious glance at the extras who nervously occupied the pavement, and staring inquisitively into the camera as they passed it in the centre of the street.

The squelching, snorting passage of heavy breath, swaying bodies and padding feet had faded into the distance before anyone moved.

'I am not,' said Ben through clenched teeth, 'going to do another take.'

'How was it?' Emma radioed Colin. 'Have we got enough there?'

'Think so,' Colin radioed back. 'We should really do the opening again—the confrontation between the dog and the cows you do not want, and it's a pity so many of the cows looked at camera. But if the reverse shot goes smoothly, you can use that as the master and with some cutaways, it should be okay.'

'Right then, let's move,' shouted Matt. 'C'mon, move, everybody. We want to go with the light as it is.'

Within what was a short space of time for the television crew and what seemed an interminable period for the extras who longed to be able to sit down somewhere, or have a cup of tea, the lights on the street were adjusted and the camera position was shifted to the bridge end of the street.

'This should be totally straightforward,' muttered Charlie to Lenny. 'There's nothing in front of us to spook the cows and they don't need bloody Lassie in this shot. I'll take 'em on down to the meadow and meet you back here in half an hour. I never thought I'd say "Thank God for Stephen", but he certainly got us out of a nasty-looking hiccup.'

'And he won't let you forget it, Boss. You can be sure of that. This is a bloody weird game, if you ask me. All this time, all this money, all these people . . . and for what? What's it all about, eh? Daft, I call it. Just plain daft; and there's my Paula, sick as a parrot 'cos she ain't been asked today.' Lenny shook his head and sucked in the air through the gap in his teeth. 'I never thought I'd say it, but I'm starting to think our Stevie's got a point.'

'Maybe, but it's paying the bills, Lenny, and that's good enough for me.'

Lenny looked at him sideways and smirked. 'They paying you extra for curling your hair, Charlie boy?'

'Standby . . . turnover . . . mark it . . . cue Charlie . . .'

Lenny opened the gate and with Gip leading the way, the cows surged out of their pen and over the bridge. Ignoring the camera perched on its truck in the middle of the road, they ambled on down into the High Street with Charlie following. On cue, Charlie saw Jilly wave at him, and as instructed, he waved back. Almost simultaneously Matt's talkback crackled a warning and a Range Rover Sport appeared round the bend beyond the village shop and roared down the High Street towards the cows.

The driver slammed on the brakes and stopped, but the cows, spooked by the sudden and rapid appearance of the car, turned in every direction but the one in which they had been headed. Onto the pavements, into the gardens that fronted the High Street, back in the direction they had come, mooing, pushing, stamping, and defecating.

Seeing a cow coming at speed towards him, Ben turned and fled up the nearest garden path and hammered desperately at the door. This was opened by a surprised Paula Spinks, resplendent in faux leopard skin trousers. Without bothering to explain, he tumbled in and slammed the door behind him.

Jilly and the woman with the pushchair dashed into the shop as mayhem broke out. Awestruck, they stared out at the scene from the safety of the shop window where they were joined by Rita.

'There'll be trouble with the village, after this,' she opined, her arms folded across her chest. 'The Tuckers have had enough complaints in the past about bringing them cows through. People don't like it. What a mess!'

'It wasn't their fault,' protested Jilly. 'Those cows were perfectly well behaved till that . . . that moron roared up in his big boy's toy.'

'That moron, as you call him, is Hugh Lester. He owns the other farm in the village.'

'Then why hasn't he got out to lend Charlie a hand?' retorted Jilly. 'It's disgraceful.'

Hugh Lester was still sitting in his car watching

196

Charlie and Lenny trying to bring the cows under control when Matt, who had marched down the street, rapped peremptorily on his window. The window slid down and a pair of cold blue eyes looked with disfavour at Matt, 'Yes?'

Matt, breathing in deeply, struggled to control his temper.

'Excuse me, sir, but didn't you see the roadblock? We're filming these cows and for everyone's safety, we temporarily stopped the traffic. Wasn't this explained to you?'

'I was stopped by an unprepossessing youth with ironmongery in his nose, who tried to prevent me from going about my lawful business, if that's what you mean by a roadblock.'

'Didn't he explain what we were doing?'

'Yes, but I don't see why that should stop me. I've met cows before. You can't just close the highway like that. I've business in Summerbridge and the sooner you get this mess cleared and the road open, the better.'

Matt was distracted from completely blowing his top by an angry shout from Stephen, running heavily down the road towards him. 'What's been going on? What have you done with my cows? Charlie? What the hell's been going on? I'll bloody kill you.'

'Well you'll have to do it later,' Charlie shouted. 'Give us a hand, for Chrissake!'

Between them, Stephen, Charlie, Lenny and Gip managed to round up the herd and Stephen, still grumbling, drove them off to the peace of the meadow, leaving Charlie and Lenny and the film crew surveying the mess. There were cowpats everywhere: on the pavements, the road, on lawns and paths; shrubs and flowerbeds had been trampled, hedges torn and gates swung off their hinges.

'Matt,' said Charlie, quietly, 'if you lot don't get this mess sorted by evening, then we're done for. There are those in the village who've been agitating to stop us driving our herd along the High Street. If we can't bring the cows through, we can't use the meadows this side of the river and that's our best grazing. Without it, the dairy herd's finished.'

36

'Oh my word, you are in a bit of a state!' Paula tutted sympathetically at the man sitting huddled and shaking, on her battered sofa.

'I'm sorry,' Ben gasped, 'I just have a thing about cows. I did tell them, but did they take any notice . . .'

'I don't like 'em much myself,' Paula smiled at him encouragingly. 'Nasty big brutes. But they don't do no harm. Although,' she chuckled, looking out of her cottage window, 'they's going to find it hard to persuade the village otherwise after today's little game. Now,' she said, turning back to her unexpected visitor, 'what you need is something to settle your nerves. Won't be a minute.'

And before he could say anything, she whisked out of the sitting room, threw off her fluffy pink mules, retrieved her stilettos from under the stairs, (where they'd been thrown when it became clear the film crew were not going to use her that afternoon) shooed her two youngest (Johnny and

Joannie Spinks, aged three and two, respectively), back up the stairs with promises of crisps and Coke if they kept quiet; collected two glasses from the kitchen, together with Lenny's carefully hoarded bottle of Jack Daniel's, checked her hair and face in the pink plastic heart-shaped mirror Lenny had bought her one Valentines, and returned to her visitor.

He'd not moved from his corner of the sofa, but the colour was returning to his face and he looked up with some bemusement at his hostess.

'There you are, Mr Dacres,' she said pouring him a liberal amount of the whisky. 'You get that down you and you'll feel better in no time.'

'Thank you,' he said, sounding feeble. 'You're very kind. Are you going to join me?'

'Lord no, I can't stand the stuff meself. My tipple is Black Velvet—you know, like what Joan Collins drinks, but since we ain't got no champagne, I'll make mine a Guinness.' And she reached over the back of the armchair and extracted a can from a cupboard.

'Are you . . . are you expecting company?'

'Company?' Paula looked at him blankly. 'Lord no. Why do you ask?'

'It's just that you look so . . . Well . . .' Ben attempted a laugh, 'For a start, you don't look as if you're about to do the housework . . .'

'No. I was hoping to get asked to do some filming this afternoon.' She leant forward, confidingly, her swelling bosoms clamouring for attention through the thin black nylon of her frou-fou blouse. 'They asked my mate, Tracy Jones, and Sarah Fields—and she's nothing to write home about, though I don't mean to be nasty. So I thought they'd

199

definitely ask me, so I got meself dressed ready, and the kiddies, just in case they wanted them, too . . .' She sighed, swallowed a mouthful of Guinness and chuckled, 'But I might have found it a bit difficult to run from they cows in these shoes. Have some more Jack Daniel's.'

Too stunned to demur, Ben held out his glass and she splashed in another generous helping. 'What . . . er . . . what part were you up for? Mrs er . . . Miss . . . ?'

'Paula, Mrs Paula Spinks. My Lenny works alongside Charlie Tucker at Marsh Farm. I expect you've met him.'

Ben shook his head.

'He's outside at the moment, running around after they cows. He don't much like cows, either. Give me a motor any day, he says. But then you can't milk a motor says I . . .' She leant forward again and again Ben found his eyes drawn to her quivering cleavage. 'I wasn't up for any particular part,' she said softly, 'but I was hoping, you know . . .' she took a large gulp of Guinness. 'But you coming here, like this . . . And my being here and not out with the cows . . . maybe it was meant to be . . . My horoscope said "Expect the unexpected today". I always read the stars, do you? And they were right, weren't they? Maybe you can help me realise my dreams, Mr Dacres.'

*　　　*　　　*

'Where is everyone? It's like a bleedin' graveyard this afternoon. And where's Ross? I wanted to speak to him.' Jason looked around the empty canteen bus and viewed the young catering assistant with disfavour.

'They're all in the village, Mr Hart. Ross called everyone out on an emergency clean-up, as I understand it. I think the cows ran amok.'

'Good for them. We should follow their example; that would liven this place up. I'll take one of those iced buns and a tea . . . milk and two sugars.'

'I'll make some fresh.'

Munching his sticky bun, Jason wandered across to the notice board hanging near the entrance. It contained little of anything to interest him: a pamphlet on the attractions of Summerbridge, a cinema programme, showing, as far as Jason could work out, one film a week, a bus timetable from Summerstoke to Summerbridge, details of The Bunch of Grapes quiz night with a note attached from Matt encouraging volunteers, a general invitation to the party that night, a handwritten note from someone offering a jacket for sale, and a card on which was written in Marcus' firm hand:

"Alison (Tucker) needs help to set up a website for Marsh Farm. Anyone able to help her?

See Marcus or Charlie if you can.

Thanks

Marcus"

Jason stared at it for a moment, then glanced across at the lad who was preoccupied with pouring spitting water from an urn into a teapot. He turned back to the notice board, swiftly pulled off the card and stuffed it in the pocket of his leather jacket.

37

'Wow, Alison, cool or what! You look wicked.' Al, still in his bike leathers, stood in the kitchen of Marsh Farm, gazing at his girlfriend.

Alison smiled happily and twirled around him. 'Hannah lent me this dress. It feels fab. I'm so looking forward to this party . . . I can't wait to dance.'

Al's smile faded. 'I hope I'm up to it. My leg's hurting like buggery at the moment.'

Alison stopped, concerned, and put her arms round his neck. 'I'm sorry. You moan so rarely, it's easy to forget. Sit down, at once. You should keep the weight off it as much as poss.' She patted a lump in his leather jacket. 'What's this?'

'The beginning of a solution to our website problems,' replied Al, unzipping his jacket and pulling out a neat and expensive-looking digital camera. 'It belongs to my aunt. It's got everything we need—lots of pixels and a decent video facility. She says we can borrow it as long as we take care of it.'

'That's brilliant. And really nice of her!'

'Yeah—it's hard to see how she and my mother are sisters.'

He held up the camera. 'There . . . stand still, look at me . . . that's it . . .' There was a flash and Al examined the result. 'Brill, the first of many . . . Alison Tucker of Marsh Farm.' He grinned. 'What a stunner . . . I'll show you how to use this, Ali, then you can take pictures whenever things happen, instead of waiting for me to be here.'

'Are you sure?' Alison replied, somewhat dubiously. 'I'd hate anything to happen to it.'

'It won't. Just don't drop it in a puddle or lose it.' Al smiled at her. 'Give us a cuddle then I'll get changed into my party gear.'

The cuddle, which was more passionate than decorous, was interrupted by an embarrassed cough.

'Sorry,' said Angela, blinking behind her glasses, her face pink. 'I didn't mean to, um . . . Stephen's just gone down to Summer Meadow to check on his cows. He says they were really upset today, so I've come on to make some tea for everybody.' She placed a large plastic carrier on the table and covered her embarrassment by busily unpacking the contents.

'Won't there be food at this do, Angela?' enquired Alison, making no move to get off Al's lap.

'Well I don't know. And if there is, it might be awfully late. So I said to Mum I'd make a fish pie. It's quick and easy, and Stephen is really hungry after all that business with the cows.'

'I'll help you.' Alison stood up, casting a warning frown at Angela. 'Al, why don't you go and get changed in my room?'

'Sure.' But to Alison's alarm, Al picked up on Angela's marked reference to the cows. 'What was this business with the cows, Angela, that got Stephen so worked up?'

Alison shot Angela such a fierce look that Angela became flustered. 'Oh . . . er . . . I . . . er . . . the cows were running all over the High Street, Charlie couldn't control them . . . so Stephen had to help him . . . they went everywhere . . . It was such a mess, he said . . . he's very angry . . .'

'It wasn't Charlie's fault at all, Angela.' Alison was cross. 'They were filming the cows walking through the village and they got spooked by a car, that's all. It could have happened with Stephen herding them. Go and get changed, Al, then you can help us. Angela, Al has managed to borrow a digital camera so we can take photographs for this website.'

As the kitchen door closed behind Al, Alison turned to Angela and snapped, 'Please, do me a favour Angela; I don't want Al's evening to be ruined because of his lousy parents, so no mention of Hugh Lester, if you don't mind. And please, could you try not to always blame Charlie when things go wrong. It doesn't help at all. I know Charlie is not perfect, but then neither is Stephen, whatever you might think.'

Angela went pink. 'I certainly won't say anything to upset Al, Alison. But I don't think you're being quite fair in saying I always blame Charlie. I don't think you appreciate how hard Stephen works to keep this farm together, for all of you, while Charlie is running around and adding to Stephen's problems half the time.'

Alison was utterly exasperated. 'What are you talking about? Without Charlie this farm would be up shit creek without a paddle and that's a fact . . .'

To the relief of both a full-blown row was averted by the cheerful entrance of Jeff, waving two bulging carrier bags.

'Here we are, my lovelies, fish suppers for the starving masses.' He looked around. 'Where are they all—I'd have thought they'd be chaffing at the trough, wanting to get off to this party?'

'Fish suppers?' Angela was put out. 'But I told Mum I'd make a fish pie; I've got all the stuff here . . .'

'Well, Jenny told me to pick up fish and chips. Put it in the freezer . . . it'll keep, won't it? And these won't.'

Angela, miffed, started to put her produce away.

'I'll give Mum a shout, Jeff, and tell her you're here; she was in the bath.' Alison headed to the hall door. 'There might be some delay before we can all leave—Charlie's not back yet and Stephen is still communing with his cows. Gran phoned to say not to expect her and Ron. He's not feeling up to much so they're going to have a quiet evening in.'

38

Veronica leant forward into her mirror, carefully creamed on her lipstick, and glanced at the reflection of her husband buttoning up his dress shirt. 'We'll take my car tonight, darling. I don't feel much like drinking and if I change my mind, we can always get a taxi back and pick it up in the morning.'

Hugh shrugged. 'As you wish. I don't want to stay to the bitter end, anyway. These affairs are a bloody pain. Give me a hand with these cuff-links, would you?'

Veronica had spent the afternoon in a fizz of excitement and indecision: to 'dance the night away' with Ben Dacres . . . but Hugh and she were already committed to a fund-raising dinner at the Pump Rooms in Bath. Hugh hated those sorts of events and only agreed to attend because the great and the good would be there. To complicate matters, Veronica had got the tickets through their friends, the Crouchers, so there was no way she could plead a headache or some other ailment— they all knew she eschewed such weakness.

But she'd agonised . . . she had to . . . she simply had to go to Ben's party and her brain spun, plotting a way in which this could be achieved. Of paramount importance was to leave Hugh at the dinner and return herself in answer to some sort of crisis. The question was, what might bring her back home early and without her husband? Cordelia? Yes . . . no other excuse would work as well, and although her relationship with her daughter was driven by complete and utter selfishness on both sides, she'd find a reason to play the maternal card, leaving Hugh behind.

She stood up, smoothing down the gold silk sheath dress that clung to her figure. Her action had its desired effect. Hugh ran his eyes appreciatively over her.

'I don't think I've seen that dress before?'

'No? This old thing, I've had it for ages.'

'What a pity we've got to go out, I wouldn't mind ripping it off you.'

Veronica smiled. 'You can,' she purred. 'Later.'

In spite of the fact the car was Veronica's, Hugh insisted on doing the driving. Stretching back in the leathery comfort of her Porsche, Veronica allowed a certain amount of desultory husband-and-wife conversation to pass before she introduced the next strand of her plot.

'You know, Hugh, I'm getting a little concerned with the amount of time Cordelia is spending with that friend of hers, Tamara Bell. Tammy she calls her—I ask you, Tammy Bell, what sort of name is that?'

'Is it the name you object to, or the girl?'

Veronica snorted. 'It's symptomatic of the sort of girl she is. Really, Hugh, I don't think she's a good influence. I asked Cordelia what they planned to do tonight and Cordelia was so vague, it made me suspicious. They're meant to be studying for their GCSEs, not gadding about town.'

'And what makes you think that's what they're planning?'

'I looked into Cordelia's overnight bag and I would say, judging from its contents, studying is not going to be a major feature of her stay with Miss Bell.'

Hugh sighed with impatience. 'Teenage girls are a complete mystery to me, Vee. Did you confront her?'

'And have her throw a hissy fit? Besides, it was too late to fix her up with anyone else. I'll talk to her tomorrow when I pick her up. Unless of course,' she gave a nasty chuckle, 'I swoop on her tonight and take her back home.'

'This is a two-seater and there's no way I'm going to travel back with Cordelia on my lap.'

'You could always take a taxi, darling, if it came to it.'

So far, so good.

Her thoughts drifted back to the time when Anthony had been knocked off his bike after a terrible row with her and Hugh. He'd refused to see them and she'd waited at the hospital for twenty-four hours till it became clear he wasn't going to relent. She'd left, not knowing whether she'd ever see him alive again and she nurtured a bitter anger for the suffering he'd caused her and his rejection. And now, for some reason she couldn't explain, he was creeping back into her thoughts and received there with a softness that unnerved her.

39

Although daylight had long since faded, the High Street of Summerstoke was brightly lit by series of flood lamps rigged the length of the street and powered by a humming generator. Emma, Matt and the film crew had withdrawn, leaving Charlie with Ross and his band of merry men to make good the damage done by the cows.

They worked tirelessly. High-powered hoses disposed of the muck; chippies repaired gates and fences; a van appeared from a local garden centre carrying an assortment of turf, shrubs and bedding plants, and every aggrieved householder was visited and compensation agreed if the repair work on offer was not acceptable. By and large, the level of satisfaction was high and successive trays of tea, sandwiches, cakes and biscuits were brought out for the workers.

As the evening progressed, Charlie exhausted as he was, started to relax. When he had first surveyed the damage, he really believed that the demise of the dairy herd was inevitable. No way would the village residents, who constantly nagged the Parish Council about the cows' passage along their High Street, allow the practice to continue.

He didn't know Ross nearly as well as he knew

Matt, but he was impressed by him and deeply grateful, as he told Marcus when he came to inspect progress.

'Yeah, well, he's the best there is,' replied Marcus shortly. 'But this shouldn't have happened. I don't blame you, Charlie, don't misunderstand me. But how on earth did that car get through, that's what I want to know? And what was Emma doing running a strange dog with the herd in the first place? Commonsense should have told her the cows might object. This afternoon has been an expensive exercise. In fact this whole shoot has been dogged with accidents and I don't like it.'

'Emma came back a short while ago, looking for Ben Dacres. He seems to have vanished off the face of the planet.'

'What? Nobody told me. What the fuck is going on?' Marcus pulled out his mobile. 'Sorry, Charlie, I need to get this sorted.'

He turned his back on Charlie and was shortly engaged in an expletive-laden conversation.

'Hi, Charlie!' Strolling down the High Street towards him was Lenny in a gleaming white T-shirt, his jeans pressed, the long fringes of his leather jacket swinging jauntily, his blond hair brushed sleekly into a pony-tail.

'Blimey, you look smart, Lenny. Off somewhere nice?'

'You're kiddin' me, Charlie, mate? You surely ain't forgotten this party? I'm off to claim my first freebie of the evening. Seven-thirty the invite says and, by my clock, seven-thirty it very nearly is.'

'Christ!' Charlie gaped at him, horrified. 'I clean forgot.'

'Well,' Lenny grinned at him, 'You ain't the only

209

one. We've got one of them actor-fellers on the sofa, sleeping off a bellyful of my Jack Daniel's.'

'What?'

'S'right. Paula says he came barging in, freaking about the cows. She gave him a swig to calm him down like. Had a couple of bevvies with him then went off to pick the kiddies up from school. When she got back, he'd consumed most of the bottle and was out for the count. Do you think I can claim a replacement bottle as compensation?'

Charlie grinned. 'I think Marcus will be so relieved to have found his star, he'll give you a crate of Jack Daniel's.'

'That's my boy!' Lenny clapped him on the shoulder. 'See you later.'

Charlie tapped Marcus. 'Marcus, Marcus, I've found him. Relax, I know where he is.'

Marcus whipped round. 'What? Where? How d'ye know? They've not seen him at the hotel; he's not been back to his caravan . . . He was last seen running towards the river. Where is he, Charlie?'

'Snoring his head off, very much the worst for a bottle of Jack Daniels, according to Lenny, on the Spinks's sofa. It would seem when the cows rioted he found refuge with Paula.'

Marcus relief was expressed with a loud crack of laughter.

'Brilliant! Thanks, Charlie. Bloody hell, what a day it's been. I think it's time for a bit of fun. Are you coming to this party? I should be there by now, welcoming the guests.'

'I'm filthy. And Isabelle was expecting me to pick her up, like right now . . .'

'I'll go and collect her, if you like,' replied Marcus. 'I can tell her what's happened and then you can shower and change without hassle. We'll see you when you're ready.'

'Thanks, Marcus,' said Charlie gratefully. 'I'll be there within the hour.'

*   *   *

'Hey, Mum, you look terrific!' Alison exclaimed as Jenny walked, rather self-consciously, into the kitchen where Jeff, Alison, Al, Stephen and Angela were sitting round the kitchen table tucking into fish and chips.

'Do you think so? You don't think this top is too much?' Jenny asked uncertainly. It was a light chiffon kaftan, with an abstract design full of colour, which floated with every move she made. More importantly for Jenny, it completely concealed the bulges and curves the tightness of her dress emphasised.

'No, it's lovely. Don't you think so, Jeff?' Alison dug him in the ribs.

He smiled up at Jenny, his mouth full of chips. 'You always look lovely to me, Jenny. But yes, that thing is very pretty.'

'You look really good, Mum,' agreed Stephen. 'You put us to shame. Do you think I should wear a tie? Only Ange thought it wouldn't be necessary to dress up too much.'

'It's only a crew party, in a pub,' protested Angela. 'They'll all be wearing jeans. If we dress up too much, we'll look silly.' As if to emphasis her point, she was wearing a pale brown corduroy pinafore dress and a white ribbed nylon sweater.

The effect, with her wispy sandy hair, little pointed face and huge glasses, made her look even

211

more like a field mouse than usual, reflected an irritated Alison, feeling cross that Angela should so unthinkingly undermine her mother's fragile confidence.

'Oh dear, do you think this is too dressy, then, Angela?' Jenny looked down at her top dubiously.

'No, no, it's lovely, Mum. I only meant . . .' Angela caught Alison's eye and went pink.

'It's a very unusual top,' she continued. 'I don't think I've seen it before. Where did it come from? I didn't know you'd been out shopping.'

'I haven't. Isabelle lent it me. And she did my shoes, look!'

Jenny lifted the hem of her dress to display a pair of what had been shabby court shoes but now transformed by swirls of paint in colours similar to the kaftan.

'Wow—they are cool!' laughed Alison. 'You'd better watch out Jeff, Ben Dacres will sweep her out from under your nose.'

'Oh Alison, don't be so daft,' chided Jenny, but she blushed a deep rosy red. To cover her confusion, she started to bundle the fish and chip debris into the bin. 'Now where's Charlie? Or has he gone straight to Isabelle's? And where are Gran and Ron? Those cars will be here soon to take us down.'

At the mention of Charlie's name, Stephen growled. 'He's still rushing around with those telly people. Trying to make good the mess they made of the High Street this afternoon. It's the last time I let him use my cows for anything. I've told him straight. That's it as far as I'm concerned. Money or no money, they can whistle in the wind for anything else . . .'

212

'What's this about the cows?' enquired Jeff. 'Did they have problems this afternoon?'

Al looked up. 'I understand it was a car that caused all the trouble?'

'Yes,' said Stephen shortly, 'It was.' He went scarlet and started to unwrap another packet of fish and chips. 'If these are going spare, I'll have another one. I'm starving.'

On tenterhooks, Alison seized the opportunity to divert the conversation. 'Yes, two of them are spare. Gran phoned when you were in the bath, Mum. She says Ron isn't feeling up to much this evening so they're going to have a quiet night in front of the telly.'

Jenny brightened, for Elsie's absence meant she wouldn't have to endure the inevitable caustic comment on her appearance. 'Not like your gran to miss a party; he must be feeling poorly.' Then, concerned, she shook her head. 'I do hope he's all right. He hasn't been looking that good for a few days.'

'It would be awful if anything happened to him,' observed Alison. 'Gran's pretty resilient, but she's devoted to Ron.'

'But they are both in their eighties,' commented Angela, sagely. 'They can't go on forever.'

*   *   *

It was Emma who answered the door to Marcus. Pale and drawn, Marcus was clearly the last person she wanted to see.

'I've heard nothing, Marcus,' she began, trying to keep her voice steady, 'Matt's gone out again with a flashlight, just in case he might have slipped into

213

the river, but I am starting to wonder whether we should call the police.'

Marcus, preoccupied with the report he'd have to make on the day's events, had temporarily forgotten the panic over the missing actor and gave her a blank look, 'The police? Whatever for?'

'Ben—he's been gone for nearly four hours, Marcus, and nobody has heard anything from him, not even Jilly, who's his pet confidante. I knew he was nervous of working with cows and we had made sure he would have very little to do with them. It was so unfortunate that arrogant shit, in his stupid great gas-guzzler, chose that moment to assert his right to roar along the Queen's highway without hindrance. Ben fled and we just don't know where he's gone. He could be lying injured somewhere . . .'

Marcus gave an impatient snort. 'No he's not. He's lying dead drunk on Jack Daniel's, on a sofa in Paula Spinks's cottage, so I suggest you get on the phone to Matt and tell him to stop wasting his time.'

The colour flooded back into Emma's thin face. Her eyes grew very bright and when she spoke, her voice wobbled. 'When did you find this out? When was he found?'

'Just now. I've come straight from the scene of the crime. Paula tells me he rushed up her garden path and she gave him a slug of Jack Daniel's to calm him down. By the time she returned from picking up her kids from school, he'd downed the lot and passed out.' He gave a short laugh. 'He was just coming to when I left to come here. I think our middle-aged Romeo is going to disappoint quite a few ladies at the party tonight.'

'Serves him bloody well right if he has a stonking hangover, I've been worried sick. Look, I better call Matt. Thanks for coming to tell me, Marcus. I suspect you're probably seething about this afternoon. It's small recompense, I know, but Colin and I've had a look at the rushes and we're confident we've got most of what we need.'

'Good, because, Emma, this afternoon has been a bloody fiasco, and not something that can be laid at the door of Jason Hart.'

Emma flushed with anger. 'No, of course not, I never suggested . . .'

'Then perhaps we can restore some professionalism to this shoot. We need to get back on schedule and not make any further unnecessary and expensive mistakes. I want nothing like this ever to happen again. I hope that's absolutely clear.'

A mutinous spark flared in Emma's eyes, 'Yes Marcus, it's clear. Very clear. As far as I'm concerned, only one mistake has been made to date, and that's not been mine. But as we'll never agree on this, you may rest assured I will do everything in my power to make sure no others are made.'

He glared at her. 'Of all the stubborn . . .'

'A question of the pot calling the kettle black, I think,' she retorted.

Isabelle, entering the sitting room, was startled. 'Marcus, I didn't realise you were here.' She looked at the two of them glaring at each other. 'Sorry, have I interrupted something? I'll leave you to it . . .'

'No, don't go, Isabelle,' Marcus turned his back on Emma and smiled. 'I've come to escort you to

215

the party. Charlie is still busy cleaning up the mess in the village and says he'll meet you there in about an hour.'

Isabelle smiled back at him. 'Oh. Right, thanks Marcus. I'll just get my coat and say goodnight to the girls. Do you want us to wait for you, Emma?'

'No thanks, Isabelle.' Ignoring Marcus, Emma stalked out of the room, saying as she went, 'I've got to phone Matt before he wastes any more of his time, and anyway, I'm not nearly ready. I'll see you there.'

40

The function room of The Foresters Arms was a long low stone barn at the back of the pub and this was where the *Silage and Strawberries* production party was being held.

Before they'd gone to clear up the mess in the High Street, Ross's band had transformed the room with coloured lights, silky drapes, paper garlands and festoons of artificial flowers.

One of the electricians, an aspiring DJ, had set up his turntables at one end of the room beyond a small dance floor, chairs had been set against the walls and a temporary bar, stocked with wine, beer, cider and soft drinks, crisps and nuts, had been erected at the other end.

'Just as well we ate before we came,' whispered Stephen to Angela as the party from Marsh Farm entered the room. 'I don't see no food as such.'

'They've done it up nice, though,' whispered Angela appreciatively. 'But there aren't many

216

people here, are there? We're very nearly the first to arrive.'

It was true. Apart from the DJ and a couple of waiters standing by, one or two crew members not known to them, and Lenny, a pint of cider in hand, the room was empty.

The family shuffled into the room and stood together, feeling awkward. 'I thought the party was meant to start at seven-thirty?' whispered Jenny. 'Where is everybody? It's nearly quarter to eight. I thought we was late enough . . .'

She was interrupted by the arrival of Rita Godwin, resplendent in an emerald green jersey that matched her spectacles, followed by her husband Rob, who was rarely persuaded to leave his armchair in front of the TV. He made straight for the bar, leaving Rita to join her friend.

'My, don't you look all dressed up fit for a royal garden party, Jenny Tucker!' She looked round the room, 'Where's lover boy? Where's anybody? That's rich, isn't it—invite us to a party and not bother to turn up!'

For the next quarter of an hour the room steadily filled with those people from the village who'd been invited and the drink flowed. In the absence of their hosts there was plenty to gossip about, given the events of the afternoon: the speediness with which the mess was cleared and damage repaired; the matter of compensation and the greed of some who'd demanded it; and the luck of those who'd had their shabby gardens given a free makeover (this with a significant look in the direction of Lenny Spinks), were all subjects of fruitful discussion, as well as the behaviour of you-know-who driving the Range Rover . . . and meaningful glances were cast in the direction of Al, of which Alison was all too aware.

It was with great relief she spotted the arrival of Hannah with her boyfriend, Nick, who, like Al, was mad on motorbikes. Neither was interested in Al's parents and would certainly not have heard anything about rioting cows.

'Where is he?' Hannah peered round the room.

'Who?' asked Alison, relieved to see Al and Nick absorbed in conversation.

'Jason Hart, of course. Don't say he's not going to turn up!'

Shortly after eight, Marcus appeared with Isabelle and his arrival seemed to cue the arrival of more or less everybody else, including Jilly Westcott and Juliet, who floated in accompanied by her son, Jamie, a tall thin, pale lad of about sixteen who was at the same school as Alison.

He nodded at Alison and pulled a face as Juliet took him by the arm and almost dragged him over to talk to a babyish-looking boy actor. Their conversation was brief; Jamie looked around the party with an expression of disdain, grinned at Alison and disappeared.

To her surprise, the young actor strolled over and stood in front of her. 'Hi', he said. 'I'm Harry Hobbs.'

'Oh?'

'You haven't heard of me?'

'Er . . . no . . .'

'Don't you guys get television in this neck of the woods?'

Alison was irritated. 'Of course; but if you mean I should know who you are, and be impressed, I don't and I'm not.'

Harry shrugged. 'Never mind . . . you're some chick. Wanna dance?'

'No thank you.' She turned to talk to Hannah, but Harry was not to be got rid of so easily.

'Why not?' he demanded. 'Everyone else here could be drawing their pensions. Come on, let's go.'

'She doesn't want to,' Al said sharply, looking up. 'Push off, kid.'

*   *   *

Emma arrived shortly after, looking distinguished in a sleeveless, deep red dress, her arms adorned with heavy brass bangles and a dark blue and red striped shawl draped around her shoulders. Matt and Colin accompanied her and yet more followed. The room filled, the music swelled, the chatter got louder as people drank more, and fought to make themselves heard. The party was well and truly underway.

'There's Jason Hart', murmured Alison to her friend.

'Where?'

'There, talking to Juliet Peters.'

'Oh my God, Ali, you've got to introduce us,' squeaked Hannah.

'I will, I promise. But later. I'm not going to pander to that over-inflated ego by rushing up to him as soon as he arrives.'

'Hi, Alison. You look lovely in that dress.' Isabelle smiled down at her.

'Thanks, Isabelle. It actually belongs to Hannah, here. You've worked wonders with Mum, by the way. She's so excited about this party, she's like a kid.'

They both glanced in the direction of Jenny,

who was standing with Jeff, laughing and chatting, surrounded by a small group of admiring men.

Alison grinned, 'I do believe my mother is flirting. Jeff had better watch out.' She looked back at Isabelle. 'Where's Charlie?'

Isabelle gave a slight shrug. 'I don't know. Marcus said he'd been delayed but that he'd be here within the hour. I do hope he gets a chance to enjoy this party. He's working flat out at the moment, what with the farm and the filming,'

'You try telling Stephen that.'

'Hi, Alison.' Marcus appeared at Isabelle's side. 'I trust you're not going to spend all evening sitting down. I'm relying on you and your mates to lead the way with the dancing.'

'You managed to appease Rita Godwin then, Marcus?' Isabelle chuckled. 'She was giving Marcus a round ticking-off for not being here promptly at the start of the evening.'

'Maybe being late for your own party is how they do things in town . . .' mimicked Marcus, 'but it don't go down well here, in the country.'

Alison grinned. 'She's right. If it wasn't for the prospect of free booze and a good gossip at your expense, everyone might have left before you got here. What kept you? Apart from,' she cast a warning glance in Al's direction, 'the business with the cows that is?'

'Ben Dacres.' And Marcus, launching into a witty resumé of Ben's misadventure, had the satisfaction of seeing both Isabelle and Alison laugh.

Emma, who was standing nearby, looked across at them with some surprise

'Oh poor Mum,' said Alison, 'She was so hoping to have a dance with him this evening.'

'I'm afraid she's going to be disappointed. When I left Charlie with him, he was barely able to stand, let alone dance.'

'I do hope Charlie gets here soon,' said Isabelle wistfully.

'I'm sure he will, but in the meantime, he said I was to look after you. Come on, let's get you another drink. And here's the food at long last . . .'

Far from Stephen and Angela's fear that there would be no food, The Foresters Arms, supported by a generous budget, pulled out the stops. Myriad dishes of delicious little delicacies arrived—mange tout stuffed with cream cheese, smoked salmon in dill pancakes, sticks of chicken satay and spicy peanut butter sauce, tiny Yorkshire puds stuffed with rare roast beef, sticky prunes wrapped in bacon, choux puffs filled with prawns . . . As plate after plate wafted in front of him, Stephen bitterly regretted the second fish supper he had wolfed down earlier.

'It's no good, Ange, I've got to have one of those,' he said finally, succumbing to a miniature version of his favourite food—tiny sausages stuck into a dainty pot of mash. He looked happily about him as he tucked in. 'I must say, whatever else, these film people know how to throw a party. And the way that High Street got put to rights. I couldn't believe it, the state it was in—I thought we'd be finished!'

Angela smiled at him. 'I'm glad it's all sorted too, Stephen. It's awful when you and Charlie fall out, and as Gran says, we've all got to pull together. Once the filming's finished we'll make this farm a success, you and me. Oh I am so looking forward to our wedding. With all this fuss, it's like everyone

221

has forgotten about it.'

'I haven't, Ange,' Stephen patted her hand. 'You and me . . . you've said it, that's our future.'

'Stephen, Angela, what a nice surprise . . . but then I guessed you'd be here.' A light musical voice interrupted them.

They both looked up to see Nicola Scudamore, exquisite in a bright flowery dress, her shining dark curls dancing around her face and her eyes sparkling with amusement.

Angela spoke first. 'Nicola,' she said without enthusiasm, 'What a nice surprise. Are you in this TV thing?'

'Yes, didn't Stephen tell you?'

Angela shot Stephen a look of surprise.

He went pink. 'Er no, I forgot . . . I've been that busy . . .'

'Forgot that you'd seen me? Oh, Stephen,' Nicola gave a tinkling laugh. 'How could you? And have you forgotten how we spent the whole afternoon together, looking round the farm?'

'It wasn't the whole afternoon,' muttered Stephen, his face going from pink to a deep red. 'I just showed you some of the animals.'

'And so sweet of you to do so, particularly as you're so busy . . .'

'Yes, well . . .'

'But I'm delighted to hear you took my advice . . .'

'Your advice?' He looked up at her, the colour draining from his face.

'Yes, I heard that the old dears at Summerstoke Manor said "no" to *The Dream*. Well done, you were obviously very persuasive.'

'What are you talking about, Nicola?' Angela

finally found a voice, but it was cold and distant, not one with which Stephen was familiar.

Nicola laughed lightly. 'Stephen told me the Merlin Players were planning to stage *A Midsummer Night's Dream* at the Manor. The Merlin Players doing Shakespeare! I ask you . . . they'd never be taken seriously again. Stephen agreed with me and said he'd see the old ladies and convince them it was a bad idea. So I say well done, Stephen. I didn't think you had it in you. Don't you agree, Angela?'

'I do,' replied Angela in a small, tight voice. 'I didn't know he had it in him, either.'

'Anyway, must go, Jason's waiting for a dance. Good to see you both again, looking so . . . so . . . well. Bye for now.' And she disappeared into a crowd.

Stephen could hardly breathe. He felt as if all his systems had shut down; he couldn't think, he couldn't move, and sat, staring hard at the floor without seeing it, frozen, waiting for Angela to say something.

It seemed a long time coming. Then a small voice on a sob broke the silence between them. 'It was bad enough you didn't tell me you'd seen Nicola and you'd spent the afternoon with her, but to lie to me about The Merlin Players. Oh, Stephen . . .'

'I didn't lie to you, Ange, I didn't . . . I just . . . I admit I went to see them and told them I was worried. I was worried, you know I was . . . I thought we was biting off more than we could chew and Nicola agreed . . .'

At the mention of Nicola's name, Angela almost spat. 'Nicola! Why is what Nicola thought more important than my feelings? What's Nicola to

223

you, Stephen? Are you still in love with her? Is it because of her you lied to me? You've deceived me and I never thought you were the sort of person who'd do that!'

'I'm not . . . not . . . no . . . believe me, Ange, you've got it all wrong . . . I love you. I wouldn't do anything to hurt you, honest.'

'Well you just have. Very badly.' Angela stood up. 'I'm going.'

Stephen jumped up, alarmed. 'Going? You can't. Where? Please Ange, let me explain . . .'

'I think I've heard enough explanations for the moment, thank you, Stephen. I need to go and think things over. This is so . . . so dreadful, I'm not sure I want to . . . to carry on . . .'

'Ange,' Stephen was agonised. 'Ange, don't say that. Don't go. I love you . . .'

'You've a funny way of showing it.' She shook her head, the tears starting to tumble down her cheeks. 'I'm going. I'll get one of those taxis waiting outside. Don't call me, Stephen, I don't want to talk to you just for now.'

And before he could move, she'd darted through the room and was gone.

41

'Hey, Isabelle, ain't this a lovely party? I can't wait to strut my stuff!'

Paula, dressed like a Christmas Barbie doll in a tiny silver skirt and sparkling lurex top, clutched her dream drink (Guinness and real champagne, a special order from Marcus by way of a 'thank-you') and gazed around the crowded room, her eyes wide. 'So many people here, ain't there, an' I don't know half of them. Where've they all come to? I hope I ain't missed nothing.'

'Have you only just got here, Paula?' Knowing how much Paula had been looking forward to this party Isabelle couldn't believe her friend could have arrived so late.

'Yes. I couldn't really leave me mum with Ben Dacres flat out on me sofa, could I? She was dead scared he'd wake and she'd have to talk to him.' As cheerful as ever, Paula was not a hostage to martyrdom. ''Twas alright, though, I just got myself dolled up good and proper and then, when Charlie took him off, I got myself over here.'

'Charlie?'

'Yeah, when the taxi driver saw the state of Mr Dacres, he said there was no way he'd take him . . . said he might throw up in his cab and it didn't matter how much they was gonna pay him, he didn't want to spend the rest of his evening cleaning out puke. You can see his point.'

'So Charlie took him? Good old Charlie, I certainly owe him . . .' said Marcus, overhearing Paula as he rejoined them. 'How's your Black Velvet, Paula?'

'Very nice, thank you, Marcus,' primly replied Paula, who found Marcus intimidating. 'Er . . . have you seen my Lenny?'

'He's over by the bar.'

'Then I'll go and find him, if you don't mind. I'm more than ready for a bit of a dance.'

Marcus grinned at Isabelle as Paula tottered off in her four-inch stilettos. 'How on earth is she going to dance in those things?'

225

'With ease, I should imagine,' laughed Isabelle, gazing after Paula. 'She loves a bop and she tells me when she and Lenny are on their uppers, they crank up the music and dance like crazy in their tiny sitting-room.' She smiled, almost wistfully. 'They're a funny pair, but they are the kindest, sweetest people I know and absolutely devoted to each other, which seems to be a rare thing these days.'

'You and Charlie seem to be doing all right.'

She looked at him gravely then smiled fleetingly, 'Yes, yes we do, don't we. But it's early days yet. I don't want to make any more mistakes.'

Marcus held out his arm. 'Well, in the meantime, how about having a dance with me?'

'I'd love to, but aren't you meant to be the host? There must be loads of other people you want to talk to? You've hardly left my side since we got here . . .'

He smiled at her. 'It's been a pleasure.'

Marcus's offer to escort Isabelle to the party had been entirely altruistic. He'd liked what he'd seen of her, but thin, fragile blondes were not his style; his ego, however, ruffled from his last encounter with Emma, needed repair and being in Isabelle's company and focussing on her, he became aware of her in a way he'd never done before. Her eyes, huge and blue, danced with warmth and laughter when she talked to her friends and when enthused, her face glowed.

'There's really something quite mediaeval about her looks,' he thought. 'Her hair, short and fine like that, looks like a halo. Put her in a white robe and she wouldn't be out of place on a Christmas card . . .' And to his own amazement, he felt a sharp stab of envy. 'Charlie really is a lucky lad . . .'

'Hi, Jools.'

Juliet turned and looked at Jason Hart without much enthusiasm. 'Hello Jason.'

He was not deterred. Still not reconciled to the prospect of three months' exile in the country, he'd consoled himself with the prospect of some fun, and fun, for him, was to see how many birds he could lay before he returned to the city. Nicola Scudamore, he was confident, was in the bag; Alison Tucker would need more long-term stalking, so tonight he thought he would have a go with this particular popsie. Juliet was outside his usual parameters, but she was strikingly pretty and from the outset he'd thought she'd be good game.

She was looking lovely this evening: her skin's creamy whiteness was enhanced by a vivid blue dress; her red-gold curls shone and danced as she moved, her huge blue eyes sparkled, and her hands fluttered like little birds as she talked to the group of admirers who'd gathered around her as soon as she arrived.

He glanced at her companions. 'You all alone this evening then, Jools?'

She gave a little snort of laughter. 'Hardly. But if you mean I'm here without Oliver, then yes, for the moment. He's coming later, he's got a constituency surgery.'

'Sounds very nasty.'

'Very boring, more like.'

'Unlike this film malarkey, you mean? I'm looking forward to seeing the out-takes from this afternoon.' He chuckled.

Ross appeared with a glass of orange juice. 'Here you are, darling. Hi Jason, enjoying the party?'

'Enjoying is not the emotion that immediately springs to mind,' replied Jason. 'Enduring more like. I reckon you had more fun in the High Street. Just my luck to miss out on the action.'

Juliet shot him a look. 'You weren't there then?'

'No, more's the pity. He looked at her, a slight smile playing across his face. 'No, I'm innocent of the cows, whatever you may think. It wasn't me in that Range Rover, honest. But,' he grinned, 'it's good material, innit?'

'How do you make that out?' Ross's pleasant expression didn't waver.

Jason snorted. 'Cows running amok, trashing the place . . . beddable Ben running for his life and drinking himself senseless on a bottle of JD . . . Emma's gonna have to rewrite that script: exit Ben, pursued by a cow.'

Juliet chuckled then looked serious. 'I've never known a shoot to be so beset with problems. Have you, Ross?'

'Certainly not such dramatic ones.' Ross replied. 'Let's hope this is the end of it, we can't afford too many more.'

'Mind you,' chipped in Jason, 'if the filming was to be called off, we'd all get to return to real life a lot sooner. What a great idea.'

The smile went out of Ross's face but before he could speak, Juliet, looking severe, interjected, 'No it's not, Jason, and don't even think of it. This filming is real life for us who are working in it. It might be playtime for you, but for everybody else it's bread and butter time.'

'My, I think I've just had my knuckles well and

truly rapped. I'm sorry, Miss, I won't be flippant again.'

Her dimples appeared. 'Oh yes you will. I don't think there is much you take seriously.'

Impulsively he seized her hand. 'Come and have a dance with me, Jools, before your old man gets here. Let's go and make whoopee on the dance floor.'

Before she could reply, they were interrupted. 'Jason, here you are . . . I thought we'd arranged to meet in the hotel foyer? It was lucky I bumped into Joe just now. He told me he'd brought you on down here with Jilly and some others. Why didn't you tell me? Oh, hi, Juliet, Ross.'

Juliet, disengaging her hand from Jason's, dimpled at her friend. 'Hi Nicola. You've arrived on cue. Jason is dying for a dance, but I'm not dancing this evening. Not yet, anyway.'

Thwarted, Jason snarled to himself. Nicola was okay, good arm-candy certainly, but he wasn't going to let her get in the way.

Juliet, feeling she'd had a fortuitous escape, turned back to her group to find Emma and Matt had joined them.

'I overheard some of that conversation with Mr Hart,' muttered Emma. 'Honestly, I've worked with some difficult customers in my time, but Jason . . .'

'Is without any redeeming qualities,' Juliet finished with a slight laugh. 'I know it's not my place, Emma, by why on earth did you cast him?'

Emma shrugged. 'It was nothing to do with me. Marcus insisted, saying it was the ingredient that clinched the commission.'

'Well let's hope Marcus doesn't have cause to regret it,' said Ross lightly. 'We'll just have to keep

Mr Hart firmly in our sights, and make sure nothing else goes wrong.'

'Juliet, darling, I'm sorry I'm so late, but I'm sure you haven't missed me.' Oliver Merfield dropped a kiss on his wife's neck. 'Hmm, you smell nice. I think I shall borrow some of your scent to spray the office with at the end of my surgery.'

'No you won't. Your expensive ways would become tabloid headlines . . .' Juliet dimpled up at her tall, lean husband. 'Darling have you met Emma Knight? She's our director. And this is Ross Manvers, our second AD, and Matt, who's the first AD.'

'It's good to meet you all at last; I've heard a lot about you.' Oliver shook their hands, then turned back to Juliet. 'Well darling, have I time for a drink, or are you aching to get on to that dance floor?'

'Oh, have a drink, Ollie. Truth to tell, I'm feeling really tired this evening. Maybe we'll dance later.'

*　　　*　　　*

Charlie was exhausted by the time he reached The Foresters Arms.

Not only had he spent the earlier part of the evening rushing around sorting the villagers and their gardens out, but at the very moment he was poised to return home and get ready for the party, he'd found himself landed with the unwelcome problem of transporting a paralytic Ben Dacres.

He had no alternative but to collect his van, bundle the weakly protesting actor into the passenger seat and bump his way over to Stowford Country Club.

Miraculously, given the quality of the van's

suspension, Ben was not sick, and when they arrived at the hotel (where they met with an arctic reception), was sufficiently compos mentis to order a pot of black coffee for himself and a large whisky for his friend.

Charlie left him to have a shower and drove back to Marsh Farm. He thought with envy of Ben's shower; the farmhouse's old-fashioned bath-tub would take far too long to fill to make the much-longed-for soak viable. He was late enough already; he had promised to pick Isabelle up at seven-thirty; Marcus would have taken her to the party, but she must be wondering where he was . . .

Shortly after nine, he turned into the car park, narrowly missing a taxi pulling away. Catching a glimpse of the passenger, he frowned, puzzled: he could have sworn it was Angela.

The room was heaving with people.

'Charlie, I'm so glad you've got here at last. You did me a huge favour.' Ross grabbed his arm. 'Let me get you a drink—you must be in desperate need of one.' And before Charlie could demur, he'd been firmly steered towards the bar. It took a little time before he could extract himself from the grateful Ross, who wanted to know precisely what had happened to Ben, before, second pint in hand, he made another attempt to find Isabelle in the crowded room.

He bumped into Jenny. 'Mum, where's Isabelle? Have you seen her?'

'Charlie, you're here at last. Everyone's been asking after you. It's a lovely party. I've been dancing with lots of different people. It's a pity Jeff's not keen, but I'm working on him.'

Charlie smiled at his mother's flushed and

excited face. 'I'm glad you're having a good time, Mum. You look jolly nice in that thing. But have you seen Isabelle?'

'Isabelle? The last time I saw here she was dancing with Marcus, but that was some time ago. No look, there she is, on the dance floor, with Oliver Merfield.'

Charlie followed his mother's gaze.

Isabelle, in a short slate–blue dress, with long dangling earrings made from mother-of-pearl buttons, was listening intently to Oliver as she swayed to the music.

Captivated by the sight of her, Charlie watched, admiring.

'She's lovely,' he thought. 'Not in the conventional way, like Juliet, but she's striking. Even the way she dresses is not like anyone else.' And not for the first time, he was assailed by self-doubt. 'What on earth does she see in me? Me, Mr Clodhopping Farmer with no conversation beyond motocross, ploughing and farrowing pigs.' He sighed heavily. He'd not eaten since lunch and he was tired out. 'Oliver's more her type, I've always thought it . . .'

Just as he had resolved to make a move towards her, Marcus came up behind Oliver and tapped his shoulder. There was laughter between the three of them and Oliver left the dance floor. Marcus took Isabelle's hand and an unexpected and searing surge of jealousy swept over Charlie. How could Marcus, his friend, his mate, look at his girl like that?

He finished his pint and the alcohol, combining with everything else, worsened his mood. He pushed his way back to the bar, where he was received with enthusiasm by various members of the TV crew—who naturally gravitated to the bar rather than the dance floor.

Here Emma found him, some time later.

'Charlie—you're here! Does Isabelle know?'

'No, she was dancing . . . she was having a good time, so I thought I'd wait my turn . . .' Charlie sounded more slurry and pathetic than he'd intended and he tried to deflect it with a shaky laugh.

Emma regarded him with exasperation. 'I don't know how long you've been here, but I think you ought to tell her. She can't understand where you are. She must have phoned your mobile half a dozen times. Are you just going to abandon her to Marcus? He certainly wouldn't be my first choice of a comfortable companion for an evening.'

Charlie stared at Emma, remorseful and ashamed. 'You're right,' he said with drunken frankness. 'I've buggered it up. I need to sober up a bit, Emma. I'll go to the bog, get some fresh air, then I'll go and find her.'

'Don't leave it too long, Charlie. She was talking about going home pretty soon. Do you want me to tell her you're here?'

'No. She'll wonder why I didn't find her as soon as I got here.'

'Well actually, Charlie, that's what I wonder, too. Honestly!'

Jenny was enjoying herself in a way she could never have imagined. She was having fun. She, a plump, middle-aged woman, was being asked to dance and people were chatting to her like they were interested in her. And without Elsie's disapproving eyes on her, her spirits were high. The only disappointments were Jeff refusing to dance and no Ben Dacres, but there, she couldn't have everything.

'Here you are, love, orange juice and lemonade.' Jeff smiled down at her as he handed her a brimming glass. 'My word, you do look hot. Do you want to sit down?'

'No, no, I'm fine, Jeff, but maybe I should get a bit of fresh air.'

They pushed their way to the door just as a pale but immaculate Ben Dacres entered the room. A faint cheer went up from those close enough to witness his arrival.

He held up his hand in acknowledgement. 'I heard there was a rumour that I was too worse for wear for the party,' he said. 'What a slur; I never miss a party. Thank you, Ross, I'll have a small whisky and water. Hair of the dog, dear boy, hair of the dog.'

He glanced around the crowd close to him and his eyes fell on Jenny. He cocked his head, struggling to recognise her. Jenny went pink with pleasure.

'Hello again, Mr Dacres. I'm glad you was able to make it to the party.'

At the sound of her voice, the penny dropped.

'My little Cancerian, I came to dance with you. That is,' he registered the proprietorial presence of Jeff, 'if your partner doesn't mind? I don't wish to usurp his position on the dance floor.'

'Not at all,' said Jeff good-humouredly. 'I'm not much of a dancer.'

'Then,' said Ben, swiftly downing the drink Ross handed to him and holding his arm out for Jenny, 'the pleasure is mine. I love to dance.'

Jeff watched him lead Jenny on to the floor; the music, being somewhat slower and more balladic than before, Ben put his arm round Jenny's waist and the couple began to waltz.

Jeff looked on, sipping his ginger beer. He was not used to Jenny looking like this: so excited, so alive, so sexy. Deep in the depths of his comfortable soul, something stirred.

He remembered, when he'd first met her—a devastatingly pretty, shy, seventeen-year-old— he had felt something similar. But not really understanding that mix of sexual attraction and envy, and seeing as Jim, his best mate, had got there first, he'd buried it. He was not given to self-analysis, but watching the two of them dance, he decided it was no longer enough to do nothing. And the first thing he'd do, he decided, was to take his place on the dance floor and reclaim his Jenny.

Perversely, at the moment of decision, his mobile buzzed. He pushed his way outside to take the call, then pushed his way back in again, made purposefully for the dance floor and tapped Jenny on the shoulder.

She turned and smiled happily to see him. 'Oh Jeff, have you come for a dance?'

'No love, sorry,' he said regretfully, noting the

actor fellow held onto Jenny's hand. 'I've had a call. I've got to go; a cow in labour's having a few problems. I'm not sure I'll be able to get back before the party's over. I could drop you off at the farm on my way out, if you like?'

Disappointment momentarily clouded Jenny's face. 'Oh Jeff, that's such a shame . . .'

'You're not going, are you, my little Cancerian? So soon? The night is young . . .' Ben was enjoying the uncritical admiration of his dancing partner and after the day's misadventures, he so much needed that sort of solace.

'I don't have to, Ben. Jeff's a vet; he's on call so he's got to go. But I could stay for another dance . . .'

'That would be wonderful.'

Jenny turned back to Jeff. 'I'll see you, tomorrow, as planned?'

Jeff nodded. He would've much preferred Jenny to accept his offer of a lift, but he was not an unreasonable man.

Alison watched Jeff give her mother a kiss on the cheek and leave. The dance floor was full, the music had changed, but still Ben Dacres managed to keep hold of Jenny.

'I don't know what it is about Mum, tonight,' she chuckled to Al, 'but she's hardly left that dance floor and now Ben Dacres is glued to her.'

Al looked across and grinned. 'From where I sit, it seems to me he needs your mother to hold him up.'

Alison laughed. 'You may well be right.'

'Why don't you go and dance, Ali? I know you want to.'

And she did: numerous people had asked her

to join them, but she didn't want to leave Al on his own. Quite apart from the fact she'd rather be with him than anyone else, there was still the lurking danger that some malicious spirit would fill him in about his father's role in that afternoon's debacle. Much as he distanced himself from his parents, their behaviour still had the power to upset him.

'Maybe I do, but I'm quite happy to stay here with you. You're not going to be around much longer. I want to make the most of you.'

'Sounds good to me.' He lightly caressed her shoulder, glancing across the room as he did so. 'Isn't that your pal, Jason Hart, over there? With that girl in the flowery dress?'

Alison looked in the direction he was indicating and, as if he felt their eyes on him, Jason Hart turned and stared, then muttered something to his companion.

Alison looked away—she didn't want him to think she was, in any way, interested. But the damage had been done. A couple of seconds later he was standing in front of her, the girl with the floral dress at his elbow.

'Hi. Want a dance?' His abrupt request took the three of them completely by surprise. The girl looked very put out, Al snorted, and Alison laughed.

'You don't waste time in small talk do you? This is Al, my boyfriend, Jason. I'm with him this evening.'

Jason nodded briefly at Al, then turned his attention back to Alison, 'Then why aren't you up there? Or are you waiting for the barn dance to start?'

'I've injured my leg, as it happens,' interjected

Al, coldly. 'Alison's free to dance if she wants to, but . . .'

'I've chosen not to. I'd rather keep Al company, thank you.'

'Come on, just for one. Your bloke won't die of loneliness. Nicola here can sit and chat to him.'

'Jason!' Nicola looked as if it was the last thing she wanted to do.

Alison regarded her with a puzzled frown. 'Nicola? Don't I know you from somewhere?'

Nicola shrugged, 'Possibly . . . I've done some TV work and . . .'

Jason interrupted her. 'This is a good bit of music, come on Alison.'

'Why don't you dance with Nicola?'

'She's tired of dancing.' A rare grin transformed his face. 'She's ready for bed. Oh come on, don't be scared, I'm not going to eat you.'

Alison allowed herself to be pulled to her feet and with a rueful smile at Al, who winked reassuringly back, she followed Jason onto the floor.

*   *   *

'I don't believe it!' Charlie stared at the front tyres of his van with disbelief. 'I just don't believe it. What fucking luck! Both of them—what have I done to deserve this?'

He had gone outside, as he had told Emma he would, to try and sober up. The night air was cold, so he had wandered into the car park to collect his jacket from the van when he had spotted the vehicle, sitting at a strange angle, as if resting on its chin.

Both front tyres were flat.

He groaned out loud. 'Bloody hell, what a bloody end to a bloody, bloody day!'

'Charlie?' It was Isabelle's voice.

He spun round. 'Isabelle?'

A silvery figure, silhouetted against the streetlight, walked towards him through the gloom of the dimly lit car park.

'I'd given up on you; I was about to go home. What happened? I know you took Ben Dacres back to the hotel, but he's been here for a while.'

He could hear the reproach in her voice and, ashamed, he put his arms around her. 'I'm sorry, Isabelle, I really am. After I'd got him up to his room, I went home to change. It all took so much longer than I thought, and then when I got here . . .'

She interrupted, seeing his van, 'Oh no, you've got a puncture?'

'Two.'

'Two! Oh Charlie, what awful luck. You must have driven over some broken glass or something. Why didn't you come and tell me? Have you been out here all this time?'

'No . . . I've only just discovered them . . . I did come in. I . . . er . . . had a drink or two. You were dancing . . . I didn't want to interrupt . . .'

Isabelle withdrew from the fold of his arms. 'I've been waiting for you all evening, Charlie Tucker.' She was cold. 'I tried your mobile goodness knows how many times; why didn't you answer? I've been worried about you; particularly when Ben Dacres turned up and you didn't. Why didn't you find me as soon as you got here?'

Charlie felt wretched. 'You were dancing with Oliver and then with Marcus, you . . . you were having a good time with them. I understand why; they're nice blokes. They're much more your sort than I am, Isabelle.'

Isabelle exploded. 'I don't believe this. I was dancing with them because you hadn't turned up. Only now it appears you had, but chose to have a drink or two, or was it three or four, Charlie, before putting me out of my misery?'

'I'm sorry, Isabelle. I was tired; I over-reacted. I wanted to be with you so much and then I saw . . . I thought you were having a good time and . . .'

'So you've already said.' Her voice wobbled. 'I don't know how many times I have to tell you it's *you* I love, Charlie; *you* I would like to have spent the evening dancing with. When will you believe me? Or maybe you don't want to believe me; maybe it's a way of telling me that you don't think we have much of a future. Well, if that's the case, far better for me to know now . . .'

'Isabelle, no . . . really, you've got it all wrong . . .'

'Have I? Have I really, Charlie? Well perhaps we'd better both have a long, clear think about it. I'm going home now. I'm sorry not to stay and help you with your tyres but I'm sure Lenny will give you a hand to fix them. Goodnight.'

And before he could think of anything to say that would stop her, she'd turned and walked swiftly back across the car park, through the lamplight, over the road into the darkness of her driveway.

43

Alison would have to have been superhuman not to have experienced a thrill seeing the envious looks Hannah cast in her direction as she danced with Jason, and it was so good to dance. The silky movement of the dress she wore made her feel sexy and she was completely into the music; it was just a pity it was Jason Hart and not Al dancing with her. She cast a look in Al's direction and could see he was talking with that Nicola girl.

The level of the music was such that conversation was manageable only by shouting in the other person's ear, which meant its scope was limited.

'Is Nicola your girlfriend?'

Jason pulled a face. 'I don't think so,' he replied. 'We've spent a night together, but that hardly qualifies her.'

Alison shook her head. 'You're a tough nut, Jason Hart. She's very pretty.'

Jason shrugged. 'So? So are you.'

'But I'm not prepared to spend the night with you.'

Jason made no reply and for a while allowed the music to take over. When it changed, Alison began to leave the floor, but Jason grabbed her wrist. 'Don't go. There's something I want to talk to you about.'

Alison glanced over at Al, who was still absorbed in conversation with Nicola.

'Okay, one more track. What is it you want to talk about?'

'This.' Jason pulled a card out of his pocket and

241

passed it to Alison.

She read it. 'That's nice of Marcus. He said he'd try and find someone.'

'And has he?'

'Not that I know of.'

'You could ask me.'

'You?' Puzzled, Alison looked at him. 'What do you know about website design?'

'My starry career has been pretty meteoric, you know. I once had a day job; I designed websites; I was very good. Have you seen mine?'

Alison nodded.

Jason looked smug. 'What did you think?'

'It's good.'

'Well then, would you like me to help with yours? It won't cost you.'

Alison frowned. 'Why should you want to help, Jason?'

'Put it down to my innate good nature. If that doesn't wash, then understand I'd jump at anything to while away the tedium of the hours spent with this little lot. It would be a challenge; making a silk purse, etc etera.'

She gave him a guarded look. 'This is important to us, Jason. It's not a joke.'

'Yeah, yeah. Whatever.'

Alison was torn. If he produced anything half as good as his website . . . but she just didn't trust him. 'Well if you mean it and you think you've got the time, that's wicked. I'll talk it over with Al.'

'What's he got to do with it?'

'He was giving me a hand, but we've got badly stuck and he's meant to be getting on with his uni work . . .'

'Then let him. I'll help you.'

242

Emma was chatting to Ross and Matt when Marcus wandered over.

'Hi, fellas, mind if I join you?'

Matt nodded affably at his boss, 'Hi Marcus, nice party.'

'Yeah, good for everyone's morale,' Ross murmured.

'Which,' said Emma, 'was at an all-time low this afternoon. Your team did an amazing job clearing up, Ross.'

'We aim to please,' he shrugged, then grinned, looking across at the dancers. 'I must admit I am more amazed at the recuperative powers of Mr Dacres.'

The other three followed his gaze. Ben and Jenny were dancing the twist.

Matt gave a crack of laughter. 'I've never seen anyone do that in real life. My God!'

'Well actually, I'm not sure I have,' grinned Ross, 'and I'm a few years older than you.'

Emma gave Marcus a cold look, 'Has Isabelle gone, then?'

Something about her tone caused him to look at her with suspicion.

'Yes, why?'

She felt uncomfortable; quite apart from their personal differences she was cross with him for so evidently flirting with Isabelle and unsettling Charlie, but she had drunk sufficient wine to remove her reserve. 'No reason, Marcus, other than the fact that you've been sticking like glue to her side all evening.'

His eyes glinted. 'I like her. I told Charlie I'd look after her. Do you have a problem with that?'

Emma breathed in deeply and then said, in measured tones, 'No, Marcus, I don't. But maybe Charlie does.'

'Charlie? What are you talking about?'

'Charlie arrived a while ago. I think you were dancing with Isabelle at the time. Anyway for whatever reason, the silly idiot, seeing the two of you together, took himself off to the bar. The last time I saw him, he was trying to sober himself up before he saw Isabelle. Did he see her before she went?'

'Not that I'm aware of, but contrary to what you are suggesting, Emma,' he said bitingly, 'I did not monopolise Isabelle all evening. She's her own woman and I think Charlie is quite capable of looking after his own interests.'

'And do you know what I think, Marcus Steel?' Emma replied coldly, 'I think you're a selfish, self-opinionated bastard.'

*   *   *

'Are you all right, Ben? You look very pale?' Jenny hovered anxiously over her dancing partner who had suddenly felt very feeble and needed to sit down.

'I'm afraid, my dear, I do feel a little . . . peculiar. It suddenly hit me, I really shouldn't have attempted that twist.'

'I'm sorry, that was my fault. I used to be really good at it. I should have been more thoughtful, you having been ill and all.'

Ben shot Jenny a sharp look. 'What do you

244

mean, I was perfectly fine.'

'You're very brave, but I heard about that accident you had yesterday. I sent you a card this morning, did you get it?'

'Card?'

'Yes, it was a get well card, with flowers on it and a rhyme inside. You probably thought it was daft, but I wanted you to know . . . well, to know we was thinking of you.'

Ben (who'd laughed at the card, reading the verse with exaggerated pathos to all and sundry) looked up at her, his face a mixture of suffering, nobility, and humility (an expression of which he was particularly proud).

'You are too good, my dear. Yes, I did receive it. It's sitting on the dressing table in my trailer. I shall treasure it. But now I feel, alas, our magical evening must come to a close. I must away to my bed, alone.'

'Yes of course, Ben, dear. Shall I tell Ross to get a car for you?'

'My angel.'

Ross responded to Jenny's request with alacrity and within a short space of time, Jenny found herself alone and ready to draw the evening to a close. She looked round the thinning crowd for the rest of her family.

*   *   *

Upon Alison's return to Al, Nicola jumped up with an impatient, 'At last. I'm longing for another dance, Jason, let's go.'

Jason allowed himself to be dragged away, 'Okay, okay, but let's get some bevvies first, I'm in

245

dire need of one.'

'Hey, I've got some great news,' Alison began, but she got no further. Al had got to his feet, his face livid and scowling.

'Why didn't you tell me?'

'Tell you what, Al?' Alison's heart sank; she knew exactly what was coming.

'That it was my father who'd caused the trouble this afternoon. I've been sitting here all evening and everyone knew what had happened. I wouldn't have come if I'd known . . .'

'Which is why I didn't tell you.' Alison was cross. 'Why should your dad be allowed to destroy our evening? We were both looking forward to this party. And anyway, how do you know everyone knew? As far as I can tell, no one actually knew who the driver was, apart from Charlie and he's hardly likely to go rushing round saying, "Do you know who the driver of that car was?—It was Hugh Lester, Al's dad!"'

'No, maybe not the crew, but the village would know; not many people drive a Range Rover Sport. Nicola could tell me what sort of car it was and how everyone is talking about the arrogant shit driving it; and there were enough of the village here tonight to put the finger on me. You should have told me, Ali. It was bonkers of me to think I could ever have any sort of life in Summerstoke. I shouldn't have come.'

'Al.' Alison's voice was soft and she put her arms around him. 'Darling Al, no one blames you for your parents, no one, my family least of all and they have the most cause. Are you going to refuse to come and see me, stay with me, sleep with me, because of your shit of a father?'

246

He looked down into her upturned face and softened a little. 'No, of course not. I love you Alison.' He kissed her, but then drew away, brooding. 'But you should have told me, Ali, you should have told me.'

'Yes, I see. But you do understand why I didn't, don't you? But I won't try and hide things from you again, Al, even if I think it's for the best. Promise.'

Unnoticed by Al and Alison, obscured as she was by a bunch of people by the door, staring at them with a look of horrified incredulity on her face, stood Veronica Lester.

44

Everything had gone as Veronica had planned.

They had arrived at the Pump Rooms, found their table and their friends and settled in to an expensive evening of good food and wine, raffle tickets and auction. Just before the dessert, Veronica made her way to the ladies and texted her daughter.

No sooner had she returned to the table than her mobile rang. She took the call; a look of surprise was followed by one of concern. With a brief, 'I'll phone you back,' she snapped it off and, in an undertone, addressed Hugh. 'I won't be a moment, darling, but that was Cordelia. I'm not sure, but I think she might need rescuing. I am just going somewhere quieter to phone her back.'

And before he could express his displeasure, she whisked away to phone her daughter.

Cordelia, as yet an immature Lester, one

prepared to deceive and play her own games but not adept enough at pulling the wool over her parents' eyes, had played right into her mother's hands.

'So, it's as I thought,' Veronica said grimly. 'You're not at Tammy's place, studying, you're in town. You're fifteen, Cordelia . . . all right, nearly sixteen . . . but that makes you an underage drinker . . . oh for goodness sake, don't talk rubbish, I know you have. How many clubs and pubs have you been to this evening? . . . No, don't attempt to lie to me. I am going to pick you up in ten minutes . . . Where are you now? Kingsmead Square? Good God, what are you doing there? Walk through to the Theatre Royal, I'll pick you up from the front . . .'

She glanced at her watch. It was close to nine-thirty. It would take her half an hour to get back home, despatch Cordelia to her room and walk down to The Foresters Arms. Ten o'clock was not too late to turn up to a party and she reckoned by the time Hugh had polished off a few brandies and got a taxi back, he would be home at midnight . . . and if she was later in, he couldn't blame her, could he, if on the way home, seeing the lights of a party to which they'd been invited, she decided to make the best of her ruined evening?

Hugh growled with considerable annoyance when he heard his wife's evening was to be curtailed, but he made no attempt to dissuade her from leaving. He said he'd get a taxi later, but Veronica was not to wait up for him, then he settled back behind a large brandy to resume his conversation on horseflesh with his mate, Gavin Croucher,

Chuckling at her ingenuity, Veronica sped lightly

248

from the building, picked up her car and collected her very sulky daughter.

It was not a comfortable ride back for either of them and by the time Veronica pulled into the drive of Summerstoke House, Cordelia was in such a temper, she tore up the stairs to her room and slammed the door.

Veronica stood at the bottom of the staircase for a moment, then stepped lightly out of the still-open front door and banged it shut, thus giving, she hoped, her daughter the firm impression that her parent was still in the house.

Her heart pounding, she smoothed her hair, pulled her pashmina around her shoulders and walked through the gates and down to The Foresters Arms, trembling with excitement.

Soon she would see him, soon she would be dancing in his arms. She almost broke into a run and would have done, but for the fear of arriving hot and dishevelled. She'd no idea who else would be there . . . she didn't care. He would be waiting for her; he would be wondering where she was, his queen of the tennis courts. He might even be thinking she wasn't going to turn up, that he might as well return to his hotel because she wasn't there . . .

She walked faster.

'Don't go, my darling,' she whispered, 'I am coming; I'm very nearly there . . .'

A number of taxis were parked outside, and as she turned onto the path leading to the entrance, a couple pulled away.

There was no one on the door to take her name and she stood there, hesitating, flinching at the wall of sound and body-heat. The room was crowded;

self-consciously she stood there, trying to spot Ben. A slender, dark-haired woman in a deep red dress came to her rescue.

'Hello, have you just got here?'

'Yes,' Veronica croaked, 'Er . . . Ben Dacres invited me, my name is Veronica . . .'

But before she could finish, the woman interrupted her. 'Oh, that's a shame, I think he's just gone . . . Joe,' she addressed a man standing close by. 'Ben's gone, hasn't he?'

The man called Joe chuckled. 'Gone in every sense, I'd say Emma. In my opinion, he should never have tried that twist with Mrs Tucker; it fair finished him off. She's a goer and no mistake.'

Veronica felt quite light-headed.

'Let me get you a drink, at least,' said the woman. 'I'm Emma Knight, by the way. What would you like?'

'White wine, thank you,' Veronica managed to croak. She was devastated. Not only was he not waiting for her, not only had she just missed him, but he had been dancing with . . . with a Tucker! How she loathed that bloody family. If she had her way, they'd be wiped off the map. And now Mother Tucker had got her paws on something that was, by every right, hers: Ben Dacres. She was the one he'd invited, she was the one he wanted to dance with and the wretched Tucker woman had driven him away.

Her mind was a maelstrom of envy, disappointment and anger. Casting her eyes around the room, willing Ben to materialise and claim her, her gaze was arrested by the familiar figure of a tall dark youth. Shocked, she stared and stared, not believing the evidence of her eyes.

It was her son. It was Anthony. What was he doing here?

In close conversation with a slight, pretty, blonde creature; as she watched, he bent down and kissed the girl.

At that moment, Emma reappeared with Veronica's wine.

Veronica clutched her arm. 'Tell me,' she asked hoarsely, 'Who's that blonde girl, over there?'

Emma looked surprised. 'That's Alison. Are you not from these parts? I assumed everyone from the village knew Alison Tucker.'

45

'I could have danced all night, I could have danced all night, and still have asked for more . . .' Jenny sang as she burned the toast, still bubbling with the pleasure of the previous evening.

It was a sullen morning, the rain so heavy it was hard to tell through the window whether it was day or night. Nobody else was about, but that was not unusual. Stephen, having milked the cows and washed down the dairy, would be in for his breakfast shortly; Charlie, his dog, Duchess, with him, was probably out early with the film crew; Alison would come down when she was called, as would Al who was sleeping on the sofa in the sitting room; and Angela, who Jenny assumed was asleep in the top room, would be down as soon as she woke.

'I must go and see how Ron is this morning,' she thought, abandoning the grill and sploshing a bit

251

more milk onto the porridge, bubbling stiffly on top of the stove. 'Now why does this porridge always go lumpy?'

The kitchen door opened and Gip, followed by Stephen, brought in the damp air and mud.

'Here, Gip, here,' Jenny produced the dog's towel and proceeded to rub her down while Stephen stripped off his dripping waterproofs,

'What a wet old morning,' she said cheerily. 'Do you want to call Angela down, dear? Tell her breakfast is ready. It's lucky she doesn't have to go into the library this morning, she'd be very late . . . She deserves a lie in; it's a pity you couldn't have one yourself . . . What a lovely party it was, wasn't it? When did you leave? I looked round for you, but you'd gone. Did you enjoy yourselves? I don't think I've ever danced so much in all my life. There you are, Gip, nice and dry. Cup of tea, dear?'

'Ta.'

There was something about the monosyllabic response that caused Jenny to turn and look at her younger son. He was sitting, slumped in the old wooden carver, staring at his feet encased in the thick woolly socks she knitted for him; his hair was matted with wind and rain and his face was shiny with the wet.

'Stephen?'

'What?'

'Is something the matter, love?'

He looked up at her; his eyes were swollen and red with crying and he was crying still.

She couldn't bear it and going to him, cradled his head in her arms. 'Oh Stephen, what is it, my baby?'

She couldn't have done that to Charlie or Alison—they would have pushed her away and held

252

their hurt to themselves, but Stephen was like her: simple and straightforward with his emotions. He clung to her and wept.

'What is it, love? What is it?' She gently stroked his head.

A pall of acrid blue smoke rose from the grill. 'Oh no, it's the toast!' She rushed to blow out the flames licking over the charred black surface of the bread.

As he watched his mother, Stephen's sobs subsided and he gazed at her, completely forlorn. 'It's me and Ange, Mum. I think . . . I think it's over.'

'Oh no?' Jenny was so shocked she dropped the grill pan with a loud clatter, sending the burnt toast skidding across the floor. 'What d'ye mean Stephen—it's over? Not you and Angela? That's just not possible.'

'It is, and it's my fault,' replied Stephen, wretched. 'It's all my fault.'

'Why what did you do that was so awful? Little Angela is devoted to you—anyone can see that?'

'I let her down, Mum. I bumped into Nicola . . . you remember Nicola, don't you? I had a real crush on her, for ages, but loving Ange has changed all that, you know that.'

'And so does Angela. So what did you do with Nicola that upset Angela so?'

'For a start, I didn't tell her I'd seen Nicola or that I'd showed her round the farm.'

'But that's hardly a reason for Angela to break off your engagement is it, Stephen? There must be more to it than that?'

Stephen went red and hung his head. 'It was because of the Merlin Players, Mum. Mrs Pagett

253

wanted me to ask Mrs Merfield if they could use the gardens of the manor to stage a Shakespeare this summer . . .'

Jenny was puzzled. 'But what's that to do with Nicola?'

'I told her that's what we was going to do and she laughed and said I had to stop them, they'd make fools of themselves, and she was right, I knew she was right . . . we can't do that sort of stuff. So I . . . so I went and told Mrs Merfield that I wanted her to not let them. But I know Ange really wanted to, so I didn't tell her what I'd done, but then Nicola did, last night at the party. And Ange thinks I did it because of Nicola, which isn't true, Mum, but Ange was so upset, she went off and said I wasn't to contact her. It was awful!' And with a loud groan he slumped against the table, his head on his hands, gazing in despair at his mother. 'What shall I do, Mum? What shall I do?'

'Oh dear, Stephen,' Jenny shook her head. 'I'm not sure I followed all that but it does seem a terrible muddle. It'll be all right, though, just you wait and see. Angela knows she's the important one, not Nicola. Let's have a nice cup of tea and see if we can't think of a way to sort this out. Come on dear, cheer up. I'm sure it's not as bad as you think.'

'It is, Mum,' mourned Stephen. 'It is. Everything's gone wrong between Ange and me since that bloody television bunch came here. If they hadn't come, Nicola wouldn't have been here. They're wrecking my life.'

*   *   *

Cold, drenching rain slanted across the valley,

254

battering man and beast alike. Charlie, hunched inside his old waterproofs, stared at the massive head of the Highland bull; the raindrops were dripping off the tips of the bull's horns and his rough red coat was soaked. The bull, arrested in the process of munching hay, stared impassively back.

'You're not bothered by this weather, are you old fellow?' Charlie said softly. 'You're not bothered by anything—you've got your woman, you've got your kid, no worries; life's a bundle of hay as far as you're concerned.'

He sighed and whistling to Duchess, resumed his trudge along the track with her dancing at his heels. Having established he was not immediately needed by the film crew, he'd set out to rescue his van. A car came up behind him and hooted. He turned.

It was his gran.

He ran back and opened the car door. 'You're out early, Gran. Where're you off to? Can I cadge a lift to The Foresters?'

'Get in, Charlie—try not to make my car any wetter than you have to, and spread out that newspaper for Duchess on the back seat, for goodness sake; she's filthy,' replied Elsie, more testy than usual.

He did as he was told, then clambered in. As they set off up the track, he repeated his question. 'Where are you headed this early, Gran?'

Elsie, preoccupied with trying to see through a windscreen completely obscured by the rain, didn't reply.

Charlie looked at her curiously. 'Gran?'

Her reply was curt. 'It's none of your business, but if you must know, I'm going to the hospital, in Bath. Ron was taken ill last night.'

255

'Gran!' Charlie was shocked. 'I didn't know. What happened? What's wrong? Have you told Mum?'

'Of course I haven't. What good would that do? She'd wring her hands and get upset and I'd have to sort her out as well. She means well, but she's a fool.'

Charlie held his tongue.

'Ron's not been well for a little while,' Elsie continued in more measured tones. 'I've tried to get him to the doctor, but he's so stubborn . . . Said it was a touch of indigestion. Last night the pain got so bad, he could hardly breathe. I thought it might be appendicitis and called the ambulance.'

'You didn't think to come and get one of us?' Charlie said gently.

'You were all at that party. There didn't seem any point in ruining your fun. I was with him—I was all he needed.'

'But you, perhaps you could have done with one of us to be with you.'

'Hmm.' It was a noncommittal grunt. 'I've buried a husband and a son, Charlie. I can cope.'

'Maybe. But what did the doctors say? Is it appendicitis?'

'Almost certainly not, though they hedge their bets, these medics. He's seeing a specialist today and they plan to run tests on him. What sort of test, I don't know, I just hope . . .' Her iron control cracked, just a fraction, and it took a few moments before she allowed herself to continue. 'Poor fellow—he's spent the night on one of those hospital trolleys, in an observation ward, they called it.'

'That's awful, Gran. A man of Ron's age—surely

they could have found him a proper bed?'

'It's they way they do things. He'll get a bed when he's put on a ward, that's what the nurse told me when I said the same thing. Anyway, Charlie, that's where I'm headed.' Attempting a lighter tone, she changed the subject. 'What are you up to today? Spending a bit of time with Isabelle and the girls, I hope?'

Although very much like his grandmother in many ways, Charlie did not possess her degree of self-control. His face dulled. 'Erm, no. Probably not.'

Elsie gave him a sharp glance. 'Why on earth not? She's a nice girl, is Isabelle. You don't want to take her for granted, Charlie. There are plenty of other fish in the sea and if you don't look after her . . .'

'I know, Gran, I know.' Charlie replied, miserably. 'You don't have to tell me. Drop me off here, please. Look, we'll talk about it another time. Will you phone me from the hospital?'

'Whatever for?'

'You can tell me how Ron is for a start. Honestly, Gran, we're all in this together, whether you like it or not. You can't go it alone and Ron wouldn't want you to.' He scribbled a number on a piece of paper. 'This is my mobile. I'll keep it on and you can phone me as soon as you get a chance. If you don't, I shall come to that hospital and hunt you down.'

Elsie favoured him with a faint smile. 'I used to despair of you, Charlie Tucker, but you've turned out not so bad. Now be off with you and make sure you go and see that girl of yours.'

'Oh, if only it were that easy,' thought Charlie,

257

watching his Gran drive on up the hill out of the village.

Apart from a scribbled note on the windscreen from the landlord of The Foresters Arms demanding the removal of the vehicle, the van was in exactly the same sorry state as he'd left it the night before. Checking the flattened tyres, he gave a long angry whistle. 'I don't fucking believe it. Who the fuck would play such a trick? The bastards, the fucking bastards!'

Firmly wedged into the valve of each of the front tyres was a matchstick.

46

Veronica was in such a disagreeable mood over breakfast, neither Hugh nor Cordelia lingered.

Cordelia fled, thankful, for once, to return to her school books; and Hugh, faced with the teeming rain, abandoned his customary ride and shut himself in his study with papers, plans, and accounts, leaving Veronica to vent her ill-humour on the cleaner. Having nearly driven that unfortunate person to tender her resignation, Veronica removed herself to the sitting room and sat, brooding, over a pile of glossy magazines.

What was it that concerned her the most? Just missing Ben by a hair's breadth? That was so unlucky she could spit. Hearing that he'd danced with that Tucker woman? She'd no idea what she looked like, they didn't move in the same circles for one thing, but the fact that a member of that family had the gall to take her place in Ben's arms rankled badly. Or was it seeing her son kissing the Tucker girl? No, worse than that, to be told they were going out with each other? If *that* was the state of play, any reconciliation with her son wouldn't, couldn't, be entertained.

They'd taken their eye off the ball, she and Hugh, as far as the Tuckers were concerned. Well, no longer. Somehow, she'd get back at them and Hugh would help her do it; she'd get them out of Marsh Farm, and nothing would stop her . . .

Her lips curled. When he found his girlfriend living in a council house, would Anthony find her such an attractive proposition? She doubted it. However much he might fight it, he was a Lester.

And as for Ben . . . she could forgive him. After all, he'd have had no idea who he was dancing with. It was simply because she had left it so late to get there . . . Get him on the tennis court; get him to come to this party she was planning, that would put her back on track.

In a better humour, she scribbled him a note apologising for having missed him at the party and suggesting a rendezvous. Addressing the envelope, she tossed it on one side to post later, returned to the kitchen, where she collected some coffee, and then went and tapped on the closed study door.

'Hugh, darling,' she sounded penitent, 'I am sorry I was in such a pig of a mood this morning. I've brought you some coffee.' She placed the cup on his desk and ruffled his hair. 'Will you forgive me?'

He frowned. 'If it wasn't for the fact I know why you were in such a foul mood, I'd have initiated divorce proceedings.'

She experienced a momentary frisson of fear.

'You do?'

'Of course, and I told Cordelia as much. It was damned unfair you had to cut short your evening to bring her back home. She was lucky she didn't have me collecting her, that's all I can say.'

'Yes, quite; but something else really upset me, darling. As we were passing the Foresters Arms, I saw Anthony. It was definitely him, Hugh, and he was kissing a girl.' Her face twisted with disgust. 'That's why he's been seen in Summerstoke; it turns out he's dating the Tucker girl.'

'What?' Hugh's explosive reaction was music to Veronica's ears. 'The little runt, the bastard; he's making a mockery of us, Vee. Why else would he . . . in bed with the Tuckers, eh? The shit, he'll live to regret it, I'll make sure of that. I'll ruin them. I'll see them chucked off that miserable farm of theirs . . .'

'So how are we going to achieve that?' enquired Veronica. 'We've not had much success so far. And now that TV company is pumping money into their farm . . . and, so I hear, they're opening the place as a rare breeds centre. They're not going to be so easy to break, Hugh.'

Hugh brooded. 'Money is always at the root of everything. That's got to be the way in . . . But also,' he suddenly brightened. 'We can strike at their jugular. Stupid, I should have acted straight away . . .'

'What have you in mind, darling?' Veronica almost purred. Hugh had absolutely no scruples in getting what he wanted; all she had to do was convince him that they wanted the same things. Slightly more difficult, she thought wryly, in the case of Ben Dacres.

'Their dairy herd. You know they rely on the Merfield land this side of the river? It's always been a contentious issue, the herd coming through twice a day. So far tradition has won out over the whingers, but yesterday I drove into the village just as that damn fool film crew were filming the herd. In the middle of the afternoon—I ask you! The cows went ape-shit, causing a heck of a lot of damage. So now is the time to strike. Complaints to the district council, health and safety . . . the lot.'

Veronica cocked her head. 'Don't tell me you're going to activate the whingers? You probably despise them more than anyone else in the village.'

'Yes, I do, and they know it, so you're going to find us a rabble-rouser, Vee. I'll put in the first complaint, but I'm sure you've contacts. One or two local faces seem to feature quite regularly at our parties.'

'So saying we're successful and Marsh Farm haven't enough viable dairy pasture . . . ? They still have the film crew and they will still open the farm to rare breeds.'

'The film crew I leave to you. Surely it's not beyond your powers of persuasion to make them see whatever they're doing on that bog of a farm, they can do in considerably more comfort up here. The ideal thing, Vee,' his face grew cunning, 'would be to infiltrate a saboteur.'

Veronica laughed. 'Hugh, be realistic! This is beginning to sound like a second-rate movie.'

'Okay . . . but we need to somehow engineer a rift between film and farm. Think about it, Vee.' He gave a short laugh. 'If they lose the herd and the filming, I can't see the rare breeds thingy having much of a life, and that would be quite easy to

261

sabotage at a distance. Endless complaints to health and safety, rumours of E-coli etc etera and they'd soon lose heart.'

Leaving Hugh phoning a local councillor who 'owed him', Veronica returned to the sitting room, deep in thought; a number of things he'd said had resonated.

Sally Green! Yes, Sally Green could be relied on to stir up discontent about the cows. Not only that but . . . Veronica frowned, trying to remember a recent conversation . . . That's right, Sally Green had rabbited on about some rift between the Tucker brothers. Maybe that could be exploited . . . through that fiancée, perhaps.

As for persuading the film unit to move, that, she suspected, wouldn't be so easy, but she wasn't daunted. The drinks party would be a golden opportunity to plant the seed, and if she could get Ben eating out of her hand . . .

47

Emma had woken early on Saturday morning with a thick head and a mind buzzing with endless replays of her last conversation with Marcus. Upon reflection it might have been more circumspect to have held her tongue—he was her boss after all and could easily replace her—but she wasn't sorry for what she'd said.

He hadn't come near her for the rest of the evening and when they had all finally gone their separate ways and she'd said 'goodnight', he'd barely acknowledged her.

Emma was glad they'd decided to work on Saturday; at least she was fully occupied, with no time to reflect too closely on the possible fallout from that confrontation. She didn't expect to see him on set; they were picking up a number of small scenes featuring Harry Hobbs, the feeling being among the directors that if these scenes were in the can, Harry could be released from the set for a couple of weeks. Everyone saw this as an advantage, even the senior actors who'd had to sacrifice part of their weekend.

This plan had already fallen foul of the weather. A dawn sequence on the banks of the River Summer was ruled out by unrelenting rain, so they retired to the set in the barn. Here the sound recordist huffed and puffed, the drumming of the rain on the tin roof of the barn penetrating his sensitive antennae.

'I ask you, a tin roof, why was that not taken into consideration?' he grumbled to Colin, waiting patiently by his camera. 'Didn't it occur to anyone we might have these problems? What's the point of building a studio if it's not soundproof? Sloppy, I call it ...'

He was finally persuaded the problem could be overcome by close miking, but the morning's start had been delayed still further.

Emma felt her mood sink. Perhaps it would be a good get–out if Marcus replaced her. Certainly there'd been very little fun in this project so far and although she had already made a number of friends, as the director at the top of the pile, she had no allies.

The first scene, between Jilly and Harry, passed off smoothly. For all his precocity, Harry on set worked well and Jilly was terrific.

'One down, two to go,' sang out Matt. 'Coffee break, everyone, while we re-rig.'

Jason and Juliet were needed for the next scene, and Emma gave a weary sigh hearing the bantering tones of Jason Hart as he entered the barn with Juliet.

'Feeling a bit peaky this morning are we, Jools? You should have done a bit of dancing; nothing like a good jig to shift the alcohol. Morning, Matt, Emma. What delightfully unfunny piece of rubbish are we wasting our time with today?'

'Haven't you got your script, Jason?' Emma asked him with impatience. 'The re-writes were distributed last night.'

'Last night? I never saw them . . .'

Matt intervened briskly. 'They would have been delivered to your room, Jason. We expect you at least to read them through before you come on set—ideally, you should learn them. That's what most actors would expect to do.'

'But then,' came the riposte, 'as you are all continually at pains to point out, I'm no actor.'

'Look, he can borrow mine,' said Juliet. 'He's not got too much to say in this one and I pretty well know it.'

'Thanks, Juliet.' Emma glanced at her and felt concern: in spite of her makeup, Juliet did look very pale. 'In the meantime, Matt, would you arrange for another set to be sent over, please. Juliet, are you feeling okay?'

Juliet nodded. 'Yes, sorry. I must have overdone it last night, although, honestly, I scarcely drank anything.'

'It must have been something you ate,' smirked

Jason.

'Right, let's get on with the rehearsal. Where's Harry?'

'I'm here, Emma.' Harry strolled onto the set. 'Just waiting around for something to happen, as usual.'

The three-handed scene took longer than it should have done, not helped by Jason's unfamiliarity with the script. Ross arrived with a spare set, but that did not help. Finally the exasperated production assistant scribbled his lines on a succession of Post-it notes, sticking them unobtrusively on different parts of the furniture. By the time they had finished, Ben, made up and ready for his scene, was waiting in the wings.

'Okay, let's get moving,' shouted Matt when the all clear from Colin had been given. 'We'll take a late lunch. Clear the . . .' but he got no further.

From outside the barn there came a loud shriek, followed by shouts of 'No, you can't go in there . . . shoo . . . shoo! He-elp . . . someone, he-elp!'

A burly electrician, standing close to the barn entrance turned to see what was causing the disturbance and froze, croaking, 'Bloody Norah!'

And Juliet, who'd been making for the door to get some fresh air, screamed and fainted on the spot.

'What on earth's going on?' shouted Matt and strode over to investigate the cause of the disturbance. He, too, stopped dead, the colour draining from his face.

'What is it, what is it?' shouted Ben in a complete funk. 'Not more bloody cows; my nerves won't stand it.'

Emma, about to go to Juliet, also froze, as did

the entire crew who could do nothing but stand and look on with fascinated horror as, completely oblivious to the panic in the yard and the effect they were having on the occupants of the building, two huge pigs, their eyes bright and curious, pushed their way through the open door.

Snuffling and grunting, they moved purposefully in clearly intending to inspect the contents of the barn for anything edible.

Fortunately for Juliet they displayed not the slightest interest in her inert body and ambled their way onto the set. With a banshee-like shriek, Ben bolted through the kitchen-set door, slamming it shut behind him.

The noise attracted the larger of the two pigs, an enormous pink, almost hairless, beast with a disturbing grin on its face, who wandered over to sniff at the door. The other, black and hairy, with a white band around its shoulders, placidly snuffled around the floor of the studio.

'Get them out of here,' squeaked Emma. 'Now!'

Matt pulled himself together. 'We can't deal with those beasts!'

The black pig turned and looked at him, nose in the air, sniffing.

'Christ, look at those jaws!' he gulped. 'Everyone, out of the building, now! Chris, go to the farmhouse and see if there's anyone there. We need help right away!'

His crew need no urging. As one they fled, skirting fearfully around the beasts and scooping Juliet up on their way out.

With trembling fingers, Matt rang Charlie. 'Your pigs—they're here . . . Here in the barn, on our set . . . I don't know what the fuck they're doing here,

Charlie, just get here right away. I want them off this set, now! What? You what . . . ? Bloody hell, I'll get Ross to send someone to pick you up. You'd better hope they don't do too much damage in the meantime . . . No, for fuck's sake, we won't frighten them . . .'

Alison, followed by Jenny, ran into the barn and stopped aghast at the sight of the animals. 'What on earth are they doing here?'

'That's a good question.' Matt was grim. 'And I want them out. What are you doing?' For Alison had produced a camera and was proceeding to take pictures of the two pigs on the set.

She grinned at him. 'A good photo-opportunity, don't you think? It will be brill for our website. Have you sent for Charlie? I'm not sure how much I can do.'

'Can't you and your mother get them out of here?'

Jenny looked at him with alarm. 'Er . . .'

'It's no use asking her,' said Alison cheerfully. 'She's useless with animals.'

'Help,' came a thin, trembling voice from behind the door against which the large pink was now meditatively banging its head. 'Help!'

'Its Ben,' cried Jenny. 'We've got to rescue him. Do something Alison.'

'I'll try.' Alison shrugged and thrust the camera into Matt's hands. 'Please Matt, it would be great if you could take some pictures for me.'

He stared at her in disbelief. 'I don't think you realise how serious this is, Alison. Get those fucking beasts out of here before they do any more damage.'

Alison shrugged and went over to the pink

267

monster and scratched her back. 'Clementine—what are you up to, you naughty girl? You won't find anything nice to eat in here . . .'

At the sound of the girl's voice, the pig stopped head-butting the door and turned to look at her. The black pig also turned and lumbered over.

'That's right Rebecca, it's me; and I've got something very nice for you, but you can't stay in here.' Alison produced a bag from inside her jacket.

The pigs, who easily came up to her waist, started to jostle and grunt, and holding the bag above her head, still talking to them in a soft, unhurried voice, Alison slowly moved with them towards the barn door.

Matt and Jenny watched their progress in tense silence.

'Help,' came the feeble cry again.

Jenny rushed to the door. 'It's alright, Ben dear, it's quite safe to come out now.'

Ben almost fell through the door into her arms. 'My angel,' he cried. 'You've saved my life!'

Jenny was enormously gratified, but honesty prevailed. 'No, Ben, don't be daft, you was in no danger. I doubt the pigs would have done you any real harm, nasty big beasts though they be.'

'I have heard,' said Ben stiffly, detaching himself from her embrace, 'pigs have a terrible bite and people can lose limbs, or worse . . .'

To Alison's great relief, because she didn't think she'd manage to coax the two pigs all the way back across the yard and into their pen unaided, Charlie arrived in one of the film unit's cars.

When the two pigs were finally safely secured, Alison and Charlie walked slowly back to the set.

'Thanks Ali, you did a good job. Clementine

and Rebecca seem none the worse for their little adventure. My God, when I think they've only got about a week to go before they farrow . . . it could have been disastrous!'

'How could they have got out, Charlie?'

'Search me. Pigs, as far as I know, haven't yet mastered the art of pulling back gate bolts.' Charlie had a set, grim expression on his face. 'If it's somebody's idea of a joke, like letting the air out of my tyres, then the sooner we find out who the comedian is the better, before there's any real damage.'

'What do you mean, letting the air out of your tyres?'

'Last night at the party, the two front tyres on my van had been deflated, Ali, with the aid of matchsticks. I'd thought I'd been unlucky and had a couple of flats, but no, some bastard had stuck matches in the valves.'

'That's just rotten.' Alison frowned. 'There've been rather a lot of accidents since the filming started, haven't there?'

'Have there?'

'Yes. I know the cow thing yesterday was Hugh Lester's fault, but before that there was that set collapsing, and before that, remember, the ram escaped from his field. I told you there was no sign of any holes and the gate was open, so you and Stephen assumed Lenny hadn't shut it properly.'

'I didn't. It was Stephen who blamed Lenny.'

'There you are then, four inexplicable accidents in less than a week.'

Charlie frowned. 'Four's too many for coincidence. It may mean nothing, but,' he pushed his hand into the pocket of his overalls, 'I found this

269

trodden into the mud under the front axle of the van.'

'This" was a yellow plastic key tag printed with a number 12.

'Charlie, Alison.' Emma crossed the yard to meet them. 'How are your pigs?'

'None the worse for their outing, thanks Emma; which is a relief since they are both due to farrow next week.'

'Farrow?'

'Give birth to lots of wriggly, noisy piglets, Emma,' Alison explained. 'They're going to be our first and we're hoping they'll be a real draw when the rare breeds opens.'

'How are things in the barn, Emma?'

'As you might imagine, Charlie: they made a bit of mess, but I think it's pretty much cleared up by now. Gave everyone a nasty fright, of course, and put the kibosh on the rest of the morning's filming. We're going to have to stretch our schedule somehow, next week, to make up for it.' Emma hesitated. 'The thing is, Charlie, Matt is on the warpath and, yet again, I find myself in the unenviable position of having to explain the delay to Marcus. I promised him there would be no further incidents, and now . . . Are you able to shed any light on how those pigs got out?'

'No, I am not, Emma.' Charlie couldn't keep the note of anger out of his voice. 'Those two sows are valuable creatures and we take the greatest care of them. Someone unbolted the gate to their pen.'

'You think it was one of us?' Emma demanded.

Charlie shrugged. 'What else am I to think?'

'I think you should tell Emma what we've just been talking about, Charlie,' chipped in Alison.

270

'What's that?'

'Oh, Alison pointed out that this is not the first "inexplicable accident".'

'No,' said Alison, 'it's the fourth in less than a week.'

'The fourth?' Emma was startled.

'Yes,' continued Alison. 'On Wednesday we had a runaway prize ram—his gate was unfastened; on Thursday that bit of your scenery collapsed—as I understand it, the pin had been pulled out of the door hinge; last night someone let down the tyres on Charlie's van, and now, this. Someone's having some fun at our expense, if you ask me.'

'And you think it might be someone in my unit?'

'I don't know.' Charlie shook his head. 'I don't have any other explanation. Alison's right—it's all too much to be a coincidence. It's like someone is targeting the farm.'

'Or the filming,' Emma frowned, 'and the awful thing is, I can think of who it might be.'

'Who?

Both Alison and Charlie stared at her, but Emma shook her head and blushed. 'No, I've said too much. It's very unfair of me. I've no evidence at all . . .'

'And all we've got is this.' Charlie showed her the tag.

Emma examined it closely and shrugged. 'It's a key tag of some sort, isn't it? Where did you find it?'

'On the ground, underneath my van . . . could have nothing to do with anything. We need to put our heads together and draw up a list of possible suspects.' Charlie looked grim. 'I want this lunatic stopped before anything else happens.'

271

'Don't you think we should tell Marcus of our suspicions?' asked Alison.

'No!'

Both Charlie and Emma spoke in unison and so decisively, Alison was taken aback. 'Oh. All right, only I thought he should be involved . . .'

'Not yet, Alison, not till we have more concrete evidence.' Emma was firm. 'I've already suggested to him that this . . . this particular person is a problem and he was completely dismissive. No, I think we'll keep it to ourselves for the moment.

48

Sally Green was surprised and flattered to be rung and invited by Veronica to lunch at the Country Club.

'Do you know, Vee, I've never eaten here before. Philip has, but he says it's very pricey and the food isn't as good as it should be . . .'

'It suits me, but if you rather go somewhere else?' Veronica drawled, bored already by her companion. She had chosen the Country Club because she knew Sally ached to be admitted to the sanctum and, more particularly, she hoped she might bump into Ben.

'No, no, this is lovely. Thank you so much for inviting me. I don't know how on earth I'm going to choose. Everything on this menu looks so delicious . . .'

Finally she settled on lobster mousse followed by fillet steak. Veronica ordered a green salad and a plain omelette.

Sally was flustered, 'Oh dear, is that all you're having? I seem so greedy—perhaps I should change my order. Waiter, I'll have the same as Mrs Lester ...'

'No, no,' Veronica intervened. 'You must have what you'd like. I eat here a lot, so the menu holds no surprises for me.' She looked up at the waiter, 'So Jacques, lobster and steak it is for my friend, and a bottle of Gabbiano pinot grigio. Thank you.'

During the course of the meal, Veronica made sure Sally's glass was never empty and listened, with apparent interest, to the small town talk that flowed from her companion's dull mind and limited interests.

Sally's colour was high, her laugh was becoming loud and prolonged and she was beginning to repeat herself, when Veronica decided it was time to start probing.

'Have you seen that fiancée of Stephen Tucker's again?'

'No, no I haven't. I did say I would drop in on her the next time I went to the library.'

'You should. It would be interesting to find out how things are between the two brothers and whether they have sorted out their difficulties.'

'Yes, yes it would. I'll pop in on Monday ...'

'I seem to recall, Sally, you suggested she and her fiancée should buy the brother out. Seems eminently sensible to me ... The farm's too small to have two bosses.'

'Yes,' Sally preened herself, 'I'm glad you agree with me, Vee. Though I suspect they'd find it hard to come up with the funds ...'

'There's always a way,' Veronica replied with a casual shrug. 'They could find someone prepared to

273

act as a sleeping partner, for example . . . you know, put up the money, but take no part in running the business.'

'Goodness,' Sally laughed loudly, for no good reason that Veronica could see, 'are there such people?'

'Oh yes. It could be a good investment; a lot of city people are interested in investing in land these days. One could put capital into the farm, agree a rate of interest and when the farm is sold . . . I mean, when the farm is making a good profit, the capital plus the interest can be paid off. More wine?'

'Goodness me, no, I've drunk far too much already.' Sally looked at the empty bottle with dismay, causing Veronica, who had confined herself to one glass, to smile inwardly.

Sally's flush deepened. 'Oh dear, how am I going to get home? I'll have to leave my car here; I can't take the risk . . . Philip would kill me if I got stopped.'

'Well you can either take a taxi, or I can give you a lift,' said Veronica, enjoying Sally's discomfiture. 'I wasn't planning to go back to Summerstoke right away, but it's not a problem . . .'

By the time Sally Green had got into Veronica's red Porsche, she was so overcome with gratitude she was prepared to do more or less anything Veronica might ask of her.

'You know,' Veronica kept her voice cool, disinterested. 'You might pass on the idea of a sleeping partner to your little friend. But Sally, you really must promise me, solemnly, not ever to mention my name . . .'

'Oh yes, Vee, no of course I won't, I promise.'

'Thing is, Sally, I've got access to that sort of capital. I don't need the income from it at the moment—we've got plenty—so it would be nice to be able to invest it in a business in our own village.'

But even Sally Green knew there was no love lost between the Lesters and the Tuckers and she stared at Veronica, a look of confusion on her face. 'Why would you want to help the Tuckers? You don't like them?'

'No,' replied Veronica evenly, 'but I am going to tell you something in complete confidence. Can I trust you?'

'Yes Vee, yes, you can.' Sally's eyes popped with excited curiosity.

'My son, Anthony is going out with the Tucker girl. In fact, he appears to be infatuated with her. Unfortunately he and I haven't seen eye to eye recently, and I want him to appreciate I'm not the ogre he thinks I am. If the Tuckers knew it was Lester money bailing them out, they would reject it out of hand. But I want to be reconciled with my son, Sally. What mother wouldn't? So if I can help the Tuckers . . .'

49

Lunch at Marsh Farm was a subdued affair, overshadowed as it was by the news about Ron, no Angela to cook for them, Stephen barely able to respond in anything but monosyllables, and Charlie preoccupied.

'Perhaps I should go and see Ron, this afternoon.' Jenny gathered the plates, sadly

275

surveying the remains. 'Do you want to come with me, Alison? We could catch the bus. It'd give your Gran a break. I could take in the rest of this pie. None of you have eaten very much and you hear terrible stories about the food in the hospital. I expect Ron could do with something nice to eat.'

'I think if Ron is having lots of tests today, Mum, we should wait till Gran says he's ready for visitors,' replied Alison. 'I'll come with you as soon as she says it's okay, and, anyway, I've got to get on with my biology essay this afternoon. I want to go to the cinema with Al this evening, but I need to finish my essay before I can even think about it.'

'Perhaps you're right; we'd better wait to hear from her first.' She looked at her two silent sons. 'I've made some apple crumble for pudding, boys. It's your favourite, Stephen. Are you going to have some?'

Stephen barely grunted in reply. Jenny sighed and served him a handsome portion.

Alison was exasperated. 'I don't know what's got into you, Stephen, but you've been a right misery guts this week.'

Not looking up from at his pudding, Stephen growled, 'Shut it, Alison.'

'I don't see why I should. I just don't know what you've got to be so miserable about. I know you don't like the film crew here, but . . .'

'You're too damn right I don't,' Stephen burst out. 'They're ruining everything. I wish they'd never come. I wish we'd never accepted their filthy money. In fact, do you know what I think? I think we should pay it all back and tell them to clear off out of here!'

'Don't be so bloody stupid,' snarled Charlie,

coming to life. 'I don't see what you've got to gripe about . . .'

'Oh don't you? Don't you?' Stephen leapt to his feet, red in the face. 'My cows, for starters. That bloody fiasco yesterday could have . . .'

'Cost us our dairy herd. I know, I know—but it didn't, did it? And that wasn't the fault of the film crew and they spent half the evening clearing up the mess, and so did I, I might point out, while you were living it up at a party being given by them.'

'Living it up—that's rich, you don't know the first of it!' Stephen was almost beside himself. 'Well let me tell you, Charlie, there'd better be no more accidents with my animals or . . . or . . .'

'Yeah, or what, Stephen?' Charlie sneered.

'I'll call the whole thing off.'

'You can't do that.' Charlie got to his feet and glared at his brother.

'Oh yes I can, you just watch me.'

'But we're partners, in case you've forgotten. We're in this together—the farm, the filming and the rare breeds.'

'Well maybe,' Stephen thumped the table, 'maybe that's something else we should call off an' all . . .'

'Stop it, just stop it you two. This is bloody stupid!' yelled Alison, a mixture of fury and fright.

'You're too right, it is, bloody stupid, and I'm not staying to take any more of his shit!' retorted Charlie and turning abruptly, made to leave. Unfortunately his heel landed on a piece of burnt toast that had lain on the floor, unnoticed since breakfast, and he went skidding across the kitchen, ending up on his back at the foot of the Rayburn.

'Yah—stupid, stupid—who looks stupid now?'

277

Stephen jeered.

Furious, Charlie got to his feet. His eyes fell on the dish of crumble on the stove; not hesitating, he scooped up a handful and hurled it at Stephen's face.

'You bastard, you fucking bastard!' yelled Stephen and spooning a large portion from his bowl, threw it at Charlie, who then retaliated with another handful.

Alison and Jenny looked on horrified as the crumble battle raged until there was no more left, and both the men and the kitchen were dripping in the slimy mess. There was a moment of complete silence then Jenny sat down and began to weep.

At once both brothers started guiltily towards her but they were stopped by Alison. 'Leave her alone. You're bastards, both of you. I'm going to take Mum into the sitting room and you can bloody well clear this mess up and make her a cup of tea.'

Alison returned to the kitchen a while later to confront her brothers only to find the kitchen clean but empty. Frustrated, she was about to leave when she heard a tap on the kitchen door.

'Come in,' she called out, puzzled. Few people ever knocked on their kitchen door. 'It's open.'

Jason Hart pocked his head round the door. 'Now there's a bit of luck: just the person I was hoping to see.'

'Oh?' Alison inwardly cursed. Jason had given her no reason to mistrust him, but she didn't feel safe in his company and she suspected if he had come to help her with the website, it was not going to be quick. It was a shame, she reflected, he'd come over after Al had gone back to Bath.

Jason, who'd watched Al's motorbike depart, was

well satisfied. 'Yeah, what better way to spend a rainy Saturday afternoon playing compootahs? I'd said I'd help you—no time like the present.'

'I'd have thought you'd have gone back to London for the weekend?'

Jason shrugged. 'I was going to, but the schedule was changed and there seemed little point. I thought I'd hang around and see what gives here. What are you up to tonight?'

'It depends.'

'On what?'

'On whether I get a biology essay finished. I said to Al if I did, we'd go to the cinema.'

He stared at her. 'My, for a pretty chick, you've sure got a deadly routine worked out. When does fun enter your life?'

Alison flushed. 'I have plenty, thank you.'

'You must show me what you call fun, sometime—I might learn something. Now, where is this computer of yours? My fingertips are itchy.'

Alison hesitated; the computer was in her bedroom and she really didn't want to take him up there. With a bit of warning, she would have brought it downstairs, but if she insisted on doing that now, it would look pretty pathetic. She could put him off. After all, she did have this essay to write, but the website had to be done and it was only three weeks to the opening day. There was no help for it.

'It's upstairs, in my room.'

'In my lady's chamber? Well, well—what's that going to do for my powers of concentration?'

50

Stephen gulped back his tears. It was no good, he couldn't cry and attach milking clusters at the same time; the large soulful eyes of his ladies were reproachful as he fumbled with unusual clumsiness. He took a deep breath, wiped his nose on his sleeve and tried to settle into the rhythm of the milking process.

The squirting of the milk into the glass jars provided a regular, comforting, soundscape; the cows settled down, breathing heavily and munching their concentrates. He loved them dearly, these cows, and as he moved among them, his befuddled mind cleared. There were only two things in his life worth fighting over—his cows, and Angela. Even the rare breeds, much as he wanted them, were unimportant compared to these two loves.

The cows, for the moment, were safe. He'd seen the clean-up job in the village; no one, he felt, could validly complain. So what was he going to do to save Angela? Life without her was unthinkable. He'd really ballsed it up! Somehow . . . somehow he had to show her she could trust him . . . that it had been a momentary blip, that Nicola really meant nothing to him, that even over the Merlin Players he was prepared to back down . . . he would do whatever she wanted. But how? How?

He groaned. If only Gran was about to tell him what to do. All his life she'd been there for him, often an irritant, it was true, like one of those blasted horseflies. His mother gave him unconditional love, but at times of trouble, he needed the clear-sighted, critical thinking of his gran. If only Ron hadn't fallen ill . . . He toyed vaguely with the idea of going to seek her out in the hospital, but gave it up—he had too much to do and it would take too long to drive to Bath, find a parking space, then find her. Maybe he'd call on her when she got back . . .

But if Ron was really ill, would she want to be bothering with him? Probably not . . . he would have to sort himself out.

What would Gran suggest? The worst thing he'd done was to persuade the old ladies not to allow the Merlin Players to stage the play in their garden and not to tell Angela that's what he'd done. Supposing . . . supposing he went to them and persuaded them to change their minds?

At the thought of confronting them again, he broke into a sweat. It would be far worse this time because he'd have to explain about his own change of heart. Supposing they still said no? Or supposing they said yes and Angela still didn't want to know?

What he needed was someone who'd tell Angela what he was going through, how he was trying to make amends.

His Mum? No, Ange knew his Mum fought his battles, no matter what. But she was in awe of Gran, and Angela, Stephen knew, would listen to her; no one else would do. But Stephen squirmed at the prospect of having to explain what he had done.

However, the way he saw it, it was his only course of action, and doing something, however difficult, was enough to lift, if only a fraction, the gloomy shroud that had enveloped him since Angela left.

*　　*　　*

Having decided on his course of action, Stephen did not hang about. Apologising to his mum, who sat, waiting alone in the kitchen for someone, anyone, of her family to turn up for supper, he dashed up to the bathroom, washed, shaved, and changed without stopping, just in case any hesitation on his part would have a fatal effect on his resolution.

Shortly after six-thirty he nervously knocked on the front door of the Manor. He knew the Merfields, sticklers for time-keeping, had pre-dinner drinks at seven then sat down to dine at seven-thirty.

The door was opened by Nanny, who like the Merfield ladies whom she had served since time immemorial, was if not in her eighties, very nearly there. Like them, the decrepitudes of old age were not given cupboard space and although her tall, thin body was stooped and stiff and her hair iron grey, her eyes were alert and shrewd behind her specs, and her energy had the likes of Paula Spinks gaping with admiration.

Unlike the other ladies of the house, her dress was simple, practical, and never varied: a dark tweed skirt and cashmere sweater for the winter, a lighter tweed skirt and sweater for the summer, and sensible leather shoes, which squeaked loudly when she walked.

'Well, this is an unexpected surprise,' she said warmly. 'Come in . . . but you're by yourself. Where's young Angela?'

'Er . . . she's not here.'

'No, I can see that. What can I do for you, dear? I'm busy with cooking supper at the moment, but you're welcome to come and chat to me in the kitchen.'

'Well, as a matter of fact, it's Mrs Merfield I've come to see.' In spite of the cool evening, Stephen perspired freely.

Nanny gave him a sharp look. 'Oh?'

'Yes, the thing is, Nanny, I need to ask them if they'd consider changing their minds about allowing their garden to be used for this Shakespeare.'

'As I understand it,' she said severely, 'they said "no" because that's what you wanted.'

'Yes,' said Stephen miserably, hanging his head. 'But I've really upset Angela. She wants it to happen and who am I to say it shouldn't? She's so cross with me . . .' his voice faltered, 'I've got to try and make it up to her somehow. So I thought if I could get . . . well . . . persuade Mrs Merfield to agree . . .' His voice trailed away and he stood, feeling increasingly uncomfortable under Nanny's gaze.

'Come and wait in the kitchen,' she said, sounding brisk but not unsympathetic. 'I think it best if I prepare the ground a little. I'll find out whether the ladies have any real objection to the idea of your theatricals in the garden. If they don't, then you can put the situation to them and ask them to change their minds.'

Stephen trailed in her wake to the kitchen, which was full of appetising smells. His stomach rumbled its appreciation.

Nanny looked at him, a twinkle in her eyes. 'You've missed your tea to come here, no doubt. Help yourself to a beer from the pantry, and tuck into that loaf—it's fresh out of the oven—and there's a good piece of cheddar.'

283

She glanced at the kitchen clock. 'It's nearly seven o'clock; the ladies will be having their gin. You stay here and finish your drink; I'll go and talk to them.'

Stephen couldn't eat or drink anything. His stomach knotted, his throat went dry, he sweated; if they said no, he wouldn't have to face them, but he so wanted to put things right.

The kitchen clock ticked on, the pans on the old cream Aga hissed gently. It seemed as if the old lady had been gone for ages. He got up and walked around the kitchen. He sat down again. He tried to read the newspaper lying on the table, but his eyes slid over the newsprint without registering anything. Then he heard Nanny's squeaking footsteps in the passageway.

'Well?' he demanded before she was hardly through the door.

She looked at him with a glimmer of amusement. 'Well Stephen, they're not averse to the idea, but,' she said, with a certain relish in her voice, 'they want you to tell them why they should change their minds.'

'Oh.'

There was a world of feeling in that monosyllabic reply.

Nanny gave him a stern look. 'Mrs Merfield has suggested you go and join them for a drink before dinner. There's twenty minutes till I serve up, so you've plenty of time. Do you know the way?'

'No,' croaked Stephen, desperate at the thought of having to face the Merfields alone again.

'Then I'll show you. Come along,' she said bracingly. 'Don't be in such a funk. It'll be alright, you'll see.

He was so nervous his legs felt as if they didn't belong to him and he didn't know how he managed to walk all the way down the passageway to the hall and across the vast flagstoned floor to the small drawing room.

'Ah, Mr Tucker, do come in and have a seat.' Mrs Merfield sat by the fire, as she had done the last time he visited, dressed in magnificent black.

'Nanny tells me you drink beer,' murmured Charlotte, who was dressed in flame orange silk. 'I do hope this suits you.' She poured him a tumbler of amber liquid and passed it to him.

'Thank you, thank you very much.' He took the glass, and stared at it, thinking there was no way he could swallow anything.

'Twice in one week, Stephen Tucker,' tittered Louisa, strikingly attired in frothy green. 'We are lucky!'

'Now then, Mr Tucker, Nanny tells me that you've had a change of heart over this theatrical business. Perhaps you'd like to tell us why you think we should reconsider?'

Stephen's mouth opened, then shut. It was no good, he couldn't think how to begin. Then Angela's face was before him, tears rolling down her cheeks.

Taking a deep breath, he began. 'I'll be honest with you, Mrs Merfield. I haven't changed my mind. I don't think the Merlin Players should do something like this . . . but what do I know? I'm only the stage manager; I don't get up and do the acting stuff. They all want to do it and, well, if they think they can, why shouldn't they have a go? It's their twentieth anniversary this year, they want to do something special and Angela thinks doing this

Shakespeare at the Manor would be special, so who am I to put a damper on their fun? It was wrong of me to persuade you to say no and it was wrong of me not to tell Angela that's what I done. She's so cross with me, she don't want anything to do with me, and I don't blame her. So all I can do is ask you to let them have a go and to say sorry to put you to all this trouble.'

He ran out of breath and not being able to think of anything else sensible to say, he took a huge sip of his beer and waited for their response, a large white foaming moustache adorning his top lip.

'Thank you, Mr Tucker. You put that very well. We will discuss the matter over dinner and let you know our decision tomorrow morning. Will that be soon enough for you?'

It was a clear dismissal. Rapidly swallowing the last of his beer, he put the glass down and got to his feet 'Yes, thank you, Mrs Merfield, ladies. Thank you. Er . . . I'll wait to hear from you, then.'

Standing outside, in the cool damp air of the evening, his brain cleared and he stopped trembling. He'd done what he could.

'I just hope to God,' he thought, 'it's enough . . . Now, Gran . . .'

*   *   *

'Gran.'

At the sound of Charlie's voice and his touch on her shoulder, Elsie woke from the light doze into which she had fallen. Instinctively she looked first at Ron, who was lying on his back, snoring slightly. Reassured, she turned her attention to Charlie.

'Charlie, what are you doing here?'

'Well, Gran, I decided to hunt you down. A day spent here, worrying, could drive the strongest person bonkers. The nurse told me it was all right to come in. How's Ron?' He looked over at the inert figure, sleeping, apparently peacefully, and glanced around the room. It was a small ward with three other occupants and Ron's privacy was dependent on a curtain half-drawn round his bed.

Elsie looked at her grandson with a measure of relief she did her best to disguise. She'd spent the whole day at Ron's bedside, talking to him when he was awake, reading to him from her newspaper, and from the brochure that she'd brought from home about the Galapagos . . . anything to keep both their spirits up. He had been given painkillers and when he slipped into sleep, Elsie, weary with anxiety, had dozed herself. It had been a long day and so the sight of a familiar face was very welcome.

'It's nice of you to come, Charlie. You didn't have to, I can manage.'

'Yes, I know you can—no-one better—but I thought a bit of company wouldn't go amiss.' Charlie pulled up a spare chair. 'I'll leave whenever you want me to. So—how's Ron, Gran?'

'I think he's worn out with all the tests he's had today: scans, probes, blood tests . . . I can't think they've got anything left to look at.'

'And any results?'

To Charlie's consternation, Elsie's eyes suddenly watered and tears started to trace the wrinkles on her face.

He was alarmed and afraid, he'd never seen the fierce old lady cry before. 'Gran? What is it? Tell me.'

Elsie pulled out a handkerchief and vigorously blew her nose.

'I'm tired,' she said, looking at him reproachfully, then regaining her composure, she took Ron's limp hand in her own, 'Ron's got to have an operation, which at his time of life, as they say, is not very clever . . .'

'Oh Gran . . . What is it? What for?'

'They're going to do it on Monday, Charlie, a keyhole, whatever that is . . .'

'But what for, Gran? What for?'

'Gallstones. They want to remove his gall bladder, which, they tell us, is a redundant organ anyway.'

'So it's not . . .'

'No,' said Elsie, firmly. 'It's not. And we're most fortunate because they going to do it on Monday, so he should be home by the weekend.' Elsie gave a deep sigh. 'Which will be so wonderful. And then, when Ron is well and truly better, we're going to the Galapagos.'

Charlie, feeling weak with relief, laughed and shook his head. 'The Galapagos? Gran, you are truly amazing!'

'No I'm not; I make mistakes like everyone else. I put off marrying Ron for twenty-five years. That wasn't at all clever. And I've been sitting here for the better part of the day thinking I might lose him . . .' She stopped abruptly and fixed him with a fierce look, 'Life's too short to waste time, Charlie. It's a cliché, I know, but don't you make that mistake; you must grab happiness when it presents itself to you, not dither and doubt. Doubt is an emotional bindweed—it'll choke the life out of us if we let it.'

288

51

Tired as she was, Elsie's sleep was fitful that night and although she knew she would not be admitted to Ron's ward before ten o'clock, she abandoned her bed when dawn broke, dressed, made herself tea, then proceeded to give the cottage a vigorous cleaning.

As Ron became increasingly unwell, she had grown increasingly fearful and although the diagnosis had been a huge relief to both of them, her mind continued to run an endless marathon of 'what ifs'. A voice, calling out from the kitchen, interrupted her morbid reverie.

'Gran, Gran, are you there?'

It was Stephen's voice.

How unusual, she reflected, Stephen rarely sought her out, but when she entered her kitchen, it was obvious all was not well.

'My goodness me,' she thought, 'what's going on? First Charlie and now Stephen . . .'

He looked awkward, 'I've just come from the dairy, Gran. I heard last night Ron was taken bad. How is he?'

'Not at all well. But since the hospital hasn't phoned, I assume he's not taken a turn for the worse. He's got gallstones, so they are planning to remove his gall bladder. I'm going in as soon as I can.' She tried not to let her voice betray how difficult it was to talk about Ron. 'It's kind of you to ask, Stephen. Now, what can I do for you?'

He was taken aback. 'Why do you ask, Gran?'

'Because, Stephen,' she was crisp. 'I can read you

like a book. What's wrong? You've got a face as grey and damp as my dishcloth.'

'Oh Gran,' groaned Stephen, 'It's Ange—she's so mad with me—and it's all my fault. She says she won't see me, so I've gone and done what I can to make things better, but I'm not sure if it's enough; if she'll forgive me . . . I've got to make her know, somehow, I've tried to make amends . . . That's why I've come to see you.'

Elsie sighed to herself. Clearly things were amiss with Charlie and Isabelle, and now Stephen and Angela. It wouldn't surprise her if she walked out of her cottage to find young Alison beside herself because of some tiff with Al. What was wrong with these young people and why couldn't they sort themselves out? She didn't remember having anyone to turn to when she and Thomas had a falling out.

'Well, Stephen, I can't make head nor tail of what you are telling me. Why don't you start at the beginning; tell me the whole of it—and mind you leave nothing out.'

*　　　*　　　*

'Stephen?' Dismayed, Angela stared at Elsie. 'But I'm not sure I want to see him, Gran, you see he and I . . . we . . .'

'Yes,' replied Elsie. 'He told me all about it. He called on me in at some unearthly hour this morning.'

It was the first time Elsie had visited Angela in her bedsit and Angela was so taken aback, she had meekly let her into her meagre room. Elsie wasted no time getting to the point.

'Did he tell you what he'd done?' Angela was defensive and cross. 'Did he explain why I'm so upset? I suppose he came to ask you to persuade me to forgive him. I'm not sure I want to . . .'

'He did tell me, dear. He behaved very badly and he knows it.'

Angela, like Stephen, was miserable. Elsie felt a strong twinge of sympathy for her. Angela's room was not a place to lift one's spirits: neat and functional it might be, but it was worn and colourless. No wonder Angela flung herself into life at the farm with such enthusiasm.

'He is very remorseful, Angela, and desperate to make amends. He went to see Mrs Merfield yesterday evening to ask her to change her mind.'

'Gosh.' Angela was impressed, in spite of herself. 'Did he? He'd find that terrifying.'

'Yes he did. He's to phone her this morning, to get her decision.'

'But it doesn't change the fact he was so two-faced about it, Gran; he didn't tell me what he'd done, that he was the reason they turned us down in the first place. And he didn't tell me he'd seen Nicola.'

'No, and he was stupid and wrong not to have done so. But he also told me you'd a bit of a tiff that day, which is why he went to see Mrs Merfield alone.' Elsie gave Angela a shrewd look. 'I suspect, dear, if that quarrel hadn't happened, he'd have told you about Nicola and you'd both have gone to see Mrs Merfield. Am I right?'

'Yes, but it wasn't my fault, Elsie. He accused me of siding with Charlie because I helped with the website.'

Impatient, Elsie tutted. 'It seems when I moved

out of that house commonsense left too. But you've got to ask yourself what's behind all this? What's making Stephen so unhappy? Two quarrels with you in one week? That's not like him—he's normally such a placid, straightforward, boy and you know he thinks the world of you.'

Angela went pink and stared at her feet. 'I do love him,' she said in a small voice. 'I was just shocked and so hurt.'

'But he didn't set out to hurt you, did he? Perhaps he didn't tell you about Nicola because he knew you'd be jealous?'

Angela blushed, remembering her reaction when she'd discovered Nicola was in the cast. She could have told Stephen and forewarned him he might bump into her.

'And he told me he thought was doing the right thing persuading Mrs Merfield not to give her permission,' continued Elsie. 'And I must say I agreed with him. He's worried the Merlin Players are over-stretching themselves. Wasn't he just being protective?'

'Yes, yes, possibly.'

'But, as I said, Angela, you've got to get to the bottom of Stephen's unhappiness. You've got to talk; otherwise you can be sure there'll be more fallings out.'

'Yes.'

Elsie stood up. 'I really must go; Ron'll be wondering where I am. I'll leave you to think about what I've said. In my opinion you're everything Stephen wants . . . your marriage is the best possible thing to happen to the farm, but nothing, remember, nothing can be taken for granted.'

52

'Oh, jolly good shot!' By her standards, Veronica's attempt to reach a high lob was feeble; she missed it and saw the dirt spray just inside the line.

Her partner might not appreciate it, but the game she was playing was a skilful one: good enough to flatter his ego when he won, and letting him do so without giving him the slightest hint she could beat him with ease.

Fortune had smiled on Veronica that Sunday morning. On her way into the club, she'd encountered Ben Dacres jogging along the drive.

Leaning out of the car window, she hailed him. 'Ben, hello. Golly, you look wonderfully fit.'

Spotting a slight crease in his brow, she hastily added, 'It's Veronica,' side-stepping the mortification of him not remembering her name a second time.

'Of course, dear lady, how could I forget Verr-roni-ca!' He smiled in his most disarming fashion. 'What a very nice little car.'

'Yes, it is, isn't it. I've driven Porsches for the last fifteen years. Nothing else suits quite so well. Ben, I was devastated to have missed you on Friday night.'

'Friday?' again the little crease appeared.

'The party—you put me on your guest list, but you'd gone by the time I arrived. I am so sorry I was late. You must have got fed up waiting for me. I wrote you a note to explain, and to remind you about our little party.'

'I don't think I've received it . . .'

Ben Dacres had been feeling distinctly unwell

since Friday—'distinctly crapulent, in fact'—as he'd informed Jilly, and the debacle with the pigs on the set had finished him off. Ordinarily he would have fled back to London to salvage what he could of the weekend, and to get a good fix of TLC from his current wife. But she was on tour with *The Rivals* and he saw little point in returning to an empty house, so he'd stayed on for the rest of the weekend.

Bored, feeling rather sorry for himself, he was in dire need of a good dose of adulation. The appearance of Veronica Lester in her Porsche, blushing and twittering and laughing inordinately (all signs with which he was very familiar) was, he thought, just what the doctor ordered, and Veronica found it gratifyingly easy to persuade him to abandon his morning jog for a game of tennis.

Ben Dacres was not a stupid man, but he was vain and self-centred, so although he might suspect he was being given an easy game, he didn't bother to wonder at Veronica's motives. When the match was over and his victory secured, it would have been churlish of him not to agree to Veronica's suggestion that they retire to the clubhouse for a pre-lunch drink; and equally churlish not to accept, with good grace, the bottle of champagne waiting for them after they'd showered. (She'd found out it was his favourite tipple whenever he was feeling under the weather.)

'Darling,' he took her hand and kissed it. 'This is so kind of you; it was threatening to be such a dreary weekend. Your health, Verr-oni-ca!'

It was the way he rolled her name around his tongue . . . She felt weak, never would she try to make him call her Vee again.

294

'Congratulations on your brilliant play,' she croaked, raising her glass, thinking, as she did so, how intoxicated she already was. 'I'm going to have to demand a return match, it was a close call.'

'My pleasure; you're a good little player. Now . . . Verr-oni-ca,' he leaned forward, his voice dropping intimately. Veronica felt her heart pounding so loudly she was convinced he'd notice. 'I want you to tell me about yourself.'

'Yes?' was all she could manage.

'You're an intriguing woman. Everything about you hints at Aries. Am I right?'

Veronica stared at him and swallowed. Astrology and all that it stood for she dismissed as arrant nonsense. She couldn't think of anything sensible to say; there was nothing sensible to say.

'Yes,' she smiled, trying to flirt. 'You are clever. How did you know?'

He looked modest. 'A hobby of mine. You're so typically Arien: slim and strong, sophisticated, energetic . . . why, even your appearance says Aries.'

'Oh?'

'Your hair is so thick and your features . . .' he paused appraising her, and Veronica blushed. She knew her nose was a trifle too long for her face and her chin receded.

'Ariens,' he continued, 'have attractively strong features and you're no exception. You're obviously busy and successful, the equal of any man, I'd say; all, very typical. You see,' he sipped his champagne. 'In my line of business it's a useful shorthand. Know someone's star-sign and you save yourself a lot of heartache, especially as you have to work with people so closely, as we do. I know you're Aries,

295

I'm a Leo.'

'Is that good?'

'Oh yes, we're very compatible. We're both fire!'

'Oh, good.' Veronica laughed happily. What did it matter that he was talking utter tosh? He thought they were compatible. 'Yes, I can see how useful it must be. Do you, er . . . know the star sign of everyone you work with?'

'No, but I can guess; I'm usually right. We've one person in the cast, who, without being indiscreet, is simply anathema. I suspect he's a Capricorn—we just don't get along.'

'Is he the reason for your beastly weekend?'

'Oh no. I've hardly seen him the last couple of days, thank God. No, it's this filming. I've never experienced anything like it. I have, you know, been subjected to the most appalling situations. Really,' he shuddered, 'I suppose it's no-one's fault, but if I meet another filthy beast face-to-face, I think I might break my contract.'

'Oh no, you mustn't do that!' Veronica's antennae were quivering. 'Filthy beasts . . . why what's been happening to you?'

Needing no further encouragement, Ben embarked on a melodramatic description of the cows running amok in Summerstoke and how he'd barely escaped from being trampled to death, and then how he'd fended off an attack from two enormous pigs.

He ended, sniffing, 'and the mud and the smell. No-one warned us about that. It's so overwhelming it makes me want to gag. I suppose that's nothing to you country folk, but for us . . .'

'No, no,' Veronica hastened to reassure him. She was not so infatuated she couldn't recognise a golden opening when she saw one. She poured him the last of the champagne. 'We've a farm, too, but smells and animals are kept strictly in their place. The Tuckers are, I'm afraid, very shambolic farmers. I'm surprised they still manage to keep going, everything about the farm is derelict.' She squeezed his hand. 'You poor things—fancy having to work in the middle of all that! What were your bosses thinking of?'

'That's what I say, often. But does anyone listen? No, I'm only an insignificant actor, trying to earn an honest crust . . . My goodness, we've finished the whole bottle. Perhaps we better have some lunch before we become too plastered to move?'

'Oh yes!' Veronica was delighted—this was beyond her wildest expectations. 'That's a lovely idea, and then I shall tell you all about my farm and you will see you don't have to put up with muck and mayhem. It can't be efficient or make good business sense to be filming under such conditions, quite apart from exposing you to discomfort and danger. I'm sure if you complained to the money men at the top, you wouldn't be ignored. You're not just an insignificant performer, you're their star . . .'

53

'It's not looking good, Jenny; you'd better warn those lads of yours: certain of the village are out for blood . . . Just the box of shortbread, is it?'

'Yes please, Rita.' Jenny fumbled in her purse. 'Ron's got something wrong with his stomach so better not chocolates. He loves a bit of shortbread

297

with his tea, so I thought that might cheer him up.'

'You off there, now?'

'Yes, Jeff's driving me. He's waiting for me outside. Then we're going over to have a look at a farm shop that's just opened off the A36, see what they're doing.'

Rita sniffed as she rang up the price of the biscuits. 'Huh—trouble with these farm shops is they're in direct competition with us village shops rather than the supermarkets. You might remember that when you open yours, Jenny Tucker.'

'Yes, Rita, but we're not selling stamps and you don't sell fresh meat, so I don't see as there's much of a problem,' replied Jenny.

'Not at the beginning, no—but just you wait and see—you'll be tempted to diversify and you'll end up selling all manner of stuff that I stock. That is,' Rita added mischievously, bringing the conversation back to the original subject, 'if you survive long enough to open a farm shop, which, if certain persons have their way, seems doubtful . . .'

'It's so unfair; the crew did a lovely job cleaning up the street. I don't see as how anybody could complain.' Jenny did her best to conceal it, but she was worried. 'And I'm sure it's not the likes of Mrs Long or Mrs Spencer who've complained. They've lived in the village all their life, they know how things are . . .'

'Of course not,' Rita agreed, a note of contempt in her voice. 'But you know the way it is. People like the Greens and the Tenbys move in . . . the next thing they've taken over the parish council and the church hall committee, with their loud voices and pushy ways, and change the way things have always been. For the better, they'd say, but it's always to suit them and the value of their houses. They don't want the cows coming through and that's that. What they're saying is that this time the film crew were on hand to clean up. But supposing it happened again, who'd clean up then? And suppose somebody got hurt?'

'Oh dear—I don't know what we can do for the best. I'll warn Stephen and Charlie, though. Thank you, Rita.'

'Are you in the filming tomorrow? They're taking over my shop, you know?'

'Yes, I got a call. I'm really excited. Are you in it, too, then?'

Rita looked disgusted. 'Yes, but not in my rightful place. Would you believe it? They've got some actress to play me. As if I couldn't handle a few lines . . . Ridiculous! I'm going to be a customer in my own shop!'

The door clanged and Jeff poked his head round. 'Everything all right, love, only you do seem to have been a very long time? Hello Rita.'

'Hello, Jeff. She's just coming. How are you, then? Busy?'

'No more than usual, Rita.'

'Didn't see much of you at the party on Friday night.

'Oh, I was there.'

'But not dancing?'

'No.'

Jenny shot warning glance at Rita, but Rita couldn't resist a parting shot. 'Well I don't know, Jeff Babington, I'm not sure Rob would be happy to see me spend the evening in the arms of another, especially the likes of Ben Dacres.'

Jeff grinned. 'Shows he's got good taste. Come on, love. Bye, Rita.'

Climbing into the car, Jenny was apologetic. 'I'm sorry about Rita—her saying that; she shouldn't have done.'

'Oh I don't mind her. She's a good friend to you, Jenny, even if she's the worst gossip I've ever met. I guess it goes with the job.'

'Yes, I suppose it does.'

Jenny sounded woebegone and Jeff felt concerned.

'I'm sorry I didn't dance with you on Friday night, Jen. To tell you the truth, I was sufficiently stirred by the sight of you in that chap's arms to stir meself and come and claim you, but then that blasted call came and that was that.'

The thought of Jeff being jealous was such a novelty, Jenny felt a warm glow, but it failed to dissipate her worry over Rita's news about village getting up a petition against the herd, and she relapsed into an uncharacteristic silence.

Jeff, not knowing the cause, misinterpreted her quietness.

Not having a great imagination and or much self-doubt, his reactions on seeing Jenny dance with that actor fellow had surprised him. For one thing Jenny appeared to be really enjoying herself with a glow about her that he associated with himself. Was she smitten with the fellow?

Nothing she'd said or done had hinted as much. They'd gone to the cinema yesterday evening and spent the night together. True, she'd been tired and they'd not spent much time lovemaking; had he read that wrong? Was she actually growing tired of him?

Certainly he was no match in looks with the actor, and nor did he have that oozy, easy charm. But Jenny was far too sensible to fall for that, wasn't she?

He glanced at her. Deep in thought, she looked far from happy. Perhaps she didn't want to be with him at all? Or maybe she was trying to think of a way to tell him that she preferred this actor.

Jeff didn't know a thing about him except that he was meant to be famous, but he didn't believe for one moment he would be serious in his intentions towards Jenny. He wouldn't look after her; he'd have his bit of fun, then drop her.

Poor Jenny, she deserved a whole lot better than that. He wouldn't treat her in that way, he would look after her, always be there for her . . . Perhaps he should have made that clear to her before? Perhaps he should speak up before it was too late, like Friday, when he had finally decided to ask her to dance and that bloody call-out put paid to the evening.

What had he thought then? That it was no longer enough to do nothing?

The first thing he had to do was to take the plunge and find out what she was thinking. He took a deep breath and said, as casually as he could manage, 'Penny for them, love?'

'Oh Jeff,' she said unhappily, 'I don't know what to do for the best . . .'

He braced himself. 'Only you know what that is,' he replied gruffly. 'I won't stand in your way. I can't pretend I won't mind . . . I will, more than you probably realise, and that's my fault . . .' He broke off, feeling suddenly choked. When he regained his composure he became aware of her astonished stare.

'Jeff, what are you talking about?'

'You and me, and . . . and that actor chap. Isn't that what you're worrying about?'

Her astonishment was visible. 'You . . . and me . . . and the actor chap? You mean Ben? No, Jeff, no.' Jenny shook her head. 'Nothing was further from my mind. I was thinking about cows! But,' she added without a trace of guile, 'I shall never forget that evening. Fancy me, dancing with Ben Dacres— me—Jenny Tucker. It was so romantic—I shall remember that for the rest of my life!'

Which was not exactly what Jeff wanted to hear and, not knowing how to respond, he lapsed into a brooding silence.

54

Dropping her children at the cinema in Summerbridge, Sally Green set out for Summerstoke. Heading out of town, she happened to glance across at the bus stop by the post office. 'My goodness me,' she exclaimed aloud. 'What luck!'

Ever since her lunch with Veronica, the difficulty of fulfilling Veronica's commission had preoccupied her: how could she engage Angela in another heart to heart? True, she could call in at the library, but it didn't seem the right sort of environment for confidences and her imagination took her no further. And then, there she was . . . fate had handed her Angela Upton on a plate, waiting at the bus stop.

Angela shivered; it was cold in the wind and she'd been waiting for ten minutes already. After dithering half the morning over her next move, she could bear it no longer and decided to catch the next bus to Summerstoke and surprise Stephen. Unfortunately, being Sunday, buses were scarce.

She thought of the cosy cab of Stephen's ancient Land Rover: he'd put a cushion on the broken passenger seat to make it more comfortable for her and he always cranked up the heater, even though he never seemed to feel the cold himself. He was always so thoughtful, so solicitous. Gran was right, he did love her, she had no doubts about that, so why had he nearly ruined it all?

The whole of the previous day she'd asked herself the same questions, over and over, but with no satisfactory answers, which led to the biggest question of all: was this breach of trust sufficiently bad for her to call off their engagement?

Gran's unexpected intervention forced her to re-examine her own role, and the revelation that Stephen had been to see Mrs Merfield a second time, without her, put a different complexion on the problem. She didn't underestimate how difficult that would be for him. She wanted to forgive him, she wanted to feel his arms around her, and she wanted him to tell her Nicola meant nothing to him, that she was the love of his life.

She was interrupted from her reverie by the peremptory summons of a car horn. Startled, she looked up to see Sally Green beckoning.

'Are you waiting for the Summerstoke bus?'

Angela nodded.

'Well jump in, I'll give you a lift.'

Angela didn't tell Sally Green about the fragile

state of her relationship with Stephen, but in the course of the journey she did reveal that the happenings at the farm were a source of growing tension and that far from the situation having improved since she last saw her, the two brothers were now not speaking to one another.

'Oh dear, I am so sorry to hear that. My advice remains the same: you and your fiancée need to buy the brother out and you need to get rid of the film unit. How can you run a serious business like a farm with people like that in your hair the entire time?'

'It's true,' Angela felt wretched. 'We don't know whether we're coming or going. But Mrs Green . . .'

'Please, call me Sally.'

'Sally. The sort of money we'd need, Sally, to buy Charlie out, let alone get rid of the TV, would be astronomical. It's impossible.'

'Nothing's impossible when you know how,' replied Sally grandly. 'Have you considered getting a bank loan?'

'We've only just reduced our debt to the bank, I don't think my . . . I don't think Stephen would like to borrow that much again.'

'Then what about a private arrangement?'

'How do you mean?'

'Find someone who is prepared to invest in your farming business; someone who will lend you the money and wait for a return until the farm shows a profit or is sold. A sort of sleeping partner.'

'Like Angels, you mean?'

'What?' It was Sally Green's turn to look puzzled.

'Angels are wealthy people who invest in theatrical productions and don't expect anything back unless the show makes a profit.'

'Oh. Well, yes, I suppose like that, except that a sleeping partner would expect to get his or her money back at some point.'

Angela looked dubious. 'I'm not sure . . .'

'From you and your fiancé's point of view, Angela, it means you have someone who's prepared to put capital into the farm, but take absolutely no part in running it. Ideal.'

'Yes, yes I can see that,' said Angela slowly. 'But are there such people? I admit I don't know anything about the world of finance, but if there are, how do you find them?'

'Well, through contacts, of course. My husband's business puts us in touch with lots of different people, some very wealthy indeed. Look, Angela, in the utmost confidence, of course, if you want me to make a few discreet enquiries, I will.'

Angela fell silent. If she and Stephen were to have a future, they had to have it on their terms, not Charlie's, not Elsie's, and certainly not the television people's. It couldn't do any harm to let Sally Green make enquiries; it wasn't committing them to anything and if, just if, she found someone to invest in them, why then everything would look a whole lot brighter . . .

'Yes, thank you,' she said finally. Thank you, Sally, I'd be very grateful.'

55

'I hope you're joking, Ali!' Al's voice sounded dangerous and Alison scowled at her mobile.

'No, I'm not, Al. I don't see what the problem is.

He's been here once already . . .'

'And you didn't tell me.'

'No, I explained to you . . .' Alison's patience was wearing thin.

'You forgot.' He sounded scornful. 'This famous geezer goes up to your bedroom, ostensibly to help set up a website, and you somehow forgot about it. It doesn't wash.'

'What doesn't wash, Al?' she snapped. 'Going to my room was no big deal . . .'

'That's not the way I see it,' he snarled.

'Fine. If that's the way you want it, fine! Come over and chaperon, if you like; it'd be far better if you were here, anyway.'

'You know I can't, I've got too much to do to spend the afternoon wasting my time on your bloody website.'

'Well in that case, Al, you can have no objection to my seeking help where I can get it. I'll speak to you later.' Furious, Alison turned her mobile off and sat on the edge of her bed, trembling with anger. She and Al rarely quarrelled and this had been volcanic.

Contrary to her expectations, Jason had behaved impeccably in her bedroom that afternoon. He had made enormous strides in getting the website launched and proposed lots of ideas for the content. He'd enthused over the pictures she'd managed to collect so far, particularly the ones of the two pigs on the set. 'It's a pity we can't get more like this,' he'd chortled. 'What a laugh! It's a pity you weren't there when the set collapsed—the look on Ben Dacres's face!'

She fully intended to tell Al but when Charlie dropped her in Bath, she was only just in time for her and Al to make the movie and finally, when they'd had time to talk, discussion about the pigs on the set and who might be behind the various acts of sabotage; the fight between Charlie and Stephen, and the news about Ron, had put Jason's visit on the back-burner.

She'd stayed the night, then caught a bus back from Bath shortly after breakfast and it was while she was on the bus that she remembered about Jason and the website, but before she'd had a chance to phone him, Jason sent her a text proposing he come over that afternoon to resume work on the website.

Al had gone ballistic.

'I suppose,' she said grumpily to Hannah, whom she phoned after she'd calmed down, 'I should be pleased he cares enough to be jealous, but this is bloody stupid. What am I supposed to do? Jason is doing a fantastic job, am I supposed to stop him? "Oh no, you can't come into my bedroom, my boyfriend wouldn't like it!" He'd refuse to have anything more to do with it, and we need this website, Hannah. We really need it.'

'Do you think he fancies you?'

'Who? Jason? No. I think flirting is second nature to him . . . he can't help himself. I think it's rather sad.'

'Then why don't I come over? I don't want to play gooseberry, but if it really is as you say, I'll come over and keep you company. That should satisfy Al, and I get to meet the great Mr Hart—I hardly saw him at the party.'

'That's awesome, Hannah. Brilliant!'

'Brilliant' was not the word that sprang to Jason Hart's mind when he arrived to find his quarry ensconced with her best friend, a plump, pretty girl who eyed him with evident interest and who was not going to be dismissed that easily.

He hadn't a clear notion how the seduction was going to proceed, he never did. He was much more the spontaneous, improvisational sort who would sort out the consequences—if there were any—after his conquest. But he was certain it was going to happen that afternoon. He'd finish the website as far as he could, then he'd roll over onto her bed and demand his reward . . . that was the loose plot. The presence of Miss Hannah rather put paid to that—unless he could persuade them that three in a bed could be fun.

With apparent good grace, he sat at the computer and did his stuff, the two girls cheering him on. When he had finished and the site was ready to be launched with what material Alison had available, he sat back, basking in their applause.

'You do need some more visuals,' he remarked. 'But they're a doddle to set up, once you've got the images. You should be able to manage, but you can holler for help if you need it.'

'Jason,' Alison's face was so alight with excitement and pleasure, he was momentarily enchanted. 'You've performed a miracle. It's wonderful. I bet it would have taken the average designer months to come up with something this good . . .'

'Definitely,' chipped in Hannah. 'It's bloody fantastic!'

Jason stood up and stretched. 'I'm so stiff!' he moaned. 'It's sitting at that bloody computer for so long. I think my shoulders and neck are seizing up.' He dropped his head on his chest and tried to rotate his shoulders 'Ow! Ow!'

His performance convinced Hannah at least.

'Shall I massage your back, Jason? That might help.'

With a grunt he threw himself face down on the bed and for a few minutes, subjected himself to an amateur pounding.

'Ow—ow! Let me take my shirt off, you're grinding the material into my skin . . .'

As he sat up to strip, he noticed Alison had taken his place at the computer and was not displaying the slightest interest in the massage session on the bed. He flung himself on his back and stared accusingly at Hannah. 'Doesn't your friend ever allow herself to have any fun? Or does she belong to one of those strange sects you find embedded deep in the countryside—no sex, no fun, we're the Seventh Immaculate Dentists and if you laugh you'll die of gum disease.'

Hannah giggled and Alison looked up, 'It depends what you mean by fun, Jason,' she said coolly. 'I wouldn't have thought it was much fun to be rolling around half-naked on my bed. It's freezing in here. I'll go and make some tea—or coffee, if you prefer?'

'Any chance of a beer?' Naked from the waist up and stretched full out on the bed, he eyed her provocatively.

'Sure.' Alison turned to go.

'Any objection if I roll a spliff?'

Alison hesitated and glanced at Hannah. It was an unspoken rule they didn't smoke in each other's house, but she didn't want to appear a wet blanket, especially as she was so much in his debt.

Hannah returned her look with a slight shrug.

Everyone was out, Alison was stuffed . . .

'Go ahead, I'll be back in a minute,' she said and took herself off to the kitchen, cursing. He was going to be difficult to get rid of and Hannah was so in his thrall, she'd be no help.

Waiting for the kettle to boil, she cast around for exit strategies. Her brothers couldn't be approached—she'd get it in the neck if they discovered weed had been smoked in the house, website or no website.

She glanced at her watch . . . shortly after four. Stephen would be in the milking shed at five and he normally came in for tea before he started. In fact, she was surprised he wasn't already in the kitchen, but then he was so unpredictable at the moment, he could be anywhere—but of course, it was Sunday and Charlie would be doing the milking.

She warmed herself against the Rayburn. How he could lie on her bed with no shirt on, it was so bloody cold today, even with the central heating on. Then an idea struck and she grinned. Maybe . . . maybe . . .

She whipped into the hall, quietly opened the door to the small utility room that housed an elderly boiler and cranked the switch off. Then she tiptoed half way up the stairs and opened a huge sash window concealed behind a blind. The cold air swept in.

Going back to the kitchen, she found a beer in the fridge and put it in the freezer while she made tea. Putting two mugs, the can of beer, a packet of gingernuts and a large glass of water on a tray, she returned to her room.

Taking a deep breath, she pushed open the door and was taken aback to see Jason, still minus his shirt, sitting astride Hannah who was lying face down on the bed, also minus her top and giggling uncontrollably. The room reeked with the choking sweet smell of marihuana, the remains of a joint smouldering in a dish by the bed.

'Sorry,' Alison said with disdain, 'am I interrupting something?'

Jason looked up. 'Come on, come and join in the fun. I'm teaching your friend here how to massage properly. We've saved the end of the joint for you. What took you so long?'

'I had to hunt for the beer,' she replied, pushing the tray onto the edge of her desk. 'I'm going to have to open the window. There'll be all hell to pay if my family discover we've been smoking weed up here.'

'I don't see as it smells any different from your farmyard, love,' Jason commented as she threw the window open. 'Your yard stinks so much I wouldn't be at all surprised to learn those cows are secret ganja smokers.' Releasing Hannah from her pinioned position, he swung his legs round to sit on the edge of the bed and watched Alison.

Hannah sat up, giggling, then shivered. 'It's really cold with that window open, Ali . . .'

'Cold! It's bloody freezing. It was bad enough before you opened it, now it's like sitting in a fucking refrigerator.'

'Then put your clothes back on,' remarked Alison. 'Here, have some tea.' She handed a mug to Hannah and passed the can of beer to Jason.

'Ta. Christ, that's frigging cold! Where did you find it—the bottom of the deep freeze?'

'Not quite. Would you rather have my tea?'

'Your tea is not what I had in mind.'

311

Alison made no reply and, shivering, Jason grabbed his sweatshirt and pulled it on. 'That's better,' he grunted, reaching for the remains of the joint and offering it to Alison. 'Fancy a toke? It might warm you up. I'll re-light it for you.'

'Thanks.'

The cold air from the staircase swept under the door and combining with the draught from open window, she reckoned the temperature of her room was rapidly approaching zero. She had hoped the intense cold would drive her unwanted visitor away, but obviously he was determined to sit it out. She might, she thought, have to revert to plan B: the glass of water.

She didn't have the guts to stand up and throw it over him, but over him, somehow, it had to go. Drenched, he'd have to give up and go, wouldn't he?

The first joint was finished and lighting the second, Jason drew a bit too deeply and started to cough.

Passing the joint to Alison, he spluttered to Hannah who was closest to the desk. 'The water, there, on the tray . . . the tray, you dumbcluck, there, give it to me . . .'

Alison couldn't have orchestrated it better.

Hannah leapt up, grabbed the tray and swung it round. The glass slid across the tray and emptied itself down Jason's chest.

56

Marcus stood in the gallery and gazed at the painting on the wall in front of him. If colour could be said to be alive, then this picture was alive, he mused, and so unlike Isabelle herself; the bold combinations of colour, the sweep of the reds, the swirls of blue. He thought of her huge blue eyes, soft, gentle—not like this painting, there was nothing gentle about this.

And there was nothing gentle about his feelings. Why he'd allowed himself to fall under Isabelle's spell on Friday night, he'd no idea. But he had, and consequently found, when he allowed himself to put work on one side, he could think about little else.

He had come to the gallery on an impulse. Unlike the opening night, there were few people about and he was able to stand and muse without interruption.

He had been furious with Emma on Friday evening, and he was still simmering at her nerve as he drove up to London on Saturday morning. He thought seriously of approaching his executive producers and suggesting they replace her. 'On what grounds?' they would ask and he knew that accusing him of trying to poach his friend's girl was not a fault he could, with any credibility, complain about.

There were the accidents on the set, and they had fallen behind schedule after only a week. But those were setbacks that couldn't be laid at Emma's door and he had to admit the rushes looked good.

No, he'd have to put up with her till the end of this series; then, if they got a further commission, he'd look for someone else.

The memory of her dark eyes, flashing with contempt, so different from Isabelle's, plagued him. 'Ah, Isabelle', he sighed. He didn't like what was happening, so why did he just not stand back? Charlie was a great guy . . . they were good friends . . . it was just that he could see, so clearly, that Charlie and Isabelle could not work out. She had unique qualities, abundantly obvious from these amazing paintings, qualities Charlie could in no way match. Charlie simply was not in her league.

So was he, Marcus, in that league?

Possibly not, he admitted, but he was sure he had a lot more to offer than Charlie. For one thing he was experienced in a way Charlie wasn't; he travelled, he was socially confident, he was part of the artistic community, he had money and a wide circle of friends—all things which would see Isabelle flourish.

'But does she like you enough to leave Charlie?' The question intruded for the millionth time. 'I don't know' he sighed aloud, 'I don't know . . .'

'Don't know what, Marcus? Don't know whether you like Isabelle's work or not?' came a cool voice at his side.

It was Polly Merfield, a tall, elegant woman, with laughing eyes and a composed air. 'I'm glad you've found her paintings worth a second visit.'

'Hi, Polly. Yes, they are very striking. Quite amazing in fact.'

As they strolled round the gallery comparing notes, it occurred to him that Polly, being a friend of Isabelle's, might be worth pumping. Brushing

314

aside the fact Polly preferred to keep her distance since their own relationship had ended, he invited her to join him for a drink when the gallery closed.

Polly hesitated, but Marcus pressed her and they arranged to meet in a wine bar near Tower Bridge.

Once settled with a cold bottle of sauvignon, it was natural for the conversation to resume where it had left off.

'I know you can't judge an artist by their work, Polly, but my experiences with the artists I know have taught me that their work is, on the whole, an expression of their temperament. I just don't see that with Isabelle's. That's why I found them such a shock . . . they seem so different from her.'

'Or the her she chooses you to see,' reflected Polly. 'I don't know how well you know her, but she has a tremendous fighting spirit and a strong rebellious streak, which comes across in her painting.'

'I first met her when my brother was using the studio at Marsh Farm. He employed her to mix paint and that, in itself, was unusual. Milo hates people around him when he's got the painting fever . . .'

'Milo's an artist whom most would describe as a genius. He probably recognised something similar in Isabelle.'

'Then poor Charlie.'

Polly was curious. 'Why do you say that?'

'Because if Isabelle is going places, what happens to Charlie?'

She cocked her head. 'I think you can separate the artist and their work. I'm sure Isabelle's work is going to do really well and people will want to lionise her. But I don't think she'll have much truck with that. She's already had experience of the fast lane; her husband, you know, was an ambitious newspaper editor, determined, striving and ruthless—a bit like you, Marcus—and she hated all the associated socialising. She's very happy, living in a village, with her children at the local school, and with Charlie. So no, I don't think you need say "Poor Charlie". And if you care about him, which I think you do, you should tell him not to worry.'

57

'That was so brave of you, telling Mrs Merfield you'd changed your mind, Stephen. Mrs Pagett will be over the moon.' Angela snuggled against Stephen and beamed up at him, the nightmare of the last twenty-four hours already a distant shadow.

In the fading light of the day they were sitting in the cab of the Land Rover, relishing their reconciliation in a lay-by next to a cow field.

'Actually, I didn't tell her I'd changed my mind,' replied Stephen, holding his Angela tightly. 'I told her I still thought it was a bad idea . . .'

'But then why did she agree? I thought you said you'd had a change of heart?'

'No, what I said was that what I thought was not important, and I'd no right to throw a spanner in the works when everyone else is prepared to give it a go. It weren't fair of me. That's what I said, Ange.'

'Oh Stephen, that makes it even more noble of you. Kiss me.'

Happily he obliged and for a few blissful

minutes, kissing replaced talking.

Maybe it was a consequence of the real fright Stephen had suffered, thinking he'd lost Angela, but this romantic interlude became more intense than ever before, and as it became more intense, Stephen became aware his body had sprung to life in a way it had never done before when he'd kissed Angela. Unbidden, his penis was swelling and throbbing and making urgent demands. His breathing changed, perspiration broke out on his brow, he had an overwhelming desire to tear off Angela's clothes, to touch her skin, her breasts, her . . . her . . . He wanted to feel himself against her, to feel her fingers on his erection, to push himself into her . . . It was agony—he didn't know what to do. What would she do? What would she think? This was new. Not yet, not yet! He couldn't face rejection again.

With an agonised yell, he abruptly pulled himself away and almost threw himself out of the car, where he doubled up on the damp muddy ground.

'What is it Stephen, what is it?' Angela shouted, frightened. 'Are you all right?'

'Ow, ow! I'm sorry, Ange, I've got cramp,' he exclaimed, and hopped around, slapping his leg till he felt sufficiently in control of himself to climb back in.

Angela looked thoughtful. 'Stephen, I've been thinking,' she began, snuggling up to him again, 'All this . . . these things that have been going wrong between us . . .'

Stephen was alarmed. 'Yes?'

'I just wonder . . . you're not happy, are you? You do want to get married to me, don't you?'

'Oh yes, Ange, yes!' he replied with fervour,

317

noting with relief that his body had returned pretty much to its previous quiescent state.

'Then it's got to do with the farm and the filming, and until we get it sorted out, I'm awfully afraid something else might happen and we might end up not getting married at all.'

A flicker of sexual desire licked his loins.

'Ange!' he said, desperately.

'I think we've got to tell the television people it's not working out and you want them to leave.'

'Charlie would never agree to that!'

'And I think we've got to find a way of buying Charlie out.'

Although Stephen had flung this at Charlie, his suggestion had not been serious. Stunned, he could think of nothing to say.

She pressed on. 'You've said yourself, often enough, you want to be able to run the farm your own way. With Charlie around we'll never be able to, and that makes you miserable. That's why there are all these fights.'

She put her hand on his thigh. (Another flicker— he tried to control it by thinking of something entirely different—the large beautiful eyes of his Jerseys.) Angela's eyes, huge and round behind her specs looked up at him in a similar way.

'I can see it Stephen, and I can't bear to see you so unhappy.'

His arm tightened around her shoulder.

'I want to marry you, Stephen. I want the farm to be me and you, not me, you, and Charlie, and I think unless we can sort that out, we might as well put off our wedding.'

'Ange, no!' Stephen was agonised. 'Don't say that. We will sort something out, we will. But what you're suggesting involves an awful lot of money. How could I possibly buy Charlie out? He's sunk the whole of what Gran gave him into the business. I don't want to have to go to the bank, cap in hand, again.'

'Maybe you won't have to, maybe there's another way we can do it . . .'

'Ange?'

'I've an idea, Stephen. Let me find things out and if it comes to anything, you'll see, it'll be a perfect solution to our problems. If that's what you want, of course?'

'Yes Ange,' he said fervently. 'Yes, I do.'

He kissed her again, noting with cautious relief his body was behaving.

Then she broke off with a wistful sigh. 'There is one other thing, Stephen.'

'What's that my love?'

She spoke hesitantly. 'I know that we've . . . well . . . more or less agreed not to . . . well, do anything till we're married . . . but, well, it would be nice to do more than kiss and cuddle in the front of this old Land Rover. Wouldn't it?'

58

Finishing his Sunday shift in the dairy, Charlie decided not go to the Grapes that evening, as he had planned, but to go and make peace with Isabelle.

By the time he'd done a last check on his pregnant porkers, showered and changed, it was after seven-thirty.

'With any luck,' he thought, as he turned into her drive, 'I'll just be in time to read the girls a bed-time story . . .'

He had a great affection for the two little girls and they for him. And helping put them to bed, he reasoned, would go some way to breaking the ice with Isabelle.

At the front door, he hesitated—should he knock and wait? He more usually went straight in, but this estrangement made everything different.

He compromised; he banged on the door, put his head round and shouted her name. The answering cries of glee from the sitting room were encouraging.

'Charlie . . . it's Charlie,' shouted Clemmie.

'Oh goody,' shrieked Becky. 'He can read us a story.'

She rushed out and grabbed his hand, pulling him into the sitting room. 'Charlie, you will read us a story, won't you?'

'Yes of course I will, but I just want to say hello to your Mum first,' Charlie smiled down at her.

'You can't,' giggled Clemmie. 'She's not here.'

'She's gone out,' explained Becky, 'with Emma and Matt and Colin.'

Barely had this unwelcome news time to sink in when the kitchen door opened and Paula, resplendent in a leather skirt, no more than four inches deep, and a bright red nylon blouse over a lacy black camisole, appeared carrying a mug of tea and a plate of biscuits.

She beamed. 'Oh hello, Charlie, you not at the Bunch of Grapes this evening? Isabelle's gone off with the film people. They're putting up a team for the quiz night. I'd have thought you'd be there to cheer them on? Isabelle said nothing about you coming here . . .'

'No, well, I've only just finished work. I . . . er . . . sort of expected Isabelle to be here.'

'Oh I'm sorry to disappoint you, Charlie, love. She phoned to ask if I could babysit and since me Mum was around, I left my kiddies with her and come over. Why don't you shoot off and join her? From what Lenny says sounds like the sparks will be flying tonight. The reg'lars have got wind of the film crew sayin' they're gonna wipe the floor with the yokels. Honestly,' she added with disgust, 'they're all behavin' like kiddies. It's worse than football.'

'Mm, I'm inclined to agree with you.' Charlie was torn. Isabelle had gone to the pub . . . because he'd planned to be there? But somehow, trying to effect a reconciliation in a war-torn pub was not attractive. Particularly, he thought, if Marcus was there. Maybe that was why she'd gone . . . not to see him, but to meet up with Marcus. Oh, the deadly effects of jealousy! He felt sick.

'Is Marcus joining them?' he asked as casually as he could manage.

'No ideal, Charlie. But Emma did say everyone was going to be there to cheer them on, so I wouldn't be surprised.'

'Maybe,' Charlie thought, 'maybe I should just wait here till she gets back . . .'

His decision was made easier by Becky, tugging at his sleeve, 'You will read us a story Charlie, won't you? I've chosen one 'specially . . .'

'And so have I,' chimed in Becky. 'Mine's the best, Charlie. Read it first, go on . . .'

He turned to Paula. 'I'm not in the mood for the

321

pub tonight, Paula. I'm quite happy to take over here. Why don't you shoot off? Go and join in the fun. Give Lenny a ring and get him to come and pick you up.'

'I reckon I'll just drink this tea then go home and watch TV with Mum, if it's all the same to you, Charlie. No disrespect, but them quizzes are so borin' and, to be honest, I don't much like the telly bunch . . .'

Her usual amiable expression was replaced by one of discontent.

'Oh, why's that?' Charlie, settling on the sofa with a little girl tucked in either side of him, looked up at her curiously.

Paula frowned unhappily. 'I don't understand why they ain't asked I, Charlie. Like, everyone else in the village what put their name down has been rung. Why haven't I? Julie Marsh—she only put her name down 'cos I persuaded her to—she's been phoned twice now and, between you, me and the gatepost, Charlie, she's no looker. It's humiliatin', that's what it is. I thought this was gonna be my big break, and it's just not happenin'. Even your Mum's been asked. Why not I?'

Paula was obviously upset and although it seemed supremely unimportant, Charlie felt sorry for her. He struggled to find something consoling to say.

'Perhaps they've something up their sleeve for you, Paula. You never know. They're pulling in people to be in the background, aren't they? You're too . . . too striking for that. You couldn't just be one of the crowd, could you? And anyway, you wouldn't want to be, would you? Don't worry—it's early days yet. I'm sure you'll be called.'

Paula brightened. 'Do you think so, Charlie? I hadn't thought of that. Happen you're right. I'll give Lenny a ring on his mobile . . . he can come and pick me up before he gets too pissed.'

*   *   *

Charlie read the girls their stories, tucked them up in bed, was persuaded to read more stories, returned to the sitting room, turned the television on, turned it off again, stretched out on the sofa, stared up at the sweep of colour on the sitting room wall that had marked Isabelle's return to life as a painter, and struggled to understand it, her, his feelings for her, and what he wanted for the future; but before he was able to come up with any earth-shattering revelations, he fell into a deep sleep.

'Charlie! Charlie!' It sounded like Isabelle's voice coming from a long way off. Someone gently shook his shoulder.

'Charlie!'

It was Isabelle. He opened his eyes to find her looking down at him, a half-smile on her face. 'Well, a fine baby-sitter you make, Charlie Tucker. This house could have burnt down around your ears and you'd have slept through it.'

"Don't dither and doubt . . . grab happiness!" His gran's words resounded in his head and he didn't hesitate. He put both arms around Isabelle as she bent over him, scooped her down on top of him, and kissed her passionately. Taken by surprise, she gasped and then responded, kissing him back with equal fervour.

When they finally broke off, he gently caressed her face. 'You were quite right to be mad with me,

Isabelle . . . what a wally! You told me not to come back until I was clear about what I wanted. Well I am clear. Unless you feel differently, I'm in it . . . for the long term.'

She smiled. 'Paint and all?'

'Paint, children, fairy stories and all! I tell you, I must have read a dozen stories to Clemmie and Becky tonight. They're insatiable; as soon as I'd finished one, another got pressed under my nose.'

She chuckled. 'You're a softy, Charlie, and they exploit it.'

'And,' he kissed her, 'all the Duke Marcuses and King Olivers of this world can come and worship at your feet and I . . . I shall kiss the tip of your nose and feel very smug.'

'Silly!' She kissed him in return. 'But you're quite wrong about those two: Oliver is a good friend to us both and he loves Juliet, you know he does. And Marcus . . . Marcus is your friend, Charlie; he looked after me because you asked him to.'

Charlie recalled the expression he'd seen on Marcus's face as he'd looked at Isabelle, but dismissing it, pulled Isabelle to him.

They were interrupted by a polite cough. Emma stood at the door.

'Sorry if I'm interrupting, but Matt is insisting on celebrating our victory tonight with a bottle of sparkling and wants to know if you're going to join us in the kitchen.'

'I think,' laughed Isabelle, rolling off the sofa and pulling Charlie to his feet, 'we're up for a bit of celebration.'

'So how was the quiz night?' Charlie asked Isabelle as they made for the kitchen.

'Quite tense, actually,' murmured Isabelle.

'Matt's quite a . . . well, competitive person, isn't he? And whenever his team won a round, he couldn't conceal his jubilation. There was quite a lot of muttering, and Emma told me after one particular round, their paper was returned with "wankers go home" scribbled across it. Not very nice.'

Charlie frowned. 'For such a bright guy, Matt hasn't got a whole heap of sense, has he? He's dependent on local goodwill . . . why muck it up? People can do daft things when their noses are out of joint.'

'Like letting your tyres down?'

They stopped outside the kitchen door.

'You heard about that?'

'Who on earth would do such a thing?'

Charlie shook his head. 'God, I don't know . . . What worries me is the only person I can think of who's got it in for me and the filming, is Stephen.'

Isabelle stared at him, shocked. 'You honestly think that Stephen would do such a thing?'

'Oh, hell, Isabelle, I don't know what to think, but he's been behaving oddly ever since they arrived. It's got so bad I can hardly talk to him. We're meant to be launching a new business in two weeks, for Chrissake. At the moment it feels as if I am doing it single-handed!'

59

Marcus left London in the early hours of the morning. He liked driving at this time of day—the roads were empty and as he drove west there was a

325

discernible lightening of the sky long before dawn.

His car was powerful and there was so little traffic on the road, he could think without distraction and the evening spent with Polly had given him plenty to think about.

She'd described him as ruthless . . . was he? Ambitious, yes; and when he knew what he wanted, he didn't hang about. But did that make him ruthless? Polly, of course, was prejudiced. He was the one who'd bought their relationship to an end. He wasn't proud of that particular episode; she deserved better.

What would have happened, he wondered, if they'd stayed together? Married, with kids, probably. Did he want that? No, not yet at least, was the candid answer.

So what was he doing trying to make love to a woman who had two children and was the girlfriend of a mate of his? It just didn't add up—unless, he thought, with scouring honesty, unless he accepted Polly was right in her assessment of his character. And if she was right about him, she was probably right about Isabelle. In which case, he, Marcus, either didn't stand a cat's chance or he would end up by making her very unhappy. In either case he would have screwed up his friendship with Charlie.

Marcus tried to weigh it all up. On the plus side, Polly had no idea of his interest in Isabelle. Nor did Charlie, nor did Isabelle herself, as far as he was aware. Just Emma, and again he saw the flash of contempt.

Why should he give a damn what she thought? Emma, he reflected, was a bit like Polly: both were strong, creative, independent women; the woman he'd left Polly for fell into the same sort of category.

No hint of fragility about them. Was that the sort of person he was normally attracted to? Was that why he was so pissed off with Emma? Because he wanted her to think well of him? Because he found her attractive?

He laughed out loud. 'Don't be so bloody stupid—you can't stand the woman. And anyway, she's not a patch on Isabelle.' And he fell to dreaming of Isabelle's golden hair and dreamy blue eyes, her gentle smile and wild, kaleidoscopic paintings.

*   *   *

'Hi Emma, do you mind if I take some photographs?'

Alison, camera in hand, appeared out of the early morning mist and picked her way across the sodden grass to join Emma on the riverbank.

'I'm trying to get some sequences for our website and Charlie suggested this could be fun.'

Standing on a riverbank at five-thirty on a cold April morning was in Emma's opinion, definitely not fun. The early dawn air was icy and penetrating, and in spite of her thick lined boots, quilted jacket and ear-muffs, she was shivering. It was barely light and crew were setting up for the first shot with the aid of flashlights.

'I can't see any reason why not,' Emma replied. 'So long as you don't get in the way, obviously, and no flash when we're filming.'

'What's the scene?'

'It's part of the title sequence—little Richie is fishing, no luck; big brother, Will, comes along, takes the rod, casts it, and lo—he lands a big silver fish . . .'

Alison snorted.

Emma smiled. 'Yes, it's a bit corny, but it'll look good. Colin wants to shoot it against the sunrise, which is why we're down here so early. We would have done this on Saturday morning, but it absolutely tipped down. So it's going to be a long day for us; when we've done this, we have to decamp to the village shop . . .'

'Coffee. Emma?'

'Thanks, Dave.' Emma smiled at the young man and took the proffered mug. 'Are Harry and Jason ready?'

'Yep—they're both here, lurking in the gloom, bellyachin'.'

'Let them,' the reply was callous. 'It's what they're paid for.'

'Coffee, Alison?'

'Great, thanks Dave, I'll come with you. Thanks, Emma, I'll be very discreet.'

'Emma,' Ross strolled over. 'I've brought the fish myself to ensure there's no hiccups. Jason needs to rehearse with it and you'll need to brief Jim, the diver.'

'Thanks, Ross.'

Matt bustled up. 'Jim's here, already kitted up. Emma, Colin wants to turn over as soon as the light hits the tree line. It ain't gonna make much difference to the diver's vision, the water is murky as hell, but he's got his headlamp. I suggest we go for a run-through in ten minutes.'

'Okay, Matt.' Over Matt's shoulder appeared a man in diver's skin. 'Hi, Jim—I suspect you're the warmest of all of us in that kit.'

'Could be,' the stunt man flashed white teeth.

328

'Ready when you are.'

'Colin,' Matt shouted. 'How ready are you?'

'Give me five,' came the returning shout.

'Jason, Harry!' Matt looked around. 'Over here, guys.

Jason, buried in a thick fleece, his hands wrapped round a large mug of coffee, slouched over, followed by Harry wielding a fishing rod with which he was throwing increasingly extravagant imaginary casts.

'Bloody hell,' snarled Jason. 'Be careful with that thing, you little prat, you nearly had my eye out.'

'Right,' snapped Emma. 'You've read the script, you know what we're after. Little Richie is sitting on the riverbank, cold and fed up—he's been trying for a fish for hours and nothing is biting. Big brother Will turns up, takes the rod from him, fixes on a bit of bait and casts the line. We cue Jim and seconds later, we see the rod bend under the weight of a fish and Will successfully pulls out this plum.'

She gestures to the props man who was holding a large, very life-like rubber fish.

'All you have to do,' he explained to an uninterested Jason, 'is jerk your rod a little and the fish will wriggle. See . . .' he demonstrated with a small piece of line attached to the fish's mouth.

'We're not taking the sound on this,' explained Matt, 'which is why you have no lines. It's all in the acting . . .'

'Okay Boss.' Harry Hobbs was chirpy. 'I've been practising casting. I reckon I'm pretty good at it. But how are you going to stop Jason casting it like a klutz?'

Jason looked at him with loathing. 'Because, you nasty little piece of discarded chewing gum, unlike

329

you, I've had plenty of practise. I grew up fishing in the docks . . .'

'Good,' said Emma briskly. 'Then as soon as Colin's ready, we'll have a run-through . . .'

Her attention was diverted by the appearance of a tall lean figure in a fleece-lined leather jacket, his collar turned up against the cold.

She nodded at him. 'Hello, Marcus. Coming to supervise?'

He regarded her impassively. 'I thought I'd take a look in. It will be expensive if things go wrong . . .'

'And why should they?' She stared defiantly at him.

He shrugged. 'You tell me. I just don't want any more "accidents?". Perhaps you'd talk me through the sequence.'

Feeling utterly humiliated, but knowing he was quite within his rights to ask her, Emma had no alternative but to go through the sequence with him.

They were standing on the riverbank, looking down into the water when there was a sudden shout behind them. Before Emma could turn, something hit her full in the small of her back and she hurtled forward into a black, wet abyss.

*   *   *

It had all happened so quickly. Marcus, listening to Emma talk, had been impressed by her professionalism. It was, he thought, a demonstration of how far he'd lost control of himself that he'd actually contemplated getting rid of her because she'd "found him out". He had been about to compliment her when there came the sudden shout

330

and, almost simultaneously, Emma shot forward and plunged, headfirst, into the river.

And Jason lay spread-eagled at his feet.

Events rapidly took on a nightmarish quality: the dark water had closed over Emma's head, rapidly forming concentric rings marking the spot. Then the surface of the river broke a little further down and Emma made a brief appearance before she vanished once more.

Amid the shouts and shrieks of panic on the riverbank, Marcus recovered and taking control, shouted. 'Jim, Jim! Here, quick!'

The stuntman, who'd not seen what happened, pushed his way through the horrified onlookers. Marcus grabbed his arm. 'It's Emma—she's gone under—look there, she's coming up. Get her out. Get her out—oh God, she's gone again . . .'

Jim didn't hesitate and, switching on his headlamp, jumped into the water.

*   *   *

Emma barely had time to register what had happened before the freezing waters of the river folded over her head. She tried to kick herself up but her heavy boots moved like weights and obeyed gravity. Down she went until she touched the riverbed. The water was in her eyes, her ears, her nose. She tried to strike out and, lungs bursting, bobbed back up and briefly broke the surface, only to go under again.

Coloured lights swam in front of her eyes; her ears were deaf to all sounds but a sort of muted roar. 'I'm going to drown,' she thought despairingly. 'I'm going to die and nobody cares . . .'

She hit the bottom again, and again started to ascend, but so much more slowly she knew it would require some superhuman effort to reach the surface.

Something grabbed her from behind and she couldn't fight herself free. That was it—she was caught in weeds and so she would die a watery death . . . 'What a shame,' she thought, sadly. 'There's so much else I'd like to do . . . Screw Marcus Steel for a start. Ah well . . .'

But whatever it was that grabbed her, pulled her upwards and in a dreamlike state, she realised they had broken the surface of the water. The last thing she registered before losing consciousness was the sound of Marcus's voice, urgent, shouting orders, in control.

'Bossy bastard,' she thought and drifted away.

*   *   *

After what felt like forever to Marcus and the rest of the agonised watchers, Jim emerged, clasping Emma's limp body.

Many arms reached out to take her from him and the crew's medic (barely able to conceal his delight that after days of handing out aspirins and sticking plasters, he'd a life-saving role at last) rushed forward to take charge.

To the horrified Marcus, it seemed as if Emma was never going to regain consciousness, but in a matter of minutes her eyes fluttered open and she moaned at the medic to stop pummelling her black and blue.

Under the medic's instruction, Emma's soaked clothing was removed and, wrapped in scarves, jumpers and a thermal sheet, she was placed in Ross's vehicle to be whisked off to Bath's A&E, where, the medic informed Marcus, she would be checked for hypothermia.

'I'm afraid, sir,' he added in a cheery voice, 'that's put paid to your filming, for today at least.'

Marcus frowned and turned to Matt, who was standing, staring after the departing vehicle in a state of shock, bereft, for once, of either action or speech.

'Matt,' Marcus said sharply. 'How long have we got?'

'Marcus?' Matt looked at him uncomprehendingly.

'How long till the sunrise?'

'Oh, erm,' Matt glanced at his watch, still confused. 'Er, just over twenty minutes, I reckon.'

'Right.' Marcus raised his voice to address the crew. 'I know you're all shaken, but I want to push on with this take. We'll sort out what precisely happened to Emma afterwards. Get yourselves a coffee and be ready to stand by in ten minutes. Okay Colin?'

'Yes. Marcus.'

Marcus turned to the stuntman, 'Jim, I can't thank you enough, I really can't. You saved Emma's life. Are you okay about going in the water again?'

'Sure, Marcus. I'll be fine. It's lucky you shouted for me when you did. That water's bloody cold.'

'I'm not standing next to him!' squealed Harry Hobbs angrily, pointing an accusing finger at Jason standing alone, a pariah, shunned by everybody. 'He might push me in an' all.'

'Don't be so bloody stupid,' Jason snarled.

'I didn't mean to push her. I tripped. It was an accident.'

'I've said, we'll sort this out later,' growled Marcus. 'If you know what's good for you, Harry, when that camera turns over I will see nothing but hero worship on your face when Jason lands the fish.'

*   *   *

Alison, who'd helped carry Emma's dripping body onto the bank, was wet and muddy, and shivering violently from cold and shock. When everyone around her resumed work she decided to leave them to it and go home; taking pictures of this particular event didn't seem so much fun any more.

About to go and collect her camera, she overheard Jason protesting angrily, 'I didn't mean to push her. It was an accident.'

She stopped, frowning, trying to remember what she'd seen. She'd been filming him at the time walking down to the riverbank. And yes, she'd seen him throw out his arms and push Emma . . . she'd seen him! She'd filmed it.

'If it were an accident,' she thought, hastening to retrieve the camera which she'd abandoned on a chair when the accident occurred, 'then the camera will show that, and if it wasn't, and it was deliberate . . .'

The chair was still there.

The camera was not.

She stared blankly at the empty chair then looked around, confused, thinking she'd made a mistake and put the camera on another chair.

A few were scattered around a monitor used

by continuity and make up. She rushed over . . .
nothing. Wildly she looked about: somebody must
have moved it to a safer place, she was daft to have
just left it . . .

The film crew, subdued and talking in hushed
voices were huddled round the small van from
which Dave dispensed coffee.

Alison ran over to them.

'I'm sorry to be a nuisance,' she said, her teeth
chattering so much she could hardly speak, 'but has
anyone seen my camera? I left it on the chair over
there,' she gesticulated in the direction of the chair,
'when Emma went into the water. But it's not there
any more.' She was almost crying. 'I just wondered
whether anyone might have moved it?'

The reaction was sympathetic, but unanimous,
no, no one had seen it, no one had moved it.

'But . . . but,' the tears started to slip down
Alison's face. 'Someone must have moved it. It's
not mine, you see . . . I've got to find it . . .'

'Positions, everyone,' Matt shouted from the
riverbank and instantly they were back in work
mode, Alison's problem on hold.

'Don't worry,' whispered Dave, handing her a
cup of tea. 'Here, drink this, you look frozen; I'll
help you look when we've finished this take.'

As if apologising for all that had gone before,
the sun rose on cue, bathing Jason and Harry in
strawberry pink light. Jason hoicked the fish out of
the waters and it twisted and turned on the end of
the line, casting golden droplets into the air.

As he'd promised, Dave helped Alison hunt
around the small encampment, but they could find
absolutely no trace of the camera.

By the time Marcus felt they had filmed enough

335

to satisfy Emma's requirements and called a halt, Alison was completely distraught and sank on a chair, her head in her hands.

Marcus strolled over. 'Hello, what's this, young Alison? I thought you'd gone home. What's wrong?'

She looked up, despairing. 'It's my camera . . . or rather it's not my camera, that's the point. It's gone missing. I put it on this chair when Emma fell into the river and it's vanished.'

Marcus frowned. 'Things don't just vanish. Are you sure you put it down here . . . everything happened so quickly . . . are you sure you didn't put it somewhere else?'

'No, I'm sure; I was videoing Jason walking towards you and saw the . . . er . . . accident. I put the camera down and ran to the riverbank.'

'You videoed the accident?' Jason came up behind Marcus. 'You got it on camera?' He looked strained and defiant.

'Yes, I think so . . . I was following you and saw you . . . saw what happened.'

'You saw me trip. Something tripped me up. Something tripped me up, Marcus,' he repeated, staring belligerently at Marcus.

'So you say, Jason. But what? There are no tree roots here; there were no cables across the grass there. What?'

'I don't know,' replied Jason angrily. 'But this fucking camera might tell us. Where's the camera, Alison? Let's see it.'

'I can't,' said Alison helplessly. 'It's gone.'

60

'So, our joker strikes again,' Charlie was thoughtful. 'And the finger points very firmly at Master Jason.'

'But he insists he tripped and that it was an accident.' Alison, still shivering, was sitting by the Rayburn, wrapped in a blanket and cradling a mug of hot honey and lemon her mother insisted she drink.

Marcus had dropped her off at the farmhouse before going to talk to Jason, with the parting consolation, 'Don't worry about the camera, Alison. If we've got a thief on the crew, we'll find them out. I'll get it back for you.'

Charlie snorted. 'Jason's very bold; I'll give him that. He nearly drowns Emma, nicks your camera and pretends to know nothing about anything.'

'But why should he take my camera?'

'Because, dear sister, he knows you've filmed him . . . he's been caught in the act! It's pretty obvious. I think this clinches it. He's our man.'

Alison said nothing but sipped her drink, frowning. 'It's possible,' she began slowly, 'it was someone else who took it.'

'Why should they?' Charlie was becoming impatient. As far as he could see, the case against Jason Hart was conclusive.

'Well, if it really was an accident and the clip shows that, then Jason is in the clear and if someone else wanted Jason to take the blame for everything, it would be in their interest to steal the camera.'

'Sounds bloody convoluted to me,' Charlie

commented. 'But at least it puts our Stevie is in the clear.'

'Did you suspect him?' Alison looked at her brother, shocked.

Charlie shrugged. 'It's because of the way he's been since the television people arrived. You've seen it for yourself. He's become impossible.'

'Maybe.' Alison paused, then, watching her brother closely, curious to see his reactions, added. 'Maybe it's because he's jealous of you?'

'Jealous? Of me?' Charlie gave a short contemptuous laugh. 'How do you work that one out?'

Alison wriggled impatiently inside her blanket. Her body ached, the loss of the camera weighed heavily on her and her brother seemed to be irritatingly obtuse. 'Well, for one thing,' she snapped, 'everyone on the crew likes you. It's always "Charlie says this and Charlie does that". You can't help it, don't get me wrong, but I think Stephen's nose gets put out of joint when he's not consulted.'

Charlie frowned. 'He doesn't exactly encourage consultation . . .'

'No, maybe not. But he should be, shouldn't he?'

Charlie grunted. 'If we waited for Stephen, nothing would ever get done.'

'That's not true, Charlie,' said Alison crossly. 'He's making a bloody good stab at running this farm. You didn't want to take it on.'

'No, you're right, I didn't, but are you seriously suggesting it's because of that Stephen is so antsy with me?'

'Not just that. I reckon Angela's got something to do with it as well.'

338

'Angela? What's it to do with Angela? I thought they were the answer to love's young dream?'

'Yeah, well up to a point they are. But I wouldn't be surprised if Stephen's in a blue funk.' For a second Alison hesitated, then plunged on. 'I reckon he and Angela are both virgins, and you, Charlie . . . well, we all know the countryside is littered with your ex-lovers. And now there's Isabelle . . .'

'Yes?' Charlie eyed her dangerously.

'It's none of my affair and I really hope it works out for you, but yet again, as far as Stephen's concerned, you're making it and he's still at the starting post. No wonder he's jealous. I'm sure it will be fine in the end, but he doesn't know that.'

Charlie stared at her, then shook his head, amazed. 'When did you work this one out? I thought you were studying to become a vet, not an Agony Auntie?'

'Think about it Charlie . . . I bet I'm right.'

'That's as maybe, but I can't do anything about it, can I? It's something they've got to work out for themselves.'

Alison shifted irritably. 'That's so bloody typical. "Nothing to do with me!" You're his brother, for Chrissake. He hasn't got Dad to tell him the facts of life . . . you should do it.'

'Me? Ali, he's thirty! He's a farmer. He knows all about the birds and the bees.'

'The mechanics, maybe, but all the other stuff: the billing and cooing and when to make the move and what to do when he . . .'

She broke off at her mother's appearance.

'Alison, love, I've run you a nice hot bath. Now go and have a good soak, I don't want you catching a cold . . . you're looking very flushed.'

339

The telephone rang in the hall.

'Answer that would you, Charlie? It's probably for you anyway, it usually is . . . Now Alison, have you finished your drink?'

'Nearly. Mum, have you got something in the oven?' Alison sniffed. 'I'm sure I can smell something burning.'

'Oh blow, it's my cake,' wailed Jenny. 'What did I go and forget that for?'

She flung open the oven door and brought out a tin. The top of the cake was black and smoking.

'What sort of cake is it, Mum?'

'Chocolate. I baked it for Ben; he looked a bit poorly yesterday so I thought I'd make him a cake.' She looked at her handiwork and sadly shook her head. 'What a shame.'

'You could cut off the burnt bits and cover it with a melted bar of chocolate.'

Jenny brightened. 'Good idea, love, he'd never know. I don't suppose he gets to eat much homemade cake. Now you go and have that bath.'

Charlie poked his head round the door. 'It's Al, Alison. He says you're not answering your mobile.'

'Oh shit!' Alison panicked. 'What do I say about the camera, Charlie? He's gonna go beserk!'

*   *   *

Alison was right, Al was furious.

'What do you mean . . . you put it down and it just vanished. Things don't just vanish . . . somebody must have taken it . . . Or you just didn't look hard enough.'

'Al, that's just not fair, I looked everywhere.'

'What a bloody stupid thing to do, to leave it

340

lying around like that; it was an expensive camera
. . .

'I know, but when Emma went into the water . . .'

'You didn't think, did you? You just didn't think.
I suppose with Mr fuckin' Hart in your viewfinder,
nothing else mattered?'

'What the hell are you talking about? What's
Jason Hart got to do with anything?'

'Everything. I wouldn't be at all surprised if he
didn't nick the camera. You filmed him pushing
Emma . . . incriminating to say the least. Have you
asked him if he took it?'

'No, of course not.'

'Why not?'

'It's not so easy, Al, to go up to someone and say,
"oh, did you nick my camera"?'

'Except it wasn't yours, it's my aunt's. If you'd
spent that much on a camera you wouldn't just have
left it lying around . . .'

'Oh yes, sorry, how could I have forgotten
how expensive it was, especially as you keep on
reminding me? Emma really should have held off
drowning till I'd found somewhere secure to leave
it. Well, I'm really sorry, Al, about your aunt's
camera. If I can't find it, don't worry, I will find a
way to replace it. Oh, and if you're interested, not
that you've asked, Emma's being kept in hospital,
overnight, with suspected hypothermia.'

She slammed down the phone, trembling
violently, and gave way to a bout of angry tears.

By the time she'd finished her bath, she felt
terrible, hot and shivery, her eyes swollen with
crying; she decided to give lunch a miss and go back
to bed to compensate for the very early start she'd
had that morning.

61

'My, you're a quick worker.' The receiver pressed to
her ear, Veronica grimaced at her reflection in the
gilt mirror adorning the wall above the hall phone.

'Well done, Sally. What a fortuitous meeting.
The next thing for you to do is seek her out again;
leave it a couple of days; then say you've found
someone who might be interested but they want to
know what sort of sum is . . . The name? Well yes,
I suppose they might . . . I have got one we can use
. . . VE Osbourne, . . . yes, Osbourne. But only if
they ask, and say you don't know much about him,
you think he's a wealthy Australian . . . But the
important thing is to find out how much they need
to raise and ask them for a business plan . . . Yes,
that's right . . . Thank you so much . . . Oh, Sally,
I nearly forgot, we're having a little party here on
Thursday, for the television people; I might have
mentioned it to you before . . . Yes, that's right
. . . just a select few . . . oh, about eight-ish . . . A
pleasure. Bye.'

Humming quietly, she put the phone down and
studied her face in the mirror, and plotted her next
move.

Over lunch Hugh mentioned he'd invited two
important clients to her drinks party on Thursday,
trusting she'd come up with the goods as far as her
'celebrity friends' were concerned.

Cordelia, sulking because her mother would
not let her invite any of her mates, ate very little,
grumbling the whole while about it being 'soup and
cheese, again!' whereupon Veronica, heartily fed

up with her daughter, seized that as an excuse to demand her premature departure from the table.

When Cordelia had flounced out of the room, declaring she would rather starve to death than eat any more of her mother's rotten food, Veronica decided (the sympathy vote being decidedly in her favour), that the time had come to float her plan.

'I don't know,' she sighed. 'I thought Anthony was trying enough as a teenager; Cordelia seems determined to be as bad, if not worse.'

'What that young lady needs,' Hugh growled, 'is a good clip across the ear.'

'And if you succumbed to your very natural inclination, my darling,' rejoined Veronica sweetly, 'you'd be prosecuted for assault, made worse, of course, by the fact she's your daughter.'

'The law's an ass!'

'I agree, it often is. Talking of our son, have you got anywhere with your actions against the Tuckers?'

'It's like stirring treacle with a plastic spoon, but I've made some headway,' Hugh replied. 'And I've heard on the grapevine that certain persons in the village are on the warpath without our prompting. The Tuckers should receive notice by Wednesday or Thursday that the parish council is to be petitioned. It'll take time, but I'm optimistic.'

'Good. Meanwhile, my sweet, I've been busy. What would you say to buying a fifty per cent share in our troublesome farm?'

He stared at her, frowning. 'Explain.'

'Actually, it was a suggestion of yours that sparked me off. Create a rift, you said, a rift between the TV crew and the Tuckers. Well, I've found something better . . . a rift between the

Tucker brothers.'

Hugh's eyes gleamed. 'Go on.'

'It would seem the two brothers have quarrelled. One is about to get married and I have it on good authority his fiancée thinks the best solution would be for the one brother to buy the other out. Only, of course, he doesn't have the capital to do so. Which is where we come in.'

'Yes?'

'Obviously he wouldn't dream of putting himself in debt to us, but if we were to be presented as anonymous investors, prepared to act as sleeping partners who would collect on the investment when the farm was in profit, or sold . . .'

'Are there such people?'

Veronica shrugged. 'People with too much money do daft things. The thing is the fiancée believes there are. She is prepared to persuade her swain it's a viable way of getting rid of the other brother.'

'Hmm,' Hugh rubbed his chin thoughtfully. 'You don't happen to know which brother is going to be bought out, do you?'

'No, 'fraid not. I really don't know the individual members of that clan,' replied Veronica with disdain.

'Find out. One's very much more clued up than the other. So let me get this straight: your suggestion, Vee, is that we should loan Tucker A the necessary, and when he's bought out Tucker B . . .'

'We demand our money back. He can't pay, thrashes around for a loan which he won't get, we buy him out and voila, the farm is ours!'

'Neat.' A cold smile flickered across his features.

344

'Have you also considered how you're going to prevent the true identity of this sleeping partner from getting out?'

'Of course. I'll use my maiden name. No one knows it: VE Osborne. VE Osborne will put up the finance; there's no way it could be traced back to us.'

Hugh smeared a large piece of Stilton onto a cracker and munched it slowly, then looked up and smiled. 'You're fiendishly clever, my dear. I've said it before and I'll say it again, I'm very glad we're batting on the same side.'

'Then you agree? It's worth a try?'

'I can't see any major flaws. Yes, I think it's worth a try.'

'Excellent. The next thing to find out is precisely what sort of sum we're talking about. It maybe we can't afford the amount they'll need.'

'We can afford it. I want that farm. Whatever it takes, we can afford it.'

62

'Hello, Mrs Tucker, what can I do for you?' The burly gatekeeper winked at Jenny. 'You after Ben Dacres, love?'

'Not exactly,' Jenny looked flustered. 'I'm meant to be at the village shop . . . they want me there for the filming this afternoon and I'm a bit late, only I wanted to drop this off.' She produced a fat parcel of tin foil from her basket. 'It's for Mr Dacres—it's a cake,' she explained. 'I wondered if he was going to be here this afternoon . . .'

'He most certainly is, he's on call for the first sequence. He'll be in his trailer; do you want to give it him, yourself?'

'Oh . . . I'm not sure I've got time. I'm quite happy to leave it with you . . .'

'No guarantee it'd get to him . . . home-made cake, straight from the farmhouse kitchen . . . he'd be lucky to see a crumb! Joe . . .' He whistled to the unit driver, sitting in a nearby car, absorbed in a model railway magazine.

Joe looked up and waved at Jenny. 'Hello, Mrs Tucker. How are you?'

'Joe, do us a favour, mate, escort this lovely lady to Mr Dacres's trailer.'

And so Jenny, who had not planned to hand over the gift in person and feeling rather embarrassed at the winks and innuendos from Joe and the gatekeeper, found herself standing outside Ben's trailer door.

From within the van she could hear a pleasant baritone raised in song. She stood for a moment, listening with pleasure. The singing broke off, but before Jenny could knock, it began again.

'Some enchanted evening' he warbled, 'You may see a stranger . . . You may see a stranger . . . Across a crowded room . . .'

It was irresistible, Jenny joined in. 'And somehow you know . . . You even know then . . .'

For a minute, the two of them crooned along together, either side of the closed door of the trailer.

'. . . That somewhere you'll see her
Again and again.
Some enchanted evening . . .'
The door opened.

'Someone may be laughing,' Ben sang.

She froze, her mouth wide open, mid–phrase, then blushed fiercely.

'Don't stop,' he begged. 'I was enjoying our duet. You've got a nice little voice, my dear.'

'I just love *South Pacific*,' she said with fervour. 'It's got some of my favourite songs.'

'Mine, too.' He nodded and smiled. 'Now, to what do I owe the honour of this visit, dear lady? Or did you come merely to serenade me on my humble doorstep?'

'Oh, no, I didn't mean to disturb you. I just thought to leave this for you with Ross, but Joe insisted on showing me to your trailer.' She offered him the silver parcel.

Bemused, he took it. 'My, it's heavy. What is it?'

'It's a cake. A chocolate cake. I do hope you like chocolate. Only you seemed a bit under the weather, Saturday, and I thought a nice bit of home-made cake would cheer you up.'

'You're so kind,' he murmured, wrinkling his brow. 'Saturday, what was I doing on Saturday?'

'On the film set,' she prompted, 'with the pigs.'

'Oh yes,' he shuddered, 'the pigs. Don't remind me.'

'Sorry. Anyway I thought you'd like some cake. Now I really must be going . . .'

'Do you have to?' His smiled was so persuasive, Jenny felt torn; but it really wasn't a good idea to be late for her first job as an extra. Money was always extremely tight and what she would earn would buy Stephen and Angela a really nice wedding present.

'I'm expected down at the village shop. I'm going to be an extra and I'm a bit late already, so yes, I'm afraid I do.' She started down the steps, 'I hope you

347

enjoy the cake.'

Ben was bored; he'd been stuck in his trailer waiting to be called for an hour and he'd no idea how much longer he'd have to wait. He'd read his paper; the novel he'd selected irritated him; there was nothing of interest on Radio Two, and it was tuning into local radio that had triggered the *South Pacific* sing-song.

Jenny's arrival had been an unexpected and very welcome diversion. He liked her . . . although, for the life of him he couldn't remember her name. Admittedly she was a bit on the plump side and a trifle shabby . . . hadn't she worn that multi-coloured sweater at least twice before? But she had a soft prettiness about her, which he liked, and she clearly thought he was the bees' knees, which made him feel good.

'No, don't go. We've unfinished business, my sweet Cancerian.'

'Oh?' Jenny's resolve started to slip.

'Once you have found her . . .' he sang, slapping a hand to his chest. 'Never let her go.'

She laughed and joined in 'Once you have found her, never let her go!' She broke off. 'But I must.' And feeling a little bit like Cinderella running away from her prince, she ran down the steps.

'Sweetheart!'

She stopped, mid-flight and turned, her heart thumping. 'Yes?'

'Have dinner with me on Thursday night?'

'Dinner?' Jenny felt the colour ebbing from her cheeks. Had anybody, ever before, asked her that question? Let's go to the Chinese, yes. How about fish'n'chips? Certainly. Indian? Pub lunch? Thai takeaway? Yes, yes, but no-one had ever said 'have dinner with me on Thursday night' and certainly no-one as handsome as Ben Dacres.

She couldn't think how to respond. 'Erm,' she croaked. 'That'd be lovely. Thanks . . . erm . . . can I let you know?'

She'd no idea where that reluctant reply had come from when her whole being shouted 'Yes—yippee!' But some deeply rooted instinct had yelped like a raw nerve, warning her that this was something that needed a considered response.

Ben looked surprised and a bit miffed; he was not used to being treated so casually. 'Fine. Just leave a note with Ross. If you can make it I'll meet you in the bar of the Country Club at eight.'

'Lovely . . . that'd be lovely. Thank you Ben, I'll let you know.' And she turned and sped away, leaving a bemused Ben staring after her.

63

Jenny ran all the way to the shop and arrived just as the woman who'd recruited them finished processing the last on her list. She looked at Jenny coldly. 'You're late, Mrs . . . er?'

'Tucker, Jenny Tucker,' Jenny was chastened. 'Yes, I'm sorry, I got, er, held up.'

'We do rely on everybody being punctual. If timekeeping is going to be a problem, we must use somebody else . . .'

'No, no,' Jenny said hastily. 'I won't be late again.'

'Hmm,' the woman ticked her list and then looked critically at Jenny. 'You too,' she sighed.

'Why is it when we tell people to come in everyday clothes, they come dressed for a party. That sweater won't do, it won't do at all.'

'I'm sorry,' said Jenny humbly. 'I've got a plastic mac in my basket. I could put that on over the top.'

'Please do. Coffee and tea over there,' she waved in direction of a van parked outside the church porch. 'We'll call you when we need you. The church hall is being used for its facilities, and for shelter if it rains, otherwise wait out here.'

She snapped her file shut and disappeared into the shop. Jenny found Rita by her side, looking sour.

'Well, what a way to talk to you, Jenny, like you're back in the infants! But it's been the same for all of us. I had to go home and change; little Miss Hoity Toity took exception to my clothes 'n' all.'

'Oh well, I suppose they know what they're doing. Let's go and get a cup of tea, shall we? I could murder a chocolate biscuit. Did you hear what happened to Emma Knight, their director, this morning?'

And Jenny, with all the authority of someone whose daughter had actually witnessed the events on the riverbank, had a large audience, for most of the extras were local and ready for a good gossip.

Time passed and having comprehensively exhausted the life and near-death drama of Emma Knight; the arrogant behaviour of the quiz team the previous night; the havoc created by the cows in the High Street (at which point Jenny went very quiet); plus the loss of their meadow now the footpath had become impassable, the group became restless.

'What's happening?' became the general

grumble. 'We've been hanging about here for an hour now. What's going on?'

Members of the crew had been in and out of the shop, but, as far as anyone could tell, none of the actors had been brought down.

'Jenny, you go and ask,' Rita nudged her. 'You know them better than us. Find out what's happening.'

'I don't really know them,' Jenny objected. 'I'm sure they wouldn't keep us hanging about for no good reason.'

'Go and find out,' insisted her friend, and egged on by the rest of the group, Jenny reluctantly approached the shop. To her relief, she spotted the unit's runner, Dave, whom she recognised from the previous week's work at the farm.

'Oh hello, Mrs Tucker,' he greeted her cheerfully. 'Come to see what we're up to?'

'Yes. I'm with the extras today, Dave, and we was wondering what the delay was, only nothing seems to be happening . . .'

Dave grinned. 'That's not unusual, Mrs Tucker. It often feels that way to me, but you can be sure there's no time wasting. Location shots can take an age to set up, but once we get going . . . And actually,' his voice dropped, 'Marcus has had to take over from Emma and he's determined to get it right. The boss has got to roll up his sleeves and he's discovered it ain't that simple, so he's going to take his time.'

'Oh, I see. Yes. But have you any idea when we're going to start?'

Dave glanced at the tea van. 'Troops getting restless, are they? Do you want me to send Sarah Thornby out to talk to them?'

351

'Who's she?'

'The assistant director. You'd have seen her earlier.'

'I think,' said Jenny thoughtfully, 'better not. She's got an unfortunate manner, that one. No, we're all right for the moment. Just let us know when you've any news. In the meantime, if it's all the same to you, I think we'll go and sit in the church hall. All this standing around is exhausting.'

*   *   *

'So how much longer did you have to wait after that?' Angela asked, looking up from the chopping board, her face streaming with onion tears.

'Nearly another hour.' Jenny, feeling quite exhausted, sat at the kitchen table nursing a mug of tea. 'Everyone was really fed up, I can tell you. But then we was called and Rita and me and Mrs Grey were chosen for the inside of the shop, which was good because we got to watch what went on. Rita was really indignant 'cos she thought she could've done a better job than the actress who played the shop-keeper, but Ben was really good and so was Jilly Westcott. She plays his mother, see.'

'So what happened, what was the scene about?'

Jenny frowned. 'That was hard to tell. They would say a few lines, then stop. Then do the same lines again . . . or sometimes just some of them and they'd move the camera and fiddle with the lights and then do the same lines all over again.'

'How awful!'

'It did seem a little slow,' admitted Jenny, 'but that was probably because I was just looking on, you know. Me and Rita had to pretend to be friends, waiting to be served.'

Angela smiled. 'That wasn't difficult, Mum.'

'No, but it was odd, pretending to be what you are, if you see what I mean. I felt very awkward and it was so hard not to look at the camera.'

'Did you have to say anything?'

'No. But what they said was so lifelike. I mean, what they did say, well, word for word it could have been me and Rita . . . and as for Ben—he could have been, well, Stephen, only older of course, talking about his cows.'

Angela, frowning, resumed her chopping and conversation was suspended until the kitchen door banged and Charlie entered the kitchen, his dog at his heels.

He nodded at them both. 'Hi Angela, Mum. You don't need to include me in tonight's supper. I'm off to Isabelle's after I've put the two porkers to bed, so I'll eat there.'

'That's nice, dear,' Jenny smiled at him. 'Charlie . . .'

'Yes, Mum?'

'Any news of poor Emma?'

'Isabelle's taking some clothing and night things for her at the hospital while I look after the two girls. I think she's being kept in for observation, but I've no other news. I've been settling in the new shorthorns so I've not had any dealings with the film crew this afternoon. I take it you didn't hear anything more at the shop?'

Jenny shook her head. 'No. But poor girl, I think they missed her. Marcus seemed very . . . well . . . short with everyone. They all seem quite scared of him.'

Charlie grinned. 'I bet he can be scary when he

353

wants. I'm going to leave Duchess here, Mum. Can you see that she gets fed when Gip does.'

'Yes, dear.'

'Charlie,' Angela looked up from stirring onions. 'Have you read the television script?'

'No,' Charlie looked at her in surprise. 'Why?'

'Oh, no reason—it's just one or two things that have been said . . . I just wonder how close it is to us all here on Marsh Farm. I know it's a sitcom. It would be awful if we were being made fun of, that's all.'

64

Isabelle was greatly reassured when she saw Emma who although pale and very tired, was chafing at having to stay overnight. Isabelle stayed and chatted for half an hour, the conversation turning, for the most part, on how Emma had ended up in the river and whether it had been intentional on Jason's part and if so, whether he could be done for attempted murder. On this jolly thought, Emma's eyes drooped so Isabelle left her to her snooze.

The sun was setting when she left the hospital building and made her way across the car park. A chill wind whistled around the parked vehicles and the sodium lights flickered gold in the encroaching gloom.

'Spring is making a jolly reluctant entry,' she thought, pulling her coat more closely around her and tucking her head down against the cold. Not looking, she bumped full tilt into the tall, dark figure of a man who emerged from round a car.

'Oops, sorry!' she said, then spluttered with surprise. 'Marcus! What are you doing here?'

He looked equally startled. 'Isabelle! Er . . . I . . . erm . . . I've come to see how Emma is . . . you heard about her accident?'

'Yes, I've just been to see her.'

'How is she?'

She thought he sounded weary. 'I think she's going to be fine, Marcus. Just very tired, but they said that's because she's suffering from shock.'

'Hardly surprising.'

'No. She'll be pleased to see you.'

'Will she?'

'Of course.'

Isabelle was puzzled; she wasn't used to this terse style from Marcus.

'Well, I must get going. I've left the girls with Charlie quite long enough. Why don't you call in and have a drink with us when you get back.'

'Thank you, I might. It's been a long, bloody day.' He made to move on then stopped. 'Oh Isabelle, I meant to ask you . . . are you interested in the Blue Fire exhibition? It opens in Bristol on Thursday and I've been sent a couple of invites. I thought I'd combine a visit with a bit of business I've got to do there, but if you'd like to take up the other ticket, I could meet you off the train and then we could grab some supper afterwards . . .'

Isabelle's heart thumped. She wasn't stupid or naïve; she recognised this invitation for what it was. She'd dismissed Charlie's jealousy of Marcus as nonsensical, but maybe . . . maybe she'd been wrong.

It was an unpleasant revelation.

She sighed. 'I really would like to go to that

exhibition, it does sound wonderful, but unless Paula is able to babysit and I can get Charlie to come too, I'll have to say no. Maybe I could persuade Charlie to go with me some other time. Thanks, Marcus. It was kind of you to think of me.'

In the gloom his face gave nothing away. He shrugged and said abruptly, 'No matter. If you change your mind, the offer's there. Cheers.' And he walked off.

Isabelle watched him go, her eyes narrowed. 'And that is the clincher: If you'd said "bring Charlie along too", then . . . But you didn't. You perfidious bastard!' she muttered. 'What sort of person do you think I am? Poor Charlie, he fucking trusted you! I trusted you . . . well not any more!'

She turned and marched towards her car. 'However,' she decided, turning on the ignition, 'I'm not going to tell Charlie about this. He and Marcus have to work together and it would be awful if I were the cause of that all breaking down. Stupid bastard . . . why me? Why doesn't he find someone else to screw! Arrogant, stupid, pig-headed man!'

*   *   *

Marcus didn't immediately go to find Emma but set off on a brisk walk around the hospital grounds. The encounter with Isabelle had rattled him. He was angry with himself; he had planned a subtle siege on Isabelle's affections before getting her to choose between him and Charlie and he had been confident that, given time, she would be won.

He was troubled by the claims of his friendship with Charlie, but he knew it was inevitable they would go their separate ways. He'd convinced himself Isabelle and Charlie's relationship was doomed . . . they had so little in common . . . and that it was up to him, Marcus, to pluck Isabelle out of Summerstoke and give her more the sort of life and stimulation he was convinced she needed.

And now he'd blown it.

His day had been long and tiring; his days as director were well behind him and he'd forgotten how much energy and clear thinking went into scenes involving location, extras, and temperamental talent. He'd been so anxious they shouldn't fall behind schedule he'd refused to postpone the shoot for a day. When they finally finished, his appreciation of Emma's skills was even greater, and his genuine anxiety about her wellbeing was exacerbated by his need for her to return to work as soon as possible.

So it was unfortunate he'd encountered Isabelle when he did and was thrown by her unexpected appearance. His invitation had been crass and he could tell from her voice, not what she wanted; not at all . . . she'd made that perfectly clear: she and Charlie were an item, no room for manoeuvre.

And supposing she told Charlie? It was quite likely she would . . . in one stupid move he'd earned her contempt and sacrificed his friendship. He groaned. He didn't like what he had done; it was a stupid infatuation and it had led to this misjudgement, and like all infatuations, he told himself sternly, it was one-sided, selfish and unhealthy.

Polly had warned him . . . yes, she had; she'd suggested he was like Isabelle's husband, that he represented a life Isabelle had already rejected, and in his arrogance he'd assumed Polly was wrong.

357

Well Isabelle had turned him down and if he had any sense, any integrity, he'd make amends and move on.

He could hear the cool rejection in her voice and although not easily embarrassed, he felt his humiliation keenly and it took him some minutes to regain his composure before he was able to turn towards the hospital.

At the entrance to the hospital shop, he hesitated. It suddenly struck him he should not go empty-handed, but for the life of him, he couldn't think what to take. He really didn't know Emma that well. If it had been Polly, or his ex, Sue, what would he have brought? 'Nothing,' was the answer, but somehow, in this instance nothing would not do. In the end he purchased a box of dark chocolates and a current affairs magazine and made his way to the ward.

*   *   *

Emma awoke from a light doze, aware that someone was looking at her. She gave a start of surprise. 'Marcus! What are you doing here?'

His expression was hard to fathom but he looked tired, she thought, and strained.

'I've come to see how you are.'

'Thank you, I'm fine. Won't you sit down?'

He pulled up a chair. 'I won't stay long . . .'

'It was nice of you to come.'

'It was the least I could do. Oh,' he offered her the chocolates and magazine, 'I don't know whether you like chocolates but apparently flowers are banned.'

'Thank you, it'll be nice to have something to

read. I didn't exactly come equipped.'

'No, I suppose you didn't.'

She pulled herself up. 'Marcus, I've only had a very garbled account of what happened. What did happen? Did Jason push me in the river? Did he do it deliberately?'

Marcus frowned. 'He says not, of course. He says he tripped and it was an accident. All I know is one moment you were standing by my side, and the next, you were nose-diving into the river and Jason was flat on his face at my feet.'

'What do you think?'

'I don't know, Emma. I didn't see him trip and I haven't had a chance to talk to him properly, yet. At the time I was more concerned with getting you out and then getting you here. You looked pretty awful.'

'But do you think he would do something so drastic, deliberately?' Emma persisted. 'It's tantamount to attempted murder, isn't it?'

Marcus's frown deepened. 'That had occurred to me. I know you feel Jason has got a thing about you, but . . .'

'Not a thing about me, Marcus.' Emma was emphatic. 'I think he's got a thing about being stuck down here filming for three months and is doing his level best to sabotage the project.' She fell silent for a moment, looking thoughtful, then continued. 'But actually, I'm inclined to believe him . . . a prank like this, if it was deliberate, could have badly backfired on him and he's not stupid.'

'Well, I'm relieved to hear you say that at least. But what evidence, Emma, do you have for thinking he wants to sabotage the series?'

Emma looked weary. 'Ask Charlie, or Alison. It

359

was they who first raised the alarm. So many things have happened this week on the farm and on the set, it has to be more than just a coincidence and, I'm afraid, everything points to Jason.'

Marcus fell silent, then looked at her, his eyes narrowing. 'Why didn't you tell me?'

'Because, Marcus, A: you'd gone to London, and B: you showed every inclination to believe my accusations were the product of an over-fertile and febrile imagination.'

He gave a short laugh. 'Yes. You have a point. Hmm . . . perhaps we'd better consult with Ross; he's closer to the actors and the crew than anyone else. He might have some ideas.' He gave an exasperated shrug. 'I have to admit, Emma, this is a bloody pain. I've no doubt the press will have got wind of your accident and will be sniffing round the set, and if word gets out about everything else . . . Oh shit!'

He sighed deeply and closed his eyes.

He looked so troubled Emma felt a surge of sympathy, which took her by surprise, considering a short while ago she'd dismissed him as the quintessential pinnacle of arrogance, and a total bastard to boot.

'We can see the press off and then sort it out ourselves, Marcus. What happened to the filming today?'

He opened his eyes. 'I took over from you, and let me tell you, it was the most exhausting thing I've done for a long time.' He suddenly grinned. 'Have you met Mrs Rita Godwin?'

'No,' Emma looked quizzical, 'Who's she?'

'Mrs Rita Godwin is the owner of the village shop. She's also on the parish council, the self-appointed spokesperson of the good souls of Summerstoke, and a chatterbox. In fact, she is more than that . . . she doesn't know when to stop talking. Her conversation contains no full stops, and I had the misfortune of having her as an extra this afternoon. Emma, I need you!'

Emma chuckled. 'That's life at the coal face, Marcus. But I'd rather do my job than yours.'

He sat forward in his chair and gazed at her intently. 'I haven't really asked you how you are, Emma. You gave me quite a shock.'

'I'm fine, really I am.'

'Have they said when you can be released?'

'I'm hoping no later than tomorrow morning, but really, Marcus, I don't see why I shouldn't go now.'

He looked dubious. 'You do look rather pale.'

'I admit I feel exhausted, but I reckon I'd make a quicker recovery in my own bed. This place is so bloody noisy . . . if sleep is what I need, I'm certainly not going to get it here. Will you help me?'

'What?' he was startled.

'I'm sure if the doctor sees I'm going to be released into a safe pair of hands . . .'

'Thanks!'

'Then they won't raise too many objections. They always say they're short of beds . . .'

'I don't know . . . supposing something happens, I don't know too much about the effects of hypothermia . . .'

'Marcus,' Emma protested. 'I am neither old nor frail. I'm going to be fine. But if I stay a minute longer here I shall get the screaming hab-dabs or contract MRSA or some such thing.' Her eyes flashed at his hesitation. 'If you won't help, Marcus, I shall discharge myself after you've gone, and

361

make my own way back, but you'll have to lend me the money for a taxi, 'cos, silly me, I completely forgot to bring my purse with me.'

A faint smile flickered across his face. 'Are you always this wilful?'

She smiled back. 'Only when I want something very badly. You'll help?'

65

'Sorry to press on, Mum,' said Angela, placing knives and forks on the table, 'but Stephen and I must eat as soon as he's in from the milking. Mrs Pagett's expecting us at seven-thirty.'

Jenny gathered up her knitting and glanced at the kitchen clock. 'Jeff's got a late surgery this evening so maybe I'll wait to eat with him, love, and we need to save some for Gran; she needs to keep her strength up, poor thing.'

'Any news of Ron?'

'Not yet. He was having his op today, so fingers crossed.'

Angela shook her head. 'We have to remember he is eighty. He's had a good innings.'

Jenny felt irritated, 'Well I for one hope he's not finished yet. He makes Gran very happy.'

As she watched Angela bustling with saucepans and dishes, she wondered whether it would be wise to confide in Angela about Ben. Ever since he'd invited her out, she'd been unable to think of little else. Should she or shouldn't she accept? She so wanted to go, she really enjoyed his company, and he made her feel, well, special. If she said no, he'd never ask her again, and she would never know what it was like to go out to a posh dinner with a star . . . But if she said yes, how would Jeff take it?

If she told Jeff, she was pretty sure he'd say go, but he'd not like it, and there again, if he weren't bothered, then she'd be really upset. But if she didn't tell him and went, it would be a bit like two-timing, and she'd not do that.

So she was in desperate need of advice. But who to ask? Rita was her best friend, but Rita was a serial gossip and with all the best intentions in the world, she couldn't keep a secret. If Jenny confided in her, it would be out round the village before the end of day that Ben Dacres had asked Jenny Tucker out to dinner.

No, Jenny concluded, nice as she was, Angela would disapprove and Jenny could guess what she'd say. What she wanted was a dispassionate assessment of the whys and wherefores, not a blanket negative . . . What about Isabelle? Jenny had been struck by Isabelle's sensitivity in helping her with what to wear for the party. Yes, she'd be a good person to ask . . .

'Is Alison here for supper?' Angela cut across her reverie.

'I don't know, love. Her light isn't on in her room, so she must have gone out.'

'I'll leave enough for her as well then, shall I?'

'Please, Angela.'

'Mum . . .'

Jenny looked up to see Angela had turned from her cooking pots and fixed her with an intense gaze. She was holding a large wooden spoon from which sauce dripped onto the floor, unnoticed by Angela but not Gip, who was on her feet in a flash to lick up the unexpected treat.

'Yes, love?'

'Do you mind if I ask you a very personal question?'

For one wild moment Jenny imagined Angela had been reading her mind. 'No, love,' she faltered, bracing herself.

'Do you think people should have sex before they get married?'

Mercifully for Jenny, who was completely taken aback by the question, the telephone rang and by the time she'd answered it and returned to the kitchen, she'd had time to collect her thoughts.

She sat down and picked up an old sweater she was turning back into a ball of wool.

'That was Al on the phone. Alison's not answering her mobile. He sounded really fed up. They had such a row earlier.'

'What about?'

'The camera he'd lent her; she put it down when Emma fell in the river and it disappeared.'

'Things don't just disappear, either she forgot where she'd left it or someone took it. No wonder Al is cross.'

'Yes.' Jenny watched Angela chopping a cabbage so vigorously the floor was sprayed with the cuttings. Gip, ever optimistic, investigated, but raw vegetables held no appeal and she retired back to her basket. Sometimes, it seemed to Jenny, Angela displayed a sorry lack of sympathy or understanding of other people. 'Anyway, I told him to give Hannah a ring. That's probably where she's gone.'

Angela made no comment but continued to chop the cabbage with such intensity she was in danger of turning it into coleslaw. Jenny knew she was waiting for her to say something.

She'd never really discussed sex with her children. They had grown up in more liberated times than she, and she trusted the school and the media to give them all the information they needed. Occasionally she wondered about Alison and Al, but consoled herself with the belief that her daughter would not do anything to jeopardise her prospective university career. Charlie, she knew, had a reputation, and her fear with him had been, until he met Isabelle, that some girl would turn up on the doorstep claiming to be having his baby. But Stephen; she didn't know about her sweet, gentle Stephen. He'd never had a proper girlfriend until Angela and she couldn't believe he was the sort of person who would take himself off and pay for sex, so . . .

'Once upon a time,' she began cautiously, concentrating on her wool-winding, 'women wouldn't have dreamed about having sex before they were married . . . Not because they didn't want to, mind, but because it was expected. The virgin bride all dressed in white . . .'

Angela stopped chopping.

'But . . .' Jenny continued, 'Men did. Or rather, some did. Times have changed though and now it seems when you get to a particular stage in your relationship, sex is seen as a natural step.' She stopped, thinking of her wonderfully rumbustuous sex life with Jeff, and blushed. 'If you want to, I think it's a good idea,' she hurried on. 'But you've both got to want it and not to pretend and if one of you is not ready, then you might as well wait, and if you love each other, it will be all right.'

'Will it?' Angela blinked at Jenny and turned

365

back to stir the pot of bubbling meat. 'Oh I do hope so. I want to have lots and lots of children, but I'm just worried that Stephen doesn't . . .' She turned back to address Jenny, waving the spoon, apparently unaware it was laden with a huge glob of ragout. 'You know . . . doesn't really, well . . . doesn't.'

Gip was at her feet, her eyes following every movement of the spoon, ready for the drop.

*   *   *

'Doesn't what?' enquired Jeff later, his mouth full of savoury mince.

Jenny blushed. 'Oh Jeff, you know. The thing is, do you think I ought to try and talk to him? Or maybe you could . . . he really looks up to you.'

'Jenny,' protested Jeff, 'I'm a vet and if asked, I will certainly assist in helping any of the farm's animals in the procreation of their species, but I draw the line at interfering with homo sapiens. This is between Stephen and Angela: they must work it out. Now,' he put down his knife and fork, 'I've something to ask you.'

But whatever he was going to ask her was put on hold by the telephone clamouring for attention.

This time it was Hannah.

'Sorry to bother you, Mrs Tucker, but is Alison at home? Only I've had Al on the phone; he thought she might be here, but she's not and I can't get her on her mobile.'

Jenny frowned, concerned. 'I don't think she is, Hannah. The light's not on in her room. Hold on a moment, I'll go and have a look. She had a very early start this morning and after all that business

366

over Emma, she might have had an early bed . . .'

She put the phone down and hurried up to her daughter's room. The bed was empty, the duvet thrown back half on the floor; on the floor a mobile phone bleeped intermittently.

Jenny sped back downstairs and picked up the phone.

'Hannah? No, she's not in her room. Her mobile is, though. Have you any idea where she might be? No . . . ?'

Her face puckered with worry, she returned to the kitchen.

Jeff looked at her and got to his feet. 'What was all that about? What's the matter, love?'

'It's Alison, Jeff. Hannah was on the phone asking where she is. Al is looking for her, too. She's not in her room and she's left her mobile behind.' She glanced out of the kitchen window. It was dark. 'It's probably just me being silly, but I'm worried, Jeff. Where is she?'

The handle of the kitchen door turned.

'This'll be her now,' Jeff said comfortably.

'Alison!' cried Jenny with relief.

'No,' said Elsie, entering the kitchen. 'It's me.'

66

It took a little while for a doctor of sufficient seniority to be found before Emma's release could be secured, but finally she was free to go.

As Marcus's car roared out of the city towards Summerstoke, he reflected, with some surprise, not only was he relieved she was out of hospital, with apparently no ill effects, but he was enjoying her company and the teasing banter of their conversation was lifting his spirits.

By taking her back to the Old Vicarage he realised he would have to confront Isabelle and Charlie much sooner than he'd planned, but he was prepared for that. He just hoped Emma could be persuaded to go straight to her room and would not witness his humiliation.

'So what's your next move going to be, Marcus?'

'After I've seen you safely tucked up in bed, you mean?'

She snorted.

'You heard what the doctor said: rest for the next twenty-four hours. I don't trust you to take his advice.'

Emma pulled a face. 'I've got work to do, and I'm fine.'

'No, Emma. We can't take the chance. If anything happened to you, how would I explain it? I'll come over tomorrow with the script, first thing, and you can talk me through it. Then I'll bring the rushes back at the end of the day. Okay?'

'Okay,' she sighed. 'Thanks, Marcus.'

'For what?'

'For . . . for being so nice . . .'

'For a change?'

'Yes,' she said simply and Marcus laughed.

'But actually,' she continued, 'I was wondering what you plan to do about Jason?'

'I'll talk to Ross about your suspicions; I promise you I am taking them seriously. As for the incident this morning, I've told Jason we need to have a chat before I decide to do anything. He's expecting me this evening . . . I'll go on over after I've dropped you off.'

'That won't be much fun.'

'No,' he said grimly, thinking about the confrontation awaiting him at the Old Vicarage. 'It won't.'

Emma led the way into the hall and Marcus, tensing, followed.

She poked her head round the sitting room door. 'Hello, Charlie.'

Marcus heard Charlie's exclamation of pleasure. 'Emma, you're back! That's fantastic. Isabelle didn't think they'd let you out till tomorrow at the earliest.'

'I persuaded them to let me go and Marcus gave a very convincing performance as a caring, responsible citizen.'

'Marcus?'

Marcus braced himself.

'Yes, he's here, he brought me home.'

'Hey, Marcus,' Charlie appeared at the door. 'I've just been reading this,' he waved a script. 'I persuaded Colin to let me read it. You sly old dog . . . you've caught us to a tee!'

Scarcely believing his fortune, Marcus breathed out. From the way Charlie was grinning, it was clear Isabelle had not said anything. Silently he blessed her and gave Charlie a faint grin. 'You don't mind?'

'Not in the least,' said Charlie cheerfully. 'Angela was worried you might be making fun of us, so I thought I'd better check it out. And so, yeah, I recognise bits of us, the dialogue is very like, and the things they get up to ring all sorts of bells, but I think it's very funny. I've no problem with it.'

'Great.'

Attracted by the noise, Isabelle appeared from

the kitchen and shrieked with surprise to see Emma.

'Yes,' explained Emma, 'Marcus was my accomplice in the great escape.'

'But she's got to go straight to bed, Isabelle,' said Marcus calmly, his heart thumping. 'Doctor's orders—and she's to stay there tomorrow. I'll call round first thing to go over the script, Emma.'

'Won't you stay for a drink, Marcus?' Isabelle's voice was civil but not warm.

Marcus gave her a penitent look. 'No thanks, Isabelle, I'll leave you to it. I've some unfinished business and it's getting late.'

*   *   *

Driving over to the Country Club and thinking through the events of the evening, he realised he had come out of the other side of his infatuation. Isabelle was a pearl, but she was not for him. His behaviour would give him many private moments of embarrassment, but he could view his rejection with something approaching equanimity. He and Charlie were still friends and he realised how much he cared about that. And also on the positive side, he was looking forward to working with Emma tomorrow morning.

Which just left the little matter of Jason Hart. His face was grim when he turned in at the Country Club. Even if he had not deliberately pushed Emma into the water, there was this matter of the sabotage accusation. He trusted Ross absolutely; he would consult with him and and if he thought Jason might be up to something . . .

At the desk, he asked for Jason. The receptionist

rang his room. There was no answer.

Frowning, Marcus told her to carry on trying and walked through the lounge to the bar to see if he might be waiting for him downstairs.

Ben, Jilly, Juliet, Nicola and a couple of other actors were sitting at a table and hailed him.

'Marcus, old man, we're about to have some dinner. Will you join us?' Ben asked cheerfully.

'No thanks, Ben,' Marcus replied courteously. 'I'm looking for Jason.'

'So am I. We were going to have dinner together,' volunteered Nicola, 'But he hasn't shown. He's not in his room, either.'

'Has anyone seen him?'

No-one had.

67

Feeling lousy, and upset after her angry exchange with Al, Alison slipped into a feverish sleep. She awoke half way through the afternoon and lay, hot and aching under her duvet, her mind running over and over the events of the morning.

What had happened to the camera? Al had no right to accuse her of 'just leaving it lying around' . . . And as for that stupid suggestion that she was in any way interested in Jason Hart . . .

The camera, where was the camera? Might he have taken it?

She sat up in bed. It was no good; she knew she'd looked everywhere, but she couldn't just lie in bed, fretting . . . she had to go and have another hunt. Maybe she'd not searched a wide enough area;

maybe she'd overlooked something.

The sun was still quite high in the sky but she felt cold and clammy. Slipping into her jeans, she pulled on an old thick sweater and a quilted gilet, tucked a small torch into her pocket, and set off in the direction of the riverbank.

Away over the fields came the noise of men whooping and whistling, and the irritated bellowing of large beasts. In a distant field she could make out two large cattle trucks; Charlie had said the Shorthorns were being delivered that afternoon and she had been planning to take photographs of the event for the website . . .

'Oh, bugger it!' she muttered crossly, and climbing over a gate, followed the vehicle tracks across the field to the location of that morning's shoot. Patches of flattened grass were the only evidence of anything having taken place there.

She stood and looked around, trying to work out where everything had been and who had been standing where when Emma went into the river.

Behind her a small copse of young oak, hazel, field maple and bramble, grew in an old shallow quarry. In front of it, to the left, the refreshment van had parked and close by there had been a small table for the monitor used by makeup and continuity.

The chair on which she'd put the camera had been to the right of the copse, about fifteen feet away from the riverbank. Emma and Marcus had stood on a river bend in between an alder with dark gold catkins and young fresh leaves, and an old ash, still leafless but with silvery keys rustling in the breeze.

A thicket of blackthorn obscured the riverbank

beyond the ash tree, stopping abruptly where the river undercut the meadow. Here an ancient levee replaced the trees and shrubs, and the bank, rising steeply above the water, was dotted with straggling shrubs and brambles and last autumn's teasels.

Alison stood where she thought she had been when the incident had taken place. She had just taken some photos of Colin setting up his camera on the bank next to Emma, and then she'd turned to pick up Jason by the coffee van. As she did so, he'd moved off towards the river.

She concentrated hard, trying to work out where everyone was and who could have taken her camera without being noticed.

'The answer, I suppose,' she thought bitterly, 'is anyone who wasn't actually involved in Emma's rescue. And we were all so intent on getting her out, I don't suppose anybody noticed what anybody else was up to.'

It was clear the camera was not anywhere on the grass; this left the copse as the most likely place to conceal something; failing that, the riverbank.

'Although,' she reflected, 'if I thought I'd been caught on camera doing something I didn't want anyone to see, I'd have chucked it in the river rather than hide it . . .'

On that depressing thought, she turned and pushed her way into the copse. It was cold out of the sunlight; the ground was muddy, and vicious briars grabbed at her clothes. Undeterred, she prodded the undergrowth, probed holes, pulled back stones, and gazed up into the branches, just in case . . .

She groaned aloud. 'Oh please, it's got to be here . . .'

'Alison?'

Startled, she swung round. Jason was standing at the edge of the copse, watching her.

She scowled. 'What are you doing here?'

'Same as you, probably,' he scowled back. 'I've come to look for the camera.'

'So you can destroy the evidence?'

'Don't be any more stupid than you can help,' he said sourly. 'Why should I deliberately knock Emma in the river? No, that camera will show I tripped.'

'Well you can carry on looking in here,' Alison shivered. 'I'm freezing. But I've searched it pretty thoroughly.'

She emerged into the sunshine and tried to warm herself. Listening to Jason cursing and crashing about in the bushes, she wondered about his unexpected appearance. Should she believe him? He did have a point: unpleasant though he might be, everything against him was circumstantial. But if he didn't push Emma deliberately, if it had been an accident, why should the camera have gone missing?

She wandered down to the ash tree on the riverbank, poked around its roots and peered into the blackthorn thicket.

Suddenly she spotted something.

'Jason,' she shouted. 'Jason, come here . . .'

He crashed out of the copse. 'What is it? Have you found it?'

'No, but look at this.' She pointed at the foot of a blackthorn bush. Just above its root, almost invisible, was a curl of nylon twine, one end knotted around the trunk.

He looked at it blankly. 'So?'

'You said you tripped,' Alison was impatient, starting feel too exhausted even to speak. 'But nobody could see why you did. But maybe you were tripped up by somebody using a length of fishing line . . .'

'What?' he stared at her.

'The light was really bad, wasn't it? The sun hadn't got up. Some joker had set this trap up, then waited for someone, anyone, not necessarily you, to walk down to the river, and then they pulled the line taut. No one would have seen it; it would have been invisible . . . Don't you see, maybe it didn't have to be you, maybe Emma wasn't a target, maybe that part was an accident? Maybe it was a joke that went wrong.'

'And I walked into it . . .'

'And everyone assumed you'd pretended to trip because . . .'

'Yes, why? I'll tell you,' he spat. 'Because they're all a load of wankers and I'm not one of them.'

'No, you're not exactly popular, are you? And you haven't tried to be, have you?'

'Luvvies, has-beens and wannabes, ain't exactly my scene, darlin',' he drawled.

'Oh sorry,' she retorted. 'From where I sit, it seems to me that's exactly where you come from. You just have a different script, with an even more vicious "kick 'em when they're down" policy. So, I must confess, I don't understand why you're whinging about your treatment. You've invited it.'

Jason's eyes narrowed and he glared at her. 'I'm not whinging. I understand the scene better than most . . . it's dog eats dog, I know that. But I'm fucked if I'm gonna be screwed for something I didn't do.'

'Okay. Fair enough. And I'll help as best I can.'
She gestured in the direction of the riverbank.
'Assuming whoever tripped you up realised the
camera might finger him, I guess he'd get rid of it,
pronto. Me, I'd have thrown it in the river . . . And
if it was a theft, the riverbank is as good a hiding
place as the copse.'

'Right, so let's scour the riverbank. You go that
way,' he waved beyond the blackthorn, 'and I'll go
in the opposite direction, and then we'll swop over,
to make doubly sure.'

'Fine,' said Alison with a firmness she was far
from feeling. She would have liked nothing better
than to leave him to it and crawl home to bed. She
ached all over, her throat felt sore, she was hot and
cold at the same time and it was becoming hard to
breathe. 'I'm getting a cold,' she thought gloomily.
'What a drag!'

They set off.

Assiduously Alison scoured the bank, every
shrub, every lump of grass, every clump of weed.
The bank got steeper and steeper until she was
high above the level of the water. Here and there
the edge was torn where clumps of turf had fallen
into the water, leaving muddy scars, fresh and raw.
More dramatically, she reached a point where
several yards of the bank had dropped below the
levee in a sort of rift, forming a platform several
inches lower.

Alison walked cautiously along this unstable
edge, her eyes searching the bank below.

Then she saw it.

The sun, now low on the horizon, was winking
off something metallic. It was the camera, dangling
from a hazel twig some feet below her, just above

the surface of the water.

'Jason,' she croaked. 'Jason, I've found it.'

She knelt down, the better to see how she could retrieve it. The camera was hopelessly out of her reach, but if she could get a long stick they might be able to hook it up. Better still, she could go and get their old rowing boat and try reaching it from the river.

Before she had time to put anything into action, she heard Jason thudding along the bank towards her and before she could warn him about the instability of the bank, he had jumped off the levee onto the platform. With an almost imperceptible ripping sound, the ground beneath them tore away from the rest of the bank and fell towards the river, carrying them with it.

Fortunately for them, previous earth falls had created a muddy ledge sticking out just above the surface of the water and on this they landed, bombarded by falling earth and clods of turf. When the muddy deluge had stopped, they were both covered with debris.

Alison, wiping the mud from her face, scowled at Jason. 'Well, that wasn't very clever, was it?'

'How was I to know that would happen?' he replied angrily. 'What a fucking nightmare this is. Is this ledge gonna give way as well?'

'I don't think so,' said Alison, standing up and cautiously testing it with her feet. 'Judging from the stuff growing on it, it's been here for some time; it's probably been built up by successive falls. But we can't be sure.'

'Great!' Jason snarled. 'Where's this fucking camera, then? Or has that gone?'

But the section of the bank from which the hazel

grew had been unaffected by the earth fall, and the camera still hung where Alison had first seen it. It was now almost within their reach.

'What we need is a stick, then we could hook it off.'

The ledge, a pile of mud and weeds, had nothing of any use to them at all, but beyond the ledge, growing above the waterline, was a young willow.

'I don't suppose you've got a knife on you?' asked Alison hopefully.

Jason snorted. 'I'm not a fuckin' boy scout.'

Alison gave him a cold look. 'No, I didn't think you were. But I thought lads from London estates always carried knives . . . part of your macho image isn't it?'

'And where did you pick up that little gem of a cliche, Miss Clever Dick?' he sneered. 'An expert on gang culture, are we?'

'Not at all,' she snapped back. 'But actually, Jason, I'm not interested in having an argument with you. In fact, I'm not interested in having any further conversation with you, ever. But what does interest me is that the sun has gone; we haven't yet retrieved the camera; and, what is more significant to me now, since I don't give a toss any longer about proving your innocence, is how the hell we're going to get out of here.'

Jason looked up. The sun had disappeared behind the trees on the ridge opposite.

'Fuck!' he said simply.

'See that sapling there,' Alison pointed at the hazel. 'Do you think you might have the strength to break it off?'

He grunted noncommittally and edged to the end of their muddy platform. It was not easy: the

378

willow was young and pliable and Jason, always in imminent danger of toppling over into the water, took some considerable time twisting, turning and pulling at it till it finally splintered and he managed to rip it off.

He turned, holding it aloft with a triumphant grin and Alison, forgetting her declared resolution of never speaking to him again, returned his grin. 'Brilliant! Do you want to try fishing for the camera? Your reach is longer than mine.'

'Sure.' He edged past her to the other end of the mud. 'Hold onto my belt; I don't want to lose my balance.'

So with Alison holding onto his belt, he leant forward and managed, after a few frustrating misses, to hook the strap of the camera, lift it off its peg, and bring it safely down.

Their relief and sense of achievement was so great for a moment neither of them could speak.

'Right,' croaked Jason, 'let's have a look . . .' He switched the camera on and the small screen instantly filled with a picture of highland cattle. He pressed the forward button again and again. The same five pictures of cattle came up every time.

'I don't understand it.' Alison frowned, frustrated. 'I took those a couple of days ago. Where's all the stuff after that?'

Jason opened a small panel on the side of the camera and groaned. 'The sod, the bastard!'

'What?'

'The card's gone. We're back where we started.'

'Not quite,' said Alison with some relief. 'I've got the camera back . . .'

'Oh yes, sorry, excuse me . . . you've got what you want, so that's all right then. But what about me, eh?'

'I was coming to that. And we know not only that you didn't deliberately push Emma, but that somebody else is definitely involved. Somebody tripped you, saw I'd filmed the incident and thought I might have got a picture of them, stole the camera, and removing the chip, threw the camera away. I'd say we're definitely not back where we started; but before we waste any more time speculating on who that person might be, Jason, we need to work out how to get off this bank. Oh,' she broke off. 'I do feel awful. I think I'm catching a cold.'

'You better not give it to me,' was his sympathetic response.

They stood together looking up at the wall of earth. The edge of the riverbank was two to three feet above their heads.

'It's not going to be so easy,' Jason shook his head.

'No,' replied Alison, worried. 'And there are no roots, nothing we can hold onto. Plus that edge looks pretty dodgy to me. Even if we did get to the top, it could come tumbling down again.'

'What about trying to get up where there is foliage—where that willow is for example?' Jason went to inspect the bank, then turned shaking his head. 'No good, it's sheer down to the water.'

'Same thing this side, too,' said Alison, her heart sinking. 'No footholds, no nothing. Bugger.'

Glumly they stared up at the grassy fringe above their heads.

'Supposing you sat on my shoulders? You should be light enough. Could you pull yourself over the edge? Then you could go and get help.'

'We could try,' replied Alison dubiously. 'I'm just worried about that edge, it might not take my weight.'

'I don't see that we've got any other choices, unless we just wait here to be found.'

'We might have to wait a very long time. There's no public footpath this side of the river, and there's no stock in the fields, so no one would have any reason to come down here. Have you got your mobile?'

'In my car,' he said tersely. 'You?'

'No, I didn't think to bring it.'

'Great!' He glared at her, then with an exasperated sigh, he crouched down, 'Right, that settles it. Come on, and try not to make my trousers any muddier than they are already.'

Alison climbed on his shoulders. With much groaning and wobbling, he slowly stood upright with Alison steadying herself against the muddy wall as he straightened. At waist height, she was able to see over the top of the bank but the first tentative attempt to lever herself onto the grass brought a heavy shower of earth down on Jason's head. He yelled and tried to dodge it, upsetting Alison's balance and she fell over his head and ended up on the edge of the water. They both sat where they'd landed, frozen with fright.

Finally Alison stirred and went to sit against the shelter of the mud face, staring out across the river.

'It's a pity we're facing the grounds of the Manor,' she said glumly. 'Closer to the village we might attract attention with my torch.'

'You've got a torch?'

'Yes,' she said producing the small flashlight. 'Though it's a fat lot of good. The only hope would be if Jamie Merfield, Juliet's son, was in the boathouse having a smoke. But,' she added, 'since Juliet's at home, that's unlikely,'

'Juliet's got a son who smokes?' asked Jason, incredulous, 'How old is he, for chrissakes?'

'He's sixteen.'

'Sixteen? Juliet's got a sixteen-year-old son? Well fuck me, she must be a lot older than she looks. Shit!'

'What's it to you how old she is?'

Jason didn't reply.

'Don't tell me you fancied her?' Alison chuckled. 'Well I'm sorry to be the bearer of bad tidings . . . she's older than you think and she's got a cool husband.'

Jason snorted. 'Bully for her.'

They fell silent and watched the light in the sky slowly fade.

'You can just see the top window of the Old Vicarage through the trees. If Isabelle was up there and happened to look out of the window, she might see this torch flashing . . .'

'Who is Isabelle and why should she be at the top of an Old Vicarage and why should she take notice of a torch flashing?'

Jason sounded petulant, and Alison thought she couldn't really blame him. Their situation, as she saw it, was pretty dire.

'Isabelle's my brother's girlfriend. She lives there, and her two little daughters have a bedroom at the top of the house. If she saw a torch flashing she might wonder what it was because she'd know it was coming from our land. Don't you think it's worth a try?'

'Too many ifs for my liking, but suit yourself,'

he sniffed and slumped, staring gloomily into the middle distance.

68

Chocolate, an elderly brown labrador, stood in the middle of the shop, gazing reproachfully at his mistress. Rita regarded him with a sigh. 'Patience, Chocolate. I'll take you out in a minute. I've still got a lot of clearing up to do.'

Huffing and puffing, she bustled round her shop, re-arranging the shelves, putting displaced goods back in their rightful place, tidying the displays and vigorously sweeping the floor. True the TV crew had volunteered to clean up after themselves, but the filming hadn't finished till early evening and Rita, wanting her domain back, had shooed them away.

By the time she was satisfied, it was nearly dark outside. She found her jacket and the dog's lead and set off.

Her usual walk was across the field now occupied by the trailer camp, but the footpath had become very slippery and too dangerous to walk along in the dark, so grumbling about her enforced change of routine, she turned instead into the Tuckers' drive, climbed over a gate and, whistling to Chocolate, made for the river bank.

*   *   *

Sitting on their muddy ledge, the black water of the river slapping only a few feet away, the air

383

temperature dropping, and the dark of the night increasingly impenetrable, there had been two courses of action open to Jason and Alison: they could have cuddled together to keep warm and become firm friends, or the reverse.

She'd suggested they sat together for warmth, he'd agreed, but taking advantage of her proximity, he'd put his arm round her waist and groped for her breast. Indignant, she'd pushed him away and removed herself as far from him as the ledge would allow.

Huddled against the bank, Jason embarked on an endless monologue that alternated between his immediate discomfort, his dislike of her and his dislike of everyone and everything to do with the filming.

In the end, Alison could stand it no longer. 'Jason, why don't you just shut it? I'm freezing cold, I feel like shit, and having to listen to you drivel on and on, is driving me nuts. God knows, I thought you were meant to be a shit-hot stand up, but you'd bore for Britain!'

'Fuck off.'

'Believe me, I would if I could, Jason. Not only am I suffering from exposure to the elements but I'm suffering from over-exposure to you. You're such a bastard, I wouldn't be at all surprised if it was you who tried to sabotage the filming . . .'

'Oh yeah. Prove it.'

'I don't have to. It all fits, apart from Emma.'

'You stupid cow: that proves I had nothing to do with anything.'

'Oh no it does not; maybe it was someone playing a trick on you, and Emma got in the way; in fact, the more I think about it, the more likely I think it is.'

'Do you know what I think? I think you're nuts; you've got a screw loose; maybe it's inbreeding. Who did your mother fuck?'

'You're foul. I can't imagine why you ever agreed to help me with my website. That was so out of character, it's not true.'

'You think so? I meant to screw you, Miss Prissy. Why else should I waste my time?'

'And you think I would let you? Why? Out of gratitude? I'm not that cheap. Because I fancied you? Don't make me choke. I thought you were a prick the first time I met you and you've proved me right, you are a prick. My one regret, Jason Hart, is that I might have played any part in proving you didn't deliberately push Emma into the river, because, given half a chance, I think you would've done if you thought you could get away with it.'

*   *   *

Rita had just reached a copse of trees and was about to turn back when she could have sworn she heard voices. She stopped still. The farmhouse was some distance away; there were no houses on the opposite side of the river and no public access to the path along which she was walking.

The trees in the copse cast tall dark shadows across the grass, the river was faintly illuminated in the moonlight, and a distant owl set up its quavering call. A no-nonsense sort of person, Rita suddenly felt slightly spooked and was about to make a hasty retreat when she heard the voices again.

'No, I've got nothing more to say to you, Jason,

so you can save your breath.'

The voice was definitely of this world, she concluded. She could have sworn it was Alison Tucker and that it came from the direction of the river.

Puzzled, she moved a little closer and heard some indistinct muttering, and then the voice spoke once more. 'I'm sorry, but I just don't believe you. You can swear as much as you like, but it's not going to change anything.' It was definitely Alison, but her voice seemed to be coming from somewhere below the level of the bank.

'Alison,' she called. 'Alison Tucker, is that you?'

There was a moment's silence and then a joyful shout. 'Yes, yes it is. Who's there?'

'It's Rita Godwin. What are you up to? Who else is with you? Where are you?'

'We're here, at the water's edge. We're not up to anything, Rita. We're trapped. The bank gave away. We've been here for hours.'

'Get some help, before we freeze to death, for Chrissake.' It was a male voice Rita didn't recognise.

She bridled. 'No need to blaspheme, if you don't mind. Is that Al?'

'No it's not, Rita. It's Jason Hart, one of the actors. Please, please get help. And tell them the edge of the bank is very crumbly. It might be easier to bring the rowing boat round.'

'My goodness me, I don't know what you've been up to, my girl, but it's lucky for you I had to take Chocolate for a walk. I'll be as quick as I can.'

Which wasn't that quick, as she put Chocolate on the lead in case she bumped into any livestock, and so could only proceed at his waddling, wheezy pace.

When Elsie entered the kitchen of Marsh Farm, she felt as cheerful as she had done for weeks. Ron had come through his operation without any apparent ill-effects and the terrible fear she'd been nursing ever since he'd become ill had evaporated. At the sight of Jenny's worried face, however, and the grave look on Jeff's, she decided her good news could wait.

'What's the matter with you, Jenny?' she said calmly, pulling off her gloves. 'You look worried. What's young Alison been up to? Any chance of a cup of tea? I've just come from the hospital.'

To her surprise, it was Jeff who made for the kettle, saying, 'You sit down, Elsie, I'll make it. Jenny's worried about Alison's whereabouts.'

'Well, that's nothing new,' Elsie observed. 'Jenny's been unaware of Alison's whereabouts for the better part of these last five years.'

'That's as maybe, Gran, but I'm worried. She's not in her room, Al doesn't know where she is and nor does Hannah. And she's left her mobile behind.'

'Her mobile? Now that is serious.'

'Elsie.' It was a warning growl from Jeff and both Jenny and Elsie looked at him, surprised. He had never actively intervened in Elsie's goading of Jenny before.

In a milder voice, Elsie continued, 'Jenny, you've had many frights over Alison before, but she's always come back safe and sound.' She glanced at the clock. 'It's only a little after eight-thirty. Not late by anyone's standards. It only got really dark

387

about half an hour ago. Maybe she went out on Bumble and went further than she intended. Have you checked? She might be in his stable rubbing him down . . .'

'I'll go and have a look.' Jeff was at the door. 'Make the tea for Elsie, love. I won't be long.'

Jenny, her face strained and hopeful, did as she was bidden. Setting the tea in front of Elsie, she gave a shaky laugh. 'I'm sorry to be making such a fuss, Gran, when you're going through so much with Ron. It's just that . . . well, I've a feeling in my bones that something's wrong . . . she was so upset at losing that camera, and with poor Emma being pushed in the river, and then that awful tiff with Al . . .'

'What's all this,' Elsie was sharp. 'I don't know any of this. What's been happening? What's this about Emma, and Alison losing a camera? And why should she being having a tiff with Al?'

Jenny attempted to fill her in on the day's events, immediately breaking off when Jeff returned. 'Well? Is she there? Is she with Bumble?'

He put his arm around her shoulder. 'No, love. The stable's in darkness and Bumble is in there. From the feel of his tack, he's not been out this evening.'

Jenny stifled a frightened sob.

Jeff hugged her. 'She's probably quite safe, love. Elsie's right, it's not that late and when you find out what she's been up to, you'll laugh at yourself for being so upset.'

'Do you know,' mused Elsie, 'I wouldn't be at all surprised if she hadn't gone off on the trail of that missing camera.'

'Oh?' Jeff gave her an interrogative look.

'Yes, if I know my granddaughter, she'd have been fretting about it. She's not one to sit and wring her hands over spilt milk; she takes after me. I wouldn't be at all surprised if she hadn't gone looking for it.'

'Down by the river—this late, Gran?'

They were interrupted by both dogs jumping up from their baskets where they'd been dozing, and dashing to the yard door, barking.

There was a tap and the door opened a fraction allowing the glimpse of a face.

'Hello, Jenny? Pull off those dogs would you, I've got Chocolate here and he's very nervous.'

'Rita?' Jenny was stunned. She could count on one hand the number of times Rita had visited her at the farm over the last thirty years, never unannounced, never at this time of the evening.

'Gip, Duchess, basket!' Jeff commanded and the dogs, with a few grumbles, obeyed.

The door opened wider to admit Rita, dragging a reluctant Chocolate behind her.

'Thank God you're here, Jenny,' she began as soon as she was inside. ''Lo Jeff, Elsie . . .'

'What is it Rita?' Jenny sat down, trembling.

'I've come for help,' Rita was bursting with excitement. 'I was walking along the river, in your meadows, 'cos Dawson's field is now impassable thanks to that encampment, when I heard voices. Fair rattled me it did, I don't mind telling you . . .'

'Voices?' Jenny felt faint.

'Whose?' demanded Elsie.

'Get to the point, Rita,' Jeff spoke abruptly. 'Jenny is half sick with worry. Was it Alison?'

'Yes,' Rita replied sulkily, resenting this summary curtailment of her story. 'I could hear her in the darkness. And,' she paused, determined to get some mileage out of it, 'then I heard a man's voice. They was coming from the river.'

'The river?' Jenny repeated with horror.

Rita glanced at her. 'Yes,' she said, satisfied with her friend's reaction. '"Who's there?" I called. "Who's there . . ."?'

'Yes, yes, Rita,' Elsie intervened. 'You've already told us it was Alison and somebody else. Where is she? You said you need help. Why? What's wrong?'

In the face of Elsie's fierce gaze, Rita abandoned her attempts at further dramatisation and said simply, 'They're down on the riverbank; leastways, they're stuck on the water's edge and can't get back up. Alison said the bank's collapsed. Near that old quarry, they are. She said the ground's very crumbly, so best to get the rowing boat out and rescue them from the river. They've been there for hours, apparently; though what she was doing there with that actor fellow, I don't know . . .'

But they had stopped listening to her.

'Right,' Jeff reached for his coat. 'Where's the boat kept, Jenny?'

'I don't know, Jeff,' Jenny replied helplessly. 'It's moored up somewhere along the bank, but only Alison and Charlie ever use it . . .'

'Elsie,' Jeff turned to her. 'Charlie's over at Isabelle's—get him here.'

'Yes, Jeff,' she replied, a glint in her eye.

'Jenny,' his voice softened, 'Get some blankets together and a thermos of sweet tea.'

'Yes, Jeff.' Her reply was faint.

He leant forward and kissed her. 'There's my brave girl. She'll be all right, you'll see.'

He turned to Rita. 'Tie up that hound of yours,

390

Rita, you're coming with me. I've got my Land Rover outside, you can show me where they are. Elsie, I've got my mobile . . . as soon as I've located them, I'll phone through. Now, any idea where I might find planks and ropes . . . ?'

69

At the Country Club, Marcus was persuaded by his actors to join them for dinner. He didn't need much persuading: he'd been up since four-thirty and had eaten almost nothing all day; and wherever Jason Hart was, Marcus was more likely to catch him if he stayed at the hotel. His conversation with Jason was not one, he felt, that could be delayed until the following day when he would have his hands full doing Emma's job.

So he left a message for Jason at reception and joined them, electing to sit between Juliet and Jilly, the two performers he had most time for.

'How's Emma?' Jilly asked.

'She's going to be fine,' replied Marcus. 'I took her back to her digs this evening.'

Their surprise and relief was heartfelt and Marcus was obliged to give a detailed account of the drama on the riverbank.

'So,' remarked Ben, his voice redolent with melodrama, 'Master Jason strikes again!'

'He said it was an accident,' pointed out Nicola. 'It was unfortunate, but if he tripped . . .'

'If—a tiny word, but on it hangs a man's reputation . . .' Ben's voice rumbled round the dining room and several heads turned.

Ben, Marcus observed, was half in his cups already. He frowned. 'If you don't mind, I don't want to discuss this any further and I don't have to remind you to be discreet and not to discuss it with anyone else. I don't want the press alerted.'

'There's just one thing I wanted to ask you, dear boy,' Ben leant forward. 'We've just been discussing why this is being shot on location? And if it had to be on location, why such a run-down, derelict farm, for Chrissake? All these beastly animals, and the stench . . . !'

'You've read the script, Ben,' Marcus replied curtly. 'The location is exactly what we want.'

'But does it have to be real muck, dear boy? I have it on good authority there's a farm near here we could use that is pristine, no stench of any description, no unwanted animals doing their own thing. Everything would be under our control . . . Surely that would be preferable?'

Juliet chuckled. 'Ben would have us move somewhere where there were no cows, no pigs, no animals of any sort, Marcus. Couldn't we re-write the script and make him an arable farmer?'

Marcus snorted but was saved from making any reply by a couple stopping by their table.

'Ben!' trilled the woman, 'what a pleasant surprise. You've not met my husband, Hugh, have you?'

A short, dark haired man, with cold blue eyes and a permanent sneer, tried to look pleasant and nodded at them.

'This is Ben Dacres, Hugh,' cried his wife. 'Ben, you'll have to introduce the rest of your table, I'm afraid I don't know everyone's names . . .' she smiled at them graciously. 'I am Veronica Lester and this is my husband, Hugh . . .'

'Of course, my dear lady, allow me . . .' Ben ticked off the names round the table, finishing with Marcus. 'And last, and probably the most important person here, Marcus Steel, our producer.'

Marcus nodded politely but without any warmth. The last thing he wanted was any fan of Ben muscling in on their table. Although, he had to admit, the woman's husband looked as if it was the last thing he wanted too. Lester? The name had a vaguely familiar ring.

'Now I do hope Ben has told you of my little party,' Veronica said graciously. 'We've invited you all for drinks at Summerstoke House on Thursday evening . . .'

'Over my dead body,' Marcus heard Juliet mutter.

'Come along, Vee,' the husband cut impatiently across the chorus of tepid thanks. 'Our food will be getting cold.'

'See you on Thursday, then.' Veronica smiled at Ben and the couple moved away, leaving a silent table behind.

When they were out of earshot, Ben leant forward to whisper, 'They're simply loaded, Marcus, and they've offered us the use of their farm as a location. They'd bend over backwards to give us what we want.'

'I'm sure you're right,' Juliet commented. 'They're the sort of people who would, if it suited them.'

Marcus turned to Juliet. 'Do you know them?'

She dimpled at him. 'Yes, I do. They are utterly ghastly. I wouldn't trust them an inch, Marcus, so I hope there's no question of us moving.'

'There's not.'

'Good, and as to their party, I have to say there is no way I would accept their hospitality.' She turned to the rest of the table. 'But don't let that stop you. I am sure the food and drink will flow. Veronica is very proud of her entertaining.'

'Why didn't you tell us about it, Ben?' asked one of the other actors, 'Or don't you want us to muscle in on your scene?'

'Sorry, friends, I just forgot,' said Ben apologetically. 'I think I was meant to get a list together.'

'What cold eyes he had,' Nicola shivered.

'He's quite unscrupulous,' commented Juliet, sotto voce, glancing across the dining room where the Lesters were sitting.

'I must admit, I'd forgotten about the invitation, too,' confessed Jilly. 'I was there when she invited us. So who's coming?'

Silence again.

Ben suddenly pulled a face. 'Lawks,' he said, 'I've double-booked myself. I've got a dinner–date that evening.'

'Well, you'll just have to un-book yourself,' said Jilly, with friendly exasperation.

'Why don't you take your date along?' suggested Juliet impishly. 'They wouldn't throw her out, after all.'

'A mistake,' giggled an actress. 'The way she looked at you, Ben, she'd gobble up any opposition for hors d'oeuvres.'

'Who's your date, Ben, anyone we know?' asked Juliet.

'Is it Mrs Tucker, the lady who baked you the cake?' Nicola smirked. A chuckle went round the table. They had all been present when Ben had produced the cake for general consumption.

Ben shuddered at the memory. 'She's a very sweet lady, but I have never eaten anything that so resembled clay before.'

'It certainly kept Harry Hobs quiet for a while. He took a huge bite and his jaws stuck together,' laughed Juliet.

'Anything that shuts that brat up is not all bad, but I don't think I'll encourage any more baking. The urge to live is too great.'

'To return to the question of this party, Ben, you, especially, have to be there. I'll go with you,' sighed Jilly, 'though I can't say I fancy it much. You'll come, won't you, Nicola? We all have to do our bit for location PR and all that, isn't that right, Marcus?'

'Yes, I'm afraid so. It's important we don't alienate the local population, so Jilly, be a sweetheart and rustle up a decent representation from the cast. I'll speak to Emma, Matt and Colin.'

'Are you going to go, Marcus?' Juliet asked him with a teasing smile.

He was saved from having to give an immediate answer by the buzzing of his mobile. Excusing himself from the table, he walked into the foyer to take the call.

'Hi, Emma, shouldn't you be asleep by now . . . What? Jason? Where? Oh bloody hell, this is all I need . . . You go back to bed, now. I need you fit and well, ASAP.'

He snapped his mobile shut and went to the reception desk. 'I've got to go, so I'll have to cancel my order for dinner. Please, give my apologies to the rest of my table.'

70

Charlie arrived back at Marsh Farm just as Jeff was loading some planks he'd found in the barn.

Their conversation was brisk and to the point.

'Where are they?' asked Charlie.

'I'm not sure about the exact location,' replied Jeff. 'Rita is a bit vague. I thought she could show us the way. She mentioned a clump of trees . . .'

'That could be the old stone workings, they were filming there this morning.'

'That makes sense. Elsie said she thought Alison would have gone looking for a camera she'd lost.'

'I can believe it.'

'As far as I can make out, the bank's given way and she and this actor fellow are trapped on the water's edge. Been there for ages, it seems. They can't get back up because the bank is crumbling. Alison suggested getting the boat out, but Jenny has no idea where it's kept.'

'It's a bit further upstream from there. I'll get the key to the padlock. Anything else you think we might need, Jeff?'

'We've got lights, blankets, and a flask of tea. Some rope would be handy.'

'In the tool shed, in a box under the bench. You get that and I'll get the key.'

Within a very short space of time, Jeff's Land Rover, with Rita wedged between Charlie and Jeff, was bumping its way across the fields towards the river.

Rita had the haziest of notions about the exact location and contradicted every direction Charlie gave Jeff, but Charlie, convinced Alison had gone back to the site of that morning's filming, overrode her and when they finally pulled up in front of the copse, Rita clambered out, saying triumphantly, 'Yes, I was right, this is the place.'

Immediately Charlie picked up a faint cry.

'Alison?' he called, suddenly feeling quite choked. 'Alison?' There was no immediate reply and stumbling towards the riverbank, he called again, 'Ali?'

'Charlie?' Her voice sounded tremulous and faint.

'Yes, Ali, it's me. We're going to get you out. I just need to work out exactly where you are so carry on talking to me. Who's with you?'

'Jason.'

'What happened?'

'I was looking for the camera.' Her voice was faint and weary. 'Then I saw it, on the edge of the bank and . . .'

'Right, sweetheart, you can stop talking, I'm right above you, now. Okay, Jeff,' he shouted and the searchlight on top of the Land Rover illuminated the whole scene in an unearthly silver light.

'Right, Charlie,' said Jeff, unloading the planks. 'Let's get these down and see if it's feasible to bring them up from here.'

Together they placed the planks on the bank and Charlie, lying flat, wriggled to the edge with a torch. As he did so, a small amount of earth sprayed the two huddled figures below him.

'Hey, what the hell are you doing?' yelped Jason. 'You'll bring the whole bank down on us. I don't want to be buried alive after all this, thank you very much.'

Alison looked up. Her face, streaked with mud, was strained and white in his torchlight. 'Oh Charlie,' she croaked. 'Thank goodness you've come. I was beginning to think I'd dreamed Rita. Did I? She's such an unlikely rescuer.'

'No,' he attempted a chuckle, though he'd never felt less like laughing. 'No, she's here with us. Ali, I'm going to chuck down some blankets and a thermos. You're right, this bank won't stand too much weight. Jeff and I will bring the boat round, but that will take a little time.'

'Oh, for Chrissake,' moaned Jason. 'I've been here long enough. Just get me out of here, will you?'

'I don't want my sister to be buried alive,' replied Charlie, his voice steely. 'The boat's going to be the best way.'

*   *   *

Jenny sat with Elsie in the kitchen. Never had the clock's ticking sounded so loud. She felt numb—Alison was her baby. What would she do, how would she cope if anything happened to her? Elsie was worried too, she could tell. She had tried to keep their spirits up, made them tea and asked after the developments on the farm. But after a while her attempts at conversation had faded and the two women sat there, listening to the clock.

Glancing at her mother-in-law, Jenny observed how very weary she looked. 'Poor Elsie! First Ron and now Alison,' she thought. 'The two people she loves most in the world . . .'

'I'm sorry,' she said. 'I haven't asked. How's Ron, Gran? How did his op go?'

To her shame and sorrow, a tear appeared in the corner of Elsie's eye and crept down her cheek.

She leant forward and grasped Elsie's hand. 'Oh, Elsie . . .'

'No, it's all right Jenny. It's all right. The operation went well. Ron is going to be all right.'

Jenny sprang to her feet and hugged her prickly-thorn of a mother-in-law.

'I'm all right; for goodness sake don't fuss. It's just that I'm very tired and yes, I think I'm very hungry. Goodness me, Jenny,' she recovered herself and sprang to her feet. 'What are we doing, sitting here drinking tea, feeling sorry for ourselves? When they come back, they're going to need something nourishing. That's what we should be doing . . . making something for them all to eat. What have we got?'

'Well, said Jenny slowly. 'There's some savoury mince Angela made that I saved for you and Alison . . .'

'We'll start with that.' Elsie, re-invigorated, started for the stove. 'Come on, it's about time I gave you a cookery lesson. You've been hopeless for far too long. But then,' she added, 'I should have taken you in hand long ago. Right, we want onions, and bacon . . . have you got those?'

'Yes Elsie,' Jenny, fired by Elsie's sudden burst of energy, got to her feet.

'Then fetch them. And some tinned tomatoes.'

As Jenny rooted around in the larder, she heard the sound of a powerful engine in the yard and seconds later, Marcus burst through the door, demanding information and action.

At the same time the phone started to ring, so leaving Elsie to deal with Marcus, Jenny ran to answer it.

It was Al.

By the time she'd put Al in the picture and returned to the kitchen, Marcus had disappeared off to the riverbank.

'Right,' said Elsie a large saucepan in her hand, 'chop those onions, fine, mind, and then we'll add them to this oil I've got warming here. While I'm stirring them—you always make the mistake of leaving 'em so they burn—you can chop up that bacon . . .'

* * *

Charlie had been right. It was a slow process. He and Jeff unlocked the battered old rowing boat, kept in a muddy inlet further upstream, and rowed down to the lip of mud on which Alison and Jason sat.

Charlie steered the boat, nose in, and Jeff, the vessel rocking violently, climbed out. He pulled the boat sideways onto the ledge and gathering Alison in his arms, lifted her up and passed her to Charlie.

'Okay, Jason,' he turned to look at the figure huddled under his blanket. 'Your carriage awaits. Can you manage, or would you like me to assist you, too?'

Jason did not stir but viewed the rocking boat with horror.

'If you think,' his voice was shaking, 'I'm going to climb into that you've got it wrong. I'm past white-knuckle rides. You can get me out of here some other way.'

Jeff tried to be patient. 'There is no other way, Jason. The bank is too unstable to think of climbing. It's the boat or nothing.'

'Come on Jason,' Charlie shouted crossly. 'We need to get Ali back home or we'll have a hospital case on our hands. What's the problem?'

'I am not,' said Jason with deliberation, 'going to get in that boat. It'll tip us all into the water. I'd rather stay here and wait till morning than face certain death by drowning.'

'But it will be no different in the morning; the only way to get you out will still be by boat, so why wait?' reasoned Jeff.

'Because Marcus can get me a motor boat, a proper job, not that leaky tub.'

'No, he can't,' a voice drawled from somewhere in the darkness above them. 'I don't want to find you laid out with hypothermia in the morning, Jason. Just get into that boat now, will you, and don't be such a boring wuss.'

'But I can't. It's not safe. Don't make me, Marcus, please . . .' Jason stood up, pleading into the darkness above his head, his voice starting to rise hysterically.

With a small, almost sorrowful sigh, Jeff stepped forward, and gave a swift and calculated jab into Jason's solar plexus. Jason crumbled and with one swift movement, Jeff swept him off his feet, lifted him over his shoulders and settled him in the stern of the rocking craft. He sat down next to Charlie and took up an oar.

'Okay, Charlie? Let's row.'

71

'Bali Ha'i may call you, Any night, any day . . .'

Jenny sang, her voice throbbing with melancholic longing for some undefined resolution to her dreams.

'In your heart, you'll hear it call you:

'Come away . . . Come away . . .'

She filled the kettle and pushed it onto the stove, then turned to the washing up stacked high in the kitchen sink.

The previous evening had been one of the longest in her life and by the time they had finished eating, it had been so late she'd left the debris and gone to bed. Stephen and Angela had arrived back shortly after the rescue party and there had been so much noise, and coming and going, quite what had exercised them all escaped her, concerned as she'd been about Alison, who'd sat there looking increasingly unwell.

So now this morning, while washing the dishes and making a hot water bottle up for Alison who was clearly very poorly, she had the space and time to re-address the big question. Did she, or did she not accept Ben Dacres's invitation?

She felt . . . she believed . . . no, she knew she'd do nothing that would hurt Jeff, or cause him to doubt her in any way . . . It was just that it was such an opportunity; one that would never come her way again; one that she would be able to treasure; setting her apart, as it certainly would, from the unexceptional experiences of everybody else she knew in their village. When she was eighty, she would be able to say: 'That night, when I dined with Ben Dacres, you know, the famous actor . . .' And people would look at her with respect; something she'd never have as plain Jenny Tucker, widow of Jim who'd died on the silage clamp.

'Your own special hopes,
Your own special dreams . . .'

The door to the yard banged. It was Elsie.

'Morning, Jenny. I'm just off to the hospital, but I wanted to see how young Alison is this morning.'

'She's none too bright, Elsie. I've just made her a hot water bottle. Do you want to take it up to her? I'll make us some tea.'

Elsie returned with furrowed brow. 'Well,' she commented, 'She's in a fine old state, I must say.'

'Yes,' Jenny was immediately anxious. Elsie seldom gave quarter to human weakness. 'She got so wet yesterday morning, then all that time on the riverbank. I do hope she's not getting pneumonia.'

'She's a strong girl, Jenny. No need to start assuming the worst. It's simply a feverish cold. You just keep her warm in bed, and make her plenty of hot drinks and she'll be as right as rain.'

'Yes, I suppose you're right,' Jenny replied, not convinced.

'She'll pick up in no time when that young man of hers comes to see her, you'll see.'

'Yes, I hope so.' Jenny frowned. Al, on the phone the previous evening, had sounded more terse and annoyed than concerned.

'The trouble is when you're on your own, it's easy to start worrying and think the sky is about to fall,' Elsie sipped her tea, her sharp eyes firmly fixed on Jenny. 'Look at me; I'm a fine example. Worrying about Ron, I had him dead and buried by the time

I turned the light out of an evening, and much good that did me, or him.'

Jenny looked at her, startled, Elsie had never confided her before. Touched, the tears started to her eyes. 'He'll be all right now, I'm sure,' she said. 'You said he'd come through the op . . . Ron's such a lovely man; you're very lucky, Elsie.'

'I know,' Elsie nodded. 'And so are you, Jenny, my girl. Your man came up trumps last night.'

Jenny blushed. 'Yes, yes he did. Charlie's never taken much notice of him before, and Jeff always thought more of Stephen; but last night, when Jeff took charge, Charlie fell in with everything he suggested and they were really good together.'

She looked at Elsie and before she was able to stop herself, blurted, 'Elsie, do you mind if I ask your advice about something?'

The request took Elsie by surprise; she couldn't remember Jenny ever having asked her advice about anything before. 'No, I don't mind, what is it?'

Jenny reddened and stammered, 'I do care for Jeff, Elsie. I mean really care for him. It's just that I don't know where it's going or what he wants. I think he'd be quite happy if we carry on the way we are. But I want more than that. You're right: there will come a time when Angela and Stephen will want this place to themselves. I'm starting to feel a bit of a spare part already. She's a lovely girl, but Angela does makes me feel, well, as if I'm nearly past it. Jeff doesn't make me feel that, and nor does Ben Dacres. The thing is, Elsie. I know it's a one-off thing and means nothing to Ben, but it would be so exciting and make me feel less, well, less dull and boring.'

Elsie struggled. The last few days had been awful and coming out the other side, she had resolved to be more generous with her family, but Jenny really did invite ridicule. 'What would, and who is this Ben, Jenny?' she added, with a touch of acerbity. 'I understand the gist of what you're saying, but the detail, and what precisely you're asking my advice about escapes me.'

Jenny, already regretting her impulse, took a gulp of tea. 'Ben Dacres,' she said, blushing at the mention of his name, 'is the star in this television thing. He's on the TV a lot, Gran; probably a bigger name than Juliet Peters. The thing is, he's been really nice to me . . . he danced with me at the party last week when Jeff wouldn't, and now he's asked me to go and have dinner with him and I don't know what to do. I really want to, but I don't want to upset Jeff, 'cos I know it doesn't mean anything.'

She glanced at Elsie, anticipating the sneer that usually greeted her when her mother-in-law considered her a fool, but Elsie looked thoughtful.

Elsie was considering her response. Jenny had laid herself right open and it would be so easy to say something caustic; it's what she'd normally do; she could sense Jenny flinching, waiting for the put down . . .

'It's like the travelling circus,' she began. 'When I was a young wife, Jenny, the circus would come to Summerstoke twice a year. They'd set up in the field where the television people have got their camp and for the week they were here, there wasn't a young woman who was safe from their flirtations. We saw them as romantic, wild folk, and compared to our own boys they had the world at their fingertips; they were exciting. Making love

405

to us women was a bit of fun to them—they didn't take it seriously, and nor did we, if we had any sense. But our men, they'd get so jealous . . . It did us all good: the women felt attractive again, and the men stopped taking us for granted.' She paused, remembering, a half-smile on her face.

'So you think I should go?'

'That's up to you. But I don't think it would do Master Jeff any harm to know someone else is interested.'

*　　　*　　　*

'Phew! That should do it,' Charlie wiped a muddy hand across his brow and viewed the trench he and Lenny had just dug.

'Should be deep enough to deter a fox. Right, Lenny, lets get the fencing in.'

'How about a swig of tea first, boss? I'm parched!'

'Five minutes.' Charlie was brisk. 'We've still got a fair bit to do. When we've finished this enclosure, we need to check the goat paddock and finish off the sheds . . .'

'Okay, okay . . . there's only so much a man can do, Charlie.'

Charlie frowned. 'Sorry, Lenny, it's just that I feel we've fallen behind a bit and the last thing I want is not be ready for Good Friday's opening. Stephen would love that.'

'Your trouble is you've bitten off more than you can chew, to be honest with you,' grumbled Lenny. 'I knows you're doin' your best, but every time that blasted film crew says jump, you do, and all this,' he waved a hand, 'takes second place. I never thought

I'd say it, but this whole malarkey has been a mixed blessing. I know they've paid you well for it, but I can tell you, the whole village is fed up.'

Charlie sighed impatiently. 'Why?'

' 'Cos they walk about as if they own the place. They want to film in the shop, they close the shop. Paula's Mum wanted to buy the kids some sweeties after school and she was turned away. Bloomin' cheek, she thought. They want to close the High Street, they close the High Street, never mind whether you're going about your lawful business or not, you have to wait.'

'You sound like Hugh Lester, Lenny.'

Ignoring the insult, Lenny carried on. 'No-one can walk their dogs in Dawson's field, the footpath's a mud slide; they walked off with the prize money at the pub quiz on Sunday night and didn't buy nobody a drink; and my Paula can't think of nothing else but that she ain't been picked to be a bloomin' extra. Why not? That's what I want to know. What's wrong with her? She's worth fifty of any of 'em that's been picked. She tries to hide it, but I can tell she's really upset. A pox on the lot of them, that's what I say . . . Right, me five minutes is up.' And having worked himself into a complete ill humour, he snapped the top back on his thermos, marched over to the trailer, and pulled at the fencing posts.

Charlie looked thoughtful. Lenny's tempers were rare; he didn't really take the village's side against the filming . . . Charlie had heard him sneer often enough at folks who'd whinged until they got a piece of the pie. No, this had to do with Paula. Maybe he should have a word with Marcus. After all, he thought, Marcus owed him. As for the rest of the dissatisfaction, Charlie shrugged. He couldn't do a lot about that, but maybe that was something else he should mention.

'People,' he thought with disgust, 'why can't they just get on with their lives? Why are they so small-minded, why make things so bloody difficult? The TV crew aren't going to be here forever, and when the series goes out, Summerstoke will be in clover.'

* * *

Alison tossed and turned all morning. She felt awful, made worse by the fact that not only Al had not rushed over after her rescue, but had not phoned her . . . her mobile was switched on and close by her bed, ready and waiting.

Alison could have phoned or texted him, but pride held her back. He'd gone off the deep end with her about the camera; she'd risked her life to get it back, and now she was stuck in bed with a bloody cold; the least he could do was to phone to see how she was. She was puzzled and hurt.

Towards lunchtime, Jenny came up with a steaming mug. 'I've made you honey and lemon, Alison. Make sure you drink it while it's hot. Can you manage a bit of lunch, love?'

'No thanks, Mum.' Food was the last thing she wanted.

'Has Al been in touch? Is he coming over? A visit from him might cheer you up; you do look miserable.'

'I feel awful, Mum, that's why.' She frowned. 'Mum, what exactly did you say to Al when he phoned last night? Only, he's not been in touch with me at all and I can't understand it.'

'Hmm,' Jenny furrowed her brows. 'There was so much going on, I'm not sure I can remember, exactly . . .'

'Try Mum; maybe he's misunderstood something.'

'Well . . . he phoned just after Charlie and Jeff went out to rescue you. I picked up the phone and he asked to speak to you, and I said that you weren't here, there'd been accident and you was stuck on the riverbank and that you'd been trapped there for hours, but for him not to worry 'cos you were all right and you weren't alone, one of the actors was stuck with you, I couldn't remember his name . . .'

'What did he say?'

'He said "Jason Hart"' And I said "that's the one" and I told him Jeff and Charlie had gone out to rescue you. He didn't say much else, but he rang off soon after.'

Alison stared at Jenny, aghast.

'What's the matter, love?'

'Jason Hart. You told Al I was with Jason Hart?'

'Yes,' replied Jenny in a soothing voice, 'I thought he'd be relieved to know you weren't alone through all that. I know I was.'

'But Mum, you're not my boyfriend. Al loathes Jason and he must wonder what on earth I was doing there with him. Oh no, this is dreadful. He probably thinks I'm two-timing him, and nothing, nothing could be further from the truth. What am I going to do?'

And she burst into tears.

72

Aided by Emma's notes, the scene Marcus undertook to direct was straightforward. The character, Will, played by Jason, is driving his van along the High Street when he sees his girlfriend, played by Nicola, walking arm in arm with another man, and as he watches, they stop outside the shop and kiss.

Having established that Jason was suffering no particular ill effects from his ordeal, Marcus gave him a late start and set about shooting everything he could without him.

Several extras were employed to give life to the street and the shop. Only the exterior of the shop was being used, so it was open for business when the actual filming was not taking place, and similarly the street, so daily life was able to follow its normal course. On a shout from Matt, the runners, Dave and Chris who was positioned within the shop, would leap in and stop all unauthorised passage.

Inevitably there were grumbles: from people in the shop who wanted to leave it but couldn't, or wanted to walk along the High Street but had to wait, or wanted to drive through but had to stop.

On one occasion the Vicar came out of the Rectory, intent on his daily purchase of pear drops and newspaper. Unaware of the filming, he collided with Nicola and her companion as they stopped to embrace.

'Cut!' bawled Matt. 'Where did he come from? Andy, what the fuck you playing at?' He spat angrily into his talk-back. 'How did the dog collar get there?'

It was unfortunate a number of the extras were close enough to hear. There were black looks and discontented mutterings. 'He's our vicar . . . how dare he speak like that . . . there's no respect . . . that's the trouble . . . arrogant sods . . . treat us like dirt . . .'

On another occasion, Colin was standing in the middle of the street, looking through the camera lens, when a 4x4 roared through, missing him by inches. It didn't stop but carried on past Marcus and up over the bridge.

'Christ,' swore Matt. 'That was the same bastard who spooked the cows the other day.'

'That,' remarked Marcus, 'was Hugh Lester. I met him yesterday evening.'

'Let's hope I don't!' retorted Matt. 'I might strangle him.'

*   *   *

It was an unusually subdued Jason who turned up on time to collect the key to his trailer from Ross.

'I've replaced the missing tag, Jason.'

'Ta.'

Ross, who'd had a lengthy conversation with Marcus, looked at him shrewdly but made no comment beyond asking him if he was okay.

'I'm fine,' came the short reply.

'Good. You'll find a fresh pair of trousers laid out in your trailer. Wardrobe decided to wash everything after yesterday's debacle. If they don't fit, go and see Maggie and she'll fix them for you.'

Jason grunted.

'Do you want some coffee brought to your trailer or are you happy to go to the bus?'

'It depends on whether I'm still being fingered as a potential murderer. If I am, I'll stay in my trailer, thank you. The role of pariah is a new one on me and it's not much fun.'

'It's okay, Jason. Marcus has made it quite clear he believes you tripped; it was an accident. That's good enough for me and I've passed that on to the rest of the crew. I expect you'll get some ribbing for the hours you spent stuck on the riverbank with Alison Tucker, though. She's a pretty little thing.'

Jason sniffed. 'If you'd had to sit listening to her snivelling and whinging for four hours, you wouldn't think that.'

Ross shrugged. 'I've never known a shoot so full of mishaps. Plenty of material for you, I guess.'

'My routine doesn't depend on things actually happening to me,' Jason snapped. 'I'd rather they didn't. This whole gig is turning into a fucking nightmare and the sooner it finishes, the better. And I'm certainly not going to be frogmarched into signing any more contracts, so the sooner Mr Marcus Steel realises that, the better.'

'I'm sorry to hear that,' replied Ross, evenly. 'Maybe, by the end of the shoot, when things are a little happier, you'll have changed your mind. Forgive my ignorance, but I thought your routine was written around life as you encounter it. You mean you make everything up? You wouldn't make use of anything or anybody on this shoot, for example?'

'Don't be naive, Ross, baby!' Jason snorted. 'This lot will provide me with a whole package. If you're not busy, perhaps you'd manage my Edinburgh gig this summer. I've got plans and it's gonna make all this worthwhile. Think about it.'

'Yes, thanks, I will.'

* * *

The morning shoot finished more or less on time and the crew, minus Marcus but including the actors needed for the afternoon, gathered in the bus for lunch.

Ross was right: there was a fair attempt to tease Jason but his short, bad-tempered response quickly killed the ribaldry.

In a lull in the conversation, Jilly spoke up. 'I've been asked by Marcus to put a list of people together who'd like to go to a party on Thursday night.'

This was greeted by a general murmur of enthusiasm.

'It's a drinks party, so I guess they expect you to eat beforehand. But there'll be lots of booze . . . Juliet says they know how to throw parties . . .'

Juliet choked, but said nothing.

'When and where, Jilly?' asked one of the drivers.

'Summerstoke House. It's the top end of the village, on the left,' volunteered Juliet. 'There's a small fountain in the drive.'

'Sounds posh,' commented Maggie, the wardrobe mistress. 'What time?'

'Eight-ish. And yes, I think they're probably a bit posh, but they want to give us a welcome to the village, so Marcus would like us to make an effort,' Jilly said firmly.

'What's the name of the people inviting us?'

asked Colin.

'Lester. Hugh and Veronica Lester.'

There was such a shriek of outrage from Matt, everyone turned to look at him. He'd choked on a large mouthful of Cornish pasty, his face was purple, inarticulate noises emanated from his mouth, and his eyes bulged.

Ross thumped his back and a chunk of pasty shot out, accompanied by the shout, 'Lester! I don't believe it. Did you say Hugh Lester, Jilly?'

'Yes, why, Matt? Do you know him already?'

'He's the bastard who nearly ran Colin down in his "look at me I'm the king of the road" wankin' Range Rover today; the same guy who sabotaged our shoot with the cows. There's no way I'm going to a sodding party at his place . . . I don't want blood on my hands.'

There was silence as the crew chewed over the conflicting claims of loyalty and self-interest; self-interest because this job meant a long time on location, and Summerstoke didn't have much to offer in the way of entertainment, Summerbridge only marginally more so, and an evening of freely flowing booze was usually irresistible.

'Oh dear,' Jilly sounded nonplussed. 'I don't think Marcus knew that when he asked me to draw up a list. I tell you what, guys, I'll ask him if he still wants us to go and if he does, I'll put a note up on the board, here in the canteen van, with my name at the top; so it's up to you if you sign up for it or not. Though I'd quite like,' she added with a gulp, 'not to be the only one to go.'

'Don't you worry, darlin',' shouted Joe, the driver. 'If you go, I will. We'll drink the bastard dry.'

'Good ideal,' shouted someone else and the noise level rose as everyone debated the relative merits of staying away to make a point, or, even better, going and emptying Mr Hugh Lester's cellar.

'Well Ben, what about you?' Jilly asked pointedly. 'You're the reason the invitation was issued in the first place . . .'

'Jilly,' hissed Ben, looking rather desperate. 'You were there when she invited us. I think a "select few" was mentioned and promised by us . . . Charming as they are, I don't think Joe the driver, Billy the sparks, or Ricky the grip were quite what she had in mind.'

'No?' Jilly grinned. 'My memory is very poor, darling, as is yours. You said you'd completely forgotten about it. But don't you think it will be so much more fun with Joe and co?'

Juliet chuckled. 'You're wicked, Jilly.'

'Thank you, darling,' Jilly purred.

Ben was dismayed. He was being boxed into a corner not of his making and it was getting increasingly difficult to extricate himself. He examined the options in a thoroughly Dacres way— what did he want? He didn't want to go to a party and be, in any way, associated with the likes of Joe and Ricky. In fact, he wasn't sure he wanted to go to the Lester mansion at all; the memory of Hugh Lester's icy stare as it had lingered on him was not a pleasant one. And Veronica Lester had a hungry glint in her eye; that unnerved him. He was happy to flirt with women, but nothing more. Sex was low on his list of priorities, and he equally definitely did not like the presence of a husband like Hugh Lester in the background.

Jenny Tucker was prettier and didn't regard him in a rapacious fashion. True she was as poor as a church mouse and rather shabby; her taste in cards was terrible, and she made totally inedible cakes; but she had a gentle appeal that made him feel good. He liked that. And he didn't have to do too much to feel generous. But he certainly couldn't take her to the Lesters' party, he was no fool. Equally, he couldn't decline the Lesters and keep his date with Jenny. It was a small community and with the Country Club the only place worth eating, word of his dinner-date, given wings by gossip or malice—it didn't matter which—would inevitably get back to the spurned hostess. He couldn't risk it.

There was no help for it. He cast his mind over the schedules for the end of the week. As luck would have it, he wasn't due on set till Friday afternoon. Right. He'd phone his agent and get her to send him an urgent email instructing him to go to London on Thursday night to discuss his forthcoming autobiography with an interested publisher.

73

'Isabelle?'

On hearing Emma's voice, accompanied by an apologetic cough, Isabelle quietly cursed, then putting down her paint rag, turned to smile at the unwelcome intruder.

Emma stood at the conservatory door. 'Sorry to disturb you, but would you mind if I invite Marcus to supper tonight?'

416

Isabelle frowned at the smudges of paint on her hands. She did mind. She was still rattled by the encounter in the car park and although Charlie appeared to believe he'd misunderstood Marcus's intentions and was ready to carry on as before, she wasn't sure she could. But she couldn't reasonably refuse Emma without going into some convoluted explanation.

'No,' she replied, unable to conceal the note of reluctance, 'I don't mind.'

Emma looked anxious. 'I won't, if you don't want me to, it's just that he's bringing today's rushes over and, well, I got the impression that if Mrs Tucker hadn't fed him yesterday night, he wouldn't have eaten anything at all, all day.' Then she shrugged, changing tack, aware she'd inadvertently revealed a softer side of herself, 'But hell, he's a big boy. He can take care of himself.'

Isabelle regarded her curiously. 'Why are you suddenly so concerned about Mr Steel? I thought you couldn't stand him?'

'No I couldn't.' Emma admitted candidly. 'But since I fell into the river, he's become a whole lot more, well, human. I think his problem is lack of regular contact with us humble mortals; he needs to keep his feet on the ground to prevent his head from disappearing into the stratosphere.'

Isabelle laughed. 'You might be right. Okay. Charlie's coming over . . . that's six of us. Who's cooking? I've completely forgotten. I hope it's not me, and you're meant to be resting . . .'

'However I can run to shoving some pizzas in the oven, opening a few bags of salad and unwrapping some cheese, if that's okay with you?'

'That's my kind of cooking,' replied Isabelle

cheerfully, turning back to her painting, adding politely, 'So, you're feeling better, Emma?'

Emma took the hint.

'Fine,' she said, 'See you later.'

'Isabelle?'

At the sound of Paula's voice, Isabelle gave a deep sigh. She needed to get on with this painting and the last thing she wanted, agreeable though her visitors might be, was constant interruption.

Whereas Emma was sensitive to this need, Paula certainly wouldn't be.

'In here, Paula . . .' Isabelle called, resigned, and turned to Emma. 'I don't think you've met Paula, yet, have you?'

The look of incredulity on Emma's face as she turned to greet Paula almost cracked Isabelle up.

Determined that the TV crew should, at no point, overlook her, Paula had taken to dressing herself as spectacularly as her wardrobe would allow.

'Joan Collins wouldn't take rejection lying down,' she'd said earlier. 'This is my big chance, Isabelle, I'm not going to let it go . . .'

Tonight her appearance was spectacular. Teetering on four-inch heels of thigh-length, black patent boots, a short purple sweater clung to her ample bosom generously exposing her midriff; a wide plastic silver belt was slung low on her hips, and a pair of black velveteen hot pants completed the ensemble.

Her facial appearance was, if anything, more amazing. Long black lashes curled back from almond-shaped blue eyes, black eyeliner delineated and elongated their shape and the eyelids were heavy with silver and purple shadow. Her cheeks

418

were patted a pale rose and her cupid lips, their shape carefully outlined, glossy with a plum lipstick.

She was only in her mid-twenties but she looked, Emma thought, quite stunned, as if she'd stepped out of a Carry On film—a parody of celluloid beauty, ageless, timeless, but nothing to do with rural life in the 21st century.

'Paula, this is Emma; she's part of the television crew,' Isabelle was casual in her introduction, sensing Paula would freeze if she learned Emma was the director.

'Paula,' she turned to Emma, 'helps me out no end. My two and her two eldest are as thick as thieves. And, believe it or not, she likes ironing!'

'I've always been practical that way,' said Paula preening slightly. 'Just as well, ain't it, Isabelle? So if you want any done,' she nodded at Emma, 'just say the word, I'd be happy to oblige.'

Emma, who made it her business never to buy anything that needed anything more than rudimentary care, and certainly couldn't remember when she'd last picked up an iron, replied faintly, 'That's very kind of you, Paula, thanks,' and made to go.

But Paula wasn't going to waste this unexpected opportunity to lobby a member of the TV crew, even if she looked as if she couldn't say boo to a goose . . .

She folded her arms, barring Emma's exit, and fixed her with a determined eye. 'If you work with that lot,' she began,' you can tell me who decides who's gonna be picked for the filming. Only I put me name down and I've been waitin' and waitin' and nothing!' She almost spat her disgust. 'Then Ros Clark, with a face like the back of a bus,

419

between you and me, not that she can help that, mind, but she doesn't even go to the movies, she's been called twice and her smirk is more than a body can bear. So why not I? That's what I'd like to know? I've always wanted to be a actress. So why won't the telly people pick I, eh?'

'Er . . . I'm not sure,' Emma floundered. 'The assistant director, Sarah Thornby, who did the recruitment, is the one who chooses who to call . . .'

'That miserable cow. Sorry if she's a friend of yours, but she looks as if she's got a mouth full of lemons, as my Mum would say. Charlie said maybe they're saving me up for something special . . . me looking so much like Joan Collins. He said I'd stand out too much, bein' part of a crowd.'

'He's probably right about that.'

'But I tell you, I'd rather be part of a crowd than not be called at all. It's humiliatin'.'

'Yes, I can see that. Er, look, I'll do what I can. But try not to get too upset if you're not called. It's very boring, being an extra.'

'That's easy for you to say, you're employed by that lot. But this is my first real chance of doing somethin'; of bein' somebody . . .' And Paula sighed, a deep miserable sigh. 'Sometimes I wish the TV hadn't come to the village.'

*   *   *

A sentiment echoed, somewhat uncharacteristically, by Alison when her grandmother looked in on her before going to visit Ron.

'Now what's behind this, young lady?' Elsie's voice was bracing but she viewed her granddaughter with concern, observing that Alison's eyes were over-bright, her face flushed, and she'd developed a hacking cough. Not one to make an unnecessary fuss, she thought she might suggest Jenny call the doctor . . . not that one could ever get them to make home visits these days . . .

'Oh Gran, it's Al. I've texted him and tried calling him, but he doesn't answer. Mum told him I was on the riverbank with that creep Jason Hart and he's obviously jumped to the wrong conclusion.'

'Now why should he do that?'

'Because he doesn't like Jason and he didn't want him coming up here to help me with my website, and he was mad with me 'cos I let him and then he hears I'm on the riverbank with him, so what else is he going to think?'

'I can understand Al objecting to Jason coming up to your bedroom, whatever the reason.'

'Yes, but he's brilliant with website design. And I got Hannah here as well, Gran, and then, when he wouldn't go, I froze him out.'

Elsie raised her brows. 'Froze him out?'

A thin wheezy chuckle came from the bed. 'I turned off all the heating, opened the windows, and Hannah threw a glass of cold water over him. He was in a right strop, shivering fit to bust a gut. He couldn't get out quick enough.'

'Didn't you tell Al this?'

'No,' replied Alison miserably, 'I didn't get a chance because we got into a mega row about the camera.'

'And you haven't told him you've found it?'

'In my text message, but he hasn't taken any notice, the bastard. Oh Gran, he was only staying down here for a week, supposing he goes back to

Durham without seeing me . . .'

'Is that likely, now? He's very fond of you, Alison, any fool can see that.'

'But he's very proud, Gran, and if he's angry, I think he'd just take off. Oh if only he'd phone me . . .'

*   *   *

Al rolled up his spare pair of jeans, and stuffing them into his rucksack, mentally ticked off the list of things he'd need for the next eight weeks. Once the term was finished, he wasn't sure if he'd ever come back to Bath; he couldn't see the point. He'd leave a note for his aunt, who'd gone to London for a couple of days, and give her Alison's telephone number so she could retrieve the camera. At least that had been found, he thought bitterly. Alison's betrayal had so affected him, he couldn't think clearly and he simmered with anger. 'At least,' he muttered, 'I don't ever have to go back to Summerstoke again. Never, ever!'

His things packed, he went downstairs and was writing the note when the doorbell rang. He stomped down the hallway and opened the door.

'Hello Anthony.'

He froze.

'Aren't you going to invite me in, darling, or must I stand here on the doorstep?'

'I don't know what you're doing here, but I have nothing to say to you.' Stony-faced, he made no move to admit his mother.

'Well, Anthony, as it happens I have something to say to you, but I'd rather have this conversation inside, if you don't mind.'

Al shifted a fraction and Veronica swept past him into her sister's sitting room.

Veronica rarely did anything on impulse, but she was opportunistic and when she'd spotted her sister carrying an overnight bag into Bath Spa station, she knew there was a chance she'd find her son at home, alone.

Preoccupied as she was with Ben Dacres—and she'd come into Bath to buy herself a new dress for the following evening's party—she could not forget the nauseating vision of her son embracing the Tucker girl.

He stood by the sitting room door, his face expressionless.

'Well, what is it?'

Veronica was disconcerted by her feelings. Anthony was thin and pale, she hadn't seen him properly for nearly nine months, and she suddenly wanted him to . . . well, for him at least to look at her more warmly. Worse, she felt an almost overwhelming urge to hug him . . .

She was horrified. Anthony had rejected her; he'd sent her away . . .

Stifling the treacherous feelings, she viewed him coldly. 'You look undernourished, Anthony, but since you've refused to accept your allowance, I suppose that's not surprising.'

He gave an impatient shrug. 'I get by.'

'But Anthony, darling, there's no need for you to get by.' She tried a different tack, softening her voice, attempting a smile. 'Listen, I want you to use your allowance. There are no strings attached. The only condition is one you'd relish, darling: not to return to Bath, or Summerstoke, until you've finished your degree. And not even then, if you still don't want to see us.'

He stared at her, frowning. 'Let me get this straight . . . You're proposing to pay me to stay away?'

'That's putting it a little baldly, darling, but in essence, yes.'

'Why?'

'Why? Because I worry about you; when all's said and done, you are my son.'

'I'm sorry, but I don't believe you. There has to be another reason . . . my being your son has never stirred you on my behalf before . . .'

'Anthony, that's a terrible thing to say!'

'But true. So what is it, Mother? I can't believe this has anything to do with my aunt, so why do you want me to stay away from Summerstoke? What are you up to?'

'Nothing, Anthony, nothing at all.' She gave a light laugh. 'Why should you want to return to Summerstoke, anyway?'

'Who says I do?'

The trouble with being opportunistic is that plans not carefully thought through may go awry, and faced with the blank obduracy of her son, anger suddenly got the better of Veronica.

'Oh don't play games, Anthony,' she snapped. 'You've a girl in Summerstoke, some common little tart . . .'

'So that's it?' Al's voice was soft and dangerous. 'Let's get to the truth of this, shall we, Mother dearest? You want to pay me to stay away from Summerstoke because you're upset I could be going out with someone you think is beneath you? How antique . . . but there's more to it than that. You've done your homework, and you know the girl is not some common little tart but Alison Tucker. A Tucker of Marsh Farm, a farm you and Dad have set your hearts on getting by fair means or foul, haven't you?'

'I've no idea what her name is,' Veronica tried once more to retrieve the situation. 'The thing is, Anthony, Anthony dear, you've only got one chance with this degree; I can't bear to think of you jeopardising your future by running after someone who is entirely unsuitable . . .'

'I think I prefer to be the judge of that, thank you. Her family are worth a million times more than you and Dad. You're completely without scruples; and as for even thinking you could pay me to stay away . . .' his lip curled. 'You're unreal, you really are. Got some little scheme going to oust the Tuckers have you? Well hard luck, I'm not going to make it easy for you. I'm sticking, whether you like it or not, and you can be sure I shall be on high alert for any of your nasty little tricks.'

He turned his back on her and stalked out of the room. 'I've got nothing more to say to you. Go, please.'

At the top of the stairs he heard the door slam behind his mother, then sat, his head bowed.

'How ironic,' he thought bitterly, 'that she offers to pay for the very thing I'd resolved to do. Oh Ali, Ali, why did you have to go after that jerk?'

His despair was arrested by the sound of the doorbell again. Angrily he got to his feet, if that was her . . . ! Descending the stairs, he tried to think of a sufficiently cutting comment that would send his parent packing, once and for all.

The doorbell sounded once more.

'All right, all right,' he snorted, 'I'm coming.'

He flung the door open, ready for battle.

'Hello, Al.'

His jaw dropped.

'May I come in?'

Too astonished to say anything, he stood aside to let Elsie pass.

74

Surprised and unusually gratified to receive Emma's invitation to supper, Marcus accepted and when he and Emma had viewed the rushes, hared off to get a bottle of wine, leaving Emma to read the scripts for the remaining episodes that had been delivered that day.

While he was gone, Charlie arrived and found Isabelle still deeply immersed in her painting.

She broke off with a sigh of pleasure when she saw him and gave herself up to the warmth of his embrace.

'How much more do you want to do this evening?' he asked, finally releasing her and looking at her work

'Another half hour should do it,' she said, grateful for his understanding. 'I am so close. Poor Clemmie and Becky have hardly seen me since Paula delivered them back.'

'They're fine. I looked in on them: they're sitting in the kitchen doing some schoolwork under the eagle eye of Colin, of all people; he's also initiating Emma into the mysteries of the Aga.'

Isabelle laughed. 'They're such a nice bunch of people. I admit I was doubtful about having them here, but I'm really glad they're about.'

'Well, that's a relief. According to Lenny, the entire village is fed up with them already.'

'There'll always be those who'll grumble; I don't think most people are bothered one way or the other. Admittedly Matt is not the most sensitive of people, but really, I think the main trouble is all this "extra" business; those who get called moan about being kept hanging about, and those that don't are green with envy.'

'Like Paula?'

'Yes, like Paula. She's so upset at not being chosen, Charlie.'

He nodded. 'Tell me about it. I've had Lenny moaning all afternoon. I was thinking of asking Marcus if he couldn't find something for her, as a favour . . .'

'You could ask him this evening.' She hesitated, 'Emma has invited him to supper, I hope you don't mind.'

He gave her a searching looking. 'I don't mind, not at all. But I get the impression you do. Not on my account, I hope. I've seen the error of my ways.'

For a moment Isabelle was tempted to tell Charlie how right he'd been about Marcus, but she stopped herself. 'No, I don't mind. Actually, I thought Emma couldn't stand him, so you could have knocked me down with a feather when she suggested it. I'd say there are some interesting developments in that quarter.'

Charlie laughed. 'From what I've seen of the two of them that seems very unlikely; it's not exactly been open hostilities, but something very close.'

Later, sitting in the kitchen eating pizzas, Charlie had to admit that Isabelle had a point.

He'd always got on well with Marcus, but he could see his manner with people he employed, or those who did not interest him, was cold or imperious. Over supper however, Marcus made an effort. He engaged Emma in good-humoured banter and chatted amiably to Colin and Matt. He had the same easy-going manner with Charlie as he'd always had, and the only person, Charlie noted, whom he seemed to treat with cautious reserve, was Isabelle.

Mindful of his intention to do something about Paula, Charlie decided it was an opportune moment to put in his bid for her.

'Marcus,' he began, 'I've a favour to ask . . .'

'Ask away,' replied Marcus. 'I owe you.'

'It's not so much for me, as for Lenny. His life is being made miserable because Paula hasn't been picked to be an extra. I realise she's probably not quite what you want, but if there is any way you could tuck her in somewhere . . .'

'Hmm,' Marcus frowned, 'I could have a word with Sarah, she's responsible for whom we use . . .'

Emma interrupted. 'I met Paula this afternoon, Charlie. There is no way she could be "tucked in" anywhere.'

'No' admitted Charlie. 'But surely . . .'

'But I read through the fresh scripts before supper, and actually, following up a suggestion of yours, Charlie, I think we can use her.'

'I suggested something?'

'Yes. You said to her we might be keeping her back for something more special. Well, it's not much, but there is a scene in the local pub. Do you think she'd be happy to play the barmaid? Not that I'm suggesting she looks like a barmaid,

428

you understand. But she's so spectacular and this is a comedy . . . She's got a couple of lines which means she doesn't come under the "extra" remit. If Marcus is okay with it, we could go ahead and audition her.'

*   *   *

Charlie had been all for phoning up Paula, there and then, but was persuaded to let the formal process take its course.

'It may just be,' explained Emma, 'that even a couple of lines will be beyond her. I've known individuals completely freeze when faced with a camera, or worse, stare into it with the fascination of a snake's dinner.'

But Charlie was confident Paula would rise to the challenge, and feeling extremely cheerful after a very convivial evening, he departed, promising Isabelle he'd return after he'd checked on the state of his pregnant porkers.

Stephen was sitting alone at the table in the Marsh Farm kitchen, his head in his hands.

He looked up as Charlie entered, his face ashen. 'It's all your fault, Charlie,' he said bitterly. 'You brought the television crew here . . .'

'This is becoming rather a common refrain, Stephen,' said Charlie. 'What life or death crisis has come up now?'

'Oh, you can mock, but this farm means everything to me. And what happens to it when our milking herd is gone, eh? Do you think the rare breeds and the holiday cottages will bring in enough to keep us going? And do you think that's real farming—'cos it certainly ain't for me. Those

429

cows are the backbone of this farm . . .'

'Yes, yes, I know that. So what's brought on this latest episode of doom and gloom?'

'Major Tenby, that's what,' replied Stephen heavily. 'He phoned this evening. He's been presented with a petition from the village. After last week's debacle, he said people are up in arms. No more cows. That's what.' He was almost in tears, 'I can't see how we can fight them, Charlie. We're going to have to let the herd go; there's no way they can eat their fill on the fields this side of the river. The television's not made our fortune, as you said it would. It's done for us.'

Charlie stared at him for a moment, then gritted his teeth. 'I've had enough of this . . . we're not giving in, Stevie. I'm fed up with this constant threat. Nobody's gonna tell us where we can graze our cows . . . we've been using those pastures for fifty years.'

Stephen looked at him, deflated. 'I don't know what you're gonna do about it, Charlie, what you can do about it . . .'

'I'm gonna do what we should have done years ago, when folks first started bellyachin'. I'm gonna get legal advice. Then we'll know where we stand. The future looks bright for the farm, Steve. Now's not the time to give in to whinging bullies.'

75

'Ali? Ali? Are you awake?' Al sat at Alison's bedside, clasping her hot little hand and watching the flushed features and restless, fluttering eyelids for signs of waking.

When Elsie filled in him on what had actually taken place between Alison and Jason Hart, he'd grabbed his gear and roared over to Marsh Farm where he found Jenny waiting in the kitchen for Dr Gordon, who was with Alison.

When the doctor joined them, he told Jenny he'd given Alison something to help her sleep; she was to be kept quiet, and he'd call again the following day. If she worsened, they were to call him, as bronchial pneumonia could not be ruled out, but they were not to worry.

So worry they did.

Jeff had a late night surgery and wasn't coming over; Stephen had gone to a meeting of the Merlin Players with Angela; Charlie was over at Isabelle's, and Elsie wasn't expected back from the hospital until nine, so Al and Jenny were alone.

During the course of the evening, they'd taken it in turns to sit with Alison, listening to her harsh, laboured breathing and occasional paroxysms of coughing; Al had persuaded Jenny to let him have his sleeping bag in Alison's room and she had agreed, retiring to bed herself, emotionally and physically exhausted.

In the middle of the night Alison had woken, calling out for him, and he had lain by her side, stroking her face and whispering words of reassurance until she had drifted off to sleep again.

She was still fast asleep when he'd got up the following morning and Elsie, looking in on her, was of the opinion that although she was clearly very poorly, she looked better and there was no point in calling Dr Gordon before his planned visit that afternoon.

431

Al had unpacked his bag of books and sat down at Alison's computer, half his brain on his work, the other half listening for her, willing her to wake and be well.

At the first stirring, he'd leapt to her side.

The eyelids finally ceased their fluttering and opened. Alison's extraordinary green eyes, over-bright with the fever, looked at him and a slight crease appeared in her brow. 'Al? Am I dreaming this? Are you really here?'

He leant forward and kissed her. 'Yes, I am. It's me, stoopid.'

She shook her head. 'I dreamt you were here last night, I woke up and you were here. You said you loved me?'

'And so I did, and so I do. Your mother let me stay in your room.'

'What? Mum? Now I know I'm dreaming!'

Al stroked her face. 'We were worried about you. I slept in my sleeping bag. I promise I didn't take advantage of your unconscious state.'

Alison gave a weak chuckle. 'What a wasted opportunity.'

Al took her hand. 'Ali, I'm sorry I was so bloody stupid over Jason. I should have known you were too sharp to be taken in by him.'

'You should have trusted me, Al.'

'Yes, I know,' he said unhappily. 'I am so sorry, Ali.'

'You were right about him, though. He's an absolute creep and he did have designs on me. He said as much when we were stuck on that riverbank.'

Al grinned. 'Your Gran told me how you got rid of him when he came to set up the website.'

'Gran?'

'Yes, she came to see me yesterday afternoon. Just after . . . my God, I'd completely forgotten . . . just after I'd had a visit from my mother!'

Alison stared up at him, perplexed. 'Your mother? Why should your mother come and see you?'

Al looked down at her, his face grim. 'I'm not sure. Let's get you well first. Then we'll tackle my mother.'

Alison plucked his sleeve. 'If it's anything to do with the farm, Al, then don't do nothing. Tell Charlie. Please, tell Charlie.'

*   *   *

'Hello, Angela.'

Hearing Sally Green's voice, Angela looked up from the catalogues she was sorting. 'Oh hello, Mrs Green . . . Sally. Er . . . was it me you wanted, or was it something from the library?'

'Well actually, Angela,' Sally Green's face was flushed and her lowered voice sounded portentous, 'I wanted to have a word with you. Are you able to take five minutes off?'

'Not really.' Angela glanced at her watch. 'But I'm due a coffee break in about fifteen minutes. Can I meet you at the Black Swan? I won't be able to say long . . .'

'I'll have a coffee waiting for you.'

'Could you make that a hot chocolate? Sorry, only I don't like coffee.'

Fifteen minutes later the hot chocolate, piled with whipped cream, was waiting.

'Now then, Angela,' Sally's small eyes gleamed.

Far from being a reluctant player, she found Veronica's game and her part in it thoroughly exciting. Her trip into Summerbridge was primarily to see Angela, but also to find a dress fit for a Lester party.

'I've some good news. My husband does have a client who might be interested in investing in your farm, but, obviously, he needs to know what that investment involves; how much money you're looking for and is there a business plan?'

'Yes of course,' Angela nodded, blinking hard, her cheeks pink. 'I'll talk to Stephen, but there shouldn't be any problem getting that information. Thank you, Mrs Green . . . Sally . . . you've been wonderful.'

'Not at all.' Sally patted Angela's hand. 'Pleased to be of service.'

'There's just one thing, though,' Angela hesitated. 'Stephen's cautious. He'll not want to sign anything, or agree to anything, unless he knows who he's dealing with . . .'

Sally saw Angela's request as entirely reasonable. 'I've never met the gentleman in question, of course, but his name is Osbourne. VE Osbourne. Victor Edward,' she improvised, 'and he owns a lot of land in Australia . . .'

76

'Thing is, Isabelle, I can't say anything to Jenny, she just gets upset. You can't blame folks. They've been very patient, but there is only so much pushing around a body can take. I mean, look at the way they treat me and my shop, I've got to the point where I don't know whether I can open for business or serve my customers . . . It's terrible for trade, and as for that woman they've got, pretending to me be, well!'

For once words failed Rita and for once Isabelle, who had merely dropped in for a pint of milk, lost her patience. 'I can't believe what I'm hearing, Rita. What's the problem? Isn't everyone getting paid for their trouble? Aren't you? And I know I'm not the only one making some welcome cash out of lodgings. What were people expecting? The money to come rolling in without having to give anything in return?'

'Well I, for one, have to work extremely hard just to stand still, Isabelle.' Rita was stiff. 'I'm quite happy with the way things are with the television people. In fact, I admit, I do very well by them. But when they're gone and I find my customers gone, what will I do? And I'm their elected representative. They come to me because of my role on the parish council. I have to represent their views, regardless of how I feel about things.'

'I didn't think,' replied Isabelle, brusquely, 'that there'd been any elections for the parish council for years. I thought people got co-opted on because nobody wants to do it.'

'That's as maybe,' replied Rita, even more stiffly, 'But we are still the village representatives and if the village expresses an opinion about something, we have to listen.'

'But is this really the opinion of the village, Rita, or just the grumbles of a disaffected minority? I, for one, am quite happy with the way things are. I think it's great . . . It's brought money and new people and excitement into the village. I bet if you were to ask around, there'd be a lot more people who feel like me. Let the extras go on strike, if that's what they want to do; I suspect their places would be very quickly taken up by people from other villages. Ask if they'd rather the filming happened elsewhere, Great Missenwall, for example? I bet there'd be a resounding "no".'

Rita sniffed. There was a great deal of truth in Isabelle's words, but she was a newcomer to the village . . . what did she know about the ways of village folk, what they would put up with, and what they wouldn't? Not everything in life could be bought . . .

'Happen you've got a point, Isabelle. But you would say that, wouldn't you? Your Charlie is thick as thieves with them people, which is why I was telling you about this planned day of action.'

'Which is going to be tomorrow? The extras will refuse to co-operate, people are going to ignore instructions about when they can and cannot walk or drive through the village, or use the shop?'

'Or go into church, or see their kiddies across the road after school, or walk their dogs where they have done for years,' added Rita.

Isabelle shrugged. 'Okay, Rita, I'll pass on the news. How much do I owe you for this pint of milk?'

*   *   *

'Sorry to hijack your lunch hour like this,' Marcus looked round at Charlie, Emma, Matt and Ross. 'But from what Charlie has told me, we're gonna need a bit of a pre-emptive action.'

436

Not knowing why this meeting had been called, they waited, curious.

'Charlie, you can explain . . .'

Charlie sighed. 'There's a growing discontent in the village about the filming. It's probably the usual bellyaching from folks who don't like to be put out in any way, but it seems to be spreading. Stephen's been told there's a petition to stop the cows coming through the village as a result of last week's mess, and now we've learnt the extras are planning a strike tomorrow; plus there's a wider move afoot to persuade the parish council to withdraw their co-operation in any more shooting around the village.'

Emma groaned, 'Oh shit.'

'What a load of wankers!' spat Matt. 'Don't they know which side their bread is buttered?'

Ross wrinkled his brow and turned to Marcus. 'What do you suggest we do?'

'I've been talking it over with Charlie, which is why I said a bit of pre-emptive action is called for. We need to be more upfront with people, ain't that right, Charlie?'

'Yes. Thing is, folks got half the picture: the glamour half. At first that was all they needed. They were so excited at the thought of the telly being here. But now it's here, and they find they're being asked to do things and they don't understand why . . . Well, you've got to explain why. Get them on your side. Then give them the choice: take it or leave it. I reckon they'll take it. Can't imagine they wouldn't.'

'Makes sense,' Ross nodded.

Emma turned to Marcus. 'So what are you proposing to do?'

437

Marcus frowned. 'The first part is easy, if you can fix this for me, Ross. Tomorrow night we hold a meeting for the village and all the extras on our books, at the village hall. We must all be there, plus Sarah and Colin, ready to explain what each of us do and what makes our job easier and what more difficult. I'll describe the *Silage* storyline and the ideas behind the series and then I'll hand over to each of you. That done, we'll invite questions and ply them with booze. Okay?'

'It's very short notice,' Ross replied. 'Are you sure the hall is available?'

'If it's not, we might be able to use the school hall,' suggested Charlie. 'The thing is, everyone should know this is happening by the end of this afternoon.'

'Okay.' Ross nodded.

'Good.' Marcus was brisk. 'So for tomorrow, Matt, Ross, I want you to re-draw the schedules. Cancel all location filming and tell Sarah to stand down the extras.'

Matt whistled. 'Blimey, Marcus, you're asking a lot.'

'I know, Matt. But if they don't turn up, we'd be in the soup anyway. Better to be pre-emptive.'

Emma nodded. 'He's right, Matt. So tomorrow, back to the interiors?'

'Yes. And Friday and Saturday as well. We've got the rest of the scripts in, so we can continue shooting all the interiors for as long as it takes.'

'Laying off the extras, indefinitely,' Charlie concurred, 'is the best way I know of getting them to see sense. Particularly if, at the meeting, you explain there's the option of offering extras work to people from other villages.'

'Wicked!' Matt chuckled, then frowned. 'Marcus, this is a major re-scheduling job. I can't do it overnight.'

'I know. Which is why I'm pulling you out of this afternoon's shoot. You and Ross had better work together. Ross, you can get your team up and running to organise tomorrow, can't you? I'm sure Charlie can help . . .'

'Sorry, Marcus, I would if I could, but I've emergencies of my own to attend to. I really can't do anything else today.' Charlie was regretful but firm and after a momentary frown, Marcus nodded.

'Okay, mate. We're grateful for what you've done already.'

'This afternoon, Marcus, how had you planned to cover that without Matt?' Emma asked, a trifle anxious.

'I'll take his place.'

'What!?' Stunned, his team stared at him.

'Why not?' Marcus demanded, stung. 'I was an AD once. I can manage for one afternoon, if Emma can bear me. And I'll tell you one thing, young Matt, I won't go strutting my stuff about how I'm the greatest the next time there's a village quiz.'

There was a moment's embarrassed silence and Matt looked rather awkward. 'Point taken,' he said gruffly.

'Right', said Marcus briskly, standing to his feet. 'If that's it, we'd better get moving. Get me tomorrow's new schedule as quickly as you can, Matt.'

'There's just one other thing, Marcus.' Ross sounded diffident. 'I know Jason has your vote of confidence over Emma's accident, but the suspicion someone is trying to sabotage our shoot is growing;

it's undermining morale and . . . er . . . I just wondered if you have anyone else in the frame?'

Marcus resumed his seat, looking serious. 'No, Ross we haven't. And you're right, we mustn't relax our vigilance. I guess we hoped the accident with Emma was not intended and whoever it was, having had a fright, would lay off for a bit. My feeling is that it's not Jason. It's so unlikely we'd have two jokers in the pack. But if anyone has any serious suggestions, I'm prepared to listen.'

77

Leaving the kids squabbling over the TV, Lenny and Paula settled down at their wobbly kitchen table to eat pizza and chips.

'Have you heard about the planned strike tomorrow, Lenny?' Paula enquired indistinctly, her cheeks bulging.

'What, the extras?' Lenny took a swig from his can and wiped his mouth with the back of his hand.

'Yeah. It's all over the village. Roz told me and Mum said Mrs Godwin was full of it. Seems they think it's time they took a stand.'

'What about?'

'How do you mean, Lenny?'

'Took a stand about what? What's their particular gripe?'

'Oh, I don't rightly know. Fed up with being pushed about, I reckon. Quite right, too.'

The telephone rang and Paula, taking another large bite of pizza, left the kitchen to answer it.

Lenny half-listened to Paula's pizza-muffled

voice.

' 'Lo . . . yes, that's right . . . No, I said you got the right number . . . this is Paula Spinks speakin' . . . That's what I said . . . You can't hear . . . just a minute, hold on, don't go away . . .'

Dashing back into the kitchen, she spat out a large piece of half-consumed pizza then ran back. The conversation resumed. 'Can you hear I better, now? Right . . . I see . . . you want I . . .'

Lenny listened with interest.

Paula sounded very subdued. 'I see . . .' she continued, 'Yes, all right. I'll be there . . . Six-thirty . . . Yes, I know where it is. Thank you. Thank you very much. No, I won't be late. Goodbye.'

He heard her put the phone down and waited for her to come back to the kitchen but she remained in the hall, quite silent.

Then she screamed.

She screamed so loudly, Lenny fell off his chair. By the time he got to her, the kids had swarmed out of the sitting room, demanding to know what was up.

She was standing by the phone, her hands cupping her face, her mouth and eyes wide with shock.

'What is it, love? What is it, my flower? What's wrong?' Lenny, terrified, pulled at her hands.

She stopped screaming, astonished at the question. 'Wrong, nothing's wrong, Lenny. That was the TV lady, she wants me tomorrow . . .'

'But there's gonna be an extras strike tomorrow, Paula. You gonna be a blackleg?'

'No, Lenny, no. They don't want me as an extra.' Paula's voice rose high with excitement. 'They want me for a audition. They want to try me out for a

441

part, Lenny. I'm gonna have lines! This is for real. This is my big moment, darlin'. I'm gonna be a actress.'

'Yahoo!' Lenny shrieked and the kids joined it. For a while the tiny cottage rocked with the noise of celebration. Crisps and Coke were found for the kids; Lenny cracked another can of cider and opened a Guinness for Paula. (He also finished her pizza, she being too excited to eat another thing).

'When I'm famous,' said Paula, beaming at Lenny, 'We'll have champagne for our tea, everyday.'

'I think I'll stick with me Scrumpy Jack if it's all the same to you, darlin'. Though I wouldn't mind a regular supply of Jack Daniels for a chaser.'

'You can have whatever you like,' she said grandly. 'And we'll have steak and chips, and scampi, whenever we feels like it . . .'

'But, my little flower,' reflected Lenny. 'If this strike goes ahead, and the television pulls out of Summerstoke, which is what folks want, you might find there'll be nothin' for you after all . . .'

Paula stared, horrified. 'You're jokin'' she gasped. 'I've been waiting for this moment, all my life. I won't let them whingin' scrubbers in the village ruin everything . . . I won't!'

'How can you stop em?'

'It's only a few who is really moanin'. The others are just going along with 'em for a bit of a laugh. I'll get onto the blower right away and tell 'em not to play silly buggers. They'll listen to I.'

Again Lenny sat listening to the rise and fall of Paula's voice as she phoned around. Finally she came back into the kitchen.

'I don't understand it,' she said, puzzled. 'The

442

strike's off . . .'

'That's good, my lovely. You done well . . .'

'No, it's nothing to do with I, Lenny. The TV people, they've phoned everybody and told them they're not needed tomorrow. And there's to be a meeting in the village hall, in the evening. I don't like the sound of this, Lenny. I don't like it at all.'

'But that lady wouldn't have phoned you if they was planning to pull out, love.'

'She's just a nobody, anyone can see that. S'why she's so bloomin' sour. She might not know what's goin' on. Oh Lenny, it would be so much worse to have been promised somethin' only to see it snatched away.'

78

'Evening, young Angela.' Jeff opened the car door and smiled.

Angela had been waiting outside her lodgings for Jeff to pick her up, something he did when there was no afternoon surgery. She climbed into the car, finding it difficult to smile normally, afraid she might burst, so full was she of her news. Fortunately Jeff didn't seem to notice.

'I've just been speaking to Jenny,' he said cheerfully. 'She says Dr Gordon's been and it seems as if we're going to have young Alison with us for a good while yet.' He chuckled. 'That's a relief, I can tell you. Jenny's been fearing the worst, and wasn't to be comforted.'

Angela was puzzled. 'Alison? What's wrong with her?'

'You don't know? She took a bad chill from her adventures on the riverbank and it looked like a dose of bronchial pneumonia; gave poor Jenny a real fright.'

'I didn't know. I wonder why Stephen didn't tell me.'

Jeff shrugged. 'Perhaps he didn't realise how serious it was. It all happened so quickly and he's very preoccupied at the moment.'

'Yes, he is. The farm means a lot to him, and to me. Oh, Uncle Jeff, I can't wait till we're married and I can be a real support to him; not just helping in my spare time.'

'You do a lot already. We all enjoy your cooking.'

'Yes. That's one of the things I'm really looking forward to, you know. Sorting that kitchen out, tidying it, redesigning it, filling the store-cupboard with jams and chutneys and homemade biscuits and cakes . . . It will be wonderful.'

Jeff laughed. 'Sounds like Stephen will have to watch his waistline.' He glanced at her. 'But it's not just Stephen you're taking on, is it? It's Jenny's kitchen, after all, and there's Alison and Charlie to be taken into consideration.'

'I know.' Angela flushed at the note of censure in his voice. 'Of course I won't do anything without Jenny's agreement, but she doesn't really like cooking, does she? And as Gran says, the house goes with the job . . .'

'Oh? That sounds like typical Elsie, but it's a bit harsh, young Angela. The farmhouse is Jenny's home.'

'Yes, yes, of course it is. I love Stephen's mum, Uncle Jeff, and she's got a home with us for as long as she wants it. Same with Alison, though she'll be off to uni pretty soon.'

'And Charlie?'

Angela thought for a moment before replying carefully, 'It's Charlie's home, too, so of course he's welcome to stay as long as he wants to. But he's handed the farm over to Stephen . . .'

'And invested all his money in developing the farm buildings.'

'Yes, that's true. But do you know, Uncle Jeff, I think Charlie would rather be out of it altogether. He and Stephen are so quarrelsome these days.'

'Isn't that due to the pressure of the TV crew being there, and the rare breeds opening?'

'Yes, of course . . . but I wonder . . . Uncle Jeff, do you think if Stephen offered to buy him out, Charlie would take the offer?'

Jeff frowned. 'That's something you'd have to ask Charlie. Remember he had the opportunity to leave before and he chose not only to stay but then invested in the farm. Why should he change his mind now? And anyway, where on earth would Stephen find that sort of money?'

Angela's conversation with Sally Green wriggled and tickled inside her, but Stephen had to be the first to know, so she said nothing and the rest of the journey was completed in silence.

Jeff was fond of Angela and he thoroughly approved of her relationship with Stephen, but this conversation disturbed him. He was the first to admit he was emotionally lazy and saw little point in initiating change; 'If it ain't broke, why fix it?' being one of his favourite maxims. But clearly a lot would change with the marriage of Stephen and Angela and the way he saw it his Jenny would

445

lose out . . . Charlie, too, seemed to be some sort of target. He did not underestimate Miss Angela's determination to make sure Stephen's interests, as she saw them, take first place. Charlie, he was sure, could look after himself, but could Jenny?

Jenny greeted him cheerfully, but she looked weary.

He gave her a warm hug and kissed her. 'You look tired, love. How's the invalid?'

'Oh, Jeff, so much better. She's just agreed to try and eat something, so Al is with her, feeding her some soup we made.'

'You made?' Angela was startled.

'Yes,' Jenny smiled. 'I've had two cookery lessons in two days. Al says he does all his own cooking in Durham and we made this potato and leek soup. I thought it was really nice.'

'Do you want me to make our supper?' Angela asked, disconcerted, 'Only if you've got plans . . .'

'Plans? Oh no, Angela. If you would like to, that is, I'd be ever so grateful.'

Angela looked relieved and donning a pinafore, went to the sink and laughed. 'Well, well! How like a student, he's left all the washing up.'

'That's because I told him to,' Jenny was reproving. 'I'm going to do it. Would you like a cup of tea, Jeff?'

'In a minute, love, I want to have a quick look at those porkers first. Charlie says he thinks they're very near their time. Put your boots on and come with me. The washing up can wait a little longer . . . you need some fresh air.'

Walking across the yard, Jenny's arm tucked in his, Jeff came to a decision, but before he could say anything, she said in a serious voice, 'Jeff, there's something I've been wanting to tell you.'

'Oh?'

Why, he thought, did he feel so apprehensive?

'It's just that I've had this invitation, from Ben Dacres, to go to dinner with him tomorrow night . . .'

He felt gutted, but replied, his voice steady, 'That's nice. Are you going?'

'I had thought I'd ask you if you minded. It would be so exciting . . . dinner with a film star . . . Me, plain old Jenny Tucker.'

'Yes, I can see that it would be, exciting, I mean. But you're not plain and you're not old, Jenny. Yes, you should go . . .'

'That's what I thought you'd say.' She shook her head. 'You're so nice, Jeff, so much nicer than me. If it was you, invited out by some fabulous actress, I'd want to scratch her eyes out . . .'

Jeff suddenly felt his spirits lift.

'So,' Jenny continued, 'I wrote him a note, this afternoon, saying thank you, but no.'

He stopped dead and turned to her. 'Jenny,' he said simply, 'you're one in a million. May I kiss you?'

'You don't have to ask, silly.'

And he kissed her, long, and tenderly.

Then quite unable to speak, they resumed their walk to the pigsties.

Jenny looked on as he examined the sows.

'Charlie's right,' he said, finally. 'They're both about to bring lots of little piglets into the world.'

'In time for the opening,' said Jenny ecstatically. 'I love piglets.'

'And I love you,' Jeff closed the door to the sty. 'Will you marry me, Jenny?'

In all the time she'd been going out with Jeff, in all the wishing for him to propose, in all the romantic settings she'd imagined for this to take place, she'd never, ever, dreamed it would be in a pigsty.

'Oh yes,' she said, thinking she'd burst. 'Yes, please.'

79

The schedule for the following day was posted late in the afternoon so when the actors and crew gathered in the bus for soup and sandwiches, there was much debate and speculation.

'So this is why Marcus took Master Matt's role this afternoon,' boomed Ben, dissatisfied. 'I do not understand why all these last-minute changes are necessary. I have to go to London tomorrow . . . to see a publisher,' he hastily added, seeing Jilly's sceptical eye upon him. 'Now I shall have to catch a much later train. How very inconvenient. There's no way I'm going to be able to go to this party.'

'How very convenient,' muttered Jilly.

'And I'm afraid,' Ross informed them, 'none of the senior crew will be there. Marcus has put a three-line whip on us. We have to be at a meeting he's organising at the village hall.'

'I'll come,' Harry Hobbs piped up. 'I thought I was going home tomorrow and now I'm stuck in this god-forsaken dump. Where's the party?'

'My dear child,' said Jilly, not unkindly, 'Sorry to disappoint you, but it's a drinks party and not for fifteen-year-old boys.'

Harry's face darkened and he muttered something extremely rude.

'I'm not going to any soddin' drinks party,' Jason snarled. 'This is too much. I thought I was going to have a day off.'

'Bristol isn't that far, Jason,' murmured Nicola. 'There are some decent night-clubs there, if you fancy it. Or we could go to Bath . . .'

'Wow-wee, lucky me.'

'Well,' sighed Jilly, 'Thanks a lot for your support. Juliet, are you going to change your mind?'

Juliet laughed. 'I was never part of the invitation, Jilly. The Lesters and my family don't get on, big time. Sorry.'

Jilly swore, then raising her voice, addressed the general assembly. 'Okay, lads and lassies, Summerstoke House party tomorrow night . . . who's coming with me?'

The roar of positives reassured her and convinced Ben his trip to London was essential.

'What are you going to do about your dinner date, Ben?' dimpled Juliet.

'My dinner date?' Ben was startled. 'Hell, I'd forgotten. Thanks for reminding me, darling. She's a sweet thing and I'd hate to stand her up. I'll send some flowers as soon as I get back to the hotel.'

*   *   *

Realising that once the family had assembled for supper, she and Stephen would have no time alone, Angela prepared the vegetables then headed for the milking parlour.

Deeply absorbed in his work, Stephen started with surprise when she kissed his unsuspecting

449

cheek.

His eyes were red and puffy and although he returned her embrace, there was nothing joyful about it.

'I've got some news, Stephen,' she began. 'Some really good news . . .'

'Oh?' His voice sounded lacklustre. 'Good news . . . I could do with that.'

'You know I said I'd check out the possibility of a sleeping partner, so we could buy Charlie out? Well, there is someone. A good friend of mine is married to a solicitor and one of his clients, a millionaire, with lots of land in Australia, is interested in investing in land over here.'

Stephen frowned. 'Sounds a bit far-fetched, Ange. Are you sure?

'Oh yes, my friend is positive. But she says they're going to need a valuation of Charlie's investment before they can progress . . . in other words, how much we'd want to borrow. And they'd like a business plan for the farm. We put one of those together when we went to the bank for the rare breeds project, so that's not too difficult, is it?'

'My business plan won't look the same without my herd,' replied Stephen, dully.

'What? Without your herd? What do you mean?'

'Major Tenby says there's a petition to stop me bringing them through the village. You know the score, Ange . . . no water meadows, no herd. This is the beginning of the end, sleeping partner or no sleeping partner.'

He looked so miserable, Angela's heart went out to him.

'Oh Stephen, don't worry, it won't come to that, I'm sure. What does Charlie say? It was his fault, after all.'

'He says he's going to take legal advice. Me, I trust lawyers no further than I can throw them. They're a tricky lot; before you've got a solution to the problem you went with in the first place, you've built up another in the shape of a huge bill for their fees. And how do you know your friend isn't going to play the same trick on us, Ange? Nobody does something for nothing—you know that . . .'

She put her arms round him, 'Oh Stephen, you look so unhappy; I can't bear it. Come here.'

She pulled him down onto a small shabby sofa at the back of the parlour.

'Ange, what are you doing . . . ? I'm in the middle of milking . . . Ange . . . someone might come . . . Ange . . . Oh!'

For Angela, determined to wipe the misery off Stephen's face was kissing him with passion, and miserable though he was, his spark ignited.

Munching quietly, the cows looked on.

Stephen returned her caresses, gentle at first, but following where she led, those kisses became more intense, till abandoning all reservation, his body asserted itself.

Far from shrinking from his erection, Angela thrust herself against him, pulling at his clothes.

The cows lowed softly, sympathetically, shifting in their stalls, fascinated.

One thing led, inevitably, to another and before the milk was half way up the last collecting jar, the two of them were semi-naked on the sofa.

It was but a short step to discover making love was as natural and easy as their first kiss.

The bovine spectators, responding to the charged atmosphere, ululated loudly and as the lovers' cries

451

of agony and ecstasy rose, they were joined by the sympathetic trumpeting of the herd who, although the producers of matriarchal milk, had not, nor would ever experience the brutal thrust of the male of their species.

Man and beast made such din. Jeff, crossing the yard with his own true love, looked across to the milking parlour wondering whether he should go and see if all was well.

True, Stephen came a little prematurely, and true, Angela found it more uncomfortable than she'd imagined, but they had done it—and that outweighed all other considerations.

In blissful content they lay on the sofa, listening to the symphonic sound of the swish-swish of the spurting milk, the rhythmic sucking of the pipes, and the rumblings of the cows.

A particularly strident bellow brought Stephen back to the real world.

He sat up and blushed violently. 'Oh Ange, I'm sorry, I . . .'

Angela, her chin reddened from his impassioned kissing, leaned back on the sofa, careless of the fact that her dungarees and knickers lay discarded on the floor, and that her bra and jumper were up under her armpits.

'Oh Stephen,' she breathed, 'Don't be. That was . . . wonderful!'

'Was it?' For the first time in his life, Stephen ignored the increasingly plaintive calls of his animals. He leant forward to kiss his love. 'Oh Ange . . . I thought it was, too . . . amazing, bloody amazing!'

80

'Right, thanks for that. Good to talk to you.' Charlie drew a long breath, put the phone down and checked his watch. It was just after five; Stephen would be in the milking parlour right now. 'I might as well,' he thought, 'put him out of his misery, although I must admit last night at supper Stevie was more cheerful than he's been for months. In fact,' he frowned, pulling on his boots, 'both him and Angela behaved pretty oddly . . . all those secretive smiles and blushes, yuk!'

'Even Mum and Jeff were in an odd mood,' he reflected, crossing the yard. 'Maybe the pressure of trying to get the farm ready for the opening is getting to us all. I haven't worked so hard in my life. It would be nice,' he sighed, 'to have a day off and go away with Isabelle, somewhere, just the two of us. But chance would be a fine thing and with the opening only eight days away . . .'

Stephen, preoccupied with his cows, barely nodded at Charlie when he entered the parlour.

'Got a moment to talk?' Charlie asked.

'Can't it wait?'

Whatever had affected Stephen the previous evening, his bonhomie did not appear to have survived the night.

Charlie shrugged. 'Suit yourself. I just thought you'd want to know what I've found out about the herd as soon as I had any news.'

Stephen stiffened and with deliberate care finished wiping a cow's teats and fixed on a cluster before straightening up and turning Charlie, his face pale.

'Tell me the worst,' he said thickly.

Charlie frowned, thought for a moment, then shook his head.

'No,' he said, 'I can't, there is no worst.'

'Stop farting about Charlie. This is no joking matter.'

'And I'm not joking. There is no worst. There is nothing Major Tenby, or any of that miserable bunch of whingers and weekenders can do to stop us driving the cows wherever we want.'

Stephen's jaw dropped. 'What?' he stammered. 'But we always thought . . . The number of times we've been threatened . . . Who says, Charlie? Are you completely sure? How come?'

'It's our own bloody fault, Stephen,' Charlie grimaced, irritated. 'We've allowed ourselves to be bullied and threatened. If we'd not been so shit-scared about losing access to those meadows and gone and got legal advice earlier, we could have told them all to get lost a long time ago.'

'But who says?' Stephen repeated. 'How do we know it's true?'

'It was so bloody simple,' Charlie snorted. 'I phoned the NFU. They put me onto this legal bod who works for them and I finally got to speak to him, just now. He said we hadn't a problem. The fact that we've been driving cows through the village for at least fifty years helps, but even that's not essential . . . we're entitled to go about our lawful business. He said if there was an undue amount of mess, we should clear it up, but he pointed out that horse riders never bother, so it would be up to us. They can't stop us, Stevie. Whatever they say, they can't stop us!'

454

Charlie could have sworn there were tears in Stephen's eyes.

'And all this time,' he said with strong emotion, 'all this time, I've been worried sick we'd lose the herd. My God, Charlie, if only I'd known . . .'

'I tell you something else, Stevie, I think it would be a good idea to renew our subscription. With the farm opening to the public, I'd feel a little happier with them behind me . . . we only got their advice because I blagged it and said that was what we're planning to do . . .'

'Whatever.' Stephen clasped Charlie's arm. He was so joyful he looked years younger and Charlie was reminded of the time, before their father had died and their struggles had begun, when they had been inseparable.

'Thanks, Charlie, that's the best news. That, and . . .' he broke off, suddenly going pink. 'I can't wait to tell Ange!'

'And I can't wait to tell Major Tenby,' replied Charlie with a grin. 'I'm off to check on my porky ladies. I'll see you at suppertime if they don't need me. And I reckon we should sit down tonight or tomorrow and draw up a final checklist. I got quite a shock to realise we've only eight days to opening.'

He turned to go, but Stephen stopped him. 'Charlie, er . . . There's something I wanted to ask you . . .' and he went bright red.

Charlie stared at him. 'Ask away, Stevie,' he said. 'And don't be embarrassed. If it's about the birds and the bees, I'll give you what advice I can . . .'

Stephen was confused. 'The birds and the be . . . Oh, no, it's not about that. Me and Ange . . . we're all right, thanks. No, it's to do with the farm, really . . .'

'Oh?' Charlie waited, poised to fend off yet another complaint about the disruption of the filming, or some other related ill.

'Yes, I was wondering, well me and Ange were talking, and, well, we was thinking maybe you're sorry you threw your lot into the farm and maybe you'd rather out?' He'd become red and anxious and was perspiring heavily.

This was so unexpected Charlie didn't have an immediate answer. He frowned. 'When I cashed in my share,' he said, thinking it through as he replied, 'I was planning to take off, but I found it harder to turn my back on the farm than I ever imagined I would. As you constantly remind us, farming's not a job, it's a life, so investing my cash in developing other aspects of the business to make it more commercially viable, has seemed like a good solution. I'm not sorry, no. I get fed up with your bellyachin' and the fact that you seem to forget we're partners and I'm not just a hired hand, but I put that down to the fact that we're both working bloody hard at the moment. As for wanting out . . . since you could never afford to pay me back, I don't ever think about it. Does that answer your question?'

'Er, yes, thanks.' But Stephen did not seem particularly comfortable and Charlie looked at him closely.

'Any particular reason for asking me this, Stephen?'

'No, no, I was just wonderin', that's all. Look Charlie, it's great news about being able to use the High Street, but I'd better get on with my milking.' And Stephen, still flustered, turned his attention back to his cows.

456

Charlie stared at him for a moment, then shrugged. 'I'll see you later. I'm in the pigpen if you need me. Lenny is fixing the signs and notices; he'll finish doing that before he clocks off.'

Stephen did not look round, but muttered, 'Okay. See you later.'

81

'Okay, darlin', you ready?' Lenny had knocked off early to take Paula to her audition.

'Yeah, I guess so,' came a small wobbly voice and Paula appeared at the top of the stairs, resplendent in her faux animal skin outfit.

Lenny wolf-whistled with admiration as she wobbled down the stairs. 'Wow, darlin', they'll give you the part as soon as they look at yer!'

She gave him a tremulous smile. 'Ooh Lenny, I do hope so. I feel really nervous. Me knees are wobbling so much I could hardly make them stairs.'

'You, nervous? I don't believe it, sweetheart. This is the moment you've been waitin' for, remember? Think of old Joanie, she'd sweep in and knock 'em for six. That's what you've gotta do.'

'Yes, Lenny, but supposin' they don't take me? I'd be the laughin' stock of the village; it'd be the end of everything.'

Lenny frowned; this was not like Paula. 'Don't talk that way, darlin'. They's not gonna say no, and if they does, it's their problem, not yours, and you've still got us . . . we think you're the greatest.'

She gave a weak smile. 'Thanks, Lenny. Well, I guess we'd better go.'

Lenny did his best to cheer her up on the drive to the farm, but she remained unusually quiet and when he dropped her off in the yard with a cheery 'Break a leg' she could only manage a wan smile.

She had been instructed to report to the company office, housed in a small barn Charlie had converted. Her stomach dancing in different directions simultaneously, she knocked on the door and tentatively pushed it open.

A tall girl, with dark curly hair, sat behind a desk, working on a computer. Seeing Paula, a startled look crossed her face, then she smiled and stood up. 'Hello. Come in. You must be Paula Spinks. I'm Rosie Martin, Marcus's PA. I'm afraid they haven't quite finished the afternoon's filming, so if you wouldn't mind waiting?'

She indicated a chair and Paula sank onto it, murmuring, 'No, no I don't mind. Thank you.'

'Can I get you anything, tea, coffee?'

Feeling worse than she did on visits to the dentist, Paula shook her head and Rosie Martin returned to her computer with a comforting, 'They won't be long, I'm sure.'

It was probably only half an hour before anything happened, but every one of those 1,800 seconds was torture to Paula and when the door finally opened, she nearly threw up. To her great relief it was Emma who entered, followed by the sour-faced Sarah Thornby.

'Oh hello, Emma, nice to see you. After all my moanin' I got a audition, which is why I'm here, see.'

Emma smiled. 'Yes I know. You look magnificent, Paula.'

Paula couldn't resist preening herself. 'I did me

458

best. Let's hope it does the trick, eh?'

'I'm sure it will.'

'Well I hope they won't be too much longer, my tummy has turned to jelly with all this waiting.'

'Yes, I'm sorry about the delay, but we've a lot of catching up to do and overruns are inevitable. In fact, after this we've got another hour to put in, so we'd better get on with it if you don't mind.'

Paula was puzzled; she wasn't sure what Emma had to do with anything. She looked at Sarah Thornby for guidance, but Sarah ignored her and spoke to Emma. 'Are you happy to do it here, Emma? It's a bit limited space- wise, but there's not much movement in the scene, is there?'

Paula's confusion grew as Emma nodded. 'Here's fine. Do you mind taking a quick break, Rosie? We shouldn't be more than twenty minutes.'

'Not at all,' said Rosie and gathering her jacket, left, grinning sympathetically at Paula.

At this display of Emma's authority and sensing she'd missed a trick somewhere, Paula viewed the pale, slim woman with bewilderment.

'Are you goin' to do this audition, Emma?'

'Normally we'd get the casting director in, but as she's in London there didn't seem any point in bringing her down just for this, so yes, I am, with Sarah to provide a second opinion, of course.'

'Yes, I see. So what exactly is your job, Emma, if you don't mind my askin'?'

Emma laughed and Sarah sighed with impatience. 'Emma is the director. I'm surprised you didn't know that, Mrs Spinks.'

'No reason why she should,' smiled Emma. 'Now Paula, this is the scene I thought we'd try out.' Sarah handed Paula a couple of sheets of script.

'Sarah will read in the other parts and cue you. Is that all right?'

Paula, as she later told Lenny, suddenly had a violent attack of the wobbles, but breathing deeply, she thought of her heroine, Joan Collins, and of Lenny, her dearest darling Lenny, 'Yes,' she said. 'Yes, that's fine.'

82

Bitterly angry at the failure of her meeting with Anthony, Veronica, never, ever, questioning her own culpability, blamed him. She'd not told Hugh . . . he'd not be sympathetic, he'd not understand why she'd gone in the first place. In fact, she wasn't sure herself, but her disastrous relationship with her son remained a running sore and unsettled her.

So she concentrated all her energies on making the party, and herself, as splendid as possible. She spent hours in the kitchen, concocting delicious little canapés and deliberating on the merits of different cocktails; she ordered vast quantities of hothouse flowers; sat half a day in the hairdresser's enhancing the colour of her hair, and at the beauty salon restoring her face and painting her nails.

On the day itself, Veronica had her cleaner, Carol Simpkins, vacuuming and polishing till every speck of dust had vanished and everything that could shine, shone.

Hugh went to the races and left her to it.

Late in the afternoon, the doorbell rang, and the daily took delivery of a bouquet and a note.

Veronica's pleasure at receiving the flowers was

short-lived; having read the note, she crumpled it up and, screeching with fury, hurled it across the hall. Without her star guest, the drinks party had turned sour before it had begun. Unfortunately she still had to go through the motions of making it as perfect as she could for those who were coming—Hugh would expect nothing less, and he'd impressed upon her the importance of his two guests.

But as far as she was concerned it was all for nothing and that was too much to bear; she became ferociously bad-tempered. Forced to acknowledge she had no star guest with whom to dazzle Hugh's clients, she was obliged to swallow her pride and phone her friend, Marion Croucher, to beg her and Gavin's attendance at an 'impromptu drinks party to welcome these clients of Hugh's'. Marion's stiff acceptance clearly indicated the last-minute excuse hadn't fooled her.

Carol had been employed to stay on to help prepare for the party and serve the drinks and the canapés. Somewhat unwisely, she became the butt of Veronica's ill-humour and was bullied and snapped at till she could take no more; even the prospect of the handsome tip she'd receive at the end of the evening was not enough of an inducement to make her stay.

An hour before the guests were due, and just before Hugh Lester's expected return, Carol undid her pinafore and announced she was leaving.

'What? You can't!' Veronica glared.

'Yes I can, Mrs Lester. I've put up with enough. I'm off.'

'But I need you. I can't manage without you.'

'You'll have to. I'm fed up with being shouted at

461

and faulted at every turn.'

'If you walk out on me, you needn't come back,' screeched Veronica.

'Don't worry, I don't plan to.'

'And you needn't come crawling to me for a reference. I'll make sure you don't get a job anywhere else.'

At that threat, Carol stared at Veronica, a peculiar smile on her face. 'Oh,' she murmured, 'I wouldn't threaten me if I was you, Mrs Lester. You might regret it.'

'I'll do what I like,' bawled Veronica. 'When I've finished with you, no-one in their right minds will want you.'

'Well, in that case, I'm sure Mr Lester will be very interested in these.'

The woman pulled out two letters from her pocket. One, the crumpled note from Ben, she'd retrieved from the hall earlier; the other was in an envelope addressed to him in Veronica's handwriting.

'That's my private correspondence,' Veronica hissed. 'What the hell are you doing with it?'

'You should be a little more careful with what you throw away. As far as I'm concerned it's a little insurance policy, just to make sure I get what's due to me. I've got your measure, Mrs Lester. I'm leaving with full payment of what's owed to me and a good reference . . .'

'Don't be so bloody stupid. I don't know what you're after but . . .'

'I told you: my wages, and a decent reference. Otherwise, Mrs Lester, I shall do as I say and pass them on to Mr Lester. I'm sure he'd be very interested . . .'

'He'd be more likely to throw you out.'

'Maybe so, but I wouldn't want to be in your shoes.' She smoothed out the crumpled note and read, with mocking exaggeration, 'Darling, I am desolate, I cannot make your soirée. I have to go to London to see a publisher about my autobiography. I cannot tell you how miserable it makes me not to be with you this evening. We will meet again soon, sweetest lady. Ben.' She looked up with a sneer. 'Very sweet.'

'He's an actor,' shouted Veronica, almost hysterical with anger. 'That's how they talk. It doesn't mean a thing.'

'No? But you're not an actor, are you Mrs Lester?' She put the crumpled note back into her pocket and pulling the other out of its envelope, read with deliberation, 'Darling Ben, desperately sorry to have missed you yesterday evening. I was so looking forward to being in your arms, dancing the night away . . .' She glanced up at Veronica. 'Need I go on?'

Veronica's face was an ugly colour. 'No, you can put your filthy inference on it, but it is all quite innocent; Mr Dacres is a good friend . . .'

'I don't happen to care what kind of friend he is, I'm not your husband,' said Carol, folding the note away and turning her head in the direction of the hall. They could both hear the front door opening. 'How convenient, I'll pass them over to Mr Lester on my way out.'

'No,' croaked Veronica. While she could explain Ben's note easily enough, her letter, revealing as it did that the night she'd left Hugh at the dinner dance to take Cordelia home, she had in fact gone on to a party to meet Ben, would be less easy to explain. 'I'll deal with this.' With a strangulated sob, she grabbed her bag. 'You'll have to wait for the reference; I can't do it now. How much do I owe you?'

'Vee . . . where are you?'

They could hear Hugh crossing the hall to the sitting room.

'I'll collect my wages and the reference tomorrow,' Carol Simpkins replied coldly. 'You can have the letters back then.' She pulled on her jacket. 'I'll let myself out the back. Enjoy your party, Mrs Lester.'

83

'Right, I think that's a wrap for this evening, Matt,' muttered Emma. 'We've got this meeting in just over an hour.'

Matt needed no prompting. 'It's a wrap,' he bawled. 'Eight o'clock start tomorrow, sore heads or no sore heads.'

'Oh yes,' Emma remarked, 'I'd forgotten about that party. Thank God we've a valid excuse not to go. You off, Ben?'

As soon as the wrap had been called, Ben had shot across the studio, divesting himself of his costume on the way. 'Got to go, darling, otherwise I'll get to town too late to do anything sensible.'

Matt's attention was caught. 'Are you coming back tonight, Ben?'

'Heavens no, I'll be back tomorrow in plenty of time for my call, don't you worry.'

'Just checking. You do know your call time is

eight, don't you?'

Ben stopped in his tracks and whirled round. 'What?' he roared. 'It can't be. My schedule clearly states my call is one-thirty. I hope this is some kind of joke, dear boy?'

Matt shrugged. 'Sorry, Ben. No joke. If you look at the schedules we issued this morning, you'll see.'

Jilly, who had joined them, chuckled. 'So you'll be able to come to Ms Lester's party after all, Ben.'

Ben scowled, he was really put out. There was no way he'd have time for a decent evening in London before he'd have to catch the last train back, and he was never very good with last trains; he needed a certain amount of beauty sleep if he wasn't to appear puffy eyed before the camera.

He considered his options as the studio closed down around him. He really didn't want to go to the Lesters' party with Uncle Tom Cobley and all. He didn't, if he was truthful, want to go there at all. His other date for the evening, the farmer's widow, had sent him a note turning him down. This rankled, particularly as it arrived after he'd wasted a bunch of flowers on her. He could go back to the hotel, but the prospect of spending an evening closeted in his room in case the Lester woman should discover he hadn't gone to London after all, did not appeal either.

'Bah!' he said loudly and crossly and stalked out of the studio to find his car.

By the time he was dropped off at the Country Club he was in a thoroughly bad mood. He phoned through to Jilly.

'I will come to this wretched party, Jilly. I've already sent her a note saying I can't make it, and a bunch of flowers . . . this evening has cost me a bloody fortune in flowers, I can tell you . . . but I guess if I turn up unexpectedly, she'll not turn me away.'

Jilly chuckled. 'No, I shouldn't think so, darling. Well, I'm relieved, I must say. It'll make it a lot easier for me to have you there.'

'But I'm not staying long. I shall plead a sparrow fart's start and come back here for dinner. Will you keep me company?'

'Of course, darling. That would be lovely, and it's always a relief to have an exit strategy.'

*   *   *

'Hello, love, are you feeling a little better after your sleep? I thought these would cheer you up.' Jenny, carrying a vase of brightly coloured spring flowers, smiled down at the pale, sleepy face of her daughter.

'Al's popped back to Bath to get some things. He told me to tell you he'd be as quick as he could.'

'Thanks, Mum. Those are lovely . . . where did they come from?'

'Ben Dacres.'

Alison frowned. 'Wow, Mum! Is he getting a bit too serious?'

Jenny laughed and sat on the edge of the bed. 'He sent them to me 'cos he'd wanted to take me out to dinner, but he's had to go up to London.'

'Mum, this is serious . . .' Alison struggled to sit up, viewing her mother with alarm.

But Jenny was unperturbed. 'No it's not, love. I admit it's very flattering to have the likes of Ben Dacres paying someone like me so much attention, but it's not serious. It might be if I kidded myself it was, but I'm not that stupid. He's just having a bit of fun, that's all, and there's no danger of my heart being broken.'

'Good.' Alison sank back onto her pillows. 'I was worried. I'd hate it if you and Uncle Jeff fell out over that middle-aged Romeo.'

Jenny looked down at her hands. 'We've never . . . er . . . really talked about me and Uncle Jeff, have we? It's, um, sort of happened and I've never asked you what you thought about it.'

'Mum, Uncle Jeff is just that: my Uncle Jeff . . . someone who's been around all my life. I think it's great you and he finally got it together, but I guess I wish . . .' Her voice tailed away.

'What, love?'

'It's none of my business, really.' Alison sighed deeply. 'I just want you to be happy and I don't know what's going to happen when Angela moves in full-time. I just wish you and Uncle Jeff would, well, you know . . .'

Ever since Jeff proposed, Jenny felt as if she existed in a different dimension . . . did her feet actually touch the ground? Could she eat and drink, talk with some semblance of normality, and nobody notice anything different? She'd persuaded Jeff to say nothing to the rest of the family until she'd talked to Alison first. Alison was still at school, still a child in Jenny's eyes, and still her responsibility. So, as she'd explained to Jeff, if her daughter expressed any reservations about the marriage, then that marriage would have to wait.

The funny thing was, reflected Jenny, after dragging his feet for so long, Jeff wanted to get married as soon as possible. He said this quite forcibly, adding if Alison was unhappy about moving, he'd take up residence with them.

With rising hope, she looked at her daughter. 'Does that mean, Alison, you won't mind if Uncle Jeff and me got married?'

To her dismay, Alison burst into tears and fell back onto her pillows.

'Ali, Alison, darling, don't cry. Please don't cry. I won't do anything you don't want me to. It's just that I thought . . . I thought . . . but we don't have to get married, yet. Not until you're ready . . .'

Alison choked and hiccupped and it sounded to Jenny's anxious ears as if Alison was laughing as much as crying.

Alison looked up her eyes shining, her face wet with tears.

'Oh Mum, don't be daft. I'm crying because you've finally got it together . . . I am so relieved; I thought it was never going to happen!'

*   *   *

Alone on the set, Emma was making notes for the following day when her mobile rang. It was Marcus.

'Hi Emma, where are you?'

'In the barn, prepping for tomorrow.'

'Do you want a lift to the village hall?'

'Well, actually Marcus, I thought I'd walk. I need some fresh air.'

'Nice idea, I'll join you. I'm in my office, I'll walk over. Be with you in five minutes.'

Emma put her phone down, smiling wryly. How very typical of the man to assume she'd want his company and that she'd be ready to go when he was. Did she mind? Not much, she admitted, putting away her notes. For whatever reason, he'd become more human since he'd rescued her from her hospital bed.

He arrived as she was locking the barn door.

'Where's everyone else?' he asked.

'They shot off back to base to grab something to eat before the meeting.'

'Why didn't you?'

'I just wanted to get ahead of myself for tomorrow. I can rustle up something later.'

'Then let's eat at the pub. Shouldn't be difficult to get a table and the food is good; I've eaten there before.'

She glanced up at his profile. Strong features, clever, high brow; whatever else, an evening in his company would not be dull. 'Fine,' she said. 'Good idea.'

As they passed the pigsties, Charlie emerged.

'Charlie,' Marcus stopped. 'We're just off to the meeting. Are you joining us?'

Charlie looked tired. His eyes had their usual twinkle, but his lean brown face was drawn and as he talked he leaned against the wall of the sty. 'Sorry, Marcus. Both girls are in labour and I can't be away from them.'

'Fair enough. Should be a fairly straightforward meeting anyway.'

'How long will your pigs take to deliver, Charlie?'

'No idea, Emma. This is their first time, as well as mine, but Jeff is on hand if I need him. Clementine is way ahead of Rebecca, so the births will be staggered, thank God.'

'But it sounds as if you're in for a long night,' commented Emma. 'Good luck.'

'And good luck with the meeting. I'm sure you'll find the village very receptive.'

'Thanks, Charlie. Come on Emma, best foot forward.'

Either side of the track from the farmhouse to the road, new paddocks had been created and quite a few were already occupied. They stopped to admire some cattle with dramatically wicked horns.

'Hmm, I wouldn't like to get too close to those,' murmured Emma. 'Give me a room full of discontented villagers any day. How are you going to run this meeting, Marcus?'

'I thought I'd do the introductions, then hand over for each of you to describe your jobs and then I'll take any questions at the end.'

'Sounds fine; and their complaints about the disruption to the village?'

'I thought I'd get Ross to deal with those. He's very beguiling and immensely patient, unlike me, and then I thought I'd put it to the vote at the end . . . we stay, with their full co-operation, or we do all the village filming elsewhere.'

She looked at him, curiously. 'And would you?'

'Oh yes. It would be a fucking pain, I admit that. But I'm not going to fart about wasting time dealing with people who are too stupid to see which side their bread's buttered.'

She gave a slight smile. 'That's a faint echo of Matt. You're going to have to keep those sorts of feelings tightly under control, Marcus. Not everyone is as convinced as you are about the importance of television, or want to have their lives disrupted in its service.'

He was silent for a moment, then said lightly, 'Are you suggesting that I'm a single-minded, arrogant bastard?'

She laughed. 'Single-minded and arrogant, yes;

but I've changed my mind about the bastard.'

'Thank you.'

She laughed again. 'Humble doesn't suit you, Marcus.' And then she added more seriously, 'But if you want to win the village over, you must play it that way. Look at how they reacted to Matt when he won the quiz. We lost a lot of goodwill and that's not ours by right.'

They reached the end of the drive and turned towards the bridge.

'I think,' Marcus was thoughtful, 'that after I open the proceedings, you should take over.'

'Me?' Emma was startled. 'Why?'

'I don't want to lose tonight. You would probably play this exercise better than I. You're more . . . well, more humane than I am; more sympathetic, without being patronising. Will you do it?'

'Are you sure?' Emma was doubtful.

'I'm sure enough to promise the dinner, afterwards, is on me,' Marcus replied. 'Thanks, Emma. Oh, and by the way, I've changed my mind about you, too.'

She laughed. 'Good. And Jason Hart?'

Marcus snorted. 'You're incorrigible. But I'll admit something: you're absolutely right about his acting abilities . . .'

'They're non-existent.'

'Yes. Working with him yesterday was an eye-opener: I could see just how non-existent they are. But I'll tell you something else, Emma.'

'What?'

'Like it or not, that doesn't show in the rushes. You manage to get something out of him and that something works.'

'Oh shit . . . hoist by my own petard!'

He laughed. ''Fraid so. But at least he's not quite so bumptious.'

'That's a small compensation, I suppose. It's a pity we can't abandon him on the riverbank more often.'

They reached the end of the drive and walked towards the bridge. 'How did Paula do in her audition?'

Emma chuckled. 'She was magnificently bad. You should have seen Sarah's face when we met her. She couldn't believe I wanted to cast her.'

'Do you?'

'Oh yes. She looks so good, it's worth a thousand words. She really doesn't have to say anything to establish who she is. A little bit of coaching and she'll manage the odd sentence without too much pain.'

'For her or for you?'

'Both.'

As they drew alongside the dilapidated gate to the Spinks' cottage, the front door opened and Paula and Lenny appeared.

'Evenin' Marcus, Mrs . . .' Lenny hailed them and the two couples fell in step.

'I assume you're off to the meeting at the hall?' remarked Marcus.

'Oh yes. What, turn down the offer of a free drink?'

'Oh, Lenny! He don't mean it,' Paula said hastily to Marcus. 'He's gonna support you lot. He's no time for whingers.'

'Pleased to hear it. I hear you had an audition today, Paula?'

'Yes,' Paula's voice sounded strangled and she glanced nervously at Emma.

'Well, congratulations. I'm sure you'll be very good.'

Paula stopped in her tracks and stared at Emma, her eyes popping. 'Emma, does that mean . . . ?'

Emma laughed. 'We haven't actually written to you, yet, Paula. Marcus has rather jumped the gun. But yes, we're going to offer you the part.'

Paula let out a piercing shriek and if someone could laugh and cry at the same time, she did. She hugged Lenny and Emma and would have hugged Marcus too, but he evaded her. When she finally calmed down, she declared, 'Just let any of them, and I mean any, try to put a stop to this filming, I'll have they guts for garters.'

84

At her insistence, Al carried Alison down to the kitchen so she could participate in the family gathering that evening. She was determined not to miss out on the reaction to Jenny's news.

It seemed to her, tucked up in an old armchair by the Rayburn, the atmosphere in the kitchen was the best it had been for ages. Angela was cooking up a storm, Al and her mother were chatting like old friends as they laid the table; even Stephen seemed restored to his old, amiable self. 'And they don't know about Mum and Uncle Jeff,' she thought gleefully. 'It's going to be so wicked!'

The door to the yard banged. Jeff entered and, quite uncharacteristically, made straight for Jenny and kissed her.

Alison grinned at Angela's startled look.

'Hello, trouble,' Jeff smiled down at Alison. 'Welcome back to the land of the living.' Pulling up a chair next to her, he patted her knee. 'You gave your poor old Mum a bit of a scare, sweetheart.'

'And me,' chimed Al.

'These Tuckers are made of strong stuff,' chuckled Jeff. 'Alison's a chip off Elsie's block, so you'd better watch where you tread, young Al.'

'Who's taking my name in vain?' demanded the octogenarian, entering the kitchen.

'Me, Elsie,' declared Jeff. 'I'm the only one brave enough.'

'Get along with you, Jeff Babington, I don't terrify anyone.'

'How's Ron, Gran?' Jenny could see Elsie was well disposed towards Jeff, but she didn't want to push it too far.

Elsie gave a rare smile. 'He's fine. He's coming home, tomorrow.'

A cheer went up at her announcement and when Stephen, clean and tidy, rejoined them, relaxed and cheerful, Alison relaxed too, relieved that for tonight the tensions within the family seemed to have lifted. She felt comfortably feeble, and listened with pleasure as conversation bubbled between folk who didn't normally waste their breath on anything not to the point.

Elsie noticed this too, and her eyes gleamed.

'Supper's nearly ready,' announced Angela. 'What about Charlie? Shall we wait, or shall I serve up?'

'He's with the pigs,' volunteered Stephen. 'He'll be back soon. Let's eat while it's hot.'

'I think we should wait a bit,' Jenny responded. 'We've had too many meals without him. I don't

474

want him to lose sight of the fact that he's part of this family.'

This was unusually assertive for Jenny and Elsie gave an approving nod, 'Quite right; it won't do us any harm to wait.'

Alison's eyes widened; Gran rarely supported her mother.

Stephen looked pained, 'But I'm really hungry,' he complained.

'Then eat a slice of bread,' was his grandmother's unsympathetic response.

Fortunately for Stephen—and for Angela, who was ready to feed her starving lover whatever disapprobation it might attract—Charlie turned up.

Stepping out of his boots and pulling off his jacket, silvery with damp, he glanced around the kitchen and smiled at his sister. 'Ali, great! Good to see you. Are you feeling better?' Then turned to his mother. 'I'm sorry I'm late for supper, Mum, I know you wanted me here, but both sows are in labour and I needed to be sure nothing was about to happen before I left them to it.'

Jeff grunted. 'I thought they were pretty near their time when I saw them yesterday evening. They'll be fine, Charlie; give them regular checks, they'll just get on with it.'

'The first baby animals to be born on the farm,' said Angela, shyly glancing at Stephen as she dished out roast potatoes. 'Let's hope there'll be lots more.'

The serious business of eating was nearly through when Elsie banged her glass for attention.

'I know that Charlie is aching to get back to his pigs, but before he does, I sense there is something in the air waiting to be told . . .'

475

She left the sentence hanging and looked meaningfully at her daughter-in-law.

Jenny, suddenly shy, felt Jeff squeeze her hand. 'You're right, Elsie, of course. You usually are.'

And Elsie, reminded of the timid young girl her son had brought home, some thirty years ago, felt an unexpected lump in her throat.

Jenny turned to her two sons. 'Charlie, Stephen . . . Jeff has asked me to marry him, and I've said yes.'

'Good,' said Elsie, 'about time, too.' Then added with a twinkle, 'Well, Jeff, I'm very glad you're making an honest woman of her. I'm sure my Jim would be very pleased.'

Loud and enthusiastic in their congratulations, Charlie and Stephen hugged their mother and pumped Jeff's hand.

Angela flung her arms around Jenny, 'Oh Mum, at last, at last! Well done!'

'I don't know why you are saying "at last" and "well done",' said Jeff, irritated. 'I always knew we'd get married. It was just a question of waiting for the right moment . . .'

'Which happened to be in the pigsty,' said Jenny, her face shining with happiness.

'Which reminds me . . .' Charlie stood up.

'No, Charlie, don't go just yet,' Stephen slapped his brother on the back. 'You must tell them our news.' Beaming he turned to the rest of his family. 'We can take the cows through the village whenever we like!'

Charlie nodded. 'I'm almost ashamed to admit this, but it's true. I spoke to the NFU this afternoon. All these years we've allowed ourselves to be frightened by bogeymen; there's no way we can be stopped from taking them along the High Street.'

'So commonsense prevails,' snorted Elsie. 'Well I'm glad you've got off your backsides and consulted someone. No one would dare suggest we couldn't go about our lawful business in my day. That's the trouble with modern villages . . . they're full of city folk and the like, who don't understand the ways of the country and try to interfere. But you wait and see, they won't give up . . . they'll invoke health and safety, or some such rubbish, and suggest your cows wear nappies, or bags to catch the dung.'

Charlie laughed. 'Thanks for the advance warning, Gran. On that mind-boggling note, I'm off . . .'

'Charlie, one other thing.' Angela's voice was high with excitement. 'We've got some good news for you, too.'

Stephen looked at her, a mixture of alarm and admiration.

'Oh?' Charlie shrugged on his jacket and turned to his boots.

'Yes . . . we've found a way of paying you back your investment, if you want to leave the farm, haven't we, Stephen?'

A sudden silence fell on the kitchen.

Elsie looked sharply at Stephen. 'Stephen, what's this?'

'Yes,' Stephen nodded agreement, but his brow was furrowed and his voice less certain. 'Yes, we have. But only if you want to, Charlie.'

Elsie turned to Charlie. He had stopped in the act of pulling on his boots, clearly taken aback, and as he straightened there was a wary look on his face, but he made no immediate reply.

'Now what's all this about?' she demanded. 'Charlie?'

'I thought you'd decided you were going to stay, love?' Jenny was troubled. 'I didn't realise you were thinking of leaving again?'

Alison frowned, upset. 'I thought you were enjoying all the new stuff on the farm, Charlie,' she croaked. 'What are you going to do? You're not going away, are you? I know you and Stephen have had your differences over the last month, but I never thought you'd pull out. And where,' she turned to Stephen, 'are you going to get that sort of money?'

'That was my next question,' said Elsie grimly. 'It's no use coming to me. I've told you often enough there is nothing more to give you and I meant it.'

Stephen flushed. 'I know, Gran. I'm not going to force Charlie to do anything he don't want to do, but we thought, me and Ange, if he didn't want to ... stay, I mean ... then he should be able to take his money out, so ...'

'So we thought we'd try and find a way of raising the money,' chipped in Angela. 'And we have ...'

'Ange has got this friend who suggested we looked for a sleeping partner ...'

'Someone who'd invest in the farm but take no part in running it and wouldn't be in a hurry for a return on their investment ...'

'Does such a person exist?' asked Elsie drily.

'Yes, Gran,' replied Stephen with the air of an amateur magician about to pull something, and not sure what, out of a hat. 'Ange's friend has found someone. An Australian millionaire who wants to invest in land here.'

Again this revelation was greeted with silence.

Angela squeezed Stephen's hand encouragingly. He looked nervously across at Charlie, who was viewing him with an impenetrable expression.

Elsie again broke the silence.

No one could have guessed from her demeanour that she was both furious and deeply worried. Furious, because it was clear to her this initiative had not come from Charlie and if he took the offer, it would be the beginning of the end for her beloved farm, and worried because the revelations of Stephen and Angela exposed how innocent they were in the world of finance and business.

'I have a couple of questions, Stephen.'

'Yes, Gran?'

'Who is this friend who's been advising Angela, and what is the name of the prospective investor?'

Stephen looked at Angela. Under Elsie's penetrating gaze, Angela reddened and defiantly lifted her chin. 'My friend knows what she's talking about; the investor is a client of her husband's. He's a lawyer.'

'And her name?'

'Sally Green.'

'Ah yes,' Elsie's tone was cold. 'The wife of a local solicitor; I didn't know she'd become a financial adviser.'

'She's been very kind,' Angela gulped. 'She's gone to a lot of trouble.'

'I daresay. That's the sort of person she is. And the name of the investor?'

'He wants to remain anonymous.' Angela tried to retain control. Their revelation was to have been the crowning moment in an evening of good news;

hailed by a grateful family as the perfect solution to what she saw as 'the Charlie problem'. Somehow, unaccountably, the moment was turning sour.

'Nevertheless, if you know his name, you should reveal it. We cannot possibly assign over half of the farm to someone we don't know, can we? We will need to check him out.'

'I'm sure you'll find his credentials are impeccable, Gran.' Angela wilted under Elsie's gimlet gaze. 'And we were only going to pursue this if Charlie wanted us to.'

'Say something, Charlie,' Stephen muttered. Charlie was still standing with one leg in a boot, frozen and pale, looking at his brother.

With a visible shake, Charlie pulled on the other boot and made for the yard door, saying gruffly, 'I've left the sows alone for long enough.'

A cold gust of air scoured the kitchen as the door opened and closed behind him.

'Stephen . . .' it was a gentle, reproachful cry from his mother. 'What are you doing?'

'A good question, Jenny,' Elsie looked sternly at Stephen. 'But before we pursue that, Stephen, I would like an answer to my last question. What is the name of the prospective investor?'

'I'm not sure, Gran . . .' Stephen looked at Angela for a prompt.

'His name is Osbourne,' she said in a small voice. 'V.E. Osbourne. That's as much as I know for the moment.'

'V.E. Osbourne?'

'Yes, we have to produce a business plan and a valuation before it can go any further.'

'And you have to ask Charlie what he wants,' croaked Alison. 'I know you don't see eye to eye on some things, Stephen, but I can't believe you've done this to Charlie. He's really upset. How could you?'

'V.E. Osbourne . . .' Al was puzzled. 'V.E. Osbourne . . .'

'I don't see what I'm supposed to have done,' Stephen spluttered. 'Charlie makes no secret of the fact he's fed up . . .'

'We all do that, Stephen,' interjected Jeff, mildly. 'I moan like hell about my surgery but there's no way I'd give it up.'

'V.E. Osbourne!' shouted Al. 'V.E. Osbourne! So that's what she's up to!'

'What are you talking about?' demanded Alison, irritated. 'Why do you keep repeating V.E. Osbourne like a demented idiot?'

'Because,' said Al, his face pale, his eyes gleaming, dark and excited, 'V.E. Osbourne is my mother. Osbourne is her maiden name. V.E. are her initials, Veronica Elizabeth . . . it's why she calls herself Vee.' He gave a loud harsh laugh. 'It's my mother who is angling to become your sleeping partner, Stephen. And you can be very sure she wouldn't remain asleep for long.'

85

Charlie, driven by the impulse to put as much distance as he could between himself and his brother, walked swiftly away from the farmhouse. If he didn't have his sows to attend to, he'd have got into his van and . . . what? Driven over to Isabelle? Gone to the Bunch of Grapes? No, even

481

if he'd been free to take off, the need to be alone, to try and make sense of what was happening, was paramount.

Once he got over the shock, he castigated himself. He should have seen it coming; all those squabbles when Stephen accused him of disloyalty or maintained he was the only one who truly had the welfare of the farm at heart; and then that odd conversation in the milking parlour earlier . . .

Charlie suspected Angela of driving this proposal. Just as Stephen had never made the effort to establish what the legal situation was with his herd and the village, so he would never have got it together to find the finance to buy Charlie out. But Charlie didn't blame Angela . . . she would only do what Stephen wanted and Stephen wanted him out. Dressing it up with 'only if it's what you want, Charlie,' didn't wash.

Neither sow got up to greet him but lay on their sides, grunting. Clementine seemed particularly uncomfortable and Charlie bent over her, stroking her gently. 'Not long now, old girl. Don't worry, I'll be on hand with the gas and air . . .'

So now it was up to him. He'd meant what he'd said earlier. Assuming his money was inextricably tied up with the farm, he'd thrown all his energy into making the various projects work and he'd been proud of what he'd achieved. The rare breeds, originally Stephen and Angela's baby, he'd embraced with enthusiasm and apart from choosing the stock, Stephen had taken a back seat in setting it up. So . . . did he want out?

His mind spun over all the schemes he'd considered before throwing his lot in with Stephen. How unrealistic or childish some of them seemed now: investing in a pub; setting up a motocross course with Lenny; running a classic motorbike shop . . .

He filled a bucket with water and gently swabbed the two sows.

So what, then? Isabelle's heart was in the village. If he did something completely different, he would have to move away from Summerstoke, there weren't too many openings locally. Maybe Marcus would have some ideas. Charlie had enjoyed working for him; perhaps he could find work as a location manager elsewhere. But Charlie knew his value to Marcus lay in his knowledge of the neighbourhood and its inhabitants.

So did he want to stay where he was and stick it out, regardless of Stephen?

Suddenly the hurt and anger overwhelmed him and swearing loudly, he repeatedly kicked the door of the sty.

'That's no way to behave around someone in labour,' came a voice from the darkness outside. 'Soft, calming music would be more the thing, don't you think?' Jeff emerged into the light and looked over the gate. 'Yep, I reckon Clementine is almost there. I'll stick around if it's all the same to you.'

Charlie shrugged ungraciously. 'Do what you want.'

Jeff had been glad of an excuse to slip away from the tension in the kitchen.

Al's revelation had, at first, been met with a shocked silence, then as the implication sunk in, Stephen had turned quite white and sat unable to speak, his mouth opening and closing like a goldfish.

Angela had refused to believe V.E. Osbourne

from Australia and Veronica Lester were one and the same person, or that Sally Green might have duped her. When she was finally convinced, she'd burst into tears and rushed out of the room. Jenny had gone after her.

Alison then laid into Stephen, accusing him of stupidity and crass insensitivity, finally declaring that if that was the way he was going to run things, there was no way she was going to hang around Marsh Farm after her mum got married.

Al beat himself up over his horrendous parent and was all for leaving, but was persuaded to stay by a tearful Alison who said that as far as she could see if Stephen wasn't so underhand and stupid, there was no way Veronica Lester could lay her greedy fingers on the farm. And all the time, Elsie looked on, as grim and formidable as Jeff had ever seen her.

So, muttering he'd promised to look at the sows, he'd fled.

Slipping his hand into his pocket, he drew out a slim flask, unscrewed the top, took a swig and offered it to Charlie.

'Thanks.' Charlie took a swig, shuddering at the whisky's smoky taste.

Apart from offering support and advice whenever it was needed, Jeff had never attempted to interfere with the way Charlie and Stephen ran their affairs. But this evening he could see disaster looming and since he was going to marry their mother, his position had changed.

In his opinion the farm needed both men. He respected Stephen's abilities as a stockman, but Stephen was not worldly-wise and although Angela would undoubtedly help him, no one was better

484

placed to keep their feet in the real world than Charlie.

'You know, Charlie,' he began when they paused for a break, 'Stephen, I'm sure, was acting from the best of motives.'

'Oh yes, and what might those be?' Charlie's tone was not encouraging.

Jeff hesitated. He could have said Stephen had Charlie's own interests at heart and was concerned Charlie might feel trapped because his capital was invested in the business. But Jeff was an honest man and he didn't believe that.

'You know he thinks of nothing else but the farm and Angela and with both he's on the brink of enormous change: his relationship with young Angela which, between you and me, I think fills him with a degree of terror, and then there's this huge turnabout on the farm.'

'And he thinks he'd be better off without me.'

'No, Charlie, I don't think he does.'

'Why else would he suggest I cashed up and left? He mentioned something along these lines earlier and I told him then I hadn't thought of leaving. To suggest it a second time is a pretty strong indication of the way his mind is working.'

Remembering his conversation with Angela the previous day, Jeff frowned. 'Actually, I don't think it's Stephen's idea at all and from the way he presented it, Charlie, I honestly don't think his heart was in it.'

'Are you suggesting it was all Angela's idea?' Charlie's voice was cold.

Jeff sighed. This was all so bloody delicate: he had to convince Charlie to stay and if Angela was sacrificed in the process it would, inevitably, sow the seed for future dissent between the two brothers.

'The thing is, Charlie, as I said before, Stephen is in a real wobble at the moment. Angela is everything you'd want of your future wife. She adores Stephen and she would take on the rest of the world if she thought that's what was needed. You and he have had quite a few humdinger rows, recently, haven't you?'

'Yes, but that doesn't mean . . .'

'No of course it doesn't, but Angela takes it all at face value, sees her Stephen is unhappy, and sets about finding a way to solve a situation which seems to cause you both so much angst.'

'Well, she's been pretty effective,' Charlie shrugged, 'and I'd be daft not to jump at it. I might not get another opportunity and if they want the farm to themselves, why should I stay?'

'Because if you do take the money and go, I predict the farm will change hands in less than a year. If that doesn't matter to you, then yes, you must go.'

'What makes you so sure of that?' Charlie stared at Jeff, 'I know Stephen is not the best businessman in the world, but he's a good farmer and, as you point out, Angela's got her head screwed on.'

'Well, for one thing, this prospective investor turns out to be Al's mum, Veronica Lester.'

'What!' Charlie shouted, shocked.

At the unexpected noise, the sty was filled with distressed grunts and snorts from the fretful sow, clearly in the last stages of labour. Jeff gently examined her. 'They're on their way, Charlie. I suggest we continue this conversation later.'

After Jeff had left the kitchen, Elsie took charge. Dispassionately viewing her granddaughter, whose tearful face was white and strained, she turned to Al. 'I think you should take Alison upstairs, Al. We don't want her having a relapse. I'll put the kettle on for a hot water bottle. And, young man,' she added with asperity, 'I would like to remind you if it hadn't been for you, this whole episode could have ended in disaster. We are very much in your debt, so we don't want to hear any further references to your tainted blood. I, for one, like and respect you, and I think you're very good for my granddaughter.'

Since this was the first time she had ever given Al her blessing, he was taken aback and blushed. 'Thanks, Mrs Bates. Yes, I'll take her up, right away. Come on Ali, your gran's right, you're not doing much good here.' And he scooped her up and carried her out.

Elsie turned her attention to her grandson, staring at the floor in front of him, still frozen with shock.

'Well, Stephen?' Her voice was matter of fact rather than challenging and he looked up. He was very pale, his eyes bright with unshed tears.

'I'm sorry, Gran,' his voice shook. 'I didn't know . . . I didn't realise. I can't believe I . . . that I could have been so . . . so . . .'

'Stupid? Gullible? Inconsiderate?'

'Yes,' his answer was barely a whisper.

'Whose idea was this?'

He looked up, his face flushing. 'Ange wants the best for me, Gran. I don't want to blame her. If I hadn't moaned so much, it wouldn't have occurred to her, so it's all my fault.'

'Yes, it is,' Elsie's tone, however was not censorious and she continued in the same measured way. 'I must say, Stephen, quite apart from nearly taking the farm to the brink of disaster, you have managed to do the same to your relationship with your brother. Buy out or no buy out, he may not want to work with you again. Why should he? How can he trust you? But let me tell you this, Stephen, it is absolutely clear to me that you need his particular skills. If he leaves, I have no faith in the future of this farm.'

Stephen went even redder and stared at his hands, unable to speak.

'You're a good stockman, a steady and reliable worker and the farm should have been safe in your hands,' Elsie went on, 'and in giving you my share of the farm as a wedding present, I was expressing my confidence in your ability to put the farm back on its feet. But now . . .'

Stephen looked up, the condemned man facing his executioner. 'Yes, Gran,' he said hoarsely.

Elsie continued, calm but cutting. 'I have no faith in your judgement, Stephen. I don't want to renege on my promise, but equally, I'm not going to jeopardise this farm . . . the farm your grandfather and I worked so hard to make successful and were so proud of . . . Stephen, it's up to you. You must talk to Charlie, sort out something with him, an arrangement that will satisfy both of you and will work. Come up with a plan, a proposal, and present it to me. But I mean what I say, Charlie has to be part of this enterprise and if he isn't, I shall hold onto my share.'

Stephen slumped, broken, and although Elsie

488

felt a twinge of sympathy, she said nothing. In her opinion Stephen needed an incentive to try and work something out with Charlie, otherwise the relationship between the two brothers would never be mended. It wasn't because Stephen didn't care for his brother, she knew that, but because he always took the easiest way out of a situation and if that meant doing nothing, then nothing is what he would do.

The door from the hall flung open and Angela rushed in followed by Jenny. Angela's face was blotched, her nose red, her mousy brown hair wild. She went straight up to Stephen and said with a sob, 'I'll understand if you want to break off our engagement. In fact I'm sure you do. I won't make it difficult for you . . .' and she started to draw off her ring.

Stephen looked startled, then distraught. He stood up and caught hold of her hands. 'No, no Ange. Don't. Don't! I don't want to lose you as well.'

Jenny glanced at Elsie, a small crease appearing in her brow. Elsie stood up and taking her daughter-in-law's arm, led her out of the room.

'Oh Stephen,' Angela sobbed. 'I'm sorry, I'm so sorry. I nearly lost you the farm . . .'

He put his arms round her. 'Hush, Ange, hush. The thing is it all came out in time and, anyway, I'm sure we'd have found out before we got much further . . .'

'But everyone is so angry. Even Jenny. She didn't say much, but I could tell. I only did it because I thought that's what you wanted, Stephen; you always said Charlie didn't like farming.'

'Yes,' replied Stephen soberly, 'but this place

belongs to Charlie as much as it does to me. He's different from me, he wants different things, but he's poured everything he's got into it, Ange. I knew that really, but I chose not to take any notice, I was happy to go along with your plan to buy him out. It's not your fault, Ange. It's mine, and now, if I want to keep the farm at all, I've got to do something about it.'

Angela looked up at him, frightened. 'What do you mean?'

'Gran's mad with me.' Stephen replied, sorrowfully, 'She thinks I've no judgement and that if Charlie isn't around, the farm won't succeed.'

'Stephen!' Angela stared at him, aghast.

'So she says I've got to sort something out with him, 'cos if I don't, then we don't get her share of the farm when we marry.'

'Oh no!' Angela wailed. 'How can she go back on her promise like that?'

Miserable, he shrugged. 'I don't blame her. We've made fools of ourselves and we put the farm at risk. Trouble is, supposing Charlie wants out? What do I do then? I've got to go and talk to him, Ange. But what do I say, what do I say?'

'You can blame it all on me,' said Angela in a small voice. 'I don't think he likes me much anyway.'

'How could anyone not like you,' said Stephen, tilting her chin and kissing her. 'I'm so lucky to have you, Ange. We'll get through this if we stick together.' Then he drew back, troubled. 'But that's the other thing Ange, you said . . . you said you wanted the farm to be just me and you, and that if we couldn't sort Charlie out, there was no point in us getting married. But Gran's made it clear, no Charlie, no shares . . . I don't want to have to choose between you and the farm, Ange.'

Angela flung her arms around him. 'You don't Stephen, you don't. I wouldn't ever make you do that. We have to persuade him to stay.'

86

Events had taken on a nightmarish quality for Veronica.

At considerable expense an agency had provided her with a couple of waiters who responded to her impatient, imperious manner with insolent shrugs and an obvious determination to do no more than what was strictly necessary for their fee.

On arriving home, Hugh had immediately disappeared into his study to take a call, had a shouting match down the phone, and re-emerged in a filthy mood.

'That was fucking Tenby,' he snarled at Veronica. 'There's sweet FA we can do about stopping those cows. Tucker's been on to the NFU. They've got the law on their side. Bastards.'

'I'm surprised you didn't check with the NFU, first,' commented Veronica, unwisely.

Hugh's list of expletives shocked even the two waiters in the room below, enjoying the sound of the domestic raging overhead.

Hugh's guests, who were to stay the night, arrived first, and they couldn't have been more different: a sheik, who spoke impeccable English with a bored, upper-class drawl, and a stout, middle-aged businessman, who glinted gold and spoke with a strong Estuary accent.

'So who else is coming tonight?' the businessman demanded. 'Our Hughie promised me a glittering night with the stars.'

Veronica gave a light laugh, mentally consigning her husband and Ben Dacres to hell. 'Oh, I don't know,' she said archly. 'The acting profession is a law unto itself. We're expecting a number . . . they're making a television series here, in the village, and one or two have become good friends.'

'Who's in it? Anyone I might have heard of?'

'Ben Dacres, Jilly Westcott.' His face remained blank. She tried again, feeling rather desperate,' Jason Hart . . . er . . . Juliet Peters . . .'

'Juliet Peters . . . she's a pretty little thing. That's more like it,' he smacked his lips and Veronica felt regretful Ms Peters was unlikely to attend this soirée, she would like to have seen her landed with this oaf.

'Ben Dacres, now he's a good actor,' remarked the sheik. 'Quite a veteran of the small screen, isn't he? I shall be interested to talk to him.'

It was an order, and Veronica gulped.

On the dot of eight o'clock, Sally Green and her husband, Philip, arrived. For a tortuous five minutes she watched the couple's heavy-handed attempts to be interesting. Sally convinced herself she'd previously met Estuary man and, refusing to relinquish the idea, badgered him for his life history.

'Now,' Veronica thought savagely, 'now I know why I don't invite them here except when we've a mass of people. Once Marsh Farm is in the bag, I shall never have her here again . . .'

To her relief, Marion and Gavin arrived

shortly after and upon learning that Gavin was an ex-Olympic equestrian, the sheik, at least, brightened.

'So where are these friends of yours, then?' Estuary man had shaken off Sally and, ignoring Marion's attempts to engage him in conversation, helped himself to another cocktail and turned to her just as Hugh hissed. 'Where the bloody hell are your actor-chums, Vee?'

Veronica did not let her charm-guard drop. She gave a little laugh, 'Oh, you know actors. They're notoriously unpunctual. Marcus—that's Marcus Steel, you know, the producer . . . we met him the other night, darling—is a hard task master and Ben, Ben Dacres, warned me they might be a little late.' There was no way she could admit to Hugh her starry cast were going to let her down and she would not be able to deliver. She was going to have to bluff and lie and brazen it out till the whole ghastly evening was over.

Then fate took a hand. The doorbell rang and a large number of people, none of whom Veronica recognised, entered the room.

She breathed a little more easily and smiled brightly at her guests. This had to be better than a complete no-show.

'Sorry we're a bit late,' remarked one of the newcomers cheerfully, 'we didn't wrap till seven, so it was a bit of a scramble to smarten up, have our tea and get here. I'm Dave, by the way, I work with Colin, the director of photography; I'm his focus puller.'

'Pleased to meet you,' said Veronica trying to feel enthusiastic. 'Is Colin amongst you?'

'No, 'fraid not,' replied Dave cheerfully. 'Bit of

a bummer for them really, but he and Emma, the director, and all the assistant directors, had to go with Marcus to a meeting. Three-line whip . . . so they're not able to come.'

'It gets worse,' thought Veronica savagely. 'Not only no star actors, but none of the senior crew members.'

'So who are you all?' she asked faintly and Dave undertook a comprehensive introduction to the various members of their party: Maggie, Fleur and Marianne from wardrobe and makeup; the runners, Chris, Dave and Annie; Joe and Frank, drivers; Ollie the clapper loader; Mary, the production assistant; Ricky the grip; Rusty, a chippy; Billy the gaffer; Gary from props; John the sparks . . .

Her head spun, she wanted to stamp her feet and order them all to leave, but there was nothing she could do but mingle, avoiding Hugh's eye, a frozen smile on her face.

The noise level rose, the cocktails vanished with astonishing rapidity, and for all that they'd had their tea, the delicate little nibbles she'd slaved over disappeared the instant they were produced.

When the cocktails had gone, Hugh was forced to produce bottles of wine, which the waiters opened with a vengeance and served liberally.

The noise was so great she didn't hear the doorbell and so was completely taken aback when Ben, Jilly, and two or three other actors walked into the room.

'Ben,' she croaked, not quite believing her eyes. She went to him, arms out-stretched. 'You've come?'

He kissed her hand. 'We finished too late for me to get to London, darling. My agent is furious, but

494

it can't be helped. At least I can be here . . . that is, if I'm allowed, having said I wasn't going to come?' He twinkled at her and with that look, all the horrors of the last twenty-four hours evaporated.

'Of course you're allowed, you silly man,' she simpered. 'I'm afraid you've missed the cocktails and the canapés, but Hugh has some fine wine or there's champagne or spirits . . .'

'I'll have a glass of champagne, if that greedy lot haven't guzzled it all,' said Jilly firmly, appearing at Ben's elbow. 'Good evening, Mrs Lester, I don't think you met our fellow actors, Amanda Barton, Ian Johnson and Nicola Scudamore, have you?'

Veronica recovered herself and her manners. Her party having been hijacked by the rough and tough, she needed this little group, with Ben at their head, to redeem her. She bestowed a gracious smile on the actress and her companions. 'Please, my friends call me Vee. You're all very welcome. I'll find you some champagne . . . Hugh!' She now had the courage to catch her husband's eye.

He was standing on the edge of a small group consisting of the sheik and Gavin Croucher, and a member of the TV crew who was doing most of the talking, and when he turned in response to her summons, she could see danger writ large in his expression.

He made his way over to her. Veronica, ignoring his glowering looks, took his arm. 'Darling, see who's just arrived—Ben Dacres—the sheik will be so pleased. He's an enormous fan of Ben's opus.'

'Is he,' said Hugh ungraciously. 'I'm glad you've got something right, Vee. He's been trapped by some jerk who talks about nothing but steam fucking trains . . .'

'And this is Jilly Westcott, you met the other evening, and Amanda Barton, Ian Johnson and Nicola . . . Scudamore? Is that right?'

Nicola nodded. Her plans to spend the evening with Jason had been thwarted. He'd contracted a cold and had gone to bed, snubbing her attempts to stay and nurse him. 'Yes,' she said, smiling. 'Thank you so much for inviting us to your lovely house.'

Her bright prettiness had its effect on Hugh and, while not quite managing a smile, to Veronica's relief he looked interested.

She continued smoothly, 'I promised to go in search of some champagne, darling . . . Take Ben over to meet the sheik and I'll join you.'

Ben's presence did indeed come to her rescue, but Veronica herself saw little of him. The sheik immediately engaged him in conversation, disclosing that as an insomniac he spent hours watching television programmes, past and present. He'd seen almost all of Ben's work and was determined to discuss it in minute detail.

Ben, a glass of champagne in one hand, which an assiduous waiter kept topped up, was more than happy to oblige him, oblivious to the sounds of an increasingly riotous party and of Veronica, who occasionally hovered into sight to view him with a hungry eye.

Estuary man, drinking deeply, made a beeline for Nicola. It didn't take her long to regret her decision to come and, making her apologies, she left in the company of another actress who wanted an early night.

Time crept on and no one else, apart from Gavin and Marion who'd departed shortly after Ben took over the sheik, showed any signs of going. Veronica,

496

normally complete mistress of her parties, looked on dismayed. True, Ben had arrived and was still here, in spite of the fact he'd told her he'd an early start and wouldn't be able to stay long, but she hadn't exchanged more than a dozen words with him since then, and as for the rest of them . . .

Finally an exasperated Hugh hissed in her ear, 'That's it! I'm not opening any more bottles. They're drinking me dry. I don't know what your idea for this party was, Vee, but as far as I'm concerned, it's been an unmitigated disaster. This was meant to be a discreet, classy affair and instead we've been overrun by hooligans and riff raff. Get rid of them.'

Veronica found an unexpected ally in the substantial shape of Jilly Westcott who was close by.

'Would you like a bit of help getting rid of the hooligans and riff raff?' She asked Veronica coldly.

Veronica couldn't be bothered to smooth over her husband's rudeness and responded with a weak, 'Thank you.'

Jilly swept across the room and taking Ben by the elbow, whispered something in his ear. He nodded, turned back briefly to the sheik, then crossed the room to Veronica.

'Dear lady,' he said taking her hand. 'Alas, I must go; I have stayed far longer than I intended. A bientôt, cherie.'

Veronica was dismayed. She had somehow hoped she could get rid of everybody and persuade Ben to remain and relax in her sitting room over a large glass of cognac.

'Won't you stay?' she stammered.

'No, sweetest, I've had my marching orders,' he

glanced at Jilly standing at his elbow.

Veronica looked imploringly at Jilly, 'My husband didn't mean you, you know . . .'

'We belong to the same family,' said Jilly firmly. 'Thank you for your hospitality, Mrs Lester; Juliet said you know how to throw parties, and she was right.'

She turned round to face the room and raised her voice. To Veronica's amazement, without any apparent effort, she topped the noise. 'Okay darlings, we've had our fun. Early call, tomorrow, don't forget. Be good boys and girls and say your thank yous.' Then she whisked Ben out.

In an extraordinarily short space of time, the room emptied, leaving behind just their houseguests and the Greens.

Sally Green and Estuary man, both very drunk, were propping each other up and swapping reminiscences, having discovered, Sally informed Veronica in a louder-than-necessary voice, that Estuary man's first wife had been a school-friend of Sally. Philip Green looked on in bored silence and Hugh, frowning, was listening to the sheik.

There were glasses and debris everywhere.

The waiters, too, had vanished.

Just as Veronica thought the situation couldn't get any worse, the sheik, Hugh at his side, came to Veronica, his hand extended.

'Thank you so much for going to all that trouble, Mrs Lester; a very interesting evening.'

'But you're not leaving us?' Veronica gulped. 'I thought you were our guest for the night?'

'That is very kind of you, but no. Mr Dacres has very kindly invited me to join him at his hotel for dinner. If no room is available there, my driver will take me back to London. It is no problem.'

'As you may have gathered, darling, the sheik is a particular fan of your friend, Mr Dacres.' Hugh gave a harsh laugh. 'I am only too pleased we've enabled his highness to meet him.'

'And for that, I am very grateful,' said the sheik with a bow. 'My man will collect my bag.'

There was no help for it, Veronica had to escort the sheik to the front door. Hugh went out with him to his car and Veronica turned to face the last of her guests.

The telephone rang.

For one wild moment, she thought it would be Ben inviting her to join him and the sheik for dinner.

It wasn't.

It was Anthony and if the phone had had a cord, it would have curled at the level of contempt in his voice. 'The arch Machiavellian, herself . . . hello, Mother.'

'What do you want?' she snapped. 'I'm busy.'

'This won't take long. Just to tell you your little game has been rumbled . . . you can forget about becoming the sleeping serpent of Marsh Farm. Really, Mother, you're slipping. VE Osbourne . . . How on earth did you think you wouldn't be found out?'

Veronica slammed the phone down and stood there, trembling.

'Sally Green,' she muttered savagely. 'How would they know otherwise? The stupid, useless woman . . . she's blown it!'

To add further pain to injury, a loud female laugh resounded around the sitting room.

'Get rid of them. Now!' Hugh hissed, slamming

the door behind him.

It was too much. Her iron self-control collapsed and for the first time in her life, Veronica Lester gave way to hysterics.

87

In the dark of the kitchen Stephen sat alone, brooding. He'd persuaded Angela to stay overnight and go to bed; exhausted and overwrought, she'd needed little coercion.

It had all gone so wrong. When the evening began he'd felt so cheerful: everything was coming together: he and Ange had . . . had finally made it; his herd was safe; and Ange had found a way to buy Charlie out. And now, now the one thing never in doubt, the one thing never questioned—that Gran's share of the farm would be his on his wedding day—had gone. It was bitter.

After a while, Jenny returned to clear away the remnants of the family supper, but except to inform him that his Gran had gone home, she hardly spoke.

Then Al appeared to collect a hot water bottle for Alison. He ignored Stephen but in a low voice described to Jenny the state Alison had been in. She was now nearly asleep so he was going to work on the website and then occupy the sleeping bag for one more night, if that was okay with her.

Clutching the bottle, he stopped at the door and turned back to Jenny. 'I just wanted to say,' his normal pallor was tinged pink,' ' 'Cos I didn't get the opportunity to before, but I think . . . I'm very pleased for you and Mr Babington, Mrs Tucker. I hope, in fact I'm sure, you'll both be very happy.'

As the door shut behind him, Stephen let out a groan. 'I've ruined it for you too, Mum, haven't I? This should have been your night. It was the moment we'd all been waiting for . . . the big announcement. And I went and screwed everything up.'

'Yes,' said Jenny, simply. 'Do you know, until Al mentioned it, I'd completely forgotten about our engagement. I've been in such a bubble for the last twenty-four hours and then, poof, not another thought.'

'I'm so sorry, Mum,' Stephen whispered. He couldn't have felt more wretched.

His mother wiped her hands and sat opposite him.

'Sorry is as sorry does, Stephen. What are you going to do about it? Do you want to do anything about it?'

He looked up, puzzled. 'What do you mean?'

'Well it seemed to me, dear, you and Angela were saying to Charlie you don't want him to be part of Marsh Farm. And if that is the case, you've made a pretty good job of it.'

Stephen didn't know what to say. Was she right, was that what he and Ange were really saying? Was that what he really wanted?

'Gran has told me about the ultimatum she's given you,' his mother continued. 'I know how much you want to take control of the farm and we always thought it was just a matter of time before Gran gave up her share. If you really want Charlie out of it, you're going to have to find a way to buy him out and Gran's told you she won't give up her share until she's ready, so, as I see it, the farm continues in the way is does now, except that you'll have no Charlie . . .'

'And a very large loan . . .' muttered Stephen.

'But that shouldn't stop you. If you really don't want Charlie to be part of the business then you owe it to him to be honest and find a way of letting him go.'

Stephen was not used to his mother talking in this way. She'd never taken much interest either in the running of the farm or the financial side of it, and when trouble occurred she preferred not to know too much until it had passed. With her children she had rarely taken a hard line on anything; she petted and soothed and loved them unconditionally. He knew he was her favourite and she'd always been the first he turned to for support.

'I've even managed to turn you against me,' he murmured sorrowfully.

'No, you haven't, dear. I've just been having a good long chat with your Gran. Probably for the first time since I married your father, and about time, too. She knows you listen to me, Stephen, even though I might not have anything very sensible to say.'

'So what do you think I should do, Mum? It's not just up to me, is it? Supposing I want Charlie to stay . . . he might not want to now. What can I do about that?'

'Oh Stephen, you two boys used to be so close. That's why your dad left his share of the farm divided between you. He never imagined you wouldn't want to work it together.' She shook her head. 'It's such a shame Charlie cashed in his share, even though he poured everything back. It never

502

felt right to me after that . . . there was you and Angela, saying you was the farmer, and there was Charlie . . .'

'But that's the way he wanted it.'

'Maybe. All I'm saying is, it's not what your father wanted. And now you've gone and broken the trust between you. That's the worst part, Stephen, you've broken trust and unless you can offer Charlie something very solid and unbreakable, I can't see him staying, can you?'

'No, Mum.' Stephen felt utterly deflated. He stood up. 'I need to have a think. I'll take a walk; I'll go check the animals. Jeff's with Charlie and he's been gone some time; it maybe the sows are farrowing. I might call in there.'

'You do that, dear. Just don't leave this to fester too long.'

*   *   *

Accompanied by Gip and Duchess, Stephen went for a long walk around the farm. He visited all the new stock in their paddocks; checked the fencing for hens and ducks; visited the goats and the two Shetlands in their stables; then sat on a gate and gazed for ages at his lovely Jerseys.

His milking herd were still in their winter quarters, a large barn near the farmhouse, and he was planning to let them out onto the lush new grass next week, before the farm opening. He decided to finish his night tour there.

Feeling more clear-headed but desperately tired, he headed back to the yard.

The earlier drizzle had vanished; the clouds had rolled back; the sable sky was speckled with stars, and the mother of pearl moon, full and glowing, illuminated his way. The pigsties were far off to his right and he could see, from the lamplight spilling from the hut, that Charlie, at least, was still there.

He hesitated, wondering if he should go across immediately, but decided he'd better put the two dogs in the house first, and turned towards the cow palace.

The large cow barn was in front of him and the moon, shining down on it, illuminated the whole of one side, casting everything else in deep shadow. He glanced up at the farmhouse. A low light burned in Alison's room and a glow came from the kitchen. Apart from that, it was in darkness. To his right, set back from the yard, was the large barn the TV people had converted into a studio. The angle of the moon silvered the roof and threw a vast deep shadow across the ground.

As he reached the edge of the yard he noticed, in the blackness of the back end of the cow barn, a stray moonbeam reflecting off the edge of the barn door.

It was open.

No sooner had he registered this, when he saw a figure slip from out of the shadow and bending low, run diagonally across the yard and disappear in the darkness of the studio barn.

It all happened so quickly, so unexpectedly, Stephen's initial reaction was to blame his overwrought mind for playing tricks with his eyesight.

And then he heard his cows.

Stephen might have been on the plump side but he was fit and the love he bore his herd lent him wings. He was at the barn door in no time, the dogs

504

barking at his heels.

Pointing in the direction of the figure, he commanded, 'Gip, Duchess, fetch.'

The dogs raced off and in seconds Gip had stopped and was growling at someone in the shadows.

The barn door was ajar and stepping inside, he trod on something soft. It was a scarf. Picking it up, he stood for a fraction of a second, accustoming his eyesight to the gloom. The cacophony of protesting cows and the sickly sweet smell in the barn after their long incarceration was almost overpowering.

The animals, curious and confused, were pushing through the inner metal gate and heading for the freedom of the yard. Stephen dashed out and slammed the barn door shut. It had no latch, no lock. It would offer no resistance against the weight of the herd.

'Charlie! Charlie! Help!' he bellowed, at the top of his voice.

*　　　*　　　*

Having safely delivered Clementine of twelve little piglets, Jeff and Charlie had switched their attention to Rebecca whose condition suddenly accelerated at the birth of her neighbour's offspring.

It was Jeff who first heard the dogs barking. He frowned. 'Sounds like your dogs are out, Charlie.'

Charlie lifted his head. 'Bloody hell, you're right, Jeff. What are they doing in the yard?'

Then came Stephen's cry for help.

Charlie rushed out, followed by Jeff. The first thing he saw was a figure against the studio barn, whimpering with fear, marked by Gip who growled

505

at the slightest movement, and Duchess barking hysterically, dancing around him. Then he heard bellowing and crashes from the cow palace and Stephen's voice shouting above the noise of the cows.

'Grab that guy,' he shouted at Jeff. 'I'll go and help Steve. Gip, come.'

With the dog's help and quantities of fresh hay, the cows were persuaded back into their quarters. As Stephen shut the metal gate, he said gruffly, 'Thanks, Charlie.'

'Lucky you were out this late,' commented Charlie, coolly.

'Yes. I was just gonna check on the cows, then . . . then come and see you. When I got to the barn, I saw the door was open and realised the cows were on the move.'

'Blimey, it could have been disastrous.'

'Yeah.'

United in relief, the antagonism between the brothers was momentarily forgotten.

'Well, Stevie, it looks like you've caught our joker. Come on . . . Jeff's grabbed him, let's go and see who it is.'

88

'What a really nice evening, thank you, Marcus,' Emma smiled as Marcus joined her at the door of the pub.

'My pleasure,' he said. 'I meant what I said. You handled that meeting very skilfully and I'm exceedingly grateful.'

'Oh, I think we were helped by Paula's loud and enthusiastic endorsement of everything we said.'

Marcus chuckled. 'Certainly it was better to have her on board than not. I dread to think what would have happened if she'd been against us—she's a real rabble-rouser. It was a flash of inspiration of yours to cast her.'

'That was coincidence. The real flash of inspiration was Ross's, promising to put woodchips down on the footpath for the dog walkers. That clinched it.'

'The man's indispensable. Now, I would like to invite you back for a coffee and brandy, but since your lodgings are only a stone's throw from here . . .'

'Then why don't you come to mine? Bearing in mind of course, Boss, that I have an 8am start.'

'Oh, I'll be gone by then.'

It was shortly after one o'clock when he let himself into his cottage. He'd just pulled off his shoes when his mobile rang.

*   *   *

'Why, Ross? Why?' Upset and puzzled, Marcus stared at the man sitting opposite him.

Ross, his shoulders hunched, stared at the floor. He had said nothing since Jeff marched him into the kitchen and when Marcus arrived, the Tucker family had left them to it.

'It just so out of character,' said Marcus helplessly. 'You're the best AD in the business, it doesn't make any sense . . . opening gates, tripping people up, letting down tyres . . . it's so . . . so juvenile. Why did you do it?'

507

Ross looked up, his face haggard. 'I'm not responsible for everything, actually, Marcus. You were wrong when you said we couldn't possibly have two jokers in the pack. We have three, including me.'

'*What!!?*'

''Fraid so. I don't think Jason let the ram out intentionally . . . he just wasn't following his country code and left the gate open, but he did sabotage the set. And Harry probably didn't mean Emma to end up in the river, but he did set up the trip for Jason.'

'How do you know that? Why should I believe you?'

Ross fumbled in his jacket and produced a camera chip. 'It's on there. You can see the brat clearly enough. He and Jason have been spoiling for a fight. It was a prank that went wrong. And Jason . . . well, I told him the chippy was in danger of losing his job and if he could shed any light on why the scenery collapsed, I promised him it would go no further. He admitted he'd done it . . . he thought the whole thing was a big laugh.'

'But you? What were you up to? What were you hoping to achieve?'

Ross gave a deep sigh. 'What did I want to achieve? I wanted Jason to be sent packing. I thought, after the scenery collapse, if I could engineer a series of accidents and Jason appeared to be responsible, you'd let him go.'

'You're not serious?'

'Yes, Marcus, I am. Jason doesn't want to be here; he despises the whole enterprise. He's not one of us and he has absolutely no loyalty, no interest in making it work. I've dealt with some self-centred shits in my time but he's unbelievable.

He's completely without principle and he'd wreck the filming, just for kicks, if it suited him. He was planning to use Ben and the others as material for his act. When they behaved badly, the better he liked it. He was gonna pillory them. He didn't give a damn; he was going to have his bit of fun and to hell with feelings and reputations. And looking after feelings and reputations, protecting the actors as much as I can from the consequences of their own idiotic behaviour, when they're on my watch— that's my job, Marcus, quite apart from running an efficient, accident-free outfit, which he was quite happy to screw up.'

'How do you know all this?'

'I saw him doing a turn at some comedy club after that first read-through. It was rubbish, but he had the audience eating out of his hand; he then told them about the filming and promised to dish dirt. At our party, after Ben had made such a prat of himself over the cows, he was on a high and talked about my working with him on his next show. He's planning to launch his new material at the Edinburgh Fringe—where it would, of course, get maximum exposure. The press would have loved that, wouldn't they? What a gift . . . at the same time as the series is launched on TV it's being rubbished, night after night, by one of its stars.'

'Why didn't you tell me this, Ross?'

Ross gave a weary sigh. 'Look Marcus, I told you right from the start Jason was giving us trouble. I emailed you, remember? By day three, because of his casual approach to the schedule, we'd fallen behind and the rest of the cast were getting irritable. You said you'd talk to him. So what happens? Mad with you, he marches off, goes into some field, has a spliff and leaves the gate open. So we get the escaping ram and then the set falling in; so much for your talk.

'I heard about the bollocking you gave Emma when she suggested Jason was responsible for the scenery collapse. You wanted him on this show so much, Marcus, it was hard to persuade you he was dangerous. The longer he was with us, the more damage he could do, so I thought I'd take a leaf out of his book with one or two further little incidents: I let down Charlie's tyres, leaving Jason's key tag behind, and opened the gate to the pig pens . . .'

'I don't think the Tuckers see that as a little incident.'

'No, I don't suppose they do, but the animals were never really in any danger, were they? And tonight I was planning to rush out in my night gear and alert everybody as soon as the cows were in the yard. Then if the scarf had been overlooked, I'd have found it and Jason would have been firmly fingered.'

'So the scarf Stephen picked up . . . ?'

'Was Jason's. Clumsy, I grant you, but I reckoned you'd accept it was all too much of a coincidence and send him packing. I have to say Marcus, if you hadn't been so keen to let Jason off the hook after he pushed Emma in the river, tonight's adventure needn't have happened.'

'Why did you take the camera?'

'I realised Alison Tucker had probably recorded the incident; I didn't want Jason to be let off the hook. With no camera evidence, it would have kept the question-mark over his head.'

'So why did you hold on to the chip?'

'Because, like everyone else, I wasn't sure

whether he'd tripped, or whether it had been another charade; I needed to know. If he had done it deliberately, I'd have produced the chip with some explanation as to where I'd found it.'

Marcus struggled to absorb the detail of Ross's story and for a while, the two men sat, both staring at the floor.

Marcus finally broke the silence. 'What am I going to do without you, Ross? I'm going to have to get in another number two, but at this stage? I'm far enough behind already and you're the best there is. Why did you have to do this? Why?'

Ross looked up. His face was white and his eyes glinted with emotion. 'I told you why. It was my watch; I wasn't going to let him hang out our dirty washing for the world to jeer at.' His voice broke. 'If you sack me, Marcus, I'm finished. I'll never get another job.'

*   *   *

Charlie had left Marcus with Ross and returned to Jeff in the pigsty; he found the sow half way through her labour. Preoccupied, the two men said little until finally Jeff stood up, stretching with fatigue. 'I'll go and grab a hot drink, Charlie, then be back. She looks fine to me. The main thing is to keep the piglets in the straw till she's finished.'

He had not been gone long when Charlie heard a slight cough. It was Stephen.

'Charlie . . .'

'What?'

'I need to talk to you.'

'Yes.'

'I know you're really mad at me. And . . . and you

511

have every reason to be . . .'

'Yes.'

'I was out tonight because I needed to think things through, sort out what I want, what I think is good for the farm, for all of us.'

'I thought you'd already decided that.' Charlie's voice was neutral, his face closed.

'No, no, I hadn't, Charlie. You have to believe me. It never occurred to me until a couple of days ago, and with us squabbling so much I thought you was really fed up being stuck here, and yes, I thought maybe I'd be better off without you, so when Ange said there might be a way of raising the money, I went along with it, but I hadn't really thought it through.'

'I see.'

'Thing is Charlie, I can't manage without you. We've always been partners and if you went, I don't know how long I'd be able to keep things going. As Gran says, I ain't got the sort of business sense you've got.'

'She said that?'

'Yes.'

'What else did she say?'

'That we had to work something out; if you leave, she's holding onto her share.'

'So that's why you want me to stay?'

'No.' Stephen was sweating. 'No, Charlie, I want to work something out 'cos I don't want you to go. You must believe me. Marsh Farm is me and you. Dad wanted it that way, that's why he divided his share between us. That's what Mum says.'

'You've been talking to her, too.'

'Yes.'

'What else did she say?'

512

'She said I had to be honest with you . . . she said I'd broken the trust between us; she said I had to offer you something solid to rebuild that trust.'

For the first time since they started this conversation, Charlie's expression flickered. 'She said that? Mum?'

'Yes.'

'And did you talk to Angela as well.'

'Yes.'

'What did she say?

'She's really sorry, Charlie; she said I could put all the blame on her. But I'm not going to. She was only suggesting something she thought I wanted.'

Charlie made no reply but knelt down to help another emerging little piglet.

'But Mum said something else that made me think.'

'What?'

'That it was a pity you'd cashed in your share; she thought things had started to go wrong then. And she was right. I started to think of the farm as mine; dreamt of the day when it would be mine and Ange's. But I was wrong, Charlie, I was wrong . . .' Stephen was on the verge of tears.

'I don't see why; I don't own any part of it any more,' Charlie replied coldly. 'True, I'd sunk all my bloody money into it, but that was my choice.'

'But that's because you belong here. This farm is still as much yours as it is mine, Charlie. Please, Charlie, don't leave. Stay here. Let's be partners again. We'll make it all legal. Fifty-fifty. Please.'

89

It was a little after six when Emma's mobile woke her. Groggy, she answered it.

'Emma,' Marcus was terse, 'I need to speak to you. How soon can you be ready?'

Any inclination to protest she'd had less than five hours' sleep and a long working day ahead, faded at the urgency in his voice. 'I can be ready in fifteen minutes. Do you want to come here for coffee?'

'No. I'll pick you up in fifteen.'

It was clear Marcus hadn't slept. He looked so haggard, Emma felt alarmed. 'What is it, Marcus? What's wrong?'

'Get into the car and I'll tell you on the way to the farm. We'll talk in my office, we won't be disturbed there.'

On the way over, he disclosed the events of the night. Like Marcus, Emma was stunned.

'I'm not surprised at Harry. He and Jason have been winding each other up since the shoot began and it's the sort of stupid trick he would play. And you know I thought Jason was responsible for the scenery collapsing. But Ross? Because he believed Jason was going to have fun at our expense? Really?'

'It was more than that. He believed if Jason when ahead with his plan to rubbish *Silage* and *Strawberries*, the press would get hold of it and the series would be badly damaged. And yes, he's concerned about Ben, Jilly and Juliet and the others. Actors are vulnerable and Ross sees it as part of his job to protect their fragile egos and reputations.'

Arriving at the farm, Marcus let Emma into his office. 'Coffee?'

'Yes, please. Where's Ross now?'

'He stayed at mine last night. In the circumstances I thought he shouldn't stay on the farm any longer. I've told him to vacate his cottage and take over one of the trailers on the base and not, under any condition, come to the farm.'

'You haven't given him his marching orders, then?' Emma was astonished.

'Not yet.' Marcus looked agonised. 'That's why I wanted to talk to you. Of course I should . . . I shouldn't hesitate. But . . .'

Emma gave him a thoughtful look. 'I have to say this is not like you, Marcus.'

'I know. Thing is, Emma, Ross is second to none in his job. How many times have we said that? If he goes at this stage in the filming, a replacement AD would struggle and we can't afford to lose any more time.'

Emma blinked. 'Are you seriously thinking of keeping him on then? How can you trust him?'

Marcus grimaced. 'I think I can, Emma. Look at it this way: on the negative side he was trying to incriminate Jason and procure his dismissal . . . however we feel about Jason, that's just not acceptable and he should be sacked. On the positive side, he thought what he was doing was for the good of the company. Misguided, yes, but not out of spite or for personal gain. More importantly, from my point of view, is what he achieves in smoothing the relations between the film unit and the village: that's incalculably valuable. His crew work hard and respect him; the actors trust him. That's my dilemma, Emma. To which do I lend more weight? If he goes, we'll be thrown into turmoil. We'll get through, of course we will, but it won't be easy.'

'Who else knows?'

'Just Charlie and Stephen Tucker, and Jeff Babington. They've agreed to say nothing to anyone else for the moment.'

'What's Ross said? Does he want to stay?'

'He knows if he goes, he'll never work in the business again. Of course he wants to stay. He's desperate.'

Emma suddenly felt very sad. 'We all confided in him. Why couldn't he have shared his fears with one of us . . . with you, Marcus? You're the one he should have gone to in the first place.'

Marcus looked ashamed and replied in a gruff voice. 'Yes, well, I wish he had. He thought I had a fixation about Jason and wouldn't have listened. Maybe he had a point.'

'And what about the Tuckers? What do they want? They're the ones who've suffered the most. If you keep him on, how will they feel? It's a question of trust, isn't it?'

'Yes, it is. I don't know what they want. They probably expect me to fire him straight off; I don't know how'd they react if we kept him on.'

'Then maybe we should ask them. Set out your predicament as you have to me and see how they feel. Then you can make a decision.'

He thought for a moment, then slowly replied, 'Yes. Thanks, Emma. That's what I'll do.' He got up to pour some more coffee. 'To tell you the truth, I feel wretched. If I'd listened to you in the first place, none of this would have happened.'

Isabelle, absorbed in mixing paint, looked up, irritated, as the distant sound of the doorbell resounded through the house.

'Bollocks!' She stood still and listened. If she didn't answer, perhaps they'd go away. A friend would have knocked and come in.

The bell rang once more. She swore again, twice for good measure, and putting down her paint, made her way back through the house. She opened the front door just as Jenny Tucker started walking away.

'Jenny!' Isabelle was astonished. Jenny, as far as she could recall, had never visited her before.

Jenny greeted her with relief. 'Oh, thank goodness, you're in, Isabelle. I hope I'm not interruptin' anythin', only I . . . I brought back that lovely top you lent me for the party.'

'Thank you, Jenny, but you needn't have made a special journey. I could have picked it up next time I was over. Or Charlie could have returned it . . .'

'Charlie, yes . . .'

There was something about the way she said 'Charlie'.

Isabelle looked at her more closely. 'Is everything all right, Jenny?'

Jenny flushed. 'Yes, well, not exactly . . . I wondered if I could have a word?'

'Of course, come in,' replied Isabelle, adding anxiously, 'Is Charlie all right?'

'Yes, I think so. He was asleep when I left; he was up all night with those two pigs of his.'

'Have they farrowed, then? Come into the

kitchen, I'll put the kettle on.'

Jenny, glancing curiously about her, followed Isabelle into the kitchen.

'Yes, they have—twelve piglets apiece, Jeff says. Imagine having twelve babies all at once!'

'Yes, imagine,' said Isabelle with smile, thinking of the work involved with her two. 'Tea or coffee?'

'Oh tea please, dear, I'm not awfully fond of coffee. What a lovely kitchen this is, Isabelle.'

'Thank you. I'm ashamed you've not been before, Jenny. I'll show you over the rest of the house next time you come.'

'That would be nice. Are you busy right now?'

'Well, yes. I've got to finish the painting I'm on as soon as I can, as I've got another commission waiting.'

'That's good. I . . . er . . . I won't keep you then.' Jenny hesitated, then, taking a deep breath, launched into the speech she'd been rehearsing on her way over. 'It's about Charlie I've come, Isabelle. Well, Charlie and Stephen. The thing is, Stephen has gone and hurt Charlie really bad . . . I could see it. He's made such a mistake and Charlie has taken it to heart. But if Charlie goes off and has no more to do with the farm, then Gran says it won't last the year and I think she might be right, so she doesn't want to give Stephen her share of the farm any more, and I can't blame her, and anyway, that's not the way Jim wanted it. He wanted the two boys to run the farm together and I think it all went wrong when Charlie sold his shares to Gran and Gran says Stephen has got to make him an offer, but supposing Charlie doesn't want to know any more? Stephen will have to borrow to return the money Charlie invested, so the farm will be saddled with enormous debt and Stephen still won't own it. I can't talk to him, nor can Gran, as he knows we want him to stay. But I know Charlie will listen to you. He says you're a clear thinker. So will you? Will you talk to him, Isabelle?'

*　　　*　　　*

'Go on, drink it up and stop making such a fuss,' said Al severely. He was sitting on the edge of Alison's bed, proffering a steaming mug of honey and lemon. 'Your mum said to drink it while it's hot.'

Alison sighed fretfully. 'All right, all right; I'm just a bit sick of honey and lemon, that's all; I must have drunk a gallon of the stuff over the last couple of days.'

'Your fault for catching a cold,' replied Al with a grin. 'Hey, I think you look a whole lot better this morning, Ali. What a relief.'

'No thanks to bloody Stephen. What a mess!'

'Hmm. But at least we've outed V.E. Osbourne.'

'Thanks to you, Al. But what do we do about Charlie and Stephen? If Charlie goes, then so do I.'

Al looked at her flushed and troubled face and put out a hand to caress her cheek. 'This has been your home all your life, Ali. Could you leave it just like that?'

'You did.'

'Yes, but I lived with the parents from hell, don't forget. And having spent half my life boarding, it wasn't so much of a wrench. And also, Ali, I'd started at uni. Whatever Charlie decides, you've got to stay put till you've done your As.'

'I shall find it very hard living under the same

roof as Stephen,' Alison looked mutinous. 'Or Angela, come to that. If they don't make it up with Charlie, I'll probably never speak to them again.'

'And what would that do to your Mum, eh? The whole family would disintegrate and your family is so . . . so . . .' Al frowned and then said diffidently, 'Well, I wish I'd had the chance to be the member of a family like yours. This has to be sorted, not walked away from, Ali.'

'But what can I do? I'm stuck here in bed.'

'I suppose you could try talking to them . . .'

'I'm not sure they'd listen, either of them. I'm their kid sister, remember.'

'No harm in trying. If I see either, I'll tell them you'd appreciate a visit.'

'Okay.' But she looked so dismal he struggled to think of something to cheer her up.

'Hey, Ali, I've been thinking . . . do you have any plans for what you're going to do after you've finished your exams?'

'Not really; Hannah's keen we should all go to Padstow and hire a caravan.'

Al pulled a face. 'Not my idea of a good time. Do you fancy taking off with me? On the bike?'

Alison's face started to glow. 'Al, do you mean it? I thought you needed to work the whole summer?'

'Yeah, well, I think I'm gonna need a break. Last summer I was going to head off down to the south of France with my mates but then I had that accident. Why don't we do the trip together? If we camp, it shouldn't be too expensive. Parlez vous franglais?'

Alison laughed. 'Un peu, Monsieur, un peu.'

90

'Good.' Isabelle gave a sigh of satisfaction and laid down her brush. 'That'll do.' She stretched, glanced at her watch and exclaimed at the time. It was nearly twelve-thirty and she'd promised Jenny she would get in touch with Charlie that morning. She groped in her overalls for her mobile, but it wasn't there, she must have left it in the kitchen. Hastening into the house, she reproached herself for her neglect. Things sounded bad at Marsh farm and supposing Charlie had been trying to reach her? As she reached the hall, there was a knock at the door and Charlie poked his head round.

'Charlie,' she went to him and wasting no words, he folded her in his arms.

* * *

Charlie hadn't lingered in bed that morning, although he had turned in just before dawn. Sleep eluded him and he had lain on his bed, staring at shadows, trying to work out his course of action. Daybreak found him roaming the fields, checking on the stock; he'd called on his pigs to give them fresh hay and water and check on the piglets, then he'd walked over to the fields where the shoots of winter wheat and barley showed fresh and bright green. When Lenny arrived he set him to work on the tractor and spent the rest of the morning whitewashing the shed that was going to be the farm shop.

Marcus phoned him, wanting a meeting with

him and Stephen, but he'd prevaricated. Until he'd sorted out his response to Stephen's offer, he couldn't deal with anything else, but he agreed to meet Marcus, with Stephen, before supper that evening.

By the end of the morning, feeling his brain and body were about to seize up, he succumbed to the overwhelming urge to go to Isabelle and share his predicament with her.

When he finally released her, Isabelle scrutinised his appearance. His lean face, normally a healthy glow, looked grey and drawn, and his brown eyes had lost their habitual twinkle.

'You look tired, Charlie,' she commented.

'That's an understatement, sweetheart. I'm knackered.'

'Come into the kitchen and I'll rustle up some lunch.'

'You sure? I know you're in the middle of a masterpiece . . .'

'Sure. Cheese on toast all right?'

'Perfect.'

She led the way into the kitchen and Charlie slumped into an old armchair.

'I don't normally see you at lunchtime, Charlie. In fact, I think this is a first. The second today.'

'Oh?'

'Yes,' she said, concentrating on slicing the bread and keeping her tone light. 'Your mother came to see me this morning. Do you know I don't think she's ever been here before.'

'Mum?' Charlie was more guarded than surprised. 'Why?'

'Ostensibly to return the top I lent her for the party last week. But actually to pour out her concerns about you.'

'I see. So you know all about it?'

'Yes . . . at least, I know what Jenny told me. She wasn't always clear. In a nutshell, as far as I can make out, Stephen came up with some hare-brained scheme to buy you out, and both Jenny and your gran think that'd be disastrous.'

'First time they've agreed about anything,' he grunted. 'The point is, Isabelle, hare-brained or not, Stephen would rather run the farm, solo. That's the bottom line. The question is, do I stay, knowing that, or do I take the money and run?'

'There is no money, though, is there? If he has to raise the finance to return your investment, he'd saddle the farm with debt and, as far as I can make out from what Jenny said, Elsie won't relinquish her share of the farm, so while Stephen might run the place solo, he still won't own it.'

'Should that bother me?'

Isabelle abandoned grating cheese and knelt by his side. 'If the farm were to fail, I think it would, Charlie. I think if you were to put your mind to it, you could do most things; I think you could set the world alight. But your heart will always be in Marsh Farm. What hurts more—that Stephen wants to go it alone? Or feeling the farm doesn't need you?'

He put out a hand and ruffled her hair. 'Stephen came to me last night, in the pig shed, and begged me to stay. Mum and Gran had both got to him. He's offered me a fifty per cent share.'

'Are you saying he made the offer under duress? That he doesn't really want you to accept?'

Charlie frowned. 'To be fair, he was pretty upset. But the point is, Isabelle, if I accept then I'm turning down the last chance to take off.

523

It's one thing to have invested in the buildings . . . my leaving wouldn't affect the farm, except if I demanded my money back. But if I take on a fifty per cent share, I'm completely tied in . . . it becomes my future. That's why I need to talk to you.'

'Charlie,' she said softly. 'You're my future. Whatever you decide, I want to be with you. If you feel you must take off, I'll be with you. If you stay on the farm, I'll be with you. That is,' she added, blushing, 'if you want me.'

'Oh Isabelle,' he said, astonished, 'How can you doubt that? I love you.'

'And I love you.' She knelt up and put her arms around him. His lips met hers and their kiss, long and intense, was broken only when the smoke and smell of burning toast became so strong it couldn't be ignored.

'Oh no!' Isabelle leapt up to rescue the smouldering ruins of their lunch.

Charlie grinned. 'I see Mum's been giving you some cookery tips, sweetheart.'

She smiled and then turned serious. 'I've been thinking, Charlie, whatever you decide to do, you might think about moving in here; make this place your home, with me and the girls.'

The effect of this proposal on Charlie was electric. He started out of the chair, his eyes burning and his face glowing. He seized hold of her. 'Is that what you want, Isabelle? Do you really mean it?'

'Of course I do, silly,' she melted into his arms. 'I can't imagine anything I'd want more.'

91

Charlie sang on his way back to the farm; suddenly everything was falling into place. The decision to move in with Isabelle cleared the logjam in his brain. He loved Marsh Farm; he might think he craved adventure, but his place was here, and who needed adventures living with Isabelle Langton?

Pulling into the yard, he was hailed by Al.

'Sorry to bother you, Charlie, only I wondered, if you've got a moment, whether you'd pop up and see Ali?'

Charlie was surprised. 'Oh, why?'

'She's fretting, to tell you the truth. She was really upset by the scene last night and she'd like to talk to you.'

'Me? Right, I'll go and see her now.'

When he poked his head around her bedroom door, she appeared to be asleep. Her eyes were shut and she looked terribly pale.

'And very young,' he thought. 'Poor little sprog, she's been really unwell.'

'Ali?' he whispered.

Her eyes flew open.

'Charlie, thank goodness you've come.'

He settled himself on the edge of her bed. 'What's all this, Ali? What's up?'

She struggled to sit upright. 'Charlie, you can't let Stephen and Angela drive you off the farm, you can't. They'd make a total mess of things without you. You heard about Veronica Lester? And this is your home; this is my home. If you go, then I do. I'm not staying here if you go . . .'

'If I don't stay here, where would you go, Ali?'

She looked mutinous. 'I don't know. I don't want to muscle in on Mum and Jeff, and Gran hasn't got the space. Maybe Isabelle would let me have a room in return for babysitting, until I go to uni.'

'That's a nice idea.' Charlie grinned. 'We could both move in at the same time, but all her spare rooms are let till the filming is done, so you'll have to wait.'

Alison looked at him, puzzled. 'What do you mean?'

Charlie's grin broadened. 'Once the farm has opened to the public, I'm moving in with Isabelle.'

Alison let out a shriek. 'Charlie! That's just fab. I really like Isabelle. That's just so good.' Her face clouded. 'But the farm? Does that mean it's all over, that you're not gonna work here anymore? I'll never speak to Stephen again if that happens.'

'If I told him that, he might change his mind about his offer,' Charlie chuckled then looked at her seriously. 'Alison, I won't pretend. I was well pissed off with Stephen, and all for leaving. But I cooled down; I know that while the actual farming is not for me . . . Stephen is welcome to all that twenty-four seven muck and graft . . . I want to stay and see the farm business flourish, and I know I can make it happen. Gran wants me to stay, Mum wants me to stay . . .'

'I want you to stay . . .'

'And Stephen wants me to stay. He's proposed we become equal partners again, and you're the first to know I'm going to accept that offer. Happy?'

Alison's response was to fling her arms around her brother, half-laughing, half-crying. 'Oh Charlie, that's wicked.'

*　　*　　*

Half an hour later Stephen went further. He burst into tears and fell on his brother's shoulder, sobbing, 'Oh Charlie, thank you, thank you for this chance . . . I won't let you down again, I won't . . . You can trust me, Charlie, you really can. I promise. I'll not do anything without consulting you. We're partners . . . I've been so gutted . . . I wouldn't have blamed you if you'd never spoken to me again.'

Charlie grinned and patted his brother on the back. 'Alison was threatening something similar. Come on Stevie, it's all right, blow your nose, Marcus is waiting for us.'

Walking across the yard, Stephen said, diffidently, 'You won't hold anything against Ange, will you, Charlie? She really did mean it for the best . . .'

'Stevie, I won't, I promise. She puts you first, beyond everything. What you've done to deserve her, I don't know, but you're a lucky fellow.'

Stephen blushed and said humbly, 'Yes, yes I am.' He blew his nose and mopped his eyes. 'What does Marcus want to see us about, d'ye reckon?'

'Ross, I should imagine.'

'What's that to do with us? Unless he's going to offer us compensation?'

Charlie shrugged. 'Possibly. Let's go and find out.'

Marcus got up to greet them and offered them a beer. Watching him, Charlie thought he looked dreadful: pale and drawn, with none of his usual assertiveness or energy.

'I've asked Emma to come and join us as soon as

527

she can get a break from filming,' he said. 'I hope that's okay.'

'Of course,' said Charlie, puzzled.

'Fine by me,' agreed Stephen. 'Thanks for the beer. I've got to be off for milking in half an hour, though.'

'Right. I'd better not waste any more time,' but in spite of these brisk words, Marcus sounded lacklustre. 'It's about Ross,' he began, 'and before I say anything else, I don't have to tell you how extremely sorry I am. I will, of course sort out compensation.'

'What for? There wasn't really much damage, Marcus,' interrupted Charlie. 'Truth to tell, Ross's gang cleared up after the pigs and he fixed my tyres . . .'

'And the way he cleaned up the High Street after my herd run amok . . .' added Stephen, taking his cue from Charlie. 'Fortunately my cows didn't get out last night . . . now that would not have been funny.'

'No. His plan was to come rushing out in his night gear and alert the household before they'd got too far.'

'So what was he up to, Marcus?' Charlie frowned. 'Why was he targeting us?'

'He wasn't targeting you, Charlie. He was using you to nail Jason.'

'*What?*' Both Charlie and Stephen stared at Marcus.

'Let me explain . . .'

Marcus went through Ross's story and then described the dilemma now confronting him.

'Under normal circumstances, I'd have fired him on the spot. But as I've explained, these aren't normal circumstances. Before I decide on what action to take, I'd like to know what you think.'

'Us? Why?' Surprised, Stephen blinked.

'You're the injured parties; if you think his actions don't merit a second chance, I'll fire him. We've got to be able to trust one another and even if I banned him from coming near the farm, or the animals; if you thought he should go, you wouldn't take kindly to my ignoring your opinion, and you'd always be suspicious about his movements.'

'What has Ross said?' asked Charlie.

'Actually Charlie, he's in a complete state, but he's working today. He's banned from the farm and he's moved his stuff into a trailer on the base. I think he's truly sorry, not for targeting Jason, it has to be said, but for everything else. He's begging for another chance, but as I pointed out, he's destroyed the trust vested in him and I'm not sure another chance is an option. That's why I wanted your opinion.'

There was a light knock at the door. Marcus opened it. 'Emma, come in.'

Surprised, Charlie looked at his friend, there was something in the way he'd said 'Emma' . . .

'Hi,' Emma nodded at Charlie and Stephen, then turned to Marcus. 'Sorry I've been longer than I thought. Jason has a cold and his sneezing on and off set slowed us down. How far have you got?'

'I've filled them in on everything, I think,' replied Marcus. 'I'm waiting for their reaction. Listen guys, if you want to think this over and let me know, that's fine. Ross is in hell at the moment, but that's not our concern.'

Stephen frowned. 'If Ross isn't given this chance, what will happen to him?'

529

'He'll find it very hard to get work in the business,' Marcus replied.

'And Jason, and the other one, the kid, who nearly did for Emma?'

'They'll get a final warning.'

'So they get another chance?'

'Yes.'

'That doesn't seem very fair to me,' said Stephen, with a glance at Charlie. 'Everyone should be given a second chance, if at all possible.'

'I agree with Stephen,' Charlie cast a faint smile at his brother. 'In the end it's your decision and you have to work with it. I guess nobody knows but us, which makes it easier for you.'

'Yes, thank you, both of you. You've been great. I'll let you know, of course, what we decide to do.'

'Just before you go,' Emma interjected, 'I'm afraid I've got some more bad news.'

'Oh?'

'We've got to do some re-shooting; there's no way we can bring the first episode in on schedule unless we work on Good Friday.'

'That's our opening day!' Stephen looked alarmed. 'I don't see how we can . . .'

'That's fine,' interrupted Charlie. 'But, without interrupting your work, can we make your presence one of our attractions? If Ross is still about,' he added with a mischievous grin, ' perhaps he could arrange for small tours of the studio and the base camp. And maybe Ben, or more particularly Jason, can be prevailed upon to sign autographs?'

For the first time that day, Marcus grinned. 'You're an opportunist and no mistake, Charlie Tucker. I'll see what we can sort out.'

After the departure of the brothers, both Emma

530

and Marcus sat, wrapped in thought.

'Well,' said Emma breaking the silence. 'I didn't expect that.'

'Nor me,' agreed Marcus. 'Charlie's a pretty compassionate sort of bloke and he's worked with Ross, so I could have predicted which way he'd jump, but Stephen . . .'

'Stubborn, unimaginative, and always making clear how much he dislikes the unit . . .'

'He was straight in there . . . we should give Ross that second chance. These Tuckers never cease to surprise me.'

'And are you?'

'What do you think, Emma?'

She sighed. 'It's your decision, of course. But personally, I'd like to maintain the status quo. I think Ross will bend over backwards to show he's entirely trustworthy. I know it's an unorthodox decision, but the shoot can only benefit from keeping him on board.'

'Fine. We'll keep him. I'll talk to him later, but I must have a word with our other two miscreants. Harry put your life at risk, I can't overlook that, and if Jason causes any more trouble, he's out.'

'Will you tell him about Ross?'

'Good lord, no, he'd kick up a hell of a stink. But I'll remind him about the clause of confidentiality in his contract. Stupid bastard.'

*   *   *

One by one the Tuckers and their respective partners gathered in the kitchen, ostensibly to eat supper and to discuss the farm opening, but with the Charlie-Stephen crisis unresolved—Alison having promised to say nothing—conversation was stilted.

A subdued Angela had taken her post by the stove to conjure up a casserole.

Jenny, pale and anxious, gathered the plates and cutlery, barely responding to the good-humoured conversation of Jeff, while he, with almost no sleep the previous night and a full day's work behind him, would have liked nothing better than to retreat to the silence and comfort of his bachelor residence.

Elsie had collected Ron from hospital and seeing him settled in bed, arrived at the farmhouse just as Alison, full of suppressed excitement, made her appearance in Al's arms, wrapped in her duvet.

'You look very flushed, my girl,' Elsie commented. 'Do you think you should be down here?'

'Oh Gran, I'm fine. How's Ron?'

Elsie gave her the ghost of a smile. 'Tucked up in bed with a cup of tea, as happy as Larry, reading cruise brochures. He's very tired, poor love, but he's in no pain.'

'How many am I laying for?' asked Jenny, distracted as she was, she'd completely lost track of numbers.

'Eleven, I think, Mum,' Angela volunteered. 'I hear Charlie's bringing Isabelle and the girls.'

Jenny gulped. If Charlie was bringing Isabelle and the girls over, that had to be good, didn't it? He wouldn't have them here if he was going to leave, would he? He wouldn't expose them to any sort of scene.

The door to the yard banged and Stephen entered. Jenny examined him, covertly. Greeting everyone with evident cheeriness, he kissed Angela on the cheek then left to change out of his overalls and wash.

Jenny breathed more easily. If Charlie was going to leave, she couldn't believe Stephen would look so relaxed; Stephen always wore his heart on his sleeve. Casting a surreptitious look around the room, she realised that Elsie and Angela, at least, looked as she felt: uncertain, anxious, hopeful, while Jeff, she noticed with a pang, looked weary.

The door banged again and Charlie ushered in Isabelle, Clemmie and Becky. The two little girls hung back, shy, so Jenny, forgetting her troubles, went to fuss over them, find some cola, and encourage them to pet the dogs.

Having completed his ablutions, Stephen returned, and Elsie, who'd decided the entire family would suffer from chronic indigestion if they ate not knowing the outcome of the quarrel, was about to call the family to attention when Charlie got there first.

'I reckon,' he announced, 'if we don't sort one little matter out before we eat, you won't appreciate Angela's delicious-looking casserole . . .'

Angela, startled and gratified, managed a weak smile.

'So I just wanted to say me and Steve really appreciate all the support and advice we've had, and we've decided to go into partnership. We're gonna divide his shares, fifty-fifty, Gran. So if you do decide to give Steve your share as a wedding present, they'll also be divided up. Steve is going to run the dairy herd and take responsibility for the rare breeds stock. I'm gonna run the rare breeds enterprise, the holiday cottages and the farm shop, and I'll help Steve out on the farm, with ploughing and stuff, when he needs me. Alison, Stephen and

I think you should hold onto your share for the moment. Then if we can't agree on something, you'll have the casting vote. That's basically it, ain't it Stephen?'

Stephen nodded and with a certain timidity, looked round at them all, his gaze finally resting on Angela. 'Yes, that's it. That's how we both want it, if it's all right with you.'

For one hesitant moment she returned Stephen's gaze, scrutinising his face. He gave her a gentle smile—whereupon she flung down her wooden spoon and threw her arms around him with an inarticulate cry, which was drowned by shouts and cheers and laughter from the rest of the family, who were in no doubt at all it was absolutely 'all right' with them.

92

One entirely unexpected consequence of Marcus giving a final warning to Jason and Harry was the abrupt departure of Harry Hobbs.

'It weren't my fault,' he snivelled. 'It's so boring here and every time I wanted to do something, someone would say I couldn't. And Emma kept changing the schedules and I didn't get to go home when I wanted to. Nobody wants to be here; everybody's grumbling. Stuck in this shit-hole, miles away from anywhere. Jason just pissed me off . . . he's the worst of the lot. I didn't mean Emma to fall in the water; it was just so boring it was doing my head in. I'm gonna jack it in, and you can't stop me.'

'So that's the situation.' Marcus looked round the group of actors who'd gathered at the bar that evening. 'Until the casting director comes up with another Richie, we'll press on with what we can do without him. However, it goes without saying, the re-shoot will mean longer days and, I'm afraid, we'll have to sacrifice one day of the Easter break.'

'Oh, that's too bad,' declared Ben. 'I was planning a small recuperative trip with my wife. Her show ends that week.'

'I'm sorry, Ben,' replied Marcus. 'We can't release you until the end of Friday. Of course, everyone will be remunerated for all this extra work.'

'We better had,' grumbled Jason, 'otherwise I'm walking.' He raised his voice, 'I've got a gig that weekend. How do I know that won't be cocked up an' all?'

'It's just the Friday we need, Jason, you have my word. I'm sorry about this, folks, but there was no way we could have anticipated someone like Harry. I'm just glad Emma survived his nasty little prank. Who knows what else he might have got up to: he could have wrecked the shoot.'

'There's the pity of it,' muttered Jason. 'If he hadn't been such a nasty piece of snot, I might have lent him a hand.'

'Oh no!' Juliet exclaimed, 'Don't say you're going to take over where Harry left off, Jason. I couldn't bear any more pigs on set.'

Without it being Marcus's intention, Harry, by his departure, had left everyone assuming he was responsible for all the accidents.

Emma caught Marcus's eye and gave a fleeting grin, before turning to Jason, 'Have you seen the report back from London on the stuff we've shot so far, Jason?'

'No,' he said sulkily, 'Why should I be interested?'

'Because, believe it or not, your performance is commended. They like you.'

'What?' Ben was outraged. 'Are you sure? Did they mention me at all?'

'The standard of acting is as high as they'd expect from such a quality cast,' said Marcus smoothly. 'It's just that they were impressed with Jason's work.'

Jason smirked and preened, 'Well it's nice to know I'm appreciated. This acting lark is money for old rope.'

'Oh for God's sake!' Ben went almost purple. 'You're insufferable!'

'Good,' replied Jason, coldly. 'That's music to my lugholes. If you continue to think that, then this whole exercise will've been worth it.'

Ben looked at him with complete loathing. 'What star sign are you?'

'What?'

'Your star sign—when's your birthday?'

'January 4th. You gonna send me a card?'

'Capricorn,' Ben shuddered. 'I knew it!'

Walking away from the studio set where the meeting had taken place, Marcus looked down at Emma, a glint in his eye. 'That was an interesting little white lie, Ms Knight . . .'

She smiled. 'It had the desired effect. It's part of my plot to draw his claws.'

536

Marcus looked at her quizzically. 'Oh?'

'Jason Hart, as we know, is an arrogant bastard whose nose was completely out of joint because he knew we all thought he was no good. I reckon if he thinks his performance is rated, his attitude will change. I admit it might make him unbearably cocky for a while, but if it means he throws his energies into trying to act Ben off the set, I can handle that.'

Marcus laughed. 'It seems to me you're very good at handling arrogant bastards, Emma. By the end of this series, we'll all be eating out of your hand.'

* * *

The week to the opening sped swiftly by.

Jason protested loudly at the thought of being on show and having to give autographs, but agreed when he overheard Ben suggesting the reason Jason wasn't keen was because he didn't think anyone would know who he was, unlike Ben, of course, and Juliet, who would be only to happy to play ball.

Ross worked as hard as he always did. The wood chips were put down on the river path and he supplied a whole load more to the farm for their footpaths and farm walk. When he encountered Charlie, he attempted to apologise, but Charlie patted him on the back and told him his trouble was he was a city lad and didn't know enough about animals, and that if he had, he wouldn't have taken liberties with them.

With the addition of the material from the camera chip, Al and Alison finished off the website, and it was launched; Angela came back one day with a pile of glossy brochures; Angela and Elsie baked, and Jenny knitted, producing strawberry hat after strawberry hat and then experimented knitting little pink piglets. Stephen let his dairy herd out of the barn, and with the delivery of two golden goats and a Shetland pony, the stock was complete. The telephone started ringing with enquiries and, suddenly, they were all infused with a sense of excitement.

Stephen took a call one evening, just as they sat down to supper, and when he returned, he looked flustered.

'Who was that, Stephen?' asked Angela, anxiously. 'You look put out.'

'So would you, my love, if you'd just had an earful from June Pagett.'

'June Pagett? Who's she?' asked Charlie, his mouth full of beef stew.

'She's the head honcho of the Merlin Players,' replied Stephen, tucking into his food, 'An' she was steaming.'

'Why?' Angela was puzzled. 'We haven't forgotten a meeting or anything, have we. The auditions haven't been set yet, have they?'

Stephen grinned. 'We did forget something, Ange. We forgot to tell her that Mrs Merfield changed her mind and agreed to let us do that Shakespeare at the Manor. Apparently she decided to have a go at persuading them herself, so is really miffed with us because Mrs Merfield told her she'd agreed ages ago. It was humiliatin', she said, and we'd caused her to . . .' he screwed up his face, remembering June Pagett's exact words, 'fret quite unnecessarily, and she hoped it wasn't going to be symptomatic of the way we'd treat her *Dream*.'

Angela giggled, but was not in the slightest remorseful.

In the library the following morning, she had an encounter of a different kind. Sally Green came looking for her.

In her drunken haze at the Lester's party, Sally had not fully understood her role in Veronica's hysterics. All she knew was she and Philip had been bundled out unceremoniously by Hugh Lester, and Philip, annoyed with her and angry at their treatment, had stated she was never to accept an invitation there again. As far as Sally was concerned, the plan to introduce Veronica, incognito, as Marsh Farm's sleeping partner, was still operational. Accordingly, she sought Angela out to see what progress had been made.

When she saw her, Angela went white, then pink, and before Sally could say anything, hissed, 'You've got a nerve, coming here. I thought you were my friend, but you were her creature. How could you? Pretending you had some millionaire in tow, when all the time it was Veronica Lester. Sleeping partner? Snake in the grass, more like . . . she'd have forced us out.'

'No, no, you've got it wrong,' protested Sally, her face crimson. 'I admit a little deception, but it was only because Vee knew the Tuckers would refuse her help. She wanted to help you, she really did, because Anthony, her son, is going out with . . . er . . .'

'Alison.'

'Yes, and she wanted to get back in his good books. That's why, Angela, dear. You mustn't leap to conclusions. She just wants to help.'

'If you believe that,' snapped Angela, 'You're even more stupid than I am.'

*   *   *

Good Friday was finally upon them. The weather, which, as Elsie remarked, had been playing 'silly buggers' all week, settled, with clear blue skies and a soft breeze, and the farm was allowed to look its best. The hedgerows burst with blossom, the oak and the ash vied with each other to produce the first green leaves; clumps of late daffodils danced in the fields and the banks along the track were carpeted with primroses.

The film crew were up early and on schedule when, mid-morning, the first car arrived.

'Here we go,' shouted Charlie, who'd been keeping lookout, his stomach a knot of nerves in case nobody came.

By mid-afternoon numbers had exceeded all expectations, and to add to their excitement, the press and local television turned up.

The tours, organised by Ross, were a huge attraction—as were the piglets, and Bumble, who attracted a bevy of small girls all afternoon.

Ben and the other actors were kept busy and Ben, who'd kept a tally of his and Jason's signings, was positively crowing by the end of the afternoon.

'I know darling, you've already told me, twice,' remarked Jilly as they finally escaped to the bus for tea. 'But Juliet must have signed more than any of us. She's still out there, poor thing.'

Juliet was rescued by Oliver, who, as the local MP, came to give the venture his blessing.

'Hello my love,' he murmured. 'How are you

both? Bearing up?'

'We're both fine,' Juliet smiled up at him. 'But I shall be glad to go home.'

'Have you told Marcus about your pregnancy yet, darling?'

'He's been very preoccupied this week, Ollie. But I will, I promise.'

*   *   *

Enjoying the balmy weather and the festive atmosphere, Emma and Marcus strolled round the paddocks enjoying the occasion and, more particularly, each other's company. The week had been hectic and in spite of his own preoccupations, Marcus had been assiduous in the support he gave Emma. This was their first opportunity to relax and, during the course of the afternoon, both became aware it wasn't just their professional relationship that had changed.

Charlie, supervising the crowds that squashed around the pens to admire his precious piglets, hailed them. 'Good to see you taking a break. It's brilliant, isn't it?'

'Yeah, brilliant.' Marcus smiled. 'The way you Tuckers pull things off never ceases to amaze me.'

Charlie shrugged. 'Graft, mate, hard graft. And sheer talent of course. Meet up for a drink later?'

'Good idea. I'll bring some bubbly over.'

Charlie grinned. 'Great. And I'll get some beer.'

Emma and Marcus wandered on.

'You and Charlie,' ventured Emma tentatively, 'you're such good mates. I'm glad . . .' She stopped, kicking herself for stirring the embers.

'Glad that he never found out I was infatuated

541

with his girl; that I was the sort of friend who planned to persuade her to dump him and choose me instead?' Marcus's voice was unemotional.

'But you didn't, did you? You pulled back.'

'I can't take credit for that,' replied Marcus somewhat bitterly. 'I wish I could.'

'What stopped you then?'

'Isabelle, herself. And you.'

'Me?'

'Yes. I shan't ever forget that look of contempt in your eyes.'

'It's not there now,' she said softly.

He tucked her arm in his. 'It is amazing to me that your good opinion matters so much. I chose gold, Emma, when I chose you and it took me some while to realise it.'

Emma blushed, but did not withdraw her arm. She felt light-headed. 'It is amazing,' she marvelled to herself. 'A few weeks ago I couldn't have imagined walking arm in arm with Marcus Steel, having such a conversation.' She suddenly remembered her drowning thoughts and blushed again.

'Penny for them?' Marcus smiled.

'I . . . er . . . was just wondering what you were up to for the rest of the weekend. Are you going back up to London?'

'Yes, why? And you?'

'Yes.'

'Perhaps you'd like to have dinner tomorrow evening? That is, if you've not had enough of me. We could go and have a look at Isabelle's exhibition—it's still on, I think—and then go on somewhere?'

'Thanks, Marcus, I'd really like that, but it

occurs to me if you're not going to be around this weekend, would you consider lending your cottage to Isabelle and Charlie for a couple of nights?'

He looked at her, his eyebrows raised. 'Yes?'

'It's just that Isabelle was lamenting the impossibility of ever being able to go away with him and obviously, he can't leave the farm at the moment, but if he was able to stay in your cottage, it would be the perfect solution. I know Alison and Al would look after the girls.'

Marcus thought it over and nodded. 'It's a good idea, I've no objection.' And he marvelled to himself how much had changed in a couple of weeks. He tried to conjure up how he'd felt about Isabelle and discovered he couldn't do it; he couldn't think of her as anything other than a friend; his mate, Charlie's girl.

Amazing.

He looked down at the slender woman leaning lightly on his arm. This was even more amazing. Never, in a million years would he, a couple of weeks ago, have thought of taking her in his arms and kissing her and yet, suddenly, that was what he wanted to do.

Wanted, more than anything.

Amazing.

Acknowledgements

Particular thanks are due to my friends in Limpley Stoke who are always wonderfully supportive; Megan Jones, who has given me of her time unstintingly; Richard Curry, my agricultural adviser; the cast and crew of *Doc Martin*, especially Stephanie Cole; those friends that have cheered me on at every stage, including Richard and Rachel Dunnill, William and Rhiannon Carey Evans, Liz and Alan Booty, Sally Muir, Wendy Hoile, Anna Humpston and Emma Booty; my sister, Belinda, who promotes the existence of Summerstoke in Canada; my lovely daughter, Isabel, who gives me much-needed critical support; my agent, Broo Doherty, and editor, Joceline Bury; and most particularly, my son, Adam, who read the first draft – a chapter a day – with great enthusiasm and always demanded more.

www.carolinekington.co.uk